# A Lethal Odyssey of Cat and Mouse

## Earl Snort

**BARLOW ADAMS SERIES BOOK III**

TotalRecall Publications, Inc.
1103 Middlecreek
Friendswood, Texas 77546
281-992-3131 281-482-5390 Fax
www.totalrecallpress.com

ISBN:  978-1-64883-0785
UPC:  6-43977-40785-6

Printed in the United States of America with simultaneous printings in Australia, Canada, and United Kingdom.

FIRST EDITION
1   2   3   4   5   6   7   8   9   10

Not a speck of this is true. It's all a pack of lies.

# To My Loving Wife

"Only you can make all this world seem right. Only you can make the darkness bright. Only you, and you alone, can thrill me like you do, and fill my heart with love for only you. Only you can make this change in me. For it's true, you are my destiny. When you hold my hand, I understand the magic that you do. You're my dream come true, my one and only you." *Only You* - Recorded by the Platters in 1955.

"Nights in white satin, never reaching the end, letters I've written, never meaning to send. Beauty I'd always missed, with these eyes before. Just what the truth is, I can't say anymore, 'cause I love you. Yes, I love you. Oh, I love you." *Nights in White Satin* - Recorded by the Moody Blues in 1967.

"Yesterday when I was young, the taste of life was sweet upon my tongue . . . . the thousand dreams I dreamed, the splendid things I planned . . . . I lived by night and shunned the naked light of day, and now I see how the years ran away . . . ." *Yesterday When I Was Young* - Recorded by Roy Clark in 1969.

"I'm at it again, telling more lies. My daddy said it was because I have worms. What if it's true? Maybe I don't even know the truth."

*Earl Snort - 2021*

## ABOUT THE AUTHOR

Earl Snort is the nom de plume of a retired law enforcement officer with more than forty years experience toting a badge and a gun. Before that, he served in the armed forces.

He and his wife have been married nearly fifty years. They reside in the South. They have one son, also a career law enforcement officer, and two grandchildren.

This is the author's third foray into the world of writing fiction. After a lifetime of writing non-fiction to document investigations of true crime, he decided to try his hand in make believe.

He hopes you enjoy the yarn.

January 2021

# LIST OF MAJOR CHARACTERS

Barlow Adams - Quayle County Deputy Sheriff

Sarah Baker Adams - Barlow's Fiancée/Wife

Solomon "Sol" Pratt - Quayle County Sheriff

Leo C. "Popeye" Potts - Criminal

Corporal Heinrich "Oliver Hardy" Orbach - El Paso County
   Deputy Sheriff

Lucas "Stan Laurel" Slocum - El Paso County Deputy Sheriff

Clarence "Slick" Oldman - Quayle County Deputy Sheriff

Archibald "Archie" Willis - Quayle County Deputy Sheriff

Joseph P. "Joe Shit the Ragman" & "Joe Rag" Schitt - Convict

Richard "Dick Wad" Wadsworth - Convict

Jarvis Reeves - Texas Ranger

Grady "Gravy Train" Triplett - Criminal colleague of Joseph
   Schitt

Rémy A. "Junior" Harvey, Jr. - Criminal

Ramón "Tee Beau" Petard - Criminal

# PROLOGUE

## Monday, January 22, 1968
## Goodbye

He was seated on a wooden bench at the Greyhound bus station in Baileyville, Texas, next to his grandmother who was holding back tears, but not very well. He could have flagged down the bus in front of his uncle's Sinclair service station in Arlo, but Grandma insisted on driving him thirteen miles east so he would have a proper send off, and so she could have these last few minutes together with him all to herself.

He was wearing his winter Class A uniform, otherwise known as dress greens. He didn't have any stripes on his sleeves, but his expert rifleman's badge was pinned on his left breast. The rest of his uniforms were stowed in his duffle bag, which was resting on the floor by his feet. He was coming off a two-week leave from training en route to Vietnam by way of Fort Ord, California.

Grandma whispered, "I will miss you while you're away, just like I missed your daddy in 1942, when he left for Africa. I prayed for him every night like I do for you. I have faith that the Lord will return you to me safe and sound. All the same, don't take any crazy chances. You hear? I mean it! Do your job and do it right, but don't jump on any hand grenades, and make sure you look out for those booby traps with punji sticks. I heard all about 'em. Promise me!"

"I promise, Grandma."

"Look me in the eye and promise me again."

He stood up and squatted down in front of her. He took both of her hands in his, while he stared into her bright blue eyes. She had crow's feet in the corners of both. A wisp of silver-grey hair had fallen over her forehead. He loved her more than any person living. He whispered back. "I promise, Grandma. I'll be back in a year. I'm already counting the days. I want you to bake me a cherry pie as soon as I get home, and you have to promise me that you will take good care of yourself. Don't forget to take your medicine. We'll go visit Chloe in her new home in Bisbee, as soon as I get back. Okay?"

"My, my. You remind me of your pa more and more. You sounded just like him when he went off to war. I promise. Now stand up and give me a hug. They're calling your bus."

*****

Leaving this time was much harder than when he left for basic training and advanced individual training at Fort Sill, Oklahoma. He knew what she meant. Who could promise that he wouldn't get hurt or killed?

She was still waving at him as the bus pulled out of the lot and headed west. A tear, and then another, and another escaped from his eyes and slowly rolled down his cheeks. He waved back. "I love you, Grandma. I'll be back, one way or another."

# CHAPTER 1

Sunday, May 2, 1971
Announcement in *The El Paso Bugle*,
Section D, Page 4, 2nd Column

M r. & Mrs. Arthur Baker of Mosby, Quayle County, are proud to announce the nuptials of their daughter, Miss Sarah Mae Baker, to Mr. Barlow Knotts Adams, son of the late Chester R. Adams and the late Matilda Lee Adams, and the grandson of the late Beatrice Adams, all of Arlo, Benson County, on Saturday, June 5, at the St. Paul Methodist Church in Mosby. A reception will follow at the Bar B Ranch.

The newlyweds plan to take a two-week honeymoon, motoring to San Antonio to see the Alamo, Houston to see an Astros baseball game against the Atlanta Braves, and New Orleans to see the French Quarter.

Miss Baker graduated from West Texas Junior College (WTJC) last year. She is employed as the event coordinator at the Quayle County Rodeo Grounds. She is also a competitor in local rodeo barrel racing events. Mr. Adams is employed as a deputy sheriff in Quayle County. He will graduate from WTJC later this month.

# CHAPTER 2

## Friday, May 21, 1971
## Mission Accomplished

At precisely 1:24 p.m., Barlow K. Adams walked across the stage in the auditorium at West Texas Junior College to receive his associate of arts degree diploma in law enforcement. The curriculum was 64 semester hours, and it took him two academic years to complete. In addition, he received a certificate from the State of Texas attesting to his successful completion of four hundred hours in Police Officers Standard Training (POST), thus qualifying him to be a law enforcement officer in Texas on an annual basis, assuming that he successfully completes forty hours of continuing education each year.

This august ceremony was witnessed by his fiancée, Sarah, her parents, Arthur and Clarice Baker, Sheriff Solomon Pratt, Chief Deputy Sheriff Alexander Snodgrass, Deputy Sheriff Archibald "Archie" Willis, and countless other friends and family members of the 117 graduates. The ceremony completed, and after 45 minutes engaged in the perfunctory 'grin and shake' with dignified faculty, beaming classmates, well wishers, flashing lightbulbs, and the requisite partaking of orange sherbet punch with sugar cookies, the man of the hour and his guests repaired to the Quayle County Sheriff's Office for their own private celebration. All eleven of the sheriff's office employees were in attendance, as well as other county employees and friends who popped in and out to say congratulations, notably including Quayle County Circuit Court Judge Maxwell Sweeney and his wife, Miss Monica.

No disrespect to Barlow, but why the big deal? Other equally lofty accomplishments had occurred within the department without ceremony, since his appointment as a deputy 22 months earlier. The answer was really quite simple. It went way beyond the fondness the other employees felt for Barlow. It had something to do with their perception of the glacial but seismic shift taking place within their guild as law enforcement officers. Changes they didn't necessarily agree with, but had no way to resist or overcome. Barlow was their first deputy hired under the new state law requiring POST certification. Powerful outside forces were now dictating what a person had to learn and do, in order to become and to remain a lawman. For better or for worse, outsiders were taking control of their guild. Today signified a pivotal point for the Quayle County Sheriff's Office, even though the day-to-day operations would not change much at all overnight.

Everyone had chipped in ten bucks to buy Barlow an appropriate gift noteworthy of his accomplishment, and of course, signifying the high esteem in which they all held for him. That was no small sum for an office gift donation. The norm was one or two bucks. It was Sheriff Sol's idea, and nobody expressed surprise or reluctance. Sheriff Sol purchased the gift.

At the appropriate time, after everyone had grazed the church-style buffet line, and the cake had been cut and devoured, Sheriff Sol called the group to order. He commended Barlow, and then good-naturedly roasted him for his foibles. This included being more worried about rattlesnakes than preserving evidence on his very first day on the job; learning the hard way that horses have to be trained before one can shoot a gun while riding; and parking a marked unit in front of a house with an armed burglar, who was not afraid to shoot it out to avoid capture.

Barlow's face went from tan to beet red. Busted! Everyone had a good yuk at his expense, even though they all knew these stories.

Then, on behalf of the entire staff, Sheriff Sol presented Barlow with the office gift. It was wrapped in a box about six inches by eight inches by two inches and it weighed about two pounds. A photograph of the inept Deputy Barney Fife in uniform (played by comedian Don Knotts in the *Andy Griffith* television show) was taped to the top as a spoof. Barlow preserved the picture but he tore the package open like a hungry panther ripping open a gazelle. He couldn't believe his eyes when he opened the box.

He was looking at a high gloss, blue steel, Smith & Wesson, Model 36 Chief Special, five-shot, .38 Special caliber revolver, with a two-inch barrel and checkered walnut grips. This was the most favored gun by plainclothes detectives and for off-duty concealed carry, and as a backup gun for on-duty uniformed officers. What a fabulous gift!

He exclaimed, "Oh my gosh! I don't know what to say. This is such a surprise. Thank you all very much."

Archie, who had been Barlow's primary training officer shouted, "Be careful, Kid. You'll shoot your eye out."

Sheriff Sol interrupted all the laughter and spoke over the crowd of well wishers. "Not yet he won't. He doesn't have any bullets! I almost forgot. Jake Buchanan, where we bought this, told me to give Barlow this box of cartridges as a gift from his pawn shop." With that, he handed Barlow a green box containing fifty round nose, 158-grain, .38 Special caliber bullets. "Jake said you need to master these standard loads in that snub nose before you move on to the hot loads."

Barlow responded, "I know Mr. Jake's right, too. I will. I'll thank him the first chance I get. I need to stop by his shop anyway to buy a holster."

The reception ended with everyone in high spirits. Barlow and Sarah went back to Barlow's house for an intimate celebration in the bedroom. She rang his bell three times, reminiscent of the Vatican ringing in the coronation of a new Pope. His whole body was as limp as a wet wash rag. She was equally as sated, but she didn't want him to know. He also didn't know that she decided he wasn't getting anymore until their wedding night. He was cut off. She wanted him to be exceptionally randy on their special night.

She went back home at five o'clock. Barlow didn't want her to leave, but he had a midnight shift to pull. At least Sarah had the compassion and presence of mind, to work out all his nervous energy and send him well on his way to Dreamland. They only had two weeks to go before it would no longer be necessary for her to leave and sleep in her own bed in her parents' home. She could hardly wait.

# CHAPTER 3

## Sunday, May 23, 1971
## Where Evil Lurks

It was two in the afternoon. Texas State Penitentiary (TSP) in Huntsville, inmate # 51739, commonly referred to as Joe Rag, who was born Joseph P. Schitt, also known as Joe Shit the Ragman to Texas lawmen and within the defunct and scattered El Diablos Motorcycle Club, formerly located in El Paso, was cooling his heels in the cell he shared with inmate # 66421, Richard Wadsworth, otherwise known as Dick Wad. They were allegedly enlightening themselves by reading a year-old copy of *Popular Mechanics* and a two-month-old copy of the *National Geographic*. What they were actually doing was planning their escape.

Joe Rag was a four-time loser and a lifer. He was serving 42 years without parole for aggravated assault on a police officer and for being a habitual felon, the jailhouse term which is commonly referred to as the 'high bitch.' Dick Wad was a two-time loser, doing forty years for his second conviction of aggravated rape. His passion and perversion was to brutally sodomize old 'blue hair' ladies after he stalked them home from the grocery, or the pharmacy, or the hairdresser's. He had many 'pelts hanging on the wall' but only two convictions for his depravity. Joe Rag was a killer. Dick Wad was not, but his victims oftentimes wished they were dead, long after he was through torturing and debasing them.

They already had the method of escape worked out. What they needed was a confederate outside the walls who would provide them with clothes, guns, money, and transportation. That was the hard part, because the prison screws determined who was allowed on an inmate's visitor's list, plus they screened all their incoming and outgoing correspondence. No contact whatsoever was allowed with ex-cons. Forget about being allowed to make a telephone call. Besides that, no incoming calls were accepted, except by an inmate's attorney of record. The problem was, court-appointed attorneys did not waste their time on lost causes. Joe Rag and Dick Wad were both lost causes.

This was all done to reduce smuggling, contract murders, escapes, and the proliferation of ongoing criminal enterprises within the prison itself, not to mention beyond. It was a worthwhile pursuit on behalf of the criminal justice system, and it slowed down criminal activity substantially, but it did not eliminate it. Where there's a will, there's always a way.

Joe Rag had the will. A few months ago, he finally got permission to correspond with a woman from Del Rio named Alice Bolton. Unbeknownst to the authorities, she was the step-sister of a fellow Diablo named Grady S. "Gravy Train" Triplett, dubiously saddled with this monicker because of his penchant for consuming large quantities of groceries, no matter how bad they looked, or smelled, or tasted. Many people opined that dog food would smell and taste better than some of the swill Gravy Train consumed. He had managed to elude the dragnet and purge of the Diablos by the authorities because, by good fortune, he had been holed up, and now continued to remain, in close proximity to a whorehouse in Ciudad Acuña, Mexico, just south of Del Rio. He had been there, trying to negotiate an agreement between the Diablos and a sophisticated Mexican wholesale marijuana cartel, to swap methamphetamines for marijuana. When the proverbial shit hit the fan, and scores of Texas lawmen declared open season on the Diablos for the attempted assassination of a judge and a fellow lawman, Gravy Train stayed put, out of harm's way. He ultimately found gainful employment as an enforcer for the Mexican marijuana enterprise, after the Diablos who weren't captured or killed just dissolved or disappeared like wisps of cigarette smoke on a windy day.

Alice Bolton was a 35-year-old wench with no criminal record. She was employed as a waitress in a steakhouse which also sold alcohol, so she had an ABC license as a server. That helped establish her bonafides in the law enforcement seal of approval department, because they had already done a criminal background check on her. All that really meant was that she had never been arrested. It didn't mean she was a virtuous person. Not by a long shot.

Alice was not blessed with a pretty face, not even slightly so, but she had a Jayne Mansfield body which she would show off and let you feel, if you treated her nicely. She was also a no exaggeration, no hyperbole, nymphomaniac. Many a time she had serviced Joe Rag and however many Diablos he was with, until they were all so raw they could barely pee without shedding a river full of tears. She never got sated first. Bottom line. The cops did not know she was Gravy Train's step-sister, so she was quickly approved as Joe Rag's one and only correspondent.

It took some time for them to work out a code, but it fell into place naturally. Alice was in a perpetual state of heat, and she loved writing X-rated epistles to Joe, which sometimes were sent back to her by the prison, until finally they had to warn her that they would remove her from Joe's list of (one) correspondents if she did not tone it down.

Eventually, their code all came together. Taking her car in for a lube job meant she had recently consummated normal (for her) missionary style sex. The name of the garage was the name of her paramour. How long she waited to get her car back was how long they had had sex. If she was rear-ended in an auto accident, she had anal sex. Blowing off steam meant giving someone a head job, and giving someone a tuna sandwich meant someone treated her to oral sex. The number of clients in the waiting room were how many men she had had sex with on a given day. The friendlier they were, the more stamina her lovers had.

Joe Rag figured that the allegory was just covert enough to give the pervs who screened his incoming letters a plausible out in the event they were challenged by their captain for letting the letters pass, and just blatant enough to keep them aroused when they read them, adding a little sunshine to their uninspired, low-paid, and dead-end days.

Eventually, Alice and Joe Rag evolved into code words which had meanings beyond the sexual realm. Gravy Train was the fat kid in school who rode his bike everywhere he went, which was eventually shortened to just the fat kid, or Fatso. Joe learned that the fat kid got a job on a farm growing herbs, meaning marijuana, in Ciudad Acuña, across from Del Rio in Mexico, and that she would wave to him once in awhile whenever she saw him riding his bike, which was really his hog.

Fatso's family must be rolling in dough, because he was riding a fancy new bike the last time she saw him. When he stopped on the street to say hello, she remembered Joe to him. He said to say hello, and that he'd like to visit, but they just live too many miles apart. Fatso also said something about not seeing any of their old classmates since the school was closed, and everybody moved away. He said that he enjoyed his new job on a farm, and that it paid pretty well. He said whenever Joe got released, he might want to consider farming as a way to get a new start, and that he could help Joe find a job.

Joe wrote back to Alice, saying if she happened to run into the fat kid, to tell him Joe said hello. He wondered if Fatso still held the private memorial service at noon on the anniversary of his mother's death, like he used to at the First Baptist Church in Conroe. Then he asked, if that wasn't coming up on June 8th? If so, that's lucky because it's on a Tuesday this year, so it shouldn't interfere with church services. Joe said he would like to pay his respects this year, but he couldn't for obvious reasons. Besides, even if it only cost a dime to fly to France, he didn't have enough money to walk across the street. Even so, he would join him in prayer at noon on the 8th. He was sure Fatso would understand.

Their plan was almost complete. If Joe got a positive response from Gravy Train, he and Dick Wad would be cruising out of here on June the 7th.

# CHAPTER 4

## Monday, May 24, 1971
## A Blessing and a Curse

Deputy Kirk Shoemaker requested and received this week off as annual leave to help his dad, a resident of Alpine, to re-roof his house. They needed to strip off two layers of old asphalt shingles, and replace them with new ones, which supposedly would last fifteen years. They both knew this was a tall tale, if not sheer fantasy, but they hoped for the best anyway.

Sheriff Sol decided to throw Barlow a bone, so he replaced Kirk with Barlow on the four-to-twelve shift. This would be Barlow's first week riding solo. He had earned it. Besides that, it could be awhile before Barlow would have another opportunity to patrol the county for an entire week. Being the FNG (fucking new guy), even after nearly two years on the job, he was still low man on the totem pole. He sucked hind tit, but he never complained. He did what he was told, and he did it well. This trait endeared him to Sheriff Sol, and to the rest of the troops.

Honestly, not much of statewide import ever occurred in Quayle County, as it related to law enforcement, nor anything else for that matter. It was a sleepy county; however, when something did flare up, it always seemed to happen when Barlow was around. Sheriff Sol considered this, so in an abundance of caution, he assigned Deputy Randy Meacham to work the same shift. They didn't normally have the luxury of two units on patrol on the same shift, but this week they did. Sheriff Sol assigned

Randy the eastern half of the county and Barlow the western half. He thought it might prove interesting to see how Barlow stacked up on his own against an experienced patrol officer.

Barlow wasn't privy to the sheriff's thinking. It wouldn't have mattered to him anyway. All Barlow knew was that he was happier than a jackass eating briars. He rolled into work at 3:15, relieving Deputy Ernie Atwater thirty minutes early. Barlow knew Randy preferred driving Unit 87, the '68 Ford, which was the newest of the three marked units, so he checked out Unit 78, the '65 Dodge, which was the oldest. He preferred the Dodge anyway. He also checked out one of the Remington, Model 870 shotguns, and was headed out the door when Randy came strolling in. Randy smiled to himself when he saw Barlow unlock the Dodge.

After going through the checklist to ensure that the cruiser was fully operational, topped off with gas, and that all the equipment in the trunk was intact, Barlow called 10-8 (in service) and made a beeline to the do-it-yourself car wash. By 3:45 he was on patrol in a sparkling clean unit, westbound on US 90. When he got out of town and had the road all to himself, he blew out all the built up carbon in the Dodge's four-barrel carburetor, topping out at 135 miles per hour before settling back down to fifty, the normal cruising speed, besides being the speed limit. The weather was a pleasant 85 degrees, with a slight wind, and clear blue skies. This is what life as a patrolman was all about. Hog heaven.

Randy, on the other hand, was satisfied and content, but not overly exuberant. He was one of Quayle County's three part-time deputies, and he was an old salt. He carried a Smith & Wesson Model 19, .357 Magnum, blue steel revolver with a four-inch barrel, and twelve extra cartridges in loops on his belt, much like thousands of other uniformed lawmen throughout the U.S. He hailed from Amarillo originally. He was fifty years old, stood five-feet, ten-inches tall, weighed 180 pounds, had blue eyes, brown hair a little on the shaggy side, and walked with a slight limp, from a serious break of his left femur from a rodeo accident when he was a senior in high school. A bronc he was riding fell during competition, and landed on his leg. He was laid up in Amarillo General Hospital for six months. His draft board classified him IV-F, so he missed out on World War Two. He was the only member of the Quayle County Sheriff's Office who did not have military service. Being IV-F was a bitter pill to swallow, but he made good use of his time by enrolling in Texas A&M and earning a bachelor's degree in biology in 1944.

He considered going to medical school, but had neither the grades nor the money. Instead, he landed a job as a fertilizer salesman for a prestigious firm in Austin which paid him well, but he hated every minute of it. In 1949, God blessed him with marriage to a beautiful woman named Betsy Rivers, a horticulturist, who owned her own nursery. They had one child named Silas, born in 1952.

Life was more than just good. Except for his job, Life was wonderful. Then suddenly, in 1962, Betsy died of breast cancer, and Randy's world came crashing down. He lost his True North. He quit his job, and sold or gave away nearly everything they owned. That summer, Randy and Silas packed everything they still possessed in his blue, 1958, Edsel Corsair sedan, and embarked on an aimless, rambling journey throughout the Southwest.

In late August, they had a flat tire about ten miles west of

Mosby on US 90. A deputy sheriff named Solomon Pratt happened by and helped change it. The temperature was hovering at 106 degrees, and all three of them nearly melted. Then when they were done, the Edsel didn't want to start, so Deputy Pratt radioed for Buck's Phillips 66 to come out and repair or tow the car. Buck couldn't get the car started either, so he towed it to his service station. Randy and Silas piled into the cruiser with Deputy Pratt, who followed Buck.

During the ride, Deputy Pratt coaxed Randy's saga out of him. It was tragic. Randy had no idea where they were headed next. He was well aware that the school year was just around the corner. He was in a dilemma, with no solution in sight. Then he learned that his car had a cracked head, and it would be several days before it could be fixed. Under the circumstances, Deputy Pratt decided to take them to the Travelers Rest Motor Lodge to have a clean and comfortable place to stay.

After check-in, they walked next door to Betty's Diner for a late lunch. During the meal, Deputy Pratt gushed about Mosby, and waxed eloquent about all the things he liked about it. The Chamber of Commerce couldn't have put together a better presentation, because it came straight from his heart without all the hype. Deputy Pratt extolled Quayle School, and talked about what it was like when he was a student there. He mentioned that there were jobs available in the community. He offered to make introductions for Randy, if he were interested. He also offered to give them a tour of the town. He said it was a great place to live, and if they tried it and didn't like it, they could always push on to someplace else after the school year.

Randy accepted Deputy Pratt's offer for a tour. He drove up and down every street and avenue, pointing out all the attractions and waving to friends. American flags and a few Texas state flags were flying at many homes and businesses. The flower boxes and flower beds had marigolds, pansies, and roses, and many other types of flowers in full bloom. Though the town was small, it looked prosperous, and the citizenry appeared to be friendly and content. Randy and Silas both liked what they saw and decided to give it a shot. They rented a two-bedroom house on Sam Houston Street. Silas began his fifth-grade year the next week. Later on, Randy concluded that the flat tire was serendipitous.

Deputy Pratt also introduced Randy to Sheriff Lincoln Hobgood, who was also suitably impressed with Randy's personality and credentials. He offered Randy a job as a part-time deputy, and Randy accepted. He also picked up another part-time job breaking horses at the Circle Y south of town on TX 651 and bordering along the Rio Grande River. The rest was history.

Silas had recently completed his freshman year at Texas A&M as a member of the Corps of Cadets, and Randy was just beginning his afternoon shift, fighting crime and corruption to help keep America safe for democracy, such as it was in Quayle County.

It was 4:15. The afternoon shift was barely underway. Randy was at the far northeast end of the county, ensuring that space aliens hadn't landed, or that a roving band of gypsies hadn't squatted on some rancher's property, and butchered half his livestock. The sheriff and chief were still at the office, feeding the administrative duties monster, due to incomplete or unfiled documents left over from the day shift. Specifically, Chief Alex was fussing over an old case file, because the fingerprint cards were out of place. Alternatively, Sheriff Sol was working on a proposal to DX Unit 78, because it had over 350,000 miles on it, even though it still ran well. He knew it would be an uphill battle getting approval from a particular county supervisor by the name of Mr. LaRue S. Dinkins, who was a notorious skinflint. Sol hoped said skinflint would lose his next election. Simultaneously, Barlow was walking back to his cruiser from the lavatory at the rest stop, located on US 90 about three miles west of Mosby, when the backdraft from a low flying eastbound rocket ship almost knocked him over. Actually, it was a black, 1965 Ford Galaxy running balls to the wall.

Barlow didn't let any moss grow under his feet. Adrenaline was pulsing through his veins in rivulets. In seconds, he was kicking up gravel and dust in hot pursuit, with the red overhead light oscillating and the siren blaring. He left the windows shut to keep out the noise. Since the cruiser had no air conditioning, it was as hot as molten lava inside the car, but he barely noticed. He was rolling at 125 miles per hour, and still picking up speed. The Ford had a good head start, and when the driver realized he'd been jumped, he goosed his engine even more. Barlow (Quayle 7) was closing, but not as quickly as he would have liked. He radioed to Quayle Base, requesting backup. He knew this could get dicey real quick, if they raced through Mosby at these speeds.

Every cop lives for a high speed pursuit, just like hounds love to chase a fox. It's in their nature. Randy (Quayle 9) called in his location from Outer Mongolia and said he was en route. Sheriff Sol leapt out of his chair in his office like he had a bad case of diarrhea and said to Chief Alex, "Let's go," as he exploded out the door. Chief Alex put his file away, and tidied up before he followed. Miss Loretta radioed that both Quayle 1 and Quayle 2 were responding.

Sheriff Sol was a minute too late. He saw and heard the Ford roar past the courthouse with Quayle 7 glued to its tail, just as he pulled out of the lot in his '69 Plymouth Fury, reverberating with the sound of a 330-horsepower engine and a four-barrel carburetor with dual exhausts, being held in check. Thank God the portion of US 90 in Mosby was four lanes wide, and that traffic was light. Quayle 2 was still unlocking his '67 Jeep Wagoneer, when Quayle 1 tore out of the lot. That was okay. The Jeep had the 290, four-barrel carburetor on the 225-horsepower engine, but the vehicle was built for driving off road or pulling a trailer, not racing. Anyway, Chief knew his job would be to pick up the pieces once things came to a screeching halt.

Quayle County is roughly 54 miles west to east on US 90. It is 42 miles to the eastern county line from Mosby. There aren't many roads in the county, to include unimproved ones. There are only two unimproved north-south roads east of Mosby, until the one just east of the Val Verde County line. Once the driver of the Ford passed TX 651 at the courthouse, his potential routes of escape greatly diminished. He pretty much committed himself to staying eastbound on US 90.

Mosby is situated way out in the middle of nowhere, and it's at least a hundred miles to anyplace much bigger than comic strip Li'l Abner Yokum's *Dogpatch USA*. Del Rio, which is located in Val Verde County, is the closest prominent city to Mosby, and it's about 120 miles southeast on US 90. At the speeds they were traveling, it wouldn't take long to get there.

Quayle 1 got on the radio. He asked if Quayle 7 could read the license plate number on the Ford.

Quayle 7 responded over the air with "Texas Adam 23541."

He said they were still maintaining a steady speed of 125 miles per hour, but had gotten up to 130 for a short distance.

Then Quayle 1 told Miss Loretta at Base, to call the Val Verde Sheriff's Office, and the Texas Department of Public Safety, and ask them to start sending units west on US 90, in a mutual assist to help intercept a black, 1965 Ford Galaxy, Texas plate A23541, traveling in excess of 125 miles per hour eastbound, currently about ten miles east of Mosby. He told Base to run a license plate check, and to report back on Frequency 2. Then he told Quayle 2, Quayle 7, and Quayle 9 to switch to Frequency 2, and to give him a radio check.

They all checked in. Quayle 9 said he was on CO 11 about fifteen miles north of US 90, just west of the Val Verde County line.

Quayle Base reported that the Ford was registered to Godfrey F. Morgenstern, of Fort Hancock in El Paso County. It was reported stolen two days ago. She also said DPS had a unit en route from Comstock, and that Val Verde was trying to contact a deputy who was 10-7 (out of service) in Langtry near the county line. Both units would respond on Frequency 2 when they got within range.

Quayle 1 radioed to Quayle 9 that he was closer to the county line than Quayle 7 or himself. He told Quayle 9 to report for further instructions when he arrived at US 90. Then he told Quayle 7 to back off the siren since the perp already knew a cop was riding his bumper and why he was there. He asked Quayle 7 if he had enough power to pull up close enough to tap the Ford's left rear bumper with his right front bumper. (The idea was to shove the perp into a right swerve off the road or into a 360-degree turn, otherwise known as a doughnut.)

Quayle 7 replied, "10-4."

Time and miles were piling up quickly. It took a couple of tries before Quayle 7 was successful. This is a tough trick to pull off at 125 miles per hour. The Ford veered off onto the right shoulder, but managed to get back onto the pavement headed eastbound. Another couple of efforts netted the same results. This driver was darn good and knew what he was doing.

The county line kept inching closer. Quayle 1 preferred to have any law enforcement action which could potentially result in injury or death, to occur in his own county, where they had more influence over the after action investigation and/or grand jury presentation, than they would elsewhere.

Next, Quayle 1 asked if Quayle 7 could roll down his right window, and then pull up abreast of the Ford in the oncoming lane. If so, he wanted Quayle 7 to point his revolver at the driver, and motion for him to pull over. If he refused, Quayle 7 was to shoot him. He told Quayle 7 that the report of the gunshot would give him ringing ears for at least a half hour, so to be prepared for it.

Once again Quayle 7 replied, "10-4." He knew his heart was pounding a hundred or more beats a minute, and that his entire body was revved up in the 'fight or flight' mode. He prayed that he wouldn't shoot a hole in his own unit. While he was trying to stay on the road, and roll down the passenger window, he heard Quayle 9 on the radio.

"Quayle 1 this is Quayle 9. I'm just inside our county line on 90. I flagged down a westbound eighteen-wheeler hauling a flatbed loaded with iron sewer pipes. He agreed to block the highway for us. 10-4?"

"10-4. You park in front of him in the westbound lane canted northwest, so you can shoot out of your driver's window. Use the window sill as a bench rest. If you have a shotgun, load it with slugs. If the perp doesn't slow down, put one through his windshield. Make sure the angle is such that you shoot at an oncoming vehicle, and not at a passing vehicle, since he's coming so fast. Otherwise, you'll probably shoot behind him, and hit Quayle 7 or me. 10-4?"

"10-4. Loading with slugs now."

"10-4. Quayle 7, belay my last order. Stay behind the Ford, but back off just a little bit. Quayle 9, we should be approaching in a couple of minutes."

Both Quayle 7 and Quayle 9 acknowledged.

Still no word from DPS or Val Verde SO. Hopefully, they wouldn't be needed.

It's pretty flat in most of Quayle County. The rocket ship pilot saw the improvised roadblock nearly a mile away. He pumped the brakes hard and jerked the wheel to the right. No worries. He would go around it. The ground on the shoulder, and even further to the right, appeared to be level, consisting of nothing more than hard baked dirt and gravel. He was doing just fine, until he crested a wide, six-foot deep, dry arroyo which he didn't see until it was too late. He had no problem flying over most of it, but after a bone-jarring landing, the undercarriage of the Ford got stuck halfway up the east side slope.

Shit! He had lost his gun in the car someplace! Frantically, he pushed open the driver's door and jumped out. He lost his footing on the sandy, uphill slope, and began to slip and slide down the west slope of the east bank of the arroyo, in a herculean effort to escape. He could not afford to get busted, for more reasons than one.

Both Barlow and Sheriff Sol knew about the arroyo, so they stayed on the paved highway. Barlow managed to get out of his unit first. He ran down the driver like a cheetah chasing a zebra, and made a leaping tackle that would make Dallas Cowboys Coach Tom Landry proud. The driver fell face first and landed hard on his stomach on the hardpan. It knocked the air out of him. Barlow landed just as hard on the driver's back, adding insult to injury. Barlow had his service revolver in his hand, and he screwed the barrel as deep as it would go into the driver's right ear. "If you so much as breathe hard, I'll blow your brains out right here in the dirt."

The perp was gasping for air. Finally, he choked out, "Don't shoot! I surrender."

Randy and Sheriff Sol arrived right after Barlow cuffed the Mario Andretti wannabe behind his back. He had wild eyes, like a rabid dog. Randy kept the shotgun trained on the perp. Sheriff Sol looked on, bent over at the waist, while sucking big drafts of air. Finally, Sheriff Sol said, "Barlow, stuff him in your back seat. (Gasp. Gasp. Gasp.) Randy, check to see if we can get this car out of here, and then thank the truck driver for all his assistance. (Gasp. Gasp.) Make sure you get his name and address, and the name of his company and their address, so we can send thank you letters. (Gasp.) Then you can send him on his way. This asshole doesn't know it, but that trucker saved his miserable life. (Gasp.) I'll go back to my unit and call Base, and tell them to cancel DPS and Val Verde. I'll also tell Loretta to get Buck Boyd out here with his wrecker. Everyone clear?" (Huff. Puff.)

Both deputies were clear.

It was 6:30. The Ford was impounded at Buck Boyd's Phillips 66 service station. Chief Alex had run NCIC, NLETS, and DPS record checks on the driver. His name was Leo C. Potts. His monicker was Popeye, because his left eye looked off to the left at an upward angle. He maintained an intense stare in two different directions, so when you looked directly at him, you weren't sure which eye to focus on.

Popeye was 32 years of age. He was five-feet, eight-inches tall, weighed 155 pounds, with brown eyes and thin, scraggly, shoulder-length hair. He looked like a pushover, but that didn't mean he wasn't dangerous. Although he wasn't all that physically imposing, he was the kind of guy who would nonchalantly stab you in the back if you ever took your eyes off of him. He was as trustworthy as a scorpion, who thought he was master of the patch of ground that you walked upon.

He was also probably one of the smartest dirtbags most cops would ever encounter. He had a bachelor's and a master's degree from UTEP, and he was supposed to be some kind of a chemistry wizard. Except for his cockeye, it was hard to understand how a person with this much talent would become such a degenerate. He was last known to reside in McNary, Texas, just south of Fort Hancock on the Mexican border, where the car was stolen. Supposedly he was a welder, not a chemist, by trade. Maybe so, but in all actuality, he was one of the missing members of the Diablos Motorcycle Club. He had a tattoo to prove it, and a criminal record to further substantiate it.

In addition, his driver's license had been revoked for five years for hit-and-run and DWI. His rap sheet included two stints in Huntsville. One was a three-year layover for burglary, and the other was ten years for rape, for which he only served five, before getting paroled. In addition, he had arrests for auto theft, distribution of a controlled substance, simple assault, grand larceny, and a dozen or so misdemeanors. The kicker was a year-old outstanding warrant from the El Paso Sheriff's Office for murder, and one from the Texas Department of Corrections for parole violation.

Chief's search of the Ford resulted in the recovery of a Colt Police Positive, .38 Special revolver, with a filed-off serial number, and a baggy with 1,250 tablets of Valium, a Schedule IV drug. All in all, this was a very big bust for Quayle County. They charged Leo with speeding 130 miles per hour in a fifty mile per hour zone; reckless driving; driving on a revoked driver's license; receipt of stolen property (auto); resisting arrest; felon in possession of a firearm; possession of a firearm with an obliterated serial number; and, possession of Schedule IV drugs with intent to distribute. Furthermore, the El Paso County Sheriff's Office was coming tomorrow to personally serve a detainer and execute the warrant for murder, plus a new one for auto theft. DOC said they would mail a copy of their warrant for parole violation.

Randy and Barlow processed Popeye for fingerprints, photographs, personal history, personal property, strip searched him, clothed him in horizontal, two-inch, black-and-white stripes and shower clogs, and lodged him in cell #1, while Chief Alex handled liaison with the other police agencies, the criminal complaint, and the evidence. Chief Alex would have interviewed Popeye, but he invoked his Miranda warning rights as soon as he was cuffed and caught his breath.

Everything was coming up roses. A great day had been had by all, except for Popeye. Time to go sup, and bask in the satisfaction a job well done. Today, in Quayle County, all was well, hunky dory even. Barlow was all smiles.

Sheriff Sol said, "Great job, Fellas. Outstanding job, actually. Chief Alex and I are calling it a day. I hate to say it Barlow, but it must be said. 'No good deed goes unpunished.' This isn't intended as punishment, but you're the rookie so you get jail duty. Randy, you hit the bricks. Keep us safe, and make us all proud. Sorry Barlow, but you're also the afternoon shift jailer for the rest of the week. It truly sucks when a deputy does his job so well that he winds up on jail duty. It's like finding out your birthday cake is full of ants before you even get to taste it. However, I do have one very small consolation for you. When you call over to Betty's for Leo's meal, order one for yourself. It's on me. Adiós."

Sheriff Sol and Chief Alex turned and sailed out the door. Randy had a Mona Lisa smile. He shook his head. Barlow was in disbelief. His mood went from euphoric to disconsolate in five seconds or less. So this is the price one pays for a few hours of excitement.

# CHAPTER 5

## Tuesday, May 25, 1971
## Bad News for Popeye

Popeye was cooling his heels in cell #1, waiting to go to court. This had to be the worst dungeon in America. He was lucky they provided him with a roll of toilet paper! He was suffocating in this airless, stuffy, ten-by-ten, concrete sweat box. There wasn't so much as a breeze to carry a fart away. To top it off, the screw babysitting him this morning was a middle-aged, portly, Mexican deputy. Popeye despised greasers worse than spooks, kikes, chinks, and queers. Damn it to Hell!

He was 'screwed, blued, and tattooed.' Gravy Train would wonder if he absconded with the pills, since he never showed up. Wingnut would be wondering, too, trying to decide if he should pack up and move the shop, in case Popeye got busted and squealed, or whether he should send someone to look for his dead body, in the event someone rubbed him out. Undoubtedly, they both would hear about his arrest in a day or two. He hoped they would know that he didn't squeal. There wouldn't be any prison safe for him anywhere, if they thought he had.

Basically, he was a soup sandwich. Completely tapped out. No dough. Ditto for the few guys from the club who were still on the outside. The club was broke, and everyone was in hiding, all scattered about. They no longer had a clubhouse or a mouthpiece on retainer.

Damn! He could use that slimy, fat fuck Elton Stonebreaker

about now. He really knew how to sway a jury. He might even find a way for him to beat the rap! Without a primo lawyer, Popeye knew he was staring down a good twenty-year sentence in this armpit of a town, with all the charges they stacked on, especially with that mad dog judge. Then, he had to beat the murder rap in El Paso! He was stuck with public defenders. Damn! He could get the death penalty!

He had to think of something fast. He thought he could probably kill that greaser guard, but he'd never get out of the building alive without some help. Even if he could break out, where the Hell would he go? Mexico, like Gravy Train? Fuck! He might as well be dead! He had to get himself under control. There had to be a way.

In honor of Popeye's escapade from one end of Quayle County to the next, District Attorney Able DeWitt convened the grand jury at nine o'clock, which was bright and early for legal work. Popeye had no idea that just one floor above him, twenty or so good citizens of Quayle County were deciding just how much blood they wanted to exact for his reckless disregard of the law, and for jeopardizing their collective safety.

Turns out it was a whole lot of blood. Buckets full. Chief Deputy Sheriff Alex Snodgrass recited chapter and verse, regarding Leo C. Potts' thirty-to-forty-minute crime spree. DA DeWitt even had the chief present the misdemeanors, even though it didn't require a grand jury to authorize prosecution on misdemeanors - only felonies, but since it was all one continuous stream of outlaw activity, DA DeWitt thought it would be easier for the grand jury to keep everything in context. One crime just morphed into another.

The grand jury was horrified. Most of them had already been

informed of the juicier portions of the one-man crime spree, fully embellished of course, but getting the poop straight from the horse's mouth, an officer of the law who was actually there, well that was like feeding raw meat to a starving wolf. Singly, but ultimately collectively, this was what they asked. "Was this man part of that outlaw biker group that tried to kill Judge Sweeney and Deputy Adams? What if Old Man Bilgewater had been halfway across the street on his walker, or poor old Miz Biddy Beanblossom, she's half blind, you know, stepped out into the street when that hooligan come racing through town? He could have run them both down! You don't suppose he was planning to sell them pills to our schoolchildren, do you? Oh my gosh! And what about that there firearm? Do you think he could have kilt somebody with it, and that's why he filed off the serial number? Did you check to see if it had been used against Deputy Adams? I heard one of them guns turned up missing. This just won't do! This is a peaceful, God-fearing community. I vote 'aye' to charge him on each and every count! I hope Judge Sweeney learns him the error of his ways, and sends him up the river for a good long time! Good riddance, I say! I heard he kilt somebody in El Paso, too!"

It took less than thirty minutes. DA DeWitt and the sheriff's office got everything on their wishlist. Mr. Leo C. Potts wasn't the only sinner in town, but by God, he was the worst one to come through here since his compadre, Joe Shit the Ragman. A Day of Reckoning was coming! Yessiree Bob!

After the grand jury vacated the courthouse, Deputy Noble "Chunk" Bustamante and Sheriff Sol escorted a heavily-shackled, wary, and wily prisoner - one Leo C. Potts, a/k/a Popeye - up to the courtroom. Court-appointed counsel, Mr.

Samuel Davis, Esquire, an extremely competent and experienced attorney, was waiting for him at the defense table. After introductions, which were brief and neutral, they had a hushed but serious confabulation.

Mr. Davis gave Mr. Potts a copy of the indictment with all eight charges filed in Quayle County. He said, "Besides these charges, you need to be prepared for service on three additional counts. One for murder, and another for auto theft from El Paso County, and a third count for parole violation filed by the Department of Corrections. Do you understand the gravity of your situation?"

Mr. Potts uttered, "Yes."

Mr. Davis articulated, "The only charges for which I will be defense counsel, are the ones filed by Quayle County, stemming from the series of incidents yesterday. Whichever way it goes, guilty or not guilty, as soon as those charges are fully resolved, you will be transported to El Paso County to face the other charges with court-appointed counsel from there. Do you understand?"

"I do."

"What do you want to do regarding the eight charges pending before you here?"

"I want you to find out the best deal you can get for me, if I plead guilty. Then I will decide."

"Are you aware that since you have already been indicted, that Judge Sweeney will probably schedule trial for Thursday or Friday of this week?"

"No! Hell no! Is there any way I could be released on bond?"

"Mr. Potts, I do not think Judge Sweeney would release you on bond even if you had $100,000 in cash to post with the clerk of court. Do you have that kind of money?"

"No, of course not. If I did, I'd sure as Hell have a better lawyer than you."

"If you did, you'd be well advised to hide that money where it would be safe. Otherwise, all you'd accomplish would be to line the pockets of your lawyer. Getting back to business, Mr. Potts, do you have a defense to any of these charges, the first being speeding 130 in a 50 MPH zone?"

"No."

"Reckless driving?"

"No."

"Revoked license?"

"No."

"Resisting arrest?"

"Not really."

"Receipt of stolen property, to wit: the car belonging to Mr. Morgenstern?"

"No."

"Felon in possession of a firearm?"

"It wasn't on me. It was in the car."

"Doesn't matter, by law. You were the only one in the car. Not only that, you were driving and it was found on the front floorboard."

"Then I guess not."

"Possessing a gun with an obliterated serial number?"

"I didn't file it off. I got it like that."

"Doesn't matter, by law."

"No. Hell no!"

"Possession of Schedule IV Drugs with intent to distribute?"

"No."

"Do you have any information to trade, such as a serious

felony about to go down, or the location of a fugitive, or someone who committed an unsolved murder, stuff like that?"

"I'm not a rat."

"Okay then. I'll be frank. In my professional opinion, you are screwed big time. Judge Maxwell 'Maximum Max' Sweeney will throw the book at you, and anything else he can get his hands on. I'd say you are looking at twenty or thirty years, probably without benefit of parole. Still want me to try to cut a deal?"

"Yes."

"Very well. I will plead you not guilty today. The judge will remand you back to jail, and schedule your trial before you even get your first shower here. You're going away for a long time, Potts. Forewarned is forearmed. Plan on having a lot of time on your hands to master the art of making license plates. I'll do what I can for you, but you haven't given me much to evoke any sympathy from a jury, or this judge. Sit tight. I'll let the DA know we're ready."

Mr. Davis motioned to the clerk of court, who stood up and said, "All rise."

As if on cue, the judge entered the courtroom with his robes flapping like the wings of an eagle, a bald eagle, exactly like the august symbol of our great nation. He took a seat on his oversized, high-back, stuffed-leather chair on rollers, behind his desk, on the side of the bar reserved for legal royalty, with his piercing blue eyes peering into the distance past his hawk-like nose, just like a bird of prey surveying his domain for a juicy rodent to devour. He scowled. It didn't look like he found a plump rabbit. It was like he spotted a coiled rattlesnake, with beady eyes and a bad disposition. Eagles devour snakes, too, poisonous or otherwise.

The clerk, also serving as the bailiff, drew to attention at his full height of five-feet, four-inches tall, and recited, "Hear ye. Hear ye. The Circuit Court for the County of Quayle, in the state of Texas, the Honorable Judge Maxwell B. Sweeney presiding, is now in session. All ye who have matters before this court come forward, and ye shall be heard. God bless America and this honorable court."

Judge Sweeney kept the people standing for about ten seconds, studying each person as if he were sizing up someone for the gallows. Finally he said, "Be seated. What case have we before the court today, Mr. Clerk?"

"Your Honor, today we have an initial appearance, arraignment, and bond hearing on Mr. Leo C. Potts, docket number 71-05-0116."

"Are all parties present, Mr. Clerk?"

"Yes, Your Honor."

"Counsels, please state your names for the record."

"District Attorney Able DeWitt representing the State, Your Honor."

"Mr. Samuel Davis, Esquire, Your Honor, court-appointed counsel, representing Mr. Leon C. Potts, who is here beside me."

"Very good. And what is the matter before the court today, Mr. DeWitt?"

"Your Honor, Mr. Potts was arrested yesterday by the sheriff's office on eight counts. They include speeding 130 miles per hour in a 50 mile per hour zone; reckless driving; driving on a revoked operator's license; resisting arrest; receipt of stolen property, to wit: the automobile he was driving; convicted felon in possession of a firearm; possession of a firearm with an obliterated serial number; and, possession of Schedule IV drugs, to wit: 1,250 twenty-milligram tablets of Valium, with intent to distribute. The grand jury indicted Mr. Potts on all these counts today, and a copy of the indictment has been provided to counsel, and to the defendant.

"In addition, although it does not impact this court at all, the El Paso County Sheriff's Office will come today and serve a detainer for Mr. Potts, as a result of two arrest warrants. One is for murder, an indictment having already been returned, and the other is for grand larceny (auto) on a criminal complaint, which was just filed yesterday. An indictment for that will be forthcoming on that charge as well. Furthermore, the Department of Corrections in El Paso County has an outstanding warrant on Mr. Potts for parole violation. The sheriff's office agreed to bring a copy of that detainer with them today, too.

"This is Mr. Pott's initial appearance. In addition, this is also his arraignment. Finally, it is my understanding that he wishes to request a bond hearing."

"My, my, Mr. Potts. What a sordid tale of woe! Let District Attorney DeWitt's recitation of that lengthy list of allegations serve as both a formal listing of charges for your initial appearance, and for your arraignment. Do you wish for the indictment to be read word for word into the record, or will the written copy provided to you suffice?"

Mr. Davis stood. "Judge, we waive formal reading of the indictment. We are prepared to enter a plea."

"Very well. Is it necessary for me to read all the counts or does the defendant wish to make a carte blanche plea?"

Mr. Davis told the defendant to rise. After he did, Mr. Davis said, "Your Honor, Mr. Potts wishes to plead 'not guilty' on all counts."

"So be it. Let the record reflect that Mr. Potts has entered a not guilty plea on all eight counts. Trial is scheduled for ten o'clock on Thursday, May 27th, 1971. I don't expect the trial to take more than two hours. Three at the very most. Let's get this done, so Mr. Potts can go tend to his business in El Paso.

"Now with respect to a bond hearing. First, let me state for the record that bond is predicated upon two issues. First, is the defendant a threat to society? In other words, is he likely to hurt himself or others? If the answer is 'yes', the judge shall not set bond. Second, is the defendant a flight risk? Will he voluntarily appear for all court appearances, or is he likely to abscond? If the answer is that he is likely to abscond, the judge shall not set bond.

"Now in this case, with detainers being filed later on today, it really does not matter if I set a bond. Assuming Mr. Potts has the means to post any bond I set, he still can't be released, until he satisfies any bonds set by the other jurisdiction. I know a lot of judges would defer making a ruling on bond in a situation like this, essentially passing the buck to the other court, to avoid looking like a hard case. I'm not going to do that. I'm going to make a ruling for the record.

"Mr. Potts, I hereby rule that I believe you to be both a threat to society, and a flight risk. I can think of no conditions, zero, which would render you both harmless to society, and compliant with the court. To be crystal clear, if the U.S. Supreme Court ruled that I had to set a bond, I would do so against my better judgment. I would set your bond at one million dollars cash, to be posted with the clerk of court. I hereby remand you to remain in the custody of the sheriff, ineligible for bond in this court.

"Are there any more matters before this court?"

DA DeWitt replied, "No, Your Honor."

"So be it. Court is adjourned."

The bald eagle swept off his perch and out the back door into his chambers, probably to feast on a succulent weasel or a groundhog.

Sheriff Sol and Chunk returned Popeye to his spartan accommodations. They both could see his wheels turning, looking for any possible means of escape. Too bad. The entire staff had been ordered to have at least two deputies present anytime he was let out of the jail cell for any reason. It sucked being Popeye. First, the jail was sweltering hot. Second, the meals were basic. No desserts. Third, the only reading material available to him were a King James Version of the Holy Bible, and the copy of his indictment. Fourth, there was no television, no radio, and no other prisoners to talk to. Fifth, the only visitor allowed was his lawyer. Sixth, the only shower he would get would be the one before his trial. Finally, the deputies were instructed not to talk to him, except for official business. No chitchat.

Sam and Able sat at the defense table to parley. It wasn't much of a parley. Able said, "Sam, you know Max is gonna max out Potts, and flush him back into the system. He deserves it, too. I don't have much sympathy. He's looking at a year in jail each, for speeding, reckless driving, driving on a revoked license, and resisting arrest. He's looking at five years each, for possession of stolen property, felon in possession of a firearm, and possession of a firearm with an obliterated serial number. He's looking at ten years for possession of the Schedule IV drugs. Actually, he could get twenty for that, if the judge wants to ding him as a repeat drug dealer. Of course, we'd have to prove the old charge in El Paso County, but he's looking at so much time already, that I don't feel like going to all that effort. So, he's facing a potential sentence of 29 years because you know Max will stack the sentences. What are you offering in mitigation?"

"I don't have anything, other than avoiding a trial. He's not going to hand anyone up. He asked me to see what I could do, so I'm finding out. Would you consider some concurrent sentences, or some reduced sentences?"

"Sorry, Sam. Max was right. This trial won't take two hours. Max will have DOC or EPSO sitting in the courtroom, ready to haul Popeye's ass straight back to El Paso just as soon as he's pronounced sentence. This is the best I can do. Tell him I will stand mute on any recommended sentence, if he pleads guilty straight up on each count. Maybe Max will toss him a bone, but I doubt it. However, you can just about guarantee Mr. Potts that Max will max him out if he is convicted in a trial. It might make a difference of three or four years. Then again, it might not."

"Okay. Thanks. I'll go down and talk to him. Let you know after while."

"Fair enough. Good luck."

Sam would rather have laid his dick on a counter and hit it with a five-pound, ball-peen hammer, than to traipse down to the dungeon and discuss anything, let alone the two bad options available to this asshole, but do it he must.

The visit didn't take long. Potts decided to plead straight up. Then he pointed his finger at Sam and whispered, "You're the world's very worst lawyer, ever. When I get out of stir, I'm gonna look you up, no matter how long it takes. When you see me, it will be too late. You'll be a gone pecan. I'll make sure it hurts real bad, too. You're a dead man walking, Mister. You just keep that in mind when we're in court Thursday, Counselor. Have a nice fucking day."

Sam prayed, "Dear God, if it be Your will, please make sure this savage gets the death penalty in El Paso. I'd pay my own way, just to be a witness to his execution. Amen."

Then he thought, "How do the cops sleep at night, putting it all on the line arresting monsters like this? Society's still not safe when these savages get incarcerated, because they inevitably get out. The death penalty is the only sentence which eliminates the possibility of recidivism, and it is sorely needed for these kind of criminals. If the general public ever saw for themselves what the police and prison guards see on a regular basis, animals like this would be laid to rest. God help us all."

# CHAPTER 6

## Wednesday, May 26, 1971
## What Barlow Doesn't Know Could Kill Him

A low-down, murdering, sociopath called Larry the Fairy, who was born in this world as Lawrence J. Krebs, Jr., further identified as inmate # 47069 at the Texas State Penitentiary in Huntsville was serving life without parole for murdering his mother.

He staked her out on a half dozen, foot-tall, two-feet-in-diameter, fire ant hills in her backyard outside of Odessa, Texas, in the sizzling July sun. He caught her when she was passed out drunk. Otherwise, he probably would not have been able to subdue her. He stripped her naked to give the ants easier access to her flesh. The little bastards bit the shit out of him while he was staking her out. He still had the welts. He gave her no water. He wanted her to suffer. Suffer she did.

She cried, and screamed, and begged until her throat was so parched, and her tongue was so thick, that she no longer could. It didn't matter. Nobody could hear her. That's because Larry and his mother lived in a filthy, derelict mobile home, way out in the prairie. No one else lived within two miles and nobody ever came around, because Mildred Krebs and her son were such despicable human beings. It was rumored that Mildred engaged in sex with her son. No one could prove it, but everyone believed it.

It took her five days to die, before her heart finally gave out. Larry sat out back under an awning, and watched, and listened to, the entire, agonizing, unthinkable, horrifying affair, while he guzzled all of Mildred's Pabst Blue Ribbon beer. It was as warm as bath water, but he didn't care. He tortured and killed her because he was strung out on methamphetamines, and his mother wouldn't give him any money to buy some more. The fact that she had no money was of no consequence. The bitch had it coming.

He got caught because the postman had a package to deliver, and no one answered the door. He stepped around to the backyard and saw something that he could never unsee. He dropped the package and ran for his life back to his truck. He barely got away from Larry, who tried to bash him with a fourteen-inch monkey wrench. The letter carrier drove to the nearest house two miles away and begged Mrs. Mulligan to call the sheriff. She did, and they came, and they had to shoot Larry because he tried to bash them with the same wrench.

The deputy who shot Larry didn't do a very good job. In fact, he did a piss-poor job. He shot Larry once in the right chest, and the bullet passed clean through without damaging anything vital. Larry survived without any debilitating injury. He was eighteen years old, and he only had one prior, which was for possession of meth. He was convicted of capital murder, but the judge commuted the sentence to life without parole due to Larry's age.

Now Larry was a prison bitch who worked in the library. He saw something in the May 2nd, *El Paso Bugle*, and he thought it might be worth a pack of smokes if he gave it to Joe Rag. He was surprised that none of the other inmates had seen this. It was probably because none of the inmates gave a hoot about the society section of the newspaper.

That afternoon, while he was making his rounds pushing the

library cart down the prison walks, he made it a point to stop by Joe Rag's cell. Joe seldom wanted a book or a magazine, and he was one mean, disagreeable, dangerous inmate. He was clearly a psychopath, even Larry could see that, but he was a rich one by inmate standards because he had many cartons of smokes. They weren't paid for by his mother or an auntie, either. Joe didn't have one red cent on his canteen account. He got his smokes from other inmates. There wasn't an inmate who didn't fear Joe Rag, and who wouldn't give Joe whatever he wanted, just to remain among the living. Larry stopped at Joe's cell.

"Hey, Joe. You want something to read? I have a good selection today."

"Don't bother me you little faggot unless you have the latest copy of Penthouse."

"I ain't got that, but I got something you'd probably like a whole lot more. I figure it's worth a pack of smokes, at least."

"Tell you what, you little bitch. How about you drop on your knees and blow me? If you do it right, I'll give you five smokes."

"Some other time, Joe. The screws might catch me, and I'd lose my job. Too many eyes watching anyway. I ain't shitting. I really got something I think you want to see. How about it? One pack of smokes. If it ain't something that grabs your attention after you read it, I'll give you a piece of ass in the showers tomorrow and you keep the smokes."

"Hand it over, and I'll decide. If you're stringing me along, both me and Dick Wad will both pack your fudge tomorrow until we decide we've had enough. Savvy?"

"Savvy. Take a look at this." With that he passed the society section of the paper folded over until you could only read one article.

Dick Wad got up out of his bunk, and walked over to the bars to see what it was that was supposed to be worth a whole pack of smokes. Joe and Dick read the article at the same time.

Joe Rag said, "Fuck a duck!"

Dick Wad asked, "Ain't that the baby cop what broke your arm?"

"It surely is. Dick, give Larry a pack out of my stash. Listen, punk. I'm keeping the article. You're keeping your mouth shut, if you know what's good for you. If anybody even mentions what's in this article to me, you're a dead man. Savvy?"

"Sure, Joe. Mum's the word."

Once Larry was gone, Joe said, "I hope I hear something good from Gravy Train, soon. Now we know when and where that pendejo will be without any backup. We're gonna fuck his bride in front of his eyes, and then we're gonna kill them both. I can hardly wait."

"Me either."

Larry might be a prison bitch, but he wasn't born yesterday. He was cunning, and he was obsequious to anyone who might do him a good turn, like a certain day captain of the screws. Soon as he rolled out of Joe's sight, he stopped to see if he could hear anything useful being uttered by Joe. Bingo! Now he knew Joe and Dick had an escape plan, and that if they got out, the deputy and his wife were dead meat. Larry also had enough savvy to sit on this information until after they escaped. That way, if things got messed up and they got caught breaking out, they'd never link him as a snitch, and do him in.

# CHAPTER 7

Thursday, May 27, 1971
Clouds Give Way to Sunshine

Barlow was still on afternoon jail duty, but he had court this morning at ten o'clock. He spent a little more time than usual getting dressed. He put a high gloss shine on his boots. His shave was close. His uniform was crisp. He stopped by Espy's Barbershop and got him a trim. He even had his mustache trimmed. He polished his badge, until it blinded him in the sun. He made sure his gun belt was on straight, and lined up perfectly with his gig line. He would be called to testify today. He wanted to look sharp, and he did.

When he walked into the jail, Chunk said, "Lookee here. Chief, you need to get a picture of this. Bronco Barlow looks like he's gonna be in the movies today. Maybe we could get some recruitment posters made up, with Barlow looking like a cowboy movie star."

"Well, if I hadda known that getting all gussied up for court was gonna cause all this commotion, I wouldn't have shined my boots, or got a haircut. All I'm tryin' to do is make a good impression on the judge and the jury. Anything wrong with that?"

Chief said, "Not a thing. We all love to see a strack troop. Even Chunk. He's just giving you the business, because he's been cooped up with that pox on humanity the past couple of days. Chunk, how many times has he called you a greaser or a beaner?

"I quit counting, Chief. If he was gonna be here much longer, I'd probably end up doin' something I'd regret. The good news is, I spoke with Diego Romero and Conrad Oglesby from EPSO when they stopped by to serve the detainers. They said they got a slam dunk on the murder rap. They got three eyewitnesses, civilians, not scumbags, who're lined up to testify. They got the gun with Popeye's prints on it. They also recovered the vic's wallet and watch from Popeye's truck. They would've had Popeye, too, but he bugged out the backdoor and outran them when they were trying to serve the arrest warrant. They say he's lookin' at a wild ride on the state's 10,000-watt lightning bolt."

Chief said, "So Barlow, this really was a significant traffic arrest. Our charges may be piddly compared to El Paso's, but we put the habeas grabbus on Popeye, not them, and they've been looking for him for two months, and I mean really looking, not just making the motions. The man he killed was the brother of one of EPPD's patrol sergeants. The vic was a convenience store owner and the father of five. Popeye got away with the contents of the till, which had less than a hundred bucks, and the vic's wallet, watch, and Masonic ring. You should feel proud.

"Oh yeah. I forgot to tell you. Popeye's pleading straight up today, hoping Judge Sweeney cuts him a little slack. You can bet that Max has already talked to El Paso's chief of detectives, and that he knows the murder file better than their own DA. Nope. Popeye won't get a break here; doesn't deserve it, either.

"Listen carefully! We need to be mindful that Leo Potts is a cunning son of a bitch, and quite capable of killing anyone who gets in his way, especially a cop. The best odds for him to continue breathing oxygen longterm, would be for him to escape before they lock him down in El Paso's cellblock for capital crime prisoners. Popeye's from El Paso. He's spent more than a few nights in their jail, and he's already familiar with the story that anyone who's ever spent even one night in that cellblock has always wound up strapped in the electric chair. No one's ever avoided it, or so the story goes.

"So, here's the deal. Barlow, you and Chunk, and Sheriff Sol and I, are all escorting Leo Potts to court. You're the only one who has to testify. You're doing the allocution. We have no intelligence that anyone will try to spring Potts, but we are taking no chances. Zero. EPSO will have two deputies in the courtroom and two on the street out front. Slick will also be out there someplace, in his own truck wearing plain clothes. You and Chunk will assist EPSO, by following their transport to their jail at the conclusion of court. Give Popeye no quarter. Same for any of his friends. Tomorrow, you're back on afternoon patrol, this time with Slick. Any questions?"

"Only one. Can we check out a Thompson for the trip to El Paso?"

"Tell him, Chunk."

"I've already checked one out, with four spare magazines. It's in the trunk of the Dodge. I'll drive. You ride shotgun, rather machine gun, this afternoon."

"Sweet."

Chief Alex responded, "Thought so. Now you two peckerwoods go get the man of the hour. Sheriff Sol and I will wait for you in the hallway up the stairs."

Chunk and Barlow prepared Popeye for court, as well as for travel to El Paso. They shackled him with leg irons and a thick leather belly band with metal loops, fastened to the leg irons, and to the wrist irons by heavy chains, which restricted the lateral movement of his feet to twelve inches, and the vertical and lateral movement of his wrists to three inches. He was still dressed in jail stripes and shower clogs. Since he wasn't coming back, they picked up the paper sack with his personal clothing and items recovered from his pockets, and brought it with. Barlow did the shackling and Chunk did the guarding with his trusty nightstick. Popeye sensed that Chunk's can of whoop-ass was ready to pop open, so he minded his P's and Q's for the time being. He figured he'd have a better chance of escape once he was in the courtroom or out of the building.

They did not remove any of the shackles in the courtroom. Chunk shoved Popeye into a chair at the defense table, before taking a position in the right front corner of the courtroom. Popeye looked around and saw the colossal, featherhead Indian high sheriff seated in the jury box, as close to the defense table as he could possibly get. His obsidian eyes and the expressionless look on his face reminded Popeye of a hungry python. It also reminded him of how much he fucking hated any kind of Indian, feather head or dot-head.

The pudgy, baldheaded cop in plainclothes wearing tortoise-rimmed glasses, who was seated at the prosecution table, did not look like he posed a threat whatsoever. He looked like a schoolteacher or a post office clerk. A bean counter. A reader and writer. Not a fucker and fighter. Certainly not a man of action, unless it was with an ink pen or a typewriter.

The baby cop who tackled him, had taken up a position in the rear of the courtroom. Popeye definitely knew who he was, and had from the very beginning. He was a dead man walking for killing five of his brothers, not to mention the frame he hung on Joe Shit and Screech, and now himself. Within the remnants of the Diablos Motorcycle Club, there was still an open hit on that douche. They didn't post it outside their remaining coterie of one-percenters, for one very good reason. They didn't have the dough to make it worth the risk for someone who didn't have a deep-seated personal interest, to execute a cop and take on the wrath of the entire cop brotherhood nationwide. All the other outlaw bikers knew what trying to kill this pendejo, and the prick judge who was going to sentence him today, had cost the Diablos. This was a vendetta contract, not a profit-for-hire hit. Baby Cop's day would come.

There were also two uniforms from the El Paso SO, seated on the bench behind the prosecution table. Popeye knew they were his chauffeurs back to the cooler in his hometown. Looked like Stan Laurel and Oliver Hardy in uniforms. They definitely didn't look like much of a threat. If he had half a chance, they'd be knocking on the gates to Hell before the end of the day.

There were also a couple of busybodies sitting a few rows behind him. Two old biddies here to enjoy the show. They would do as hostages, if need be. Wouldn't that just serve them right, the skinny old, fraidy cat ghouls?

The last thing Popeye noted before the bailiff, the clerk, and the two mouthpieces showed up, was that he had no confederates. If he were going to make a break here, it would be all on his lonesome. It was just about what he expected.

Sam Davis, Esquire, took the seat next to him. He whispered, "Have you changed your mind?"

"No."

The bailiff stood and called the court to order. He announced and blessed the court. Today, Judge Sweeney entered the courtroom like he was gliding on a magic carpet. Smooth and serene. He actually had a smile on his face. He sat down promptly and told everyone to take a seat. After the clerk read the docket number in the case between one Leo C. Potts and the State, and counsels had identified themselves before the court, he asked, "Mr. DeWitt, are you prepared for trial today?"

"I am, Your Honor, but Mr. Davis needs to address the court first."

"Speak, Mr. Davis."

Sam Davis rose, tugging the defendant up with him. He stated, "Your Honor, my client wishes to change his plea from 'not guilty' to 'guilty' on all counts. There is no plea agreement between the State and my client. Mr. Potts wishes to throw himself on the mercy of the court."

"Is this true, Mr. Potts? You want to plead 'straight up' as it were, to all counts?"

"I do."

"Are you pleading guilty because you are, in fact, guilty?"

"Yes."

"Has anyone threatened you, if you did not plead guilty, or promised you a more lenient sentence if you do?"

"No."

"We shall see. Have a seat.

"Mr. DeWitt, call your witness for the allocution."

"The State calls Deputy Sheriff Barlow K. Adams to the stand."

Barlow stepped up to the bar, placed his left hand on the Bible and raised his right. The clerk swore him in. He took his seat in the witness box.

DA DeWitt stated, "Deputy Adams, tell the court what happened at approximately 4:15 on the afternoon of Monday,

May 24, 1971, in Quayle County, Texas, which resulted in the arrest of Mr. Leo C. Potts. Before you do, however, please point to the defendant to affirm positive identification."

Barlow pointed to Popeye and said, "Mr. Potts is the man who is seated next to his attorney, Mr. Davis. He's the only person in the courtroom who is wearing jail stripes.

"I was at the rest area on US 90, which is approximately three miles west of Mosby. I heard a motor vehicle approaching at a high rate of speed. I looked up and saw a black, 1965, Ford Galaxy, Texas license number A23541, barreling eastbound towards Mosby. I turned on my emergency equipment in the marked unit I was driving and fell into pursuit. The car did not pull over. It took me a couple of miles to catch up with it. The top speed we attained was 130 miles per hour, although for the most part we were going about 125. I got on the radio and called for backup.

"The defendant did not slow down when we entered Mosby. He continued on at more than 100 miles per hour, changing to the fast lane, dodging the two motorists who were also headed eastbound. One time it looked like the Ford was going to crash into Mr. Taft's delivery van, but the defendant managed to get around it, just before he ran up and nearly rear-ended a green '62, Bel Air station wagon. That, in particular, is why I charged him with reckless driving.

"About the time we left town, and the road went back down from four lanes to two, I saw Sheriff Pratt fall in behind me. I also knew Chief Deputy Snodgrass was following, and that Deputy Meacham was vectoring in from CO 11, just west of the Quayle/Val Verde County line.

"Deputy Meacham arrived at the county line about five

minutes before the rest of us. He flagged down a tractor trailer hauling iron sewer pipes, whose driver agreed to set up a roadblock. When we were about a mile out, the defendant saw the roadblock. He moved over onto the shoulder of the road and even farther to the south, still maintaining a speed of over one hundred miles per hour. It was obvious that he intended to go around the eighteen-wheeler.

"There's an arroyo just before the county line. When the defendant finally saw it, he braked hard, and tried to reduce the impact. He sailed over the west bank, but the undercarriage of the car got hung up on the east bank. The defendant scrambled out of the car, and fled over the embankment. I chased him on foot, and caught up with him before he could escape. I subdued and arrested him. Then I cuffed him, just as Sheriff Pratt and Deputy Meacham ran up. That's why I charged him with resisting arrest.

"I put the defendant in my cruiser. Deputy Meacham, Sheriff Pratt, and Chief Snodgrass searched the vehicle, which was stolen from a Mr. Morgenstern of Fort Hancock in El Paso County. They also found a Colt, .38 Special revolver with an obliterated serial number, and a baggie containing 1,250, twenty-milligram tablets of Valium, which is a Schedule IV drug. As a result, we also charged the defendant with receiving stolen property as it relates to the Ford, felon in possession of a firearm since the defendant has two felony convictions, and with possession of a firearm with an obliterated serial number. Oh, yeah. We also learned the defendant was driving on a revoked license. We charged him with that, too."

Judge Sweeney asked, "Mr. Davis do you have any questions for this officer?"

"No, Your Honor."

"Mr. Potts, is this a true rendition of what happened here on that day, as it relates to your arrest?"

"Pretty much."

"Don't sit down, Mr. Potts. Is there anything the witness said that was incorrect, or that he failed to address?"

"Well, Your Honor, he didn't tell you he knocked the wind out of me when he body-slammed me down on the ground, nearly breaking all my ribs, or that he screwed his gun barrel into my ear real hard, and threatened to blow my brains out if I so much as moved."

"I see. Did you need medical assistance as a result of this rough behavior?"

"No."

"Well then, we'll chalk that up to what can happen when a defendant resists arrest, after a harrowing, lengthy, high speed pursuit, in which numerous lives were put into jeopardy by a fleeing felon. Deputy Adams, you may step down.

"Mr. Davis, do you or the defendant have anything you'd like to add before I pronounce sentence?"

"Judge, I will speak on behalf of my client. He doesn't dispute his guilt. He also acknowledges that he's 'stubbed his toe' several times in the past, as it relates to the law. He's learned his lesson, Your Honor. He is filled with remorse as a result of his bad behavior. He implores you to sentence him below the statutory limits, because putting him behind bars until he is a geriatric, would be like swatting a fly with a sledgehammer. He understands that what he did was wrong. Thirty years in prison is way too grievous, when a third of that would drive the point home, serving justice for all, and still give him time to turn his life around. Thank you, Your Honor."

"Mr. Davis, you get an A-Plus on your eloquent plea for a man who has never respected the law, nor others, nor even himself, I suspect. He's a sociopath, who will never reform, nor will he refrain from doing harm to others. He belongs behind bars for as long as we can legally incarcerate him for the protection of others. I have no doubt he will commence preying on weaker inmates, the minute he arrives in prison.

"Mr. Potts, I hereby sentence you to hard labor in prison for one year for speeding 130 miles per hour in a 50 mile per hour zone; one year for reckless driving; one year for driving on a revoked license, with a recommendation to the Department of Motor Vehicles that they further revoke your driving privileges for another five years; one year for resisting arrest; five years for receiving stolen property; five years for being a felon in possession of a firearm; five years for possession of a firearm with an obliterated serial number; and, ten years for possession of Schedule IV drugs with intent to distribute. All sentences will run consecutively. I know you're a smart man, but I did the math for you. That is a total of 29 years. The only reason that's all you got, is because that's all the law allows.

"I hereby remand you into the custody of the El Paso County Sheriff's Office on the detainers they filed for murder, auto theft, and parole violation, and thence to the Texas Department of Corrections in Huntsville, to serve out this sentence.

"Furthermore, I order the District Attorney's Office to monitor your cases in El Paso. If, by some perversion of Nature, you are acquitted on those charges, I hereby order the District Attorney to file charges against you for being an habitual offender. You are a menace to society, Mr. Potts! It is my unwavering belief that you should never be allowed to draw a breath of air as a free man for so long as you may live, so help me, God!

"Sheriff, remove this convict from my courtroom forthwith!

"Court adjourned!"

# CHAPTER 8

Thursday, May 27, 1971
When Expecting the Worst Is Not Enough

Judge Sweeney handed Sheriff Sol an envelope containing an original, certified, exemplified, Judgment & Commitment Order, affirming his verbal decree, to accompany Leo C. Potts to the El Paso County Sheriff's Office, and thence onto the Department of Corrections after his case in El Paso was adjudicated, and he took up residence in the Texas State Penitentiary for as long, or as short, as that time might be.

Judge Sweeney had had no doubts as to what sentence he would impose, just as soon as he had learned all the facts surrounding Leo Potts' escapade throughout the breadth of Quayle County. As Paul Harvey would say, 'the rest of the story' from El Paso County served to further cement his opinion with rebar. At least two hours before the hearing, he told the county clerk to prepare the order, sign it, crimp his own seal on it, and to bring it to his chambers for him to do likewise. This was Judge Sweeney's standard operating procedure. He did this before all his sentencings, so he could hasten the convict's departure to prison and, thus, remove him from Quayle County posthaste. He firmly believed that 'one rotten apple can spoil the barrel.'

The lawmen waited for the court to clear. It didn't take long. Chief Alex and Barlow stepped outside the courtroom, to ensure that no one was lying in wait. El Paso uniformed Deputy Lucas Slocum and Corporal Heinrich Orbach, amazingly close doppelgängers to the slapstick comedian movie stars of the 1930's, Stanley Laurel and Oliver Hardy, respectively, walked over and introduced themselves to Sheriff Sol and Chunk, who now were hovering over Potts like they expected him to make a break for it any minute.

Corporal Orbach asked if it would be possible to take Potts back to the lockup, so they could switch his outfit to one of theirs, which had red-and-white horizontal stripes. 'Inmate' was stenciled in black vertically along the outside legs of the trousers and horizontally across the chest of the shirt. The back of the long sleeve, pullover shirt was stenciled with 'El Paso County Jail.' In the big city of El Paso, red and white stripes were reserved for dangerous, high-risk inmates. Black and white was for generic inmates. The footwear for all was a cheap pair of thin-soled flip flops, that anyone could purchase for 69 cents at a Five-&-Dime store. They were even flimsier than the ones issued in Quayle County. Orbach stated that they would also put their own restraints on him.

Sheriff Sol readily assented.

Then Corporal Orbach requested, "Sheriff, it's getting close to eleven o'clock. Our jail feeds at noon and six o'clock. We can't get him back for lunch, and if we have any snafus, we'll miss dinner. Would it be okay if we fed Potts here? Sheriff Brady doesn't feed inmates who are not present at mealtime."

Sheriff Sol asked, "Chunk, what's on Betty's blue plate special today?"

"Hot ham and cheese sandwich, pickle spear, Charley's potato chips, peach cobbler, and a soft drink or cup of coffee or iced tea, all for a buck. The choice of soft drink includes Royal Crown Cola, Bubble Up, Nehi Grape, Orange Crush, or Barq's Root Beer."

"Sounds good. You fellas hungry, too?"

Deputy Slocum said, "I am." Corporal Orbach nodded that he was, also.

Sheriff Sol queried, "What about your deputies who're parked out on the street?"

Corporal Orbach answered, "I'm sure they are, too."

"Very well. I'll have Loretta phone in carry out orders for everyone. It's on Quayle SO today. After we get Potts back in lockup, Lucas, why don't you mosey on out to your colleagues and ask them to join us for lunch at the jail?

"Chunk, why don't you take a gander out in the hallway, and make sure the coast is clear? I want to get our prisoner back in a secure location as soon as possible."

Five minutes later, Potts was back in cell #1. With no air conditioning and only one window in the jail, which had just been opened, it was absolutely sweltering. Corporal Orbach handed Potts his new outfit and told him to get changed. He did. The shirt was way too small, and the trousers were big enough that Oliver Hardy could have worn them. The problem was further exacerbated because the waistband had elastic in it to hold them up, but it had long since lost its elasticity, and they were way too loose. Also, the flip flops were ridiculously large. They must have been at least size thirteen.

Potts stood in the cell, with the sleeves bunched up under his armpits, and three inches short of his hands. The body of the shirt was skintight and only extended down as far as his navel. He was holding his trousers up by hand, to keep them from falling down around his knees. He yelled, "You fucker! You did this on purpose!"

Corporal Orbach yelled back, "Aw, ain't that too fucking bad?

The property clerk told me one size fits all. I guess that means now you have something to do with your hands, besides playing with your insignificant, little cock. Don't worry, asswipe. We'll cinch up the belly band, good and tight. Oh, yeah. If you need to take a dump, you better do it here. We ain't making no pit stops on the way back to El Paso. If you shit yourself, you wear it. You'll also clean it up, or you'll wear it in your hair, too!"

"Fuck you, asshole. You're on my shit list!"

"Imagine that, you worthless prick! You're on everyone's shit list! Better get used to it, while you're still able to breathe without suffering. This is as good as it's ever gonna get for you, putz."

Barlow started walking back towards the jailer's room. He motioned to Corporal Orbach, and said, "Come wait in here with me. Your partner or Chunk should be back with our food soon. Don't let this guy get under your skin. His days are numbered, and he knows it."

Corporal Orbach followed begrudgingly, eyes locked on Potts, as if he were a skunk turd resting on top of a pineapple upside down cake at a piano recital soirée. 'Shake it off,' he told himself. This was not his turf. He needed to cool it. This boil on his ass would be singing a different tune once he stepped inside the cellblock for capital crime prisoners in El Paso.

It wasn't long before Chunk arrived. He handed Potts his meal, wrapped in paper with a plastic spoon, and an RC Cola in a paper cup. Then he suggested that Corporal Orbach join the rest of the deputies in the office for lunch, where they had air conditioning. Chunk stated that he and Barlow would stay in the lockup with Potts. Then, when everyone was done eating, ask Chief to let them back in. They could put their irons on Potts before hauling his ass back to El Paso.

This suited Orbach to a T. Chunk led him out of the jail. Chunk returned to the jailer's room, carrying a sack with their meals. Barlow and he ate in peace. Potts was quiet, too. Chunk said, "This is one escort job that I will be glad to get behind me."

Barlow replied, "Me, too. It sounds like things in El Paso are a little rough around the edges."

"All the big cities are, Kid. Be thankful you're in Podunk. We have a whole lot less friction."

They were on the road by 12:45. Loretta phoned the EPSO radio room and notified them of the departure. EPSO led the motorcade in a week-old, marked, 1971, Dodge Charger, which sported a 440 cubic-inch engine, and was purchased for traffic duty to catch speeders on the new interstate highway. It was driven by the hotshot traffic cop, Deputy Enos 'The Penis' Peterson, who most of the deputies hated because he was a dick, with Deputy Quinton Grossman, who was a good guy, riding shotgun. In a perfect world, the roles would have been reversed, but Peterson had seniority and rank over Grossman.

Corporal Orbach drove a marked, well-used, and poorly-maintained, 1970, Econoline prisoner transport van, which had a sluggish, 240 cubic-inch engine. Deputy Slocum rode shotgun. Speed was not one of the van's distinguishing characteristics. Noise was. Learning to deal with the incessant rattling, the origins of which could never be fathomed, was endured like suffering with an abscessed tooth. Another marquee feature was a buckboard-like, rough and tumble ride, similar to a washing machine on spin cycle, which could shake the silver fillings out of a miser's tooth. The prison van's position was 'in the rocking chair.'

Chunk drove Quayle County's trusty and faithful, marked,

1965, Dodge Polara, with more than 350,000 miles on it, because they finally had a new Dodge on order, and they wanted to maximize their usage of the old one before DX-ing it. Barlow rode 'machine gun.' They were in drag.

Slick was way behind them all in his own truck, the pristine, 1941 Studebaker, playing utility outfielder. On the very remote chance that something went awry, it was his job to clean up the mess. He planned to eat supper with Chunk and Barlow at Pfiester's German Bistro after they dropped Popeye off.

The temperature was a balmy 88 degrees, bordering on hot. The humidity was twenty percent. Wind was out of the west at two miles per hour. The sky was cobalt blue and bereft of clouds. No shade anywhere.

Chunk and Barlow had all four windows rolled down as far as they would go, plus they pushed the vent windows out as far as possible. The rushing breeze was a tad noisy, but temperature-wise they were comfortable. Forget the good times radio. The wind made it difficult to hear, unless one turned the volume way up. Anyway, they were in an area where the radio stations were too far away to be picked up without some static during the daytime, and they would be, until they got closer to Alpine.

It didn't matter. Life was good. Rolling along at fifty miles per hour, a quarter-mile behind the jail van for 300 miles before turning around to go home, was nowhere near one of the crappiest assignments either of them had ever performed. Besides that, Chunk knew of a fabulous German restaurant, which served family style meals. It was situated on the eastern outskirts of El Paso. This was where they planned to sup, just as soon as Popeye was safely ensconced in the El Paso County Jail.

Enos the Penis couldn't contain himself. The new Charger

was just too much fun to hotrod. It was absolutely impossible to hold it down to fifty miles per hour. There were just too many horses under the hood begging to stretch out their legs. He alternated between goosing it up well over a hundred for a minute, and then dropping back to an agonizingly slow forty or forty-five for thirty seconds to give that fat fuck, Orbach 'The Whore Back,' time to catch up, which, of course, he never did. Whore Back was dogging it like usual.

Damn, he hated working with Whore Back! Enos the Penis wished the slug would just go ahead and retire. He already had 33 years on the job. His kids were grown. His house was probably paid for. His hobby was playing putt putt golf, for Christ's sake! What's next - shuffleboard? Why wouldn't he just shuffle on out the door with his pension, which was a huge gift from God, because he never did anything to earn it, and make room for someone who would do the job the way it was meant to be done?

They had driven less than ten miles, and already the lead car was out of view, except for the occasional glimpse. No worries. Corporal Orbach didn't trust that dickhead, Enos the Penis, to be there in an emergency anyway. He was 'all hat and no cattle.' All he was good for, was pissing off the public with his imperious attitude, and his fervor for writing chickenshit tickets. No violation was too minor to be overlooked. Nobody got a break. Katy bar the door if the sheriff ever promoted him!

Boom! Flop, flop, flop, flop, flop.

Lucas, who was looking at the right outside mirror, shouted, "Pull over! The right rear tire is flat."

Corporal Orbach had already figured it out by sound and feel, and was in the process of doing just that.

Chunk and Barlow had both heard it explode. Chunk also

prepared to stop. Barlow had even seen the tire blow. What he didn't know was if it blew out on its own accord, or if somebody shot it out. He wasn't taking any chances. What were the odds? They were still in Quayle County! This could be a very long day.

The van came to a complete halt on the right shoulder of the road. Chunk stopped too, but he was about twenty feet behind it and four feet onto the roadway to afford protection from motorists coming from behind, if there were any, but there weren't. Chunk remained seated behind the wheel, watching the road ahead.

Barlow stepped out of the car with the Thompson in both hands, safety off, barrel pointed down towards the ground. It was then that Barlow could see that the lead car was nowhere in sight. What were those guys thinking? Barlow scanned 270 degrees. He could not see the left side of the van from his vantage point. He did not see anyone or anything suspicious. He knew Chunk could see what he couldn't, and that he would have reacted already if anything were wrong.

Deputy Slocum stepped out of the van. He did not appear alarmed. He walked to the right rear wheel and said, "Another flat tire! This van is jinxed! It's the third one in the past two months! You all mind if we put the prisoner in the back of your unit while we change the tire?"

Barlow responded, "No problemo. We're still in Quayle County. We could radio for a wrecker if you want."

"Nope. We got it. Thanks anyway. I recently came to the conclusion that they put the spare tire mount on the back door, to make it easier for us to get to it. I've never had three flat tires on the same vehicle in my entire life. Something's wrong with this one. Besides that, it rides like a cement mixer, except without all the normal comforts, such as a decent seat, or enough legroom for anyone taller than a midget. I hate this van. Rest of the guys don't like it, either."

Barlow heard Corporal Orbach get out of the van, but he couldn't see him. Then he saw Chunk get out of the cruiser, and walk around the rear and open the right rear door. Slocum was busy unlocking the side doors of the van to transfer Potts to the cruiser.

Barlow asked, "What happened to your lead car?"

Slocum said, "No telling. I think they were having a hard time keeping that muscle car down to a low roar." He opened the doors.

Potts looked like he was struggling to step down onto the ground due to the leg irons, even though he was only a foot from it. Wearing those flimsy, gigantic sandals didn't help. It looked like he fell part way but he recovered, and stood up straight.

Corporal Orbach finally walked around the van into Barlow's view, and began to fiddle with the spare wheel mount. He looked up and ordered, "Lucas, hurry up, and get that piece of shit in their car. We haven't got all day."

Just then Potts stumbled. He was about six feet away from the van. Barlow instinctively pointed the Thompson at him. Slocum, who was on Potts' left side and a half-step behind him, bent down to give him some assistance. Slocum's Smith & Wesson, .38 Special, Model 10, service revolver was dangling like a loose piece of fruit from his holster, which he wore on the right side of his waist. It had a strap which was snapped, but the strap was designed to hold the gun in place, not to prevent anyone from unsnapping it.

Potts recognized his opportunity immediately. He twisted left and grabbed the revolver in his right hand at the same moment Slocum lifted him up from the ground. Then Potts, who was stronger than Slocum and much more vicious, jerked Slocum in front of him, and held him in place by the back of his belt with his left hand, using him like a shield.

They all saw what was happening and started to react.

Chunk's field of fire was blocked by Barlow's position in front of him.

Barlow could not shoot the fully automatic submachine gun for fear of hitting Slocum.

Corporal Orbach drew his sidearm, a Colt Diamondback, .38 Special revolver, yelling, "Lucas, look out!" He ran towards Slocum and Potts with his firearm fully extended, as if in preparation to fire. He was less than eight feet away, so this didn't make any sense. If he had a clear shot, he should have taken it. He probably didn't, and just reacted by instinct to the threat. It was both brave and foolhardy.

Due to the restraints, Potts only had a few inches with which to point the gun, and no way to aim it. It didn't matter. They were only three feet apart and the corporal was a large target. Potts fired once and hit Corporal Orbach just above his sternum in his aorta. He dropped like a safe being pushed out the side door of a messenger car on an express train. He bled out in less than a minute in spurts that were eight inches high, until there was no more pressure from a heart which had stopped pumping.

Slocum tried to jerk away, but Potts jammed the gun deep into his right rib cage and cocked it. The clicking sound of a cylinder being rotated to line up the next chamber with a live round directly in front of the barrel for ignition, combined with the snap of the hammer being locked wide open for single-action fire, is distinctive and unmistakable to those who have ever heard it. It's reminiscent of the danger one senses when a rattlesnake shakes its tail. It was only a few decibels, but it sounded as loud as a bull fart at the crack of dawn. Everyone froze in place and stopped breathing, except for Corporal Orbach, who had already stopped breathing, and was also frozen in time and place for all of Eternity.

Potts' eyes were fixed on Barlow when he screamed, "Give me the keys to the car and the cuffs right now, or I shoot this pig here where he stands before I shoot the both of you! Do it now or you all die!"

In the pandemonium, Chunk had stepped right about a foot from behind Barlow, but he still didn't have a clear shot. The good news was neither did Potts have a clear shot at him.

Barlow had barely moved since he stepped out of the unit. Right now he would have traded the Thompson for Sarah's .22 caliber revolver, because the submachine gun was as useless as holding a vacuum cleaner, so long as Potts held Slocum as a shield. Barlow aimed the Thompson directly at Potts' forehead, but the margin for error was just too small. He was racking his brain for a solution.

Then the solution appeared as if by Divine Intervention. Metaphorically speaking, it was an angel with a sword, like the one which prevented Balaam's ass from carrying him where God told him not to go.

Slick rolled up in his shiny old truck. He was dressed in blue jeans, a chambray shirt, and a blue jean jacket, with scruffy old boots, and a sweat-stained Stetson. He stopped in the middle of the road between the cruiser and the van. He leaned over and stuck his head out the passenger window. He asked, like only a rube or country bumpkin could ask, completely oblivious to the obvious, "Everything all right here? Anyone need help?"

Potts yelled back. "Get out of the truck, old man, and get your ass over here."

"Whatever you say, young fella."

Slick put the stick in first gear, turned off the ignition, set the emergency brake, and stepped out of his truck. He stood every bit of five-feet, five-inches tall, and he weighed nearly a buck thirty soaking wet. His jacket was buttoned from the bottom up to the third hole. He was thin enough, that it didn't look like he was hiding anything underneath. He walked between his truck and the van, and stopped and stared at Potts. Then he took two measured steps towards Potts and Slocum. Simultaneously, he pulled his .45 Long Colt caliber Peacemaker revolver, with its six-inch barrel from a shoulder holster. He cocked it, fired, and planted the 250-grain lead ball into Potts' right eyeball socket in one liquid, smooth, easy motion. He didn't even wait for the barrel to quit smoking before he re-holstered. This all happened by the time he completed his third step.

"Golly, fellas, hope I didn't steal your thunder. Need anything else? I can go back and fetch the sheriff if you all want me to."

Deputy Slocum, who was covered with blood, brains, and bone splinters, especially on his face, and who was shaking uncontrollably with fear and shock, hurried over, and shook Slick's right hand with both of his. "Thank you, Sir. You just saved my life. He killed my partner. Nothing I could do. I'm indebted to you forever. You were just so . . . calm and deliberate. I never seen anything like this before."

"De nada. Sorry about your partner. If Barlow hadn't been

toting that bass fiddle over there, he'd have cleaned that sidewinder's gizzard with that .41 Smith and Wesson of his. Believe me. He saved my skin about a year ago."

"You know each other?"

Barlow replied, "Deputy Sheriff Lucas Slocum, meet Deputy Sheriff Clarence Oldman, otherwise known far and wide as Slick. He's a genuine hero by all accounts, which you just witnessed for yourself. He's very modest, if you hadn't noticed. He's pulled my chestnuts out of the fire, too."

Chunk walked over and said, "Look, we gotta get the sheriff out here.

"Slick, how about you and Lucas have a seat in your truck?

"Barlow, would you take a position at the front of the van and keep oncoming traffic moving east? I'll call this in. Then I'll cover the rear."

Lucas exclaimed, "I gotta get my gun! I gotta change the flat! Sheriff Brady's gonna want me to get back to El Paso! I gotta tell Heinrich's wife!"

Slick responded, "Luke, we'll take care of all that. You're in shock. We'll get your gun back to you after the crime scene's been photographed and processed. Come on. Let's go sit down. Sheriff Sol will be here in a few minutes."

"What about my face? I got blood all over it. I gotta wash up."

Slick replied, "Not yet, Amigo."

Then he took Lucas by the arm, and led him back to his truck. Barlow took his post and Chunk returned to the cruiser.

Chunk keyed the mike. "Quayle Base from Quayle 57."

"Come in. Quayle 57."

"Quayle Base, we're about two miles east of the county line. Ask Quayle 1 and Quayle 2 to respond Code 2. Also call Quayle

3's next door neighbor and ask him to meet us."

Chief Alex overheard the radio traffic. He said, "Find out if Quayle 10 is there."

Loretta asked the Chief, "Who is Quayle 3's neighbor?"

"Pete Ricketts. It means somebody's dead."

"Oh, my gosh!

"Quayle 57. Is Quayle 10 with you?"

"10-4."

"10-4. Everyone's en route."

"Roger that."

Sheriff Sol was out the door before Chief Alex could even turn around. Chief didn't dawdle, but Sol was already peeling out of the parking lot by the time he got to his unit.

Ten miles in five minutes. Soon as he arrived, Sol leapt out of the car like a leopard. Chunk was waiting in the roadway.

"Show me what happened."

Chunk lead him to the shoulder of the road, where he could see the right side of the van and the two bodies.

"The van had a flat. We decided to put Potts in the cruiser, while Corporal Orbach and Deputy Slocum changed the tire. I opened the right rear door of the cruiser, and was standing there. Barlow was standing in front of me, by the front passenger door with the Thompson trained on Potts once Slocum got him out of the van. Corporal Orbach was removing the spare from the back door of the van. Potts stumbled and fell over there where his body is. Slocum bent over to help him up, and then when Potts stood up, he twisted to his left, and snatched Slocum's gun out of his holster. Then . . . ."

"Wait a minute. I don't recall what type of rig Slocum is wearing."

"He has on a Don Hume gun belt with a Bill Jordan style holster. It's fine. Nothing out of the ordinary. I think Slocum probably had a momentary lapse in judgment and just got too close trying to help Potts up, and he took advantage of it."

"Okay. Then what?"

"Then Corporal Orbach looked up and yelled out. Potts grabbed Slocum with his left hand, and used him as a shield. He had the gun trained on Corporal Orbach. Then Corporal Orbach pulled his gun and ran towards Potts holding it straight out like he intended to shoot, but he never did. Potts shot once, and hit Corporal Orbach in the chest. He went down. I couldn't shoot, because Barlow was standing in front of me. Barlow couldn't shoot the submachine gun, because he'd have taken out Slocum, too. Soon as Corporal Orbach fell, Potts jammed the gun into Slocum's rib cage. We were in a Mexican standoff.

"Then Slick drove up. Potts ordered Slick out of the truck. Slick got out, and walked up slowly, like a rube, and then quick as a rattlesnake, he pulled his gun out from under his jacket and shot Potts in the head. That's it in a nutshell."

"Where's the other two deputies, Peterson and the other guy?"

"Your guess is as good as mine. They were nowhere in sight once we pulled over."

"Hmmm. That doesn't go over well with me. I'll need to address that with Sheriff Brady."

Just then, Chief Alex showed up. Sheriff Sol briefed him. Then he said, "Lucas, you ride with me back to the jail, just as soon as Chief Alex can get some pictures of you standing where you were when everything went western.

"Chief, take some close-ups of his face and uniform.

"Lucas, we need to get you checked out by Doc Boykin, just to make sure you're okay."

"I'm okay, Sheriff. I'd rather help out here."

"I know you would, but I'm not asking. My county. My rules.

"Slick, you come back with me, too.

"Chief, the rest of you process the scene.

"Barlow, your primary job is to move traffic along if someone stops and wants to gawk.

"Pete Ricketts should be here very soon. Tell him to take Corporal Orbach first.

"I'll call Sheriff Brady when I get back to the jail. If the other two deputies ever do show up, tell them to stand by here, and then you call me. I'll have orders for them from Sheriff Brady. And Chief, if they don't follow your directions to the letter, arrest them and stuff them in the cruiser. I mean it! We'll sort it out later back at the jail.

"Soon as you're done here, get on back to the jail, but call me first. Oh yeah, get that tire changed, too. Any questions?"

Chief responded, "All clear, Sheriff."

# CHAPTER 9

## Thursday, May 27, 1971
## Closing the Books on Popeye

Once they got back to the jail, Sheriff Sol turned Lucas over to Slick to be examined by Doc Boykin. Then he told Loretta that "all of our guys are okay." He was a little out of character, because before she could ask any questions, he walked into his office and closed the door. He called Sheriff Brady's office, and after a couple of minutes, Adrian Brady picked up the phone.

"Hello, Sol. I'm surprised to hear from you. I was told our guys were already on their way back. Everything okay?"

"I wish it were. Your van had a flat before they left Quayle County. Slocum was transferring Potts to our cruiser, which was the follow-up vehicle. Potts managed to get Slocum's weapon away from him. Orbach charged Potts. Potts killed Orbach. One of my guys killed Potts. I've got Slocum in our office, waiting for the doctor to arrive to examine him. My chief's conducting the crime scene. What do you want to do?"

"What about Peterson and Grossman. Where are they?"

"Couldn't say. They were so far out in front of the van, that neither Slocum nor any of my guys could see 'em. We're waiting for them to turn around and come back. They've been gone at least forty-five minutes. I told my guys to radio in if they do return, and that I would pass along your instructions."

"If they do return, tell them to proceed directly to

Headquarters forthwith. After they turn in the prowl car, they are to report to Lieutenant Robles in Internal Affairs.

"Is Slocum okay?"

"Physically, I think he's fine. Emotionally, he's in bad shape. That's why I'm having the doc come to the jail to check him out. Maybe give him a sedative."

"Slocum and Orbach have worked together as partners for a dozen years or so. They were like Pete and Repeat. Have you formally interviewed him yet?"

"No. I need to, but I wanted to talk to you first, plus I'm not sure he's up to it right now."

"What's your take on the matter? Is he at fault?"

"Some would say 'yes.' Others 'no.' Me? I say 'no.' This is why.

"Going back to the beginning, Orbach put the restraints on Potts, and he had him trussed up like a shark in a deep water fishnet. Absolutely no fault there.

"My guys said Potts fell to the ground when Slocum was following him back to our cruiser. I think Slocum was trying to do the right thing and lift Potts up back on his feet. They're both right handed. Slocum was behind Potts to his left. Even though Potts couldn't move his hands more than a couple of inches either way, it was enough so that when Slocum stood him up, Potts used that momentum to jerk and twist to his left and draw Slocum's gun out of his holster. I'm pretty sure he outmuscled Slocum. Then, he grabbed hold of Slocum's belt with his left hand, and used him like a shield. So even though Slocum's gun was used, I have a hard time finding fault with what he did. He wasn't reckless. What are we supposed to do, disarm our transport officers?"

"Agreed."

"The rest of it is, my cruiser driver, Deputy Bustamante, was standing directly behind his partner, Deputy Adams. Bustamante was holding open the right rear door for Potts. He never had a shot when Potts broke bad.

"Adams was standing next to the front passenger door. He had a Thompson trained on Potts, but he couldn't shoot for fear of hitting Slocum. I can find fault with the positioning of my two deputies, but not enough to administer discipline. However, I can assure you that we will go over this scenario at an office meeting very soon, and come up with a better method to safely put a dangerous prisoner into the backseat of a cruiser henceforth.

"When Potts made his break, Corporal Orbach was taking the spare off the rear door mount. He was quick to react. He drew his service revolver and charged Potts. It was a bold and brave move, but they were only eight feet apart. Why would he do that? He never fired his weapon. When Potts shot him, they were only three feet apart. Maybe Orbach could have escorted Potts together with Slocum, but Jiminy Cricket, officers escort handcuffed prisoners on their own a thousand times a day throughout the country! I can't find much fault with that!

"I don't know why Orbach charged, or why he didn't shoot. That's the real issue that we will probably never resolve. Maybe he didn't have a clear shot, either. The only thing I do know is that he tried to rescue his partner, and he lost his life in the process. I'm saying that Orbach should get your highest medal for valor, if you all give out awards."

"Who shot Potts?"

"One of my senior deputies named Clarence Oldman. I had him tail the motorcade in his privately-owned vehicle. He was dressed in civvies. He rolled up to the scene, and acted like some dimwit. Potts ordered him out of his truck. Deputy Oldman got out, and shot Potts in the eye before he knew what hit him."

"Son of a bitch! I need to meet Deputy Oldman and thank him in person. We need to honor him. By the way, would you punish Slocum?"

"No. He just lost his best friend. He blames himself. That's more than enough punishment for a lifetime. If he worked for me, I'd do whatever I could to keep him from eating his gun or becoming a drunk. You know as well as I do that this very same thing could have happened to any of us somewhere along the line."

"I agree. He's got his time in, but he's too young to retire. I'll see if he'd like a transfer from transportation to courtroom security, or admin, or property, or even patrol. Not the jail or detectives. I could bump him up to corporal, if I see he's making the adjustment."

Miss Loretta knocked on Sheriff Sol's door. He motioned her in. He said, "Just a moment, Adrian. I may have some more information." He placed his hand over the mouthpiece and asked, "What is it, Loretta?"

"The other deputies just showed up. Chief is done with the crime scene. Both bodies are at the funeral home. What orders do you have?"

"Stand by.

"Adrian. The crime scene is complete. Peterson and Grossman showed up. What shall I tell them?"

"I've changed my mind. Tell Corporal Peterson as per my instructions, he is ordered to drive the van back to HQ. Grossman will drive the prowl car. I'm giving them six hours to return the vehicles to the lot, clean and topped off, before reporting to Lieutenant Robles."

"Roger that. What about Slocum?"

"I'm sending my Chief, Derrick Hornsby, to pick him up. If possible, he'll bring Slocum's wife. Her first name is Myra. He should be there between nine and ten o'clock."

"We'll be standing by. Tell Chief Hornsby to switch to Frequency 2 when he crosses into Quayle County, and to give us a shout."

"Will do. Thanks, Sol. We'll stay in touch."

Sheriff Sol relayed the word to Loretta, to pass along with respect to the two El Paso deputies. He also told her to tell the Quayle deputies to return to the jail.

It was going to be another very long day. He called Joanna and told her what had happened, and not to wait supper for him. She said she planned to have spaghetti and meatballs and a tossed salad with French bread. She would make enough to serve a dozen and bring it up to the jail. He told her to bring paper plates and plastic utensils. She said, "Not my first rodeo, Cowboy." Sol smiled. He told her goodbye, and hung up. He knew he had married well.

Doc Boykin examined Slocum. He was fine, physically. Doc gave him a prescription bottle with a half-dozen five-milligram Valiums. He told him to take one now and the others as needed, if he started feeling anxious. Also, not to drink alcohol or drive when he was sedated.

Chief gave Barlow Slocum's gun, and told him to fire three rounds into the dirt, and to retrieve all the bullets, and the shell casings, for comparison purposes with the shot fired by Potts, assuming that they recover the expended round from Orbach's body. He also told Barlow to unload and clean the revolver before returning it, and the two remaining live rounds, to Slocum.

Barlow, Chunk, and Slick wrote their statements. Slocum insisted on making his before he medicated.

Chunk stayed to eat Joanna's spaghetti dinner before heading home two hours late. He couldn't pass it up. Besides, his boy had an American Legion baseball game and he knew his wife, Rosa, would have fed the family sandwiches or hotdogs, before going to the ballpark behind the school. He still had time to get there before the first pitch.

Slick ate enough for two.

Loretta volunteered to stay over to help Joanna, or Mrs. Slocum, if she came.

Myra Slocum did come with Chief Derrick Hornsby. They said they weren't hungry, as they had stopped at a Kentucky Fried Chicken in Alpine for a quick bite. She and Lucas huddled together in the rolling, wooden, courtroom chairs in Sheriff Sol's office. They were so quiet, it was like they weren't even there.

Chief Hornsby said that when he had left to pick up Myra, Sheriff Brady had gone to notify Mrs. Orbach.

Chief Alex took Chief Hornsby to Ricketts' Mortuary & Funeral Home to view the bodies. Chief Hornsby took his own photos. He asked if there would be a problem transporting both bodies to El Paso, so their coroner, who was a forensic pathologist, could autopsy them. Chief Alex said that would be fine, so long as Quayle SO received a copy of the report. No problem there. Pete Ricketts was all smiles. He would be well compensated by the El Paso Coroner's Office to transport the bodies first thing in the morning.

It was eleven o'clock. Before Chief Hornsby and the Slocums

departed, Chief Hornsby called Sheriff Brady. When Hornsby hung up, he said, "Sheriff Brady and the entire staff of the El Paso Sheriff's Office thank you all for everything you've done. He said he is sending escort cars to lead the hearse back to El Paso. They will be here at nine o'clock tomorrow morning. Could you notify Mr. Ricketts?"

Sheriff Sol replied, "Of course."

Chief Hornsby continued, "Sheriff Brady hopes the autopsies can be completed tomorrow. The funeral is scheduled with full police honors for Monday, at eleven o'clock. There will be a big turnout. Sheriff Brady would be honored, Sheriff, if you and any of your staff, particularly those who were with Corporal Orbach when he died, could attend. Of course, all are welcome. He wants you all to be seated next to him. He said you could let him know tomorrow if you can come."

Sheriff Sol replied, "Tell Sheriff Brady that we're honored, and that the three deputies and I will be there."

"Thanks, Sheriff. Adiós."

"Adiós."

As soon as they drove away, Chief asked, "Ready to go home, Sheriff?"

"You go ahead. I have some calls to make."

"Who, besides Pete Ricketts?"

"The other five sheriffs between here and El Paso County, to see if they would like to have an escort unit pick up the motorcade at their respective county lines, and to drop off when they've come to the boundary to the next county. That's what we're doing. It's a small enough thing to do for a peace officer who's fallen in the line of duty, especially for one who fell in our county, and was as brave as Corporal Orbach."

"Won't those sheriffs think they've been had if they learn Potts is in the same hearse?"

"They would if he was, but he won't be. Soon as Chunk shows up in the morning, I'll have Archie drop him off at the funeral home. Chunk will ride with Pete's son, or whomever he selects to drive his old hearse, to drop Potts off at the El Paso County Morgue. It could be in the back of a raggedy old pickup truck, as far as I am concerned. They will depart as soon after eight o'clock as they can, to drop off Potts before the honor motorcade arrives. It will be very low key. We don't want to do anything to diminish the ceremonial aspect of Corporal Orbach's ride or arrival."

"Who's going to lead the motorcade from our mortuary?"

"I will. I'll pick up one of our marked units. It's the least I can do."

"You need anything from me?"

"No. You've done enough already. Go on home. I'll see you tomorrow. Same to you all too, Barlow, Slick. I've got it until Archie shows up. Thanks for everything. I am so grateful that we are not making these arrangements for one of you. Get out of here, now. I need some time alone."

# CHAPTER 10

## Friday, May 28, 1971
## A Private Toast to Corporal Orbach

It was midnight when Barlow rolled into his driveway. The Mosby grapevine was operating at full tilt. He knew this because Sarah's car was parked along the street in front of his house, and the lights were on inside and out. Tonight he did not think there was anything she could say or do to cheer him up. He hoped that he was wrong.

When he walked in, she was sitting cross-legged on the couch, with her bare feet tucked up under her dress. He saw that she had been reading a romance novel. The radio was on low. Somehow she had managed to tune into a classical music station. Normally, he listened to rock and roll, or country and western. He didn't know they even had a classical station within listening distance, but he was glad they did. The timeless music, with no vocals, was soothing. If George Jones or Hank Williams were on the air, singing their sad, unrequited love songs, he'd probably slit his wrists.

She stood up and walked over to him. She pushed the brim of his Stetson up off his forehead. She put her arms around him and nestled into his hug. He felt so solid and strong. She held on tightly, while she transmitted her love and joy just being in his embrace, to his sorrowful, dejected soul. It gave him solace. He thanked God again for bringing them together.

When they broke off, she said, "We heard. Dad gave me a

bottle of Henry McKenna to give to you. Take off your gun belt and sit down, while I pour us a wee taste."

He unfastened his gun belt and set it down on the floor by the couch. He put his hat in the easy chair. Then he sat down and stretched out his legs. He used his toes to push off his boots. She returned with two whiskey sour glasses and the uncorked bottle of elixir. She poured them both a couple of ounces. After she handed one glass to him, she sat down beside him and scootched up tight. He held up his glass and said, "Here's to Corporal Heinrich Orbach. May his soul rest in peace for all of eternity."

She whispered, "Amen." They both took a sip, and savored the warm, smooth liquid coursing though their bodies. After a reverent pause, she said, "Tell me about him."

He said, "I don't know much. I just met him today. I think he was born and raised in El Paso. He was 57 years old. He looked just like Oliver Hardy. I understand he served in the Navy as a cook before World War Two. I know he joined the sheriff's office in 1937. He tried to re-up in the Navy when the war broke out, but he was too fat by then. He was IV-F. Imagine that! A fat cook! Anyway, all I know is he was married, and he has three kids. Two boys and a girl. They're all grown. He spent most of his career working in the jail. He'd been working prisoner transport for at least twelve years, because that's how long he and his partner have been working together. He seemed like a good guy to me. I think prisoner transport was the perfect job for him. I do know he was well liked in the sheriff's office. I think he surprised everyone today. No one would have expected him to charge a prisoner holding a gun on him to rescue his partner, but he did. 'You can't judge a book by its cover.' He died quickly. I wish I could have saved him."

They finished the first drink, and Sarah poured a second.

"What about his partner?"

"I know less about him. I spent more time around Orbach. He's a good guy, too. His name is Lucas Slocum. It's really weird because he looks like Stan Laurel. Together they looked like the comedy team. A pair of jokes, except they weren't. Lucas is younger. 47, I think. He's a World War Two Army vet. He's married, and has some kids, but I don't know anything about them. He was trying to help that slimy, despicable, craven, Diablo oxygen thief to get back up after he fell down. The bastard jerked around, and got Slocum's service revolver. It happened so quickly. I had the machine gun pointed right at him, but I couldn't shoot without taking out Slocum, too. Otherwise, I would have stitched him up like a quilt. I've never felt so helpless my whole life, except for when I was a kid, and my folks got killed in that car wreck. Thank goodness Slick put him down. Shot him once in the eye. Instant annihilation, but it was too late to save Corporal Orbach. Sarah, I swear that I will never be so unprepared, ever again."

"I know you won't, Sweetie. This was not your doing. Keep that in mind. 'Bad things happen to good people.' You know that."

"I do, but if I had left that Thompson in the car, and had been pointing my revolver at Potts, I could have erased him from the gene pool before he had time to shoot Orbach. That weighs heavy on my heart."

"I know it does, but remember what you told me when you shot Clinton Dumfries? You said it could have gone either way, and that God didn't take you home because He still had more things for you to do on this Earth. You said we're all logged into His Book of Life, and that when your time comes up, it comes up.

Predestination, I think you said. If that's true, God called Corporal Orbach home because it was his time to go."

"Touché. I really hate it, when you pin my ears back with my own words, especially when it involves my immutable beliefs. You know that? Busted! I cannot argue with biblical teaching, or the cosmos. Let's have one more drink, and then maybe you can help me forget my sorrow by giving me some of your sweet lovin'."

"Nope. No can do."

"What? Don't tease me tonight. I'm hurting, Babe."

"Me, too. Did you ever think of that? Cowboy up. You only have to wait another eight days until you make an honest woman out of me. Then I will rock your universe, Mr. Adams."

"Verily, verily, sweet maiden. I knoweth not anyone more honest than thee. Thou art America's righteous poster child, plus thou art more beautiful and seductive than Elizabeth Taylor and Raquel Welch all rolled into one. I could really useth your magic touch. Please. What dost thou sayeth?"

"Mr. Adams, sweet talking me will not work, even in King James' English. I want you large and in charge next Saturday night. Savvy? 'Absence makes the heart grow fonder,' or is that adage, 'Absence makes the hard grow down yonder?' Know what I mean, Jelly Bean? You have to wait. I promise it will be worth it. Good night. Gotta go." With that she slipped on her shoes, picked up her purse and book, and headed for the door.

"Good night, you meanie. Don't worry about me. My celibate self will manage to survive somehow."

"Celibate, my foot! You've only been without for a week. Your eyes are still bright blue. They haven't turned milky yet. I know you can get through it. Talk to you tomorrow. Bye!"

# CHAPTER 11

## Monday, May 31, 1971
## The Final Fare Thee Well for Corporal Orbach

Monday was a very early morning. The sky was black with a thousand stars. No moon. No clouds. No wind. Barlow and Sarah arrived at the jail at 3:45.

Sarah had said on Saturday that she was planning to attend the funeral. Barlow told Sheriff Sol. He mentioned it to Joanna. She said she was going, too. Then April Snodgrass told Chief Alex that she was going. She had checked. Chunk's wife, Rosa, was staying at home with their three kids. She was happy to oblige. Rosa agreed to babysit all the kids.

It was understandable. None of the wives had even seen Corporal Orbach, but his murder in their county, by a Diablos Motorcycle Club gang member, hit way too close to home. They all accepted that their husbands had a dangerous job. Problem was, it was not too far a stretch of the imagination for them to picture themselves sitting where the Widow Orbach sat today.

Sheriff Sol called Sheriff Brady. He said he would have seats reserved for the Quayle wives next to their husbands next to him, hopefully all in the first row.

Sheriff Sol had planned to drive the newest marked cruiser with Slick, Chunk, and Barlow in tow, so they could 'wave the (Quayle County Sheriff's Office) flag', show their colors, in a manner of speaking, during the motorcade to the cemetery, but bringing along the wives changed everything. He knew police motorcycles would escort the hearse, followed by marked units with uniformed lawmen from throughout the region. They would all be there in a show of respect and solidarity.

There would also be a Navy Honor Guard, and civilians in POV's, and Feds in dark suits with black armbands in unmarked units, but the spectacle would be in the variety and number of police uniforms and marked units for all to see, especially the outlaw bikers, who would not be present, but they would see it on television, and on the front page of the newspaper, and they would understand that 'the gloves were off' in the foreseeable future, no matter where they lay their heads. Call it an amplified vendetta between cops and outlaw bikers.

Sheriff Sol decided to have Chief Alex, also in uniform, drive the ladies in his Jeep Wagoneer, which had air conditioning. The marked units did not. Chief could put his red ball on the roof and turn it on during the procession to identify the vehicle as law enforcement.

Sheriff Sol led. He goosed it a little bit. Chief Alex followed. The ladies were cool and did not get wind blown. They stopped briefly along the way for coffee and a light breakfast. Sheriff Sol passed out half-inch wide, black, elastic bands for the deputies to wear across their badges. Black bands were not an issue item provided to lawmen when they got sworn in. They also weren't an item one could purchase in the local drugstore at the checkout counter next to all the magazines and candy bars.

They arrived in El Paso at 10:15. The area around St. Gabriel's Catholic Church was already crowded and chaotic like this was the state fair. You could tell it wasn't though, because there were no vendors, and because the pedestrians were either cops, or folks all dressed in black. Nothing in between. With parking being at a premium, they finally found empty spaces two blocks away, in front of a barbershop owned by an understanding and compassionate barber.

The funeral was held at St. Gabriel's, which was the largest Catholic church in El Paso. The pews and balconies seated a little over a thousand. It was also in the center of the city. The Orbach family actually belonged to St. Brigid's Catholic Church, but it was a small, neighborhood affair on the west side of town, barely seating a hundred. Bishop Martin recognized immediately that pilgrims far and wide would attend the ceremony, so he suggested to Father Fritz that the larger venue would better serve the needs of the mourners. Father Fritz gratefully accepted on behalf of the grieving family, who was still in shock.

St. Gabriel's was bursting at the seams. In fact, by the time the ceremony began, there was standing room only, with an overflow crowd gathered out front. The Quayle County coterie couldn't locate Sheriff Brady, but they did find Chief Derrick Hornsby, who thanked them for coming. He apologized regarding seating arrangements. He said Corporal Orbach's family was larger than they had anticipated and needed the entire first row. The honored police guests would be seated in the second row. Chief Hornsby escorted them to their seats, and introduced them to his wife, Monique, and to Sheriff Brady's wife, Sharon. He said the audience would be asked to remain seated at the end of the service, after the casket was carried out to the hearse, to allow the law enforcement officers to return to their vehicles so they could line up as escorts. Just get in line, wives included, and follow the cops in front of them out the door. EPPD traffic officers would direct them to the staging area.

The funeral ceremony included mass. It was a long, drawn

out, sad affair. As expected, the eulogy was presented by Sheriff Brady. His remarks about Corporal Heinrich Orbach were poignant. He had had an interesting and full life.

Sheriff Brady cleared his throat and began. "Heinrich was born in El Paso in 1913, the oldest of six children. His folks, Walther and Elsa Orbach, were German immigrants. Walther was a baker by trade.

"Heinrich had a happy childhood. One thing he especially loved was baseball. He began playing at age seven. He was the catcher for the El Paso High School team, which went 18 and 6, in 1930, and 15 and 9, in 1931, when Heinrich was a starter. He batted .280 his senior year. Heinrich also loved baking and cooking, which he learned from his father, but even more importantly, he loved a special someone.

"He met his wife, Theresa Kleinpeter, at school. They became sweethearts when they were in the eighth grade. They both graduated in 1931, but they didn't marry right away. No, indeed! Mr. Kleinpeter felt that Heinrich needed to prove himself first, so Theresa worked in her family's corner grocery, and Heinrich joined the U.S. Navy to prove himself, and to see the world. He was assigned to the Asiatic Fleet as a cook on a surface vessel, the USS Canopus, which was a submarine tender. The ship's primary mission was to rendezvous with submarines at sea, and replenish them with supplies.

"The Pacific was a dangerous place between 1931 and 1937, during Heinrich's tour of duty. The Philippines and China were both hotspots. In 1931, hostilities broke out between Japan and China. Not only that, but during that period of history, China consisted of autonomous fiefdoms, and they were engaged in a bloody civil war. It was not a unified nation. Not even close.

Banditry was prolific. Life for a Chinese peasant was tenuous, trying to survive in the midst of predatory Japanese soldiers, Chinese warlords, and opportunistic gangsters.

"In 1932, the Canopus was part of a task force assigned to rescue Americans and other foreign nationals living in Shanghai. This was just one of many exciting adventures in which Heinrich was involved during his service in the Navy. For his six years of faithful service, during which time he never came home because of his assignment on the ocean so far, far away, he was awarded the Good Conduct Medal and the Navy Chinese Service Medal. He was a petty officer third class at the time he mustered out with an honorable discharge and a tidy little nest egg. Indeed, Heinrich had proved himself worthy.

"Heinrich returned home to all of us here in El Paso, and married his long suffering sweetheart. He was subsequently appointed to the position of deputy sheriff in the El Paso County Sheriff's Office. Sheriff Ambrose put him where he thought he was best suited, which was in the jail supervising inmates in the kitchen. He served in that position until 1959, when he was promoted to corporal in prisoner transport, and that's what he was doing the day he died. Altogether, he had 33 years of service. He could have retired at any time, but he loved his work, and he chose not to do so.

"Heinrich served the public well and faithfully. He died at the hands of a maniacal prisoner, who was facing the death penalty for the armed robbery and the horrendous murder of an El Paso citizen, Lazarus Santos, a loving husband, father of five, and proprietor of a convenience store. Heinrich's murder occurred during the transport of said murderer to the El Paso County Jail. Heinrich attempted to rescue his beloved partner, Deputy Lucas

Slocum, whose sidearm had been wrested away from him by the prisoner. Heinrich charged the prisoner face to face, in an effort to subdue him. He was fatally shot at a distance of three feet. A Quayle County deputy sheriff, to whom we all owe a great debt of gratitude, shot and killed the prisoner, ending his vicious, predatory activities forever. 'Greater love hath no man than this, that a man lay down his life for his friends.'

"Heinrich leaves behind his loving wife, three children, six grandchildren, and many others, to include a grateful public.

"God rest his soul, etc., etc. . . ."

There was nary a dry eye in the house by the time the honor guard had escorted the casket and the pall bearers outside to the hearse. The lawmen filed out silently behind them, and returned to their units. EPPD officers assisted them to line up in a motorcade that was six blocks long. EPPD, EPSO, and DPS provided a motorcycle escort, and they blocked off all the intersections en route to the cemetery. Barlow saw marked units from as far away as Tucson and Albuquerque and Dallas and San Antonio and Amarillo. He counted 136 marked units. He also saw two old friends, Texas Ranger Sergeant Trey Winfield, and Sheriff Dan Elliott from Eddie County, New Mexico.

Once all the mourners had assembled at the grave site, the priest prayed. The mourners bowed. The Navy presented a folded flag to a silently weeping widow, after they rendered a 21-gun salute. A lone bagpiper piped Taps. The sun was high in the sky. The heat from the sunshine was smoldering, but the soulful melody rendered by the piper chilled the mourners all the way down, deep into their bone marrow. And then it stopped. Dead silence. Everyone stood still, not sure if it was over. It was. The cumulative impact of the reverent ceremony, extensive motorcade, and music from the bagpipes was sobering and dramatic.

It ended without a whisper. Mourners walked slowly and somberly back to their vehicles. The Quayle County contingent nodded their goodbyes, and headed back home. They departed at 3:30. It was a long, quiet, solemn ride.

# CHAPTER 12

## Tuesday, June 1, 1971
## Wheels in Motion

It was 8:15. Breakfast had been served. Inmates who were privileged to have jobs were already doing them, but not Joe Rag or Dick Wad. Not today. Dick had a fever, not bad enough for bed rest in the infirmary, but bad enough to keep him sequestered in his cell. The nurse thought Joe Rag might come down with whatever Dick had because they were cellmates, so Joe remained in lockdown, too.

Larry the Fairy served as G cellblock letter carrier, in addition to being G cellblock librarian, and G cellblock's most notorious sissy. Normally, he just shoved the letters through the bars because his clients were at work, stamping license plates, or preparing meals, or working the fields, or washing clothes in the laundry, and so forth. Today he was surprised to see both Joe Rag and Dick Wad still in their cell. Dick was asleep. Joe was just sitting there on his bunk, staring into infinity, smoking a cigarette.

"Hey, Joe. You got a letter today. Looks like your sweetie still loves you. What a lucky girl! Does she take it in the ass like me? Need me to ring your bell?"

"Give me the letter, faggot. I'll punk you, and then slit your throat, and pull your tongue through it like a Colombian necktie if you piss me off!"

In a high falsetto voice, Larry replied, "Well, I was going to offer to blow you here, right through the bars, but I can see you're in way too foul a mood for that. Just take your stupid old letter!"

Larry handed him the letter, and continued down a few more cells. When he was out of sight, he stopped. He was anxious to know if the letter contained anything juicy, but he sure didn't want Joe to know he was loitering and listening. He heard Joe rip the envelope open. There was a two-minute delay. Then he could hear the squeaky springs of one of the bunks.

"Wake up, Shithead."

Pause. Crickets. Louder. "Wake up, Dick. We need to talk."

"What's up? I feel like shit. You woke me up."

"I finally got a letter from Alice. Gravy Train will meet us at noon on Tuesday. He'll be driving a '66 powder blue Dodge van. He'll help us find and kill that rat bastard and his new, blushing bride. We're gonna fuck that bitch in every hole she has and make him watch. Then we'll kill 'em both, and bury 'em out in the desert. No one will ever find 'em. Once it's done, we'll go to work with Gravy Train on his ranch in Ciudad Acuña. You be well enough to go by then? We may never get another chance like this again."

"I'll be ready, but I ain't gonna be no fuckin' sodbuster. Let's get that straight right now."

"You really are a dick wad, aren't you? We'll be the fuckin' muscle, the enforcers. Comprenden?"

That was all Larry needed to hear. He moseyed on down the walk without making a sound, dropping off more letters. If Joe Rag ever found out Larry had overheard this conversation, he'd be dead within 24 hours. He'd definitely wait until after they escaped to cash in this little tidbit. Those douchebags would never be taken alive once they broke out. He didn't even want to know how they planned to do that. The knowledge alone could get a guy killed, if anyone knew he had it.

Once they had escaped, he'd make up a bullshit story about how he learned of the hit and tip off the captain responsible for G block. He'd be a fuckin' hero, responsible for saving that cop's life, and his wife's. They'd owe him big time. He'd get him a nice spot cleaning the front offices and sleeping in A block with all the other top shelf trusties. Live high on the hog. Joe Rag might be a stone cold killer, but he wasn't very fuckin' smart. That's for damn sure.

# CHAPTER 13

### Wednesday, June 2, 1971
### Squeezing In Some Play Time

It was eight o'clock Wednesday morning. Barlow had just completed his shift. His mind was racing. He couldn't relax. No way he could go to sleep right now, even though he knew he needed to.

He was scheduled to work the midnight shift all week, Monday through Friday. The wedding was on Saturday, and their two-week honeymoon began Sunday morning. By mutual consent, even blessed by Sarah's folks, Barlow's free time was his own until Friday afternoon at four o'clock, when the walk-through at the church was scheduled. That would also signal the beginning of crunch time.

Amazing! He was excused from wedding prep because Sarah didn't want him involved. Only he knew why, and he wasn't talking. Her folks thought she was just being bitchy. She didn't defend herself. She simply insisted that she get her way, so she did. Who wants to fight while you're preparing for a wedding? Sarah believed she was protecting her own interests. She expected vim and vigor from him come Saturday night. Tired and sleepy men are poor performers. She certainly wasn't going to tell her folks how she knew that. But, what if she were the one too worn out to perform like a porn star? He couldn't imagine that, but whichever way it went, he was keeping his trap shut.

Sarah and her mother, seconded by her sister-in-law, Darla,

were reinforced by aunts and close female friends, and fortified with prodigious amounts of patience, fortitude, muscle, and errand-running provided by her dad and her brother, Cordell. All had been working day and night, allegedly to prepare for the wedding at the church, but mostly for the reception at the ranch. Even the ranch hands, Pedro, Angel, and Pancho had been pressed into coolie labor.

Barlow's job had been threefold: to agree with whatever Sarah wanted; to select a best man and two ushers; and to pay for the tuxedo rentals and corsages, plus gifts for the wedding party. Even then, he had very little input. Sarah picked out everything except for the best man and ushers. What she really wanted was his blessing. Fortunately, she had common sense and good taste.

The tuxes were black with black bow ties and black cummerbunds, except for Barlow's. His tie and cummerbund were red. All the male corsages were a single red rosebud. The ladies' corsages consisted of three red rosebuds.

For gifts, the guys were getting cigarette lighters engraved with the date and 'Thanks from Barlow and Sarah.' The ladies were getting silver Cross ballpoint pens with the same engraving. At least these were gifts which had a fifty-fifty chance of getting put to use. Who needs another knickknack to collect dust on a bookshelf?

Barlow had asked Archie to be his best man, and Sheriff Sol and Slick to be ushers. They all said yes. It was a tough decision. He loved and owed them all more than he could ever repay. Sheriff Sol was his boss, a kind and just boss. He owed Sol his job and fealty. Barlow had been involved in several gunfights with Slick, and if he were ever in another, he hoped Slick would be there at his side. Barlow had spent the greater portion of his on duty time with Arch, who had coached him through the lens of nearly fifty years of law enforcement wisdom, and had kept him from straying either too far left or right. These three were his very best male friends.

Sarah had asked her best friend from the third grade, Beth Anne Dahlgren, to be her maid of honor. Beth was starting her senior year at Texas Tech, where she was studying chemistry. Her boyfriend, also a Red Raider, was pre-med from Dallas. Her two bridesmaids were Darla and her cousin, Candace Duffy. Candace lived in Del Rio, where she was employed as a beautician. She was engaged to be married to a railroad brakeman named Haywood Jeffries.

When the wedding preparations started, they had planned to send invitations to a hundred guests. Barlow's family included his sister, Chloe, her husband, Wilbert, their three-year-old son, Oliver, his Uncle Clive and Aunt Marilyn, and their two kids, Nicole and Ira. A grand total of seven. All the other relatives were Sarah's. His friends were all on the sheriff's office, but they were her friends, too. She had known them longer than he. Simple. He thought it was simple! But it turned out not so much.

Sarah's family had been in this community all their lives. They had scads of friends. One hundred guests became a hundred-twenty, then a hundred-fifty, then two hundred, and even some more after that. Good thing the shindig was going to be outdoors, and that they had as many sheep as it called for to provide for the mountains of wedding barbecue that were necessary.

Barlow had talked to Arthur, his soon-to-be father-in-law, and had offered to buy the beer, or the bourbon, or whatever was needed. Arthur said nothing doing. He explained that the reception gradually morphed from what Sarah had in mind, to what mommy dearest had in mind. He said one day Barlow would walk in his shoes, if he had any daughters. Boys are easier, but girls steal your heart. Anyway, Sarah wanted a church wedding with a ranch reception, and Clarice wanted the same thing except on a much larger scale. They were both getting what they wanted. There had been very little friction, and for that he was ever so thankful.

So, this morning before going to bed, Barlow decided to do something he should have done the day he graduated. He was going to shoot his new off duty gun for the first time, which still lay dormant in the box. This was only Barlow's third firearm, but the other two got fired the very same day he acquired them. That's the way God intended it, too. At least that's what St. Smith and St. Wesson were reported to have said.

First, he stopped by Jake's Pawn shop. He thanked Jake for the box of bullets. He bought three more boxes with the same standard load, a Bianchi leather, inside-the-waist holster, a small, zippered, leather pouch large enough to hold 25, .38 Special cartridges, and a packet of 25-yard pistol targets. He already had the cleaning kit. Then he drove to the informal range everyone in the community used, located at a dry arroyo called Dog Canyon. To get there, start at the rodeo grounds on US 90. Turn south on a dirt road across from the entrance, and follow it all the way to the end. Easy peasy.

For decades, countless shooters had gone there and shot hundreds of thousands of rounds of all calibers and gauges, in sport and in practice, and in settling scores of bets, as to who was the better marksman. There was a variety of target stands to choose from, and even some homemade benches, but no shade.

The restroom was in the low lying bushes, where the rattlesnakes actually did find some shade.

Barlow tacked up a target, and paced off ten yards. He loaded, aimed, and fired a full cylinder of five rounds, taking his time, and using a two-handed police combat stance. He had a two-inch grouping. Maybe a little less. Everything was within the ten ring.

He reloaded, and did it again. This time his shots filled in the first group. He took down this target, and put up another. He stepped back another five yards. This time his grouping spread out. Four shots were inside of three inches, but they were still within the nine ring. The fifth was a flyer at seven o'clock in the seven ring. A jerk. He knew it as soon as he fired that shot.

He reloaded and did it again. All five shots were in the nine ring.

Barlow observed that the sights were small and narrow, and that it took a little bit longer to acquire the target than it did with his .41 caliber service revolver, which had target sights, and a four-inch bull barrel. Also, the grips on the .38 were small. This gun packed a lot more wallop than he would have imagined for a .38. Of course, he should have expected that with a gun that only had a two-inch barrel. He waited a few minutes for his hands to stop stinging. Then he put up another target.

This time he stayed at the fifteen yard line, but he fired the full cylinder, rapid fire in ten seconds or less. His shots spread out to the eight ring, but they were patterned in a circle, just like he wanted. It would be more like this in a gunfight. Nobody would use this revolver out past 25 yards, probably not even that far, unless he was mighty good or a damned fool. He concluded that fifteen yards was his limit to shoot well with this weapon, at least until he had more practice. A man's got to know his limitations, and now he knew his with this weapon.

He emptied the remainder of this box of ammo doing rapid fire drills. Then he picked up his trash and went home. He cleaned his new gun, loaded it, and placed it in the new holster. He counted out 25 rounds from the new box and put them in the leather pouch. He placed the works in his sock drawer.

This is the gun he would take with him on the honeymoon. Of course, he would have his Winchester .30-30 hidden in the pouch along the front of the seat of his truck, but the .38 would be on his person at all times. He was very thankful the guys and gal in his office gifted this gun to him. It was like having a paid up insurance policy.

# CHAPTER 14

## Thursday, June 3, 1971
## Family Reunion

Barlow's kinfolk arrived in Mosby sometime in the afternoon. It was a two-day drive for both parties, one coming east from Bisbee, and the other south from the Texas panhandle. Barlow had arranged for them to have adjacent cabins at the Travelers Rest Motor Lodge. He had left written instructions at the front desk for them, so they could find their way to his house at 62 West Zachary Taylor Avenue, and to the Bakers' Bar B Ranch. He figured nobody could get lost going to the church, since it was one of the four largest buildings in town, all of which were located at Mosby's epicenter at the intersection of US 90 and TX 651. He invited them to stop by his house any time after four o'clock for a cookout. He said he hoped to eat around six.

Sarah arrived at three. Barlow was still asleep. The house was tidy, but it didn't meet the conscientious female standard for the elimination of dust and musty odors before company comes over, so she went to work like a whirling dervish, dusting and sanitizing every surface, and spraying an aerosol in each room, that the advertisement guaranteed would make the house smell like spring wildflowers in a New England meadow, in the golden sunshine, with butterflies and enchanted fairies flittering about, but without mosquitoes or wasps, and absolutely no fornicating snakes. None! It promised to make handsome men fawn all over the purchaser, plus it was a reliable repellant against snarky biddies, and other jealous females.

She let him sleep until 3:30, at which time she woke him up, and sent him to the bathroom to shower and clean up, with a stern warning not to leave a mess. Barlow was still half asleep. Even so, the deep recesses of his lizard brain remembered how to prepare for Army SAMI (Saturday morning inspection) and he aimed to please. When he was finished and walked out of the bathroom, it looked just like Mr. Clean had been the last occupant in there. No matter. It got a squirt of New England sunshine, too.

Sarah had thought of everything. Nothing was overlooked. She brought a galvanized tub, which they rinsed out with the hose, and placed under the shade tree out back, before filling it with RC Colas, Bubble Up, Orange Crush, and Miller Hi Life, which was Uncle Clive's favorite. Then Barlow made a quick trip to the grocery, where he picked up three bags of crushed ice to keep the drinks frosty cold. He already had a bottle of Jose Cuervo for Bert, and one of Old Crow for Sarah and himself. He knew Aunt Marilyn drank beer sometimes, but he did not know Chloe's preference. She didn't drink any adult beverages when he visited her two years ago.

Sarah also brought a bowl of her mother's potato salad and a peach pie baked by Darla. She knew Barlow had taken care of the rest, to include the ice cream. She began making the tomato, cucumber, onion, and vinegar salad. The front door opened. She heard Barlow welcoming the entire family, who had decided to come all together. She wiped her hands on her apron and walked into the living room.

Both families arriving at the same time made Barlow's introductions easy. "Sarah, this my Aunt Marilyn and Uncle

Clive. They took very good care of me, when I could have been a ward of the state. These are my cousins, Nicole and Ira. This is Chloe and Bert and my nephew, Oliver. You all, this is Sarah, my one and only. My betrothed. She takes my breath away every time I look at her. I can't believe I'm such a lucky dog."

Chloe said, "Me either, Brother. She is entirely out of your league. You better treat her like she's made out of spun gold."

Sarah responded by giving Chloe a hug, followed by a hug to everyone else. "I am so glad to finally meet all of you. Barlow talks about you all more than you will ever know. We are so happy that you all could come to our wedding. Is anyone thirsty?"

Uncle Clive said, "Barlow, now that I've seen Sarah for myself, I know why you ran off and never came back."

Aunt Marilyn responded, "Shush up, you lecherous, old goat! You're embarrassing her. Look how she's blushing. Sarah, I apologize for my husband's poor manners."

Nicole said, "Mama, Daddy's right. Miss Sarah is so beautiful."

Ira piped in, "Mama, Miss Sarah said we can have something to drink. Is that okay? I'm thirsty."

Barlow intercepted, "Come with me, anyone who's thirsty. I'll show you where the drinks are. Sarah, maybe you could show the ladies the rest of the house. Come on you all, out in the backyard with me."

It was a free-for-all once Barlow pointed out the tub full of iced beverages under the tree. Ditto for the bottles of distilled spirits, and glasses, and the insulated container of ice on the counter next to the refrigerator as they walked through the kitchen to the back door. The ladies were on their own. Barlow and the men and the kids all relocated to the backyard, where Barlow put some charcoal in the grill and started a fire. Tonight they were having Georgia-style, sweet barbecued chicken breasts, which had been marinating in apple juice. The tangy gravy was made from tomato sauce, brown sugar, molasses, sweet onions, vinegar, a touch of salt, and a drop or two of Tabasco. Maybe three, or four. Taster's choice.

Once Barlow started the fire in the grill, Bert passed out a couple of H. Upmann Churchill cigars with Maduro wrappers, and then three more smaller fires got lit. Ira and Happy found one another, and an engaging game of fetch was started. Once Nicole found an Orange Crush, she went back inside to be with the womenfolk.

It was a great get together. The food was exceptionally tasty, 'the platter licked clean' even, but it paled in comparison with the camaraderie emanating from every direction. Barlow tried to be discreet in nursing just one bourbon on the rocks, but he got busted and had to come clean that he was working his final midnight shift for the next two weeks. It didn't slow the party down one bit, because it was more about being together after such a long time apart, than it was about imbibing adult beverages.

Sarah hit it off fine with all her new relatives, especially the womenfolk, and before the night ended they were all good friends. Barlow silently hoped that Chloe and Aunt Marilyn didn't tell too many embarrassing things about him. He'd know for sure if Sarah casually mentioned how awful it would be for someone, if he split the seat of his trousers wide open in church when he was walking down the aisle to be baptized, or what if some kid ate dry dog food because some smarty-pants told him it would help grow hair on his chest. Heck! He'd know just by the way she looked at him.

It was eleven o'clock before the clan headed back to the Travelers Rest Motor Lodge. Sarah stayed to help him clean up what little mess was left behind. Chloe and Aunt Marilyn had already seen to it that there wasn't much left to do.

Sarah was out the door at 11:15. She couldn't resist, though. Out by her car, she gave Barlow a French kiss and a squeeze that almost made him split his trousers a second time. Then she left. She took Happy with her, so he would have companionship the next couple of weeks. Barlow was left all alone. First time ever since he brought Happy home. The house seemed so empty.

Barlow took another quick shower and suited up. He was out the door by 11:35. Made it to work on time after all. Wide awake and sober, too!

# CHAPTER 15

## Saturday, June 5, 1971
## The Big Day

B arlow reported to the church at eight o'clock, as requested. Pastor Llewellyn was the only one there.

The wedding was at ten. He supposed they didn't want him to get lost. Or get cold feet and run off. Or have to park in the back forty. Something like that. Maybe because the tuxedos were all delivered to the church, and they thought he would have difficulty with the suspenders or bow tie.

Whatever the reason, all his cylinders were pinging on pure adrenaline. Too wound up to eat breakfast at home. Now suddenly he was famished. He thought about running over to Crabtree's, where they all got together the night before to break bread after the rehearsal. Sort of a small-town Texas version of a rehearsal dinner. It was the only place large enough in town, where they could feed everyone who needed to be fed, all at the same time. They reserved the whole restaurant from six to eight. People sat in fours at the tables and booths, and ordered off the menu. Made it easier for the waitresses and the cooks. Also, they didn't serve alcohol, so it kept the cost down. Since he was footing the bill, that was a bonus. Now, he considered running over there for a quick bite, but if the rest of them showed up and he wasn't here, they'd probably have Sheriff Sol put out a BOLO (Be On the Lookout) on him.

He went to the men's dressing room for the choir. That's

where the tuxes were. That was also pretty much where he was sequestered. Sarah and the womenfolk would all be jammed into the women's dressing room. Barlow wasn't allowed to see Sarah until she walked down the aisle. Some superstition about her turning into a pumpkin or something.

He sneaked into the women's dressing room, and placed a small, decorated box on the table, along with a wedding card addressed to Sarah. The box contained his wedding gift for her. It was a half-carat, round, solitary emerald necklace, with a pink gold chain, created by Mosby's craftsman jeweler and favorite son, Linus Farmer, to match her engagement ring. He hoped she would wear it in the ceremony. Then he returned to his designated sequestration area like a trusted inmate.

He was staring out the window to the parking lot and noticed that everyone in the wedding party seemed to be arriving all at once. He saw Clarice's big, mint green, Imperial roll up. He turned around so he would not see Sarah, and wind up putting a hex on her. Just then the door opened. Sheriff Sol entered, carrying a great big cardboard box filled with sandwiches, and doughnuts, and snacks, to tide the men over before the reception later on. Sheriff Sol was a lifesaver. He was followed by Pastor Llewellyn, who was carrying a percolator and a can full of Maxwell House coffee. Things always seem to work out in the House of the Lord.

Then it seemed like all the sudden, after the solitude, there was a flurry of activity within the church. The florist showed up. Then the photographer. Nadine from the beauty shop arrived. Then the organist. A cadre of female helper bees descended and bustled around, all in a dither.

Slick and Archie arrived. They all put on their tuxes. It was a good thing for one party that the trousers had elastic in the waistband. Sheriff Sol helped tie everyone's bow tie. Barlow felt weird wearing rented Corfam shoes, which allegedly never had to be shined. They didn't compare with the spit shine he put on his low quarters in the Army. Guess it was a good thing he wore black socks instead of white cotton boot socks.

Then Sheriff Sol and Slick hurried downstairs because guests started to arrive. They had to do the ushering. They didn't ask if the party were a friend of the groom or the bride, because they wouldn't have had enough room on the bride's side of the aisle, and folks might start to think that the few folks on the groom's side all had leprosy.

That's when the swarm of butterflies made their presence known. Barlow's stomach was all fluttery and turning somersaults. He thought he might upchuck for a few moments. His mouth went from a parched desert dry, to salivating rushing, white water creeks. He was a little dizzy. He never felt like this, before or after, any of his dicey situations, either in Vietnam or here in Mosby. That's when Archie came to the rescue.

He said, "Hey, Bud, you look a little peakish to me. Sit down here, while I pour you a glass of water. Think how good this is gonna feel once it's all over. It will go so fast, and your mind will be so discombobulated, that you won't remember half of it. That's okay. Big weddings are for the bride.

"All you have to do, is stand up tall and proud, and repeat after the preacher reads the vows, a line at a time, and say 'I do' and not drop the ring, and kiss your gorgeous bride, and walk down the aisle after it's over without fainting, or barfing all over yourself, or Sarah's million-dollar dress, that she will only wear this one time, and then it's over, and you're a toad that just turned into a prince, and Sarah is Cinderella, and all your dreams come true, and you live happily ever after. Piece of cake.

"What's to sweat? You done things a lot scarier than this. Remember, don't lock your knees. If you feel a little faint, just imagine that everyone in the church except you and Sarah are naked as the day they were born. Especially the organist. What's her name? Oh yeah. Mrs. Bellweather. She only weighs three hundred pounds, maybe four hundred. She'd squish you flat if she sat on you, just like Wiley T. Coyote in the *Roadrunner* cartoons. Just think about that. Think of her husband, Old Pencil Dick Bellwether, hisself. Weighs what, a buck twenty? Imagine them rutting like a sow and a weasel. I bet he don't let her get on top. Whaddaya say? That ought to help you crack a smile and relax."

That's all it took. Barlow began laughing, and liked to never have stopped, sort of hysterical-like. He got the hiccups. Had to drink some more water and wash his face. Comb his hair again.

Then he heard the music. Mrs. Bellweather began playing Johann Pachelbel's *Canon in D Major* on the enormous pipe organ. It sounded like it came straight from heaven. That was the signal. The preacher, and Archie, and Barlow slipped into the sanctuary through the preacher's hidden entrance, like a trio of wraiths, and assumed their positions while the guests were staring at the front entrance, waiting for a glimpse of the bridesmaids.

They did not disappoint. Beth Anne came in first, followed by Darla, and then Candace. They were wearing pink, sleeveless, form fitting dresses that accentuated all their curves and beauty. Their hair was perfectly coiffed. They looked radiant. That started the waterworks. And the flashbulbs. These women all looked like fashion models. They took their positions. Barlow was getting choked up. He tried to imagine Mrs. Bellweather like Archie suggested, but he drew a blank. At least he was able to keep himself in check. He glanced over at Archie who had a sly grin on his face. It said, "Gotcha!"

Mr. Pachelbel's job was done. Everyone was tuned up, and in the right frame of mind. Dead silence for twenty seconds or so. The anticipation was as high as it could go. Everyone had stopped breathing. At least Barlow had. Then Mrs. Bellweather began playing Wilhelm Richard Wagner's rendition of *The Bridal Chorus - Here Comes the Bride*, in its two-minute, seventeen-second entirety.

The sanctuary doors opened, and Arthur escorted Sarah down the aisle. Her pearl white dress was similar to her bridesmaids', sleeveless and form fitting, but with lace trim throughout, and a short train. Her hair was coiffed in French braids, that the sheer veil could not conceal. Her nails were filed and polished in a French manicure. She was wearing the necklace, and a blue garter no one could see, same as her grandmother's gold barrette.

Barlow had never seen Sarah look so elegant, graceful, radiant, breathtakingly beautiful. No words could adequately describe her. She was born a natural beauty, with flawless skin and green eyes, with teeth so perfect she could have been a dental poster girl. She usually wore very little makeup. She didn't need to, but today she was exquisitely made up by a beautician. She was an apparition straight from heaven. Barlow was awestruck. He seared this visage of her in her wedding dress in his mind forever. He never wanted to forget this moment.

Sarah was beaming, just like she was the first time he went to her house to take her out on a date, only more so, like a princess from a fairy tale. Arthur was beaming, too. He looked like the Marlboro Man, who had borrowed James Bond's tuxedo. He brought Sarah to the alter, where he presented her to Barlow. Then he took his seat next to his beautiful and stunning wife, Clarice. Sarah was the spitting image of her mother, only 25 years younger. Those had been 25 very good years to Clarice. As far as age goes, they looked like they could have been sisters.

The ceremony was traditional and simple. It went off without a hitch. They exchanged vows and wedding bands of pink gold handcrafted by, who else? None other than Linus Farmer. Pastor Llewellyn pronounced them husband and wife. Barlow kissed the blushing bride. They walked down the aisle and ducked into the women's dressing room, while they waited for the guests to file out and make their way to the reception at the Bar B, which was scheduled to begin just as soon as the first guest arrived.

The wedding party had more pictures to pose for before they changed clothes, so the tuxes could be returned to the rental place.

Sarah's breathtaking gown was placed in its hang-up bag to be dry cleaned, and stored for posterity. Sarah chose not to wear her bridal dress to the reception, which was outdoors at the ranch. She was afraid it would get ruined, so instead, she wore a cobalt blue satin, sleeveless, formfitting cocktail dress and her new cobalt blue lizard skin Tony Lama cowboy boots. Barlow wished she could wear her wedding dress all day today and anytime she wanted. She looked that good in it. He was sort of sad the ceremony was over for that reason alone. Nevertheless, her cocktail dress was ravishing.

Finally, the photographs were completed. Everyone but the preacher and Sarah and Barlow had gone. Barlow paid Pastor

Llewellyn the customary honorarium. He blessed them both and wished them well. He said he would see them in church when they returned from their honeymoon. The preacher left for home to attend to his aging mother, and the newlyweds headed for the Bar B.

Sarah scrunched up as close as she could to Barlow, and lay her head on his chest. She said she thought this day would never arrive. Barlow concurred. Then he asked if she was gonna give it up tonight. She asked, "What do you think?" Then he said he had heard that the best way to get a woman to quit screwing was to marry her. Then she bit him hard on his chest, and said he was so awful that he didn't deserve any, but she still might give him some, if he convinced her that he truly loved her. Then he asked what would it take to convince her, and she said that was for her to know and for him to find out, and he had until they returned to their home to figure it out. Then they arrived at the ranch and had to straighten up. That's when she French kissed him and squeezed his love muscle, and held on until she felt it getting stiff, and then she ran to the crowd of well wishers before he could react.

Barlow smiled, and walked slowly by himself to join the festivities.

It was one helluva party. Everyone was eating and drinking and making merry. Arthur had hired a country and western band from Alpine. People danced, and made toasts, and congratulated the newlyweds time and again. Before folks got too merry, Sarah and Barlow cut the wedding cake, which was five tiers of lemon cake with lemon curd between the layers and vanilla buttercream icing.

Afterwards, Sarah tossed her bouquet, which was caught by

Candace, who scrambled like a wide receiver to catch it. Barlow tossed Sarah's garter, which was caught by one of the guitar players in the band.

Then Arthur and Clarice had Angel walk Barlow's wedding gift out of the barn. Boyo, an eight-year-old sorrel, gelding quarter horse, with a cream-colored mane and tail, that Barlow borrowed to hunt down rustlers, had never looked spiffier. He was adorned with Sarah's wedding gift, which was a saddle and tack from El Paso Saddlery.

Barlow was stunned. This was way too much! He got tears in his eyes. He stammered his profound thanks to them all. Then Sarah showed the guests what Barlow gave her. All the ladies had to get close so they could see it clearly. Then Cordell told Barlow to mount up and see how the saddle fit. He did. Barlow's rear end fit that saddle like they took a mold of it. He trotted around the curtilage twice to get the feel of it. He dismounted, and began to walk Boyo back to the barn. Sarah handed Barlow an apple. He gave it to Boyo. Boyo munched it all gone and nuzzled up against Barlow's chest, getting apple juice and horse saliva all over his shirt. Maybe a little horse snot, too. That gave everyone a big laugh. Then Angel told Barlow that he would feed Boyo and put him back in his stall.

That's the way it was. The perfect party.

Before it was over, Happy escaped from the house and licked Barlow until he was as clean as any dog can make his master. It was so good to be together again. Barlow missed him so much, and it had only been two days. Judge Sweeney and Miss Monica walked over. He said, "I just knew you and that dog would be a perfect match. You all were made for each other, just like you and Sarah. The Mrs. and I congratulate you both, and wish you many happy years together."

Then Sarah started to cry for the umpteenth time today. Miss Monica gave her a big squeeze. That was the way the party went, beginning to end. There were so many friends and family to visit with, and to thank.

By six o'clock, the guests were sated, and began to make their way home. All the bottles of distilled spirits were dead soldiers. The beer was almost gone. Most of the grub was consumed. Barlow and Sarah had thanked everyone personally, not least of which were all their family members.

Barlow was sad when his family excused themselves, so they could get an early start home in the morning. He hadn't had enough time to spend with them. They understood. They were proud of him. They gushed over Sarah. Barlow and Sarah promised them they would visit just as soon as they could. Chloe hugged Barlow tight, and wept on his shoulder. She was almost inconsolable. Sarah cut in and hugged Chloe. She whispered something to her. Whatever it was, it worked like magic. Chloe regained her composure. She was smiling, and crying, when they left.

Arthur and Clarice came up. She said, "Sarah, it's time for you and Barlow to go. The house will really seem empty until you all come back from your honeymoon. We are so happy for you both. We've waited for this day almost as long as you have. Call us when you have a chance. We'd love to hear all about what you've seen, and what you've done. Have fun, but be careful. I love you both." Then she began weeping softly.

Arthur hugged her tightly. He was choked up, too. All he said was, "That goes for me, too. This is one of the happiest days in our lives. See you all in two weeks. Happy and Boyo are in good hands. Vamoose, you two, before this gets any more difficult."

With that, Barlow and Sarah left to begin their new life together. Sarah hugged Barlow with all her might all the way home. This time Barlow kept his wise cracks to himself. How could being filled with so much joy also hurt so much? He was thinking of his folks and Grandma Bea. He hoped they had watched from above.

# CHAPTER 16

## Saturday, June 5, 1971
## Their Brand New Life Begins

It felt strange to them both when they arrived at their home. Same house. Same them. Same feelings for one another. Different circumstances.

Sarah had moved in a lot of her clothes and other belongings, things she knew she would need right away, a little at a time, but mostly Friday night a week ago. It was abundantly clear that she had way more clothes than Barlow did. Not a problem. The master bedroom closet was bigger than the one in the office. He said he would move his stuff in there. She said no, she could take the office closet, but they both knew that wouldn't work, so he moved all of his stuff when she wasn't there, without another word spoken. This was a non-issue.

Tonight, he insisted on carrying her over the threshold. She was surprised that he was such a romantic. She was also a little embarrassed, because it was still daylight, but fortunately no one, Mrs. Peabody specifically, seemed to be around to notice.

Once they were inside, she asked if he wanted something cold to drink. He said no, but asked if she did. She said yes, so he went to the kitchen, and opened the fridge. It was nearly empty, because he knew they would be gone for two weeks. No eggs. No bread. No fruit. No lunchmeat, etc. He did have some cold soft drinks. And something else. A bottle of champagne, and two stemmed, narrow, fluted glasses. No note.

He said, "Someone left us a rather pricey surprise. I wonder who did that."

She asked, "What is it?"

"Pink champagne, and two crystal champagne glasses."

She responded, "Well, I'm certain my dad did the B-and-E. He borrowed my keys before we left the house this morning; however, someone else, maybe Chloe or your Uncle Clive, could have given him the stuff, and asked him to do it as a surprise. Hurry up, Mr. Adams. I'm thirsty. We can find out tomorrow, so we can thank the right people."

"One chilled, pink champagne coming up for the lady who was going to change into something more comfortable."

"None of my clothes feel comfortable right now. That's why I took them all off. I decided to wrap this throw around me that my mom got for us, to take care of the chill."

He picked up the pace, and picked up the drinks, and skedaddled on out into the living room. Didn't spill a bubbly drop. The only light was coming from one of the table lamps. Sure enough, she was sitting there like Lady Godiva, with nothing on but the new cotton throw, which had a picture of General Washington crossing the Delaware. He was looking over the bow of a rowboat. The way it was folded, George may have had a woodie. Barlow couldn't tell for sure. He knew for sure he had one.

"You naughty girl! What if your mother saw you right now in the living room, with nothing but George Washington to feel you up?"

"Hand me my drink. You sit over there in the easy chair. Maybe it was my mother who told me this might be the best way to hold your attention tonight."

"Just a sec. Hold that thought. I want to call your mother and thank her."

"Don't bother her tonight, Cowboy. Did you ever consider that she might be doing this very same thing for Daddy right now? He might not appreciate the interruption. She said several times today that our wedding reminded her of when she and Daddy got married. That's girl speak for saying she plans to get some tonight. Now that nobody else is home, it wouldn't surprise me if she decided to do it on the couch or the kitchen table. Take a walk on the wild side."

"Mrs. Adams, I do believe you have a runaway imagination that's focused in the erotic realm right now. Drink up. I'll get the bottle, and pour us another glass."

"Like you don't? Look at you, Cowboy! I do believe you are about to burst the zipper in your new dress pants. Better get that bad boy under control! I still haven't been convinced that you really love me. You might not get anything more than a peck on the cheek tonight. That would be such a waste, since I spent so much time getting all gussied up for you today. You probably didn't even notice."

He poured them a second drink, but this time he sat down next to her. They clinked glasses and had another sip.

"Mrs. Adams, you looked like a fairy angel that floated down from Heaven. You looked so good walking down the aisle, that I had to bite my lip to hold back tears. I've never, ever, seen a woman look so beautiful in public. I will never forget it. I seared your image in my brain forever."

"Why, Mr. Adams, you're giving me chills down the center of my back. I think I have a touch of the vapors. But whatever do you mean, about never seeing a woman look so beautiful in public? Does that suggest that you have in private? I may be getting a little jealous."

"Mrs. Adams, I was referring to the way you look, when you have nothing on at all, except for a smile. You're so beautiful that I'd like to hire an artist to paint your portrait in your nudies, and hang it up over the couch we're sitting on, except then I would have to share all of your radiance with anyone who stopped by. Nope. No can do. I cannot share that part of you with anyone else in the world. All that sweet pulchritude is mine alone."

"Mr. Adams, I would say that you know how to charm the panties off a girl, except I'm not wearing any. I'm smitten. Let's finish off that bottle of champagne before it gets warm. Then I shall go to the bedroom, where you can give me a foot massage. We'll see where that takes us."

He jumped up, and poured what was left into their glasses. They slammed them like they were shots of tequila. Then he scooped her up and carried her into the bedroom. He set her on the bed. She apparently forgot about the foot massage. She began helping him to undress. Then she pulled down the covers and got under them. She told him to hurry up. He did, except he was all thumbs. Finally, he got undressed, and climbed into bed.

She pulled him on top of her and began kissing him, softly biting his lips like he was made out of chocolate. His body did what comes natural. He was in her. All rational thought ceased for both of them. He put everything into it, and so did she. The intensity of the heat overwhelmed them both. What started like a house on fire ended like two competitive swimmers, neck and neck, who completed the match at the same time, except they were all tangled up together. Out of breath. No sound except the rushing of the waves in their ears. Soaking wet. Exhausted.

He started to roll over, except she squeezed her arms tighter around him, and clenched him with her legs. "Not so fast, Mr. Adams. I've missed you so much. I've been aching for you. I want to hold you as close to me as I can, until I fall asleep."

Before long she did just that. Fall fast asleep. He lay perfectly still, listening to her breathe. She was so precious. Eventually, he rolled beside her. She never stirred. He was wide awake and ready for some more loving. This would have to suffice until tomorrow, and the day after that, and the day after that. A minor sacrifice. He could never get enough of her. He lay as still as he could and watched her steady breathing. Slow. In and out. In and out. In and out. Then he fell asleep. It was only 8:45.

# CHAPTER 17

## Sunday, June 6, 1971
## The Long Awaited Honeymoon Begins

Sarah awoke bright-eyed and bushy-tailed at 0515 hours. Barlow was still fast asleep. Under normal circumstances, Happy would have been there to wash her face with his slobbery tongue, but today he was not. She slipped out of bed, still in her nudies, as quietly as she could, so as not to awaken Barlow, and tiptoed to the bathroom to attend to the call of nature, brush her teeth, rinse with the obligatory Listerine, and brush her hair. Nothing like medicine breath to encourage the pheromones of your new groom to ping! Not! But, it certainly beats gorilla breath!

Then she slipped back into bed. If Barlow was awake, he was playing possum, and very well at that. Maybe he was paying her back for conking out on him last night, after torturing him for two weeks. She certainly deserved it. He was lying on his back with his arms stretched out wide, like he was hanging from a crucifix. She slowly slipped her hand over his manhood, and squeezed it ever so slightly to test it for tensile strength. He was already two-thirds to where she wanted him to be. Even so, he did not stir.

She slipped down further under the sheet, and began licking all around his magic instrument, before taking him in her mouth, and practicing her expertise in the fine art of fellatio. That did the trick. Mission accomplished! He sat straight up in bed.

"I thought I was dreaming. I need to go to the bathroom."

"Uh uh."

"Please. I promise, I will satisfy all your needs."

"No, Cowboy. I'm mounting up. Just be still, while I scratch my itch. I think you must have drugged me last night. I couldn't stay awake. Sorry about that. Now shush up, while I ride this horse 'til it carries me past the farthest beyond. You better not go squishy on me until I'm finished!" All the while she was talking, she was sweeping the sheets off the bed, and placing her saddle on his horse, until it was cinched up just right. Then she lightly kicked her heels into his thighs, and began to canter.

"Sarah, I'm harder than an encrypted messianic message, written in the Cyrillic alphabet. I'm so hard that, now I'm awake, it's bringing tears to my eyes it hurts so much."

"Nope."

He planned to beg some more, but what she was doing suddenly enveloped his entire being. It commandeered his very essence. Then, the next thing he knew, he was rocking and bucking to make the erogenous feeling expand and intensify, until he was no longer in control. Something inside of him had taken over and transformed him into a raging, head-butting ram. Sarah was riding him hard, like she was neck and neck in a horserace, and the finish line was finally in sight. Her eyes were screwed shut, like she was trying to keep water from seeping under her eyelids while she was swimming underwater. She was breathing hard. Her fingernails were piercing his chest. He didn't care. It didn't hurt a bit.

Then, he could feel the geyser beginning to tremble from deep within. He was bathed in sweat. He was running low on oxygen, because he had quit breathing. He concentrated with all his might to keep the volcano at bay. The feeling was so good, and he wanted so bad to release the locks on his own dam, but he dared not. He was reaching his limit. The aching he had in the beginning, which had subsided to a low roar, was now excruciating pain. He didn't know if he was going to get off, or flood the bedroom with pee. Maybe both.

Suddenly Sarah said, "Oh, Lordy," and thrust two more times before collapsing on his chest. He erupted involuntarily, and continued to erupt. Four, five, six, seven, eight times. The sensation was overwhelmingly gratifying, but his rod was still steel hard, and it hurt like the dickens, so instead of lying there, basking in all the out-of-this world physical sensations, and maybe drifting off to sleep, he bounded out of bed into the bathroom to release the pressure. Ahhh! It had hurt so bad, the relief in and of itself was almost a second sexual gratification.

He hurried back to bed, ready for a second round. He held her close.

"What time is it anyway?"

"Well, it was time for you to make me joyful to be a married woman, and not some fallen angel. You already did that, mighty well I might add. Now, it's time to figure out exactly where we're going today. Where will we rest our weary bones tonight, Mr. Adams?"

"So basically the only reason you got married, was so you could get laid anytime you felt like it."

"That pretty much sums it up. Also, sometimes my feet get cold at night, and I like to put them on you to warm them up."

"Anything else?"

"Well, I really love Happy, but to get him, I had to take you. It was an all or nothing sort of thing, so I took the whole enchilada. Hope I don't wind up with buyer's remorse."

"I figured as much. The last thing Happy said to me before he was dropped off at the ranch, was to be sure I got all the trim I wanted before I got out of bed in the morning, so I could stay focused on whatever it was I had to do that day." He squeezed her right cheek (in her nether region.)

"Happy said that, did he?"

"If I'm lyin' I'm dyin'. Okay, Sweetie, my turn to be on top. Roll over, and spread your wings. Now that my bladder is empty, I have some urgent 'bidnezz' to attend to."

She smiled, and rolled over to comply with his wishes. "Well, all righty then. Let's see whatcha got, Cowboy. See if you can make my kitten purr like a Singer sewing machine."

Round two was slower, deliberate, controlled, gratifying, like a six-course meal, consumed in a fine restaurant, on a table with a white tablecloth, paired with a good red wine in crystal glasses, and perfected with soft music in the background. Round one had been a brawl in a biker bar, with tequila shooters, and beer chasers, and cigar smoke swirling over a pool table with torn felt and broken cue sticks, and balls scattered all over the concrete floor, wet with stale beer and spilled blood, and patrolled by a junkyard dog. It felt wonderful just to survive. Then he rang her bell just as loud again, and both times were exactly like she liked it, which was crazy because they were absolutely different.

"What time is it now, Cowboy?"

"It's getting daylight now. That's what time it is. Check the clock in the kitchen. Better not walk naked in front of a window, unless the curtains are pulled shut."

"I can if I want to. I'm a married woman now. I'm no longer worried that Mrs. Peabody might rat me out to my daddy."

"What would all the upstanding church ladies think? My

gosh! A shameless hussy showing off her perfect body, that would give a blind man a diamond cutter in a New York second, in a respectable neighborhood only a mile from the church where she got married!"

"Nice of you to notice, Mr. Ronnie Lee Milsap. Come on. It's 6:30. Let's hurry up, and get our stuff together, and pack your truck. We can eat at Betty's before we head east. How long do you think it will take to get to Fredericksburg?"

"Oh, it's roughly three hundred miles. That's about six hours without stops, if we don't have a flat, or run into road construction, or detours. Of course, we'll have to get gas, eat lunch, maybe have a potty stop or two. If we can get to Betty's by 7:30 and beat the Saturday morning crowd, we could probably be on the road no later than 8:30. Figure nine hours after stops. We should get there by 5:30. That should be plenty early enough to find lodging before we eat. By the way, Archie says they have the best German food there in all of Texas."

"Excellent. Sounds like a nice drive and a fun evening. I'm getting in the shower first, all by myself, to make sure you don't delay us anymore with all your sexual shenanigans, Mr. Adams. Why don't you get the rest of your stuff together while I am indisposed? Then I shall do likewise, while you get cleaned up. It shouldn't take us an hour to do what we need to do."

Most of what they were taking had already been packed. Not only that, they both packed light. Showers only take five minutes when you are young, sitting on G, and looking at O. They stripped and made the bed, and washed the few dirty dishes they had. Barlow put their luggage under a tarp, and tied it down so it wouldn't get dusty, or slide back and forth in the bed. They packed a small cooler with a half-gallon of water, and six Royal

Crown Colas in ice. Breakfast was scrambled eggs and bacon for Sarah, and sausage biscuits for Barlow. They both had coffee and orange juice. They pulled out of town at 8:25 on the dot. Let the good times roll!

The weather was typical for June - sunny with clear blue skies. No wind. The temperature was already ninety degrees. No humidity here, but they heard it would be as humid as a steam bath in San Antonio, and Fredericksburg was only about an hour west of that. They reckoned that heat, coupled with the humidity, would probably smother them, so they mentally prepared themselves as best they could.

Sarah wore a sleeveless sun dress and sneakers. She had a gauzy white cover up to avoid a sunburn. She had a scarf for her hair, so it wouldn't get all tangled and snarled in the truck, when they were rolling down the highway with the windows rolled all the way down, and the vent windows pushed wide open.

No way Barlow was dressing like some Japanese tourist in baggy shorts, Hawaiian flowery shirt, straw hat, black socks and dress shoes, with two cameras dangling around his neck. His one concession was to carry Arthur's 35-millimeter in his hand while they were browsing. (Barlow would have said gawking, if he were talking about any other tourists.) He dressed like he always did when he wasn't at work - jeans, long sleeve shirt, cowboy boots, cowboy hat, and a jean jacket when he needed to cover up the snub nose revolver, which he wore in the front of his jeans in an inside-the-waist holster. Most of the time he could pull his shirttail out of his jeans about an inch, and that was enough to roll over and conceal it. He wore his badge on a round, leather belt clip, except off duty he turned it backwards, and clipped it to his jeans under his belt so it wouldn't be as noticeable.

They had a fabulous drive. They were accustomed to desert weather. You don't miss what you don't have - like an air conditioned vehicle. They arrived in Fredericksburg at 5:20. No flats. No traffic jams. No construction. They checked into a creek-stone, three-story hotel called the Gasthaus, built in 1855. They got a room on the second floor facing the main drag. No air conditioning, but the ceilings were tall, and the room faced north. The windows were large and they opened wide. They had a nice breeze, and an oscillating fan, so it was comfortable. Most of the city was similarly constructed. Neither of them had ever seen a city like it. Built by German immigrants in the mid-1850s.

They walked up and down the covered boardwalks and browsed the shops. Sarah shot an entire roll of film. They ate in a German restaurant, gorging on a German sampler meal, washing it down with dark German beer. It was fantastic. They stopped in a German pub and sampled more German beer, after they presented their driver's licenses to prove they were 21. The waitress wasn't wearing her glasses, and it was pretty dark inside, so she couldn't read what their licenses said, specifically that Sarah would not turn 21 until July 4th. The beer was cold and delicious and went down like mountain spring water. The German draft beers had a higher alcohol content than domestic American beers, but who knew? Certainly not Sarah!

Everyone was so nice, both residents and tourists. They met two other vacationing couples - one from Pennsylvania and the other from Chicago. Everyone was jovial. About ten o'clock, they realized they were more than a little tipsy. Maybe the room was spinning a little bit for Sarah. Time to stumble back to the hotel before they had to low crawl.

Barlow had planned on getting a little more loving. Sarah had planned to give him some. They were too tired. They both got naked and fell into bed. They were both asleep within five minutes. What a day!

# CHAPTER 18

## Monday, June 7, 1971
## Breaking Loose

It was 0730. After breakfast, Joe Rag and Dick Wad assembled at the usual location in the rear of G Cafeteria with the other nine inmates from G Dorm, awaiting correctional officer (CO) escort to Laundry #2, the smaller of two laundries at TSP Huntsville, where they both worked in the transportation section. Specifically, their duties consisted of rolling the big laundry carts piled high with dirty clothes they collected from the cellblocks, to the laundry, and then back to the dorms piled high with clean clothes, after they had been washed. It required them to walk their legs off, but it was considered a cushy job because it allowed them quite a bit of freedom. It also provided them the opportunity to function as middlemen, delivering contraband throughout a substantial section of the prison, for which they received remuneration from the receiving inmates, usually in the form of cigarettes. Of course, any inmate caught in possession of contraband would suffer a loss of privileges and serve time in the hole, so there was always a risk. Nevertheless, 'nothing ventured, nothing gained.'

The prison laundries throughout Texas laundered inmate and correctional officer uniforms. Getting your uniforms cleaned for free was a perk for state correctional officers, which state troopers did not receive. However, TSP Huntsville was different from all the others. At Huntsville, the state paid a private laundry to clean CO uniforms. The concept at TSP Huntsville was to prevent the inmates from stealing or sabotaging the CO uniforms, a phenomenon which apparently was unheard of elsewhere.

At least that is how it was explained. It had absolutely nothing to do with the fact that a powerful state senator named J. Cornelius Cobb, brother to TSP Huntsville Warden Kermit O. Cobb, who was married to Lucille Pinckney, sister of Darren F. Pinckney, who was the owner of the chain of Pinckney's Stay Kleen Laundry Services, and which had, by happenstance, the state contract to wash, and starch, and press CO uniforms for TSP Huntsville.

This was all strictly legitimate, and nothing more than a way to put taxpayer money back into the hands of the community. It was simply a coincidence that the senator's sister-in-law was the sister of the businessman, who was awarded the contract to clean the correctional officer uniforms for twice what it would have cost at the state capital in Austin. Anyone who thought otherwise was either misinformed or a black-hearted Republican.

The state contract called for a Pinckney laundry truck to stop by both TSP Huntsville laundries before noon on Mondays, Wednesdays, and Fridays, to drop off paper-wrapped bundles of clean uniforms, and to pick up duffle bags full of dirty uniforms. Generally speaking, the trucks received a cursory search at the front gate both coming and going. Some guards were more diligent than others, but in the course of time, regular guards and regular drivers became chummy with each other, and the guards became lax. It's human nature. 'Familiarity breeds contempt.' That being said, new drivers and/or vehicles which had never been there before, or only aperiodically, or who were not following their normal protocols, were given more thorough searches.

Usually the more stringent searches were conducted on outgoing vehicles, because the prison did not want any inmates to escape. Of course, nobody in his right mind would ever try to break into a prison. How stupid would that be? Therefore, the only thing to worry about with respect to an incoming vehicle, from a guard's perspective, was contraband, but the laundry trucks were deemed to be low risk, beginning with Warden Cobb and trickling on down to the newest employee, something akin to the game 'follow the leader.'

Specifically, as it related to laundry vehicles, and as a backup security precaution, after the truck was cleared by the front gate, the protocol called for a CO to meet the truck at each laundry upon arrival, and to verify the number of bundles coming in, and the number of duffle bags going out. All the 'heavy lifting' was performed by inmates. Inventory sheets would be signed by the drivers and the COs verifying the count. Each party would receive a copy. The prison copy would be hole-punched and duly filed in ascending order in the proper manila folder, and placed in a metal filing cabinet under lock and key in the admin building. How's that for control? What could possibly go wrong? The 'civilian' drivers were under CO observation from entry to exit. The system worked like a Swiss watch, or so management maintained.

In practice, the laundry truck, normally driven by Gustavo Santana, and today was no different, arrived at Laundry #1 about a quarter to eleven. CO Emilio Lopez was standing by on the dock with three beefy inmates to do the actual work. These included Fatso Watson, Jesus Rojas, and Damarius Washington. CO Lopez was diligent, by the book, no nonsense. He and Santana bracketed the rear doors of the truck and counted every bundle coming out, and every duffle bag going in. Absolutely no monkey business. Protocol faithfully followed. Military precision.

Job completed, Santana drove to the rear of the compound to Laundry #2, where he was greeted by Joe Rag and Dick Wad, the regular inmates for Laundry #2, and inmate Angel 'Cementhead' Rivera.

Santana did not recognize Cementhead because he was new. He came highly recommended as a laundry transportation helper by Joe Rag and Dick Wad to CO Franklin 'Big Frankie' Duckworth, the Laundry #2 transportation supervisor. Normally Big Frankie would have been there to greet Santana instead of Cementhead, except Big Frankie had urgent business in the john, due to the dozen Carter's Little Pills that Dick Wad had crushed, and slipped into Big Frankie's coffee thermos. This was the ultimate cleansing of one's bowels in the entire state of Texas, for the 20th century to date. It was a real shit storm, but what can you do?

Normally, Cementhead, who was built like the Incredible Hulk, but whose IQ was in the low seventies, would never have been given a job which required adding sums greater than he could count on his fingers. His true aptitude was in lifting heavy weight, and in following orders literally 'to the T.' One would never tell him, "I want you to go over there, and rip that asshole's head right off his shoulders," unless that's exactly what you wanted him to do.

Everyone in G Dorm knew that, including Big Frankie, who wasn't exactly known as a Mensa candidate himself, but Big Frankie was 64 years old. He was sixty pounds overweight. He had arthritis and piles. He had a cavity in a molar that was giving him grief. His lower back and the bunions on his feet hurt. His wife was grumpy everyday, except for payday, when he gave her his check. He had nineteen years on the job. He needed one more to get the magic twenty, and age 65. Then he could retire and enjoy the rest of his life in near poverty, with a wife who looked like forty miles of bad road, who was perpetually on the rag, and whose cooking tasted worse than warmed up elephant barf. Joe Rag and Dick Wad treated Big Frankie like he was a VIP. Besides that, they kept the other inmates in line. If Joe and Dick wanted Cementhead, it wasn't any sweat off his balls. Let them have Cementhead. Eleven-and-a-half months and counting. And that's how come Cementhead was there this morning.

Cementhead's job was to keep Santana occupied and out of sight of the rear doors of the truck for at least two minutes, after the dirty laundry had been loaded, so Joe Rag and Dick Wad could hide under the pile of duffle bags.

Joe Rag told Cementhead that they had to escape, because his wife was having his baby (in which the pregnancy was problematic because it took two years to gestate.) He had to get back to Dallas, because she said she was running off with her new boyfriend. The new boyfriend was some major league badass, and Dick Wad was coming with him in case the boyfriend broke bad, like with a machine gun or something. This was Joe's only chance to salvage his marriage to this Playboy bunny he had met in Alcoholics Anonymous, and accidentally knocked up, before he got railroaded by some crooked cops. It was a sad tale full of woe, and Cementhead swallowed it hook, line, and sinker.

To pull everything off, they had to convince Santana that it was okay for Cementhead to fill in for CO Duckworth. They did that by having another inmate, William 'Sly Willy' Peters, dress in a purloined CO uniform and stand inside the laundry door to acknowledge that Cementhead was authorized to do the inventory this one time all by himself, only because CO Duckworth was indisposed with a serious case of diarrhea. Santana was welcome to step inside the restroom and smell for himself, but he didn't recommend it. Sly Willy said he had to stay inside and keep an eye on the rest of the inmates, because they were shorthanded. Otherwise, Santana would have to wait until they could get another CO to break loose from whatever he was doing, but it was lunchtime, and it might take fifteen or twenty minutes. As expected, Santana was in a hurry, so he agreed to break protocol only this one time, saying that he hoped CO Duckworth got to feeling better soon.

For their cooperation, and because there was always a chance that their collusion would come to light, and that punishment would ensue, Joe Rag willed his three-and-a-half cartons of cigarettes that he couldn't take with him, to be split evenly between Cementhead and Sly Willie. He even turned over his stash to Sly Willie Sunday night, so he could hide them someplace other than in his cell, in case he got busted. He knew Sly Willie wouldn't try to cheat Cementhead, because that would be tantamount to embracing a death sentence, which would be meted out with a godawful beating. The logic for Sly Willie not stepping out of the laundry was to keep Santana from getting a good look at his face. Joe Rag always thought of everything, and he never failed to 'cover all the bases.'

As for the rest of the inmates in Laundry #2, they 'saw no evil; heard no evil; spoke no evil.' To do otherwise, would have been the height of folly. If Cementhead didn't seek revenge, one of Joe Rag's biker brethren would. They knew they would escape punishment by the screws if they just kept their mouths shut, versus a death sentence by the inmates if they were even suspected of squealing.

Actually, the escape went off better than anyone could have imagined. The offloading and on loading proceeded normally, except for Cementhead filling in for Big Frankie. When Santana went to climb back into the cab, Cementhead slowed him up by offering him a cigarette, and asking him about the tattoo on his left forearm, depicting a scorpion stinging a rattlesnake who had it in his mouth.

Cementhead asked, "Which one won?"

Santana asked, "What do you mean?"

"Did the scorpion kill the snake, or did the snake eat the scorpion?"

"What do you think?"

"I think the scorpion won. How about you?"

"I think they killed each other. I got this tattoo to remind me that you might kill your enemy, but it could cost you your own life, too. When I was younger, I thought it was important to let everyone know what a badass I was. Now, I believe it is best to 'live and let live' if you can. Comprenden?"

"Comprenden."

"So long. Maybe I'll see you the next time if Big Frankie isn't well yet."

"So long."

That's all it took for Joe Rag and Dick Wad to burrow themselves deep under the mountain of duffle bags. The guard at the gate opened the back door and gave it a glance before pushing it shut. Joe Rag thought, "Adiós, you dumb sons a bitches."

# CHAPTER 19

## Monday, June 7, 1971
## New Sights and Adventures

Monday morning started gradually with the sun silently creeping up over the horizon in the east, eventually spreading its glow to the north side of the Gasthaus, and into the open windows of Room 203, said blinds of which were unshuttered because the newlyweds didn't think to do so before they piled into bed the night before. After a passionate bout of demonstrating their unbridled appreciation for one another, they showered and packed up, and bounded down the stairs, and into the dining room.

They feasted on French toast with Canadian maple syrup, and little German sausages, and Florida orange juice, and a carafe of Arabica coffee. Since it wasn't much more than a hundred miles to San Antonio, they lounged around, taking their old sweet time, lallygagging over breakfast. Sarah snapped more pictures, and she bought a souvenir coffee cup at the lobby when they settled their account at the front desk. She thought about giving her mom a quick call from a pay phone, but she didn't.

It was smooth sailing all the way from Fredericksburg, until they entered the outskirts of San Antonio from the north on US 281, at which time they began to encounter stop and go traffic. Barlow had studied the inset of the San Antonio map, on the backside of the official Texas state map, dated 1969, but it was only two inches square, and minus a lot of detail. Nevertheless, they found the Alamo without much trouble, even though it was surrounded by much taller buildings. From there, they began searching for a quaint or historic hotel within walking distance, and voila! Only four blocks away, and there it was. The Travis and Crockett Hotel, circa 1890, a large, five-story, stone edifice on a corner lot. It was exactly what they had hoped to find.

Sarah waited in the truck while Barlow went in to see if there 'was any room in the inn.' Indeed there were vacancies, several in fact, although they were quite pricey. However, this hotel had refrigerated air, a large lobby with Persian rugs and overstuffed leather chairs, and a tobacconist shop. It also featured a cozy bar with Victorian paintings of nude women lounging in a forest glen, on Cleopatra-style, damask-covered, chaise lounges, plus a gift shop, and an elegant dining room with crystal chandeliers. Furthermore, it offered secure, covered parking next door.

Barlow checked them in for one night. He would have felt more at home had he been wearing a tuxedo instead of blue jeans, but he looked around, and noticed that he wasn't the only cowboy in the joint. It was Texas, after all.

The desk clerk rang a bell. A bellman materialized from a concealed door in the wood paneling. He was dressed like a Prussian general in a bright red coat, with yards of gold trim, and gold buttons, and a matching pillbox cap. Made Barlow's Class A Army uniform look a mite shabby, even with all his ribbons. He was pushing a four-foot-long dolly. His name tag said his name was Carlos. He accompanied Barlow out to his truck, where he collected their belongings and rolled them up to their room on the fourth floor. Not only that, he folded down the bed covers, and placed a gold-wrapped chocolate on both the pillows. Nobody had ever humped Barlow's bags before, and he was a little embarrassed, but he saw that this was the custom here, and 'when in Rome do as the Romans do' so he did. He figured the guy expected a tip, but he had no idea what was customary, so he slipped him two bucks, and the guy began to fade away, looking as happy as the proverbial cat who ate the canary.

Sarah was as dumbfounded as Barlow with the opulence and red carpet treatment, but she hid it better, smiling sweetly at Carlos, and thanking him by name as he left. Barlow glanced up just in time to see drool begin to drip out of Carlos' mouth and onto the front of his elegant uniform, while he letched at Sarah on his way out the door. Barlow thought, "You weaselly little pervert! Detach your beady bulbs from my wife's derrière, before I blacken both of your eyes!"

Sarah saw the expression on Barlow's face. She smiled and said, "My, my, Mr. Adams. Did Carlos make you a little jealous in his fancy red uniform?"

"Did you see what he did to you? He undressed you with his eyes, and feasted on you, like you were a piece of Black Forest cake à la mode!"

"Barlow, Carlos and all the other lechers like him can look, but they can't touch. You know that. Would you rather I be so ugly that other men feel sorry for you? Why don't you forget about Carlos, and come over here, so I can give you a squeeze and a kiss, before we go sightseeing?"

That put the smile back on his face. She looked so good, he wanted to lick all over her naked body like she was an ice cream cone. She knew it, too. When they hugged, she gave him a French kiss full of promise, and then she broke off abruptly, before he could wrap her up so tight she couldn't escape. He knew all her tricks, so he feigned nonchalance. Better off if she didn't know how horny she just made him.

She said, "Mr. Adams, I could spend all afternoon here in this splendiferous boudoir with you, and work you over so bad you would not wake up for twelve hours. It's very tempting, because you make me so wet whenever I get close to you. However, if we're going to see the Alamo today, we need to get going. We still need to eat lunch, too."

"Well, we could stay here another night if you want. The Astros will be at home for nine days in a row."

"Mr. Adams, you are so sweet. That's one of the reasons I love you so much. However, you haven't told me what this hotel costs for one night. I bet it's way more than the $19.23 we spent last night, and that's more than double what a night costs at the Travelers Rest Motor Lodge. We probably ought to enjoy this beautiful hotel for the night, and move onto someplace cheaper from here on out."

"Well, you don't want to know what the Travis and Crockett charges for a room, so don't ask. We're here because this is our honeymoon, and we are supposed to have the time of our lives. It will probably be a long time before we have an opportunity to stay at a swanky place like this again."

"Barlow, I want to know how much this place costs, but don't tell me until we stay someplace more reasonable, or I won't enjoy myself. There is one thing that I wanted to run by you before we go to the Alamo."

"What's that?"

"Neither one of us has been to the beach, unless you got to go in Vietnam. Corpus Christi is only 150 miles from here. What if we went to the beach for a night or two before we go to Houston? I'd really like to see it. You know, walk on the beach, swim in the ocean. Please?"

"Of course! I never thought of it. I'd love to take you to the beach. I did have a few days at the beach on R and R while I was in Vietnam. It's really amazing, but there are a lot of nasty creatures in the ocean. You should have said something."

"I didn't think about it until just now. Thank you. You make me so happy. Now let's go get something to eat. I'm famished!"

The rest of the day consisted of holding hands while they walked, touching toes under the table while they ate, and assimilating just how small the Alamo actually is, and what the prairie must have looked like with two thousand, pissed-off Mexican soldiers standing in array for battle.

Barlow was in awe of the Texians' sacrifice. He couldn't imagine what it must have been like for the two hundred defenders facing those odds with single shot, black powder rifles, where it takes about a minute to reload, and then you have to scrub your barrel out after three or four shots to get the fouling out, before you can reload again, and continue firing for another three or four shots. At least today, an inferior force has a better chance of survival fighting with modern weapons. And, although both sides possessed cannons, the Mexicans used theirs to blow holes in the walls to knock them down, and with the fort surrounded on all sides, there was no place for a Texian to hide, or flee, once the Mexicans did breach the walls.

Truth is, a tactical retreat made a whole lot more sense to Barlow, where you live to fight another day when the odds are not so lopsidedly stacked against you. However, different versions of the story exist, so maybe they never really had that option. Also, at the time, nobody imagined that Sam Houston's Texian and American volunteers would quietly descend upon, and conquer, General Santa Anna's massive army at the Battle of San Jacinto, in the vicinity of modern day Houston, a month later to win independence for Texas, from Mexico.

The sightseeing tour was sobering, especially to Barlow, who was a combat veteran. Hats off to all the Texian and American soldiers who fought and died on this hallowed soil.

That night back at the hotel, they had a marvelous dining experience. They had a steak and lobster dinner with baked potatoes, a tossed salad, and iced tea, with a raspberry sorbet for dessert, on a table with a sparkling white linen tablecloth. The background was filled with soft classical music.

Red wine would have been nice, but they ordered no alcohol because Sarah hadn't turned 21 since the night before. They didn't suppose they could slip that minor detail past the waitress here, like they managed to pull off in Fredericksburg. Here, the restaurant had ample lighting, not to mention a lit candle in the middle of the table, so they decided not to push their luck. Anyway, the meal was wonderful, even without an adult beverage, and certainly one they'd never forget.

Afterwards, Barlow bought a pint of Makers Mark next door at a package store that was real proud of their assortment of top shelf liquors. He also patronized the hotel's tobacconist and bought a half dozen Romeo & Juliet, Churchill style cigars in Maduro wrappers at a buck each, which was three times what his everyday smokes at home cost (and he didn't buy cheap cigars!). Then they walked back to the lobby and enjoyed the big city hotel ambiance, in comfy leather chairs while Barlow smoked. They also enjoyed a taste or two of Makers Mark neat, using two of the white ceramic cups placed next to the lobby coffee urn. Not that anyone noticed, but they never uttered a word while they soaked in this rhapsody of elegance. It was a fabulous way to cap off an evening in public.

In the privacy of their luxurious room, with a four-foot tall, overstuffed, queen-size, canopied bed, they came up with a different way of topping off the evening, and they didn't waste any time getting around to it. Sarah was naked before Barlow even got his shirt unbuttoned. She told him to pull back the covers, climb up on the bed, and lie on his back, so she could get his boots and jeans off, as well as other things.

Soon, he was as bare as a plucked chicken. She climbed up on top of the bed, and checked the tensile strength of his throbbing joystick, using every female, black magic, witchy woman trick she knew. When she was satisfied that he had endured all the pleasure, and the pain that he could endure without overflowing with joy, as it were, she turned the tables on him, and suggested that it might be nice if he were to give her a licking so she would keep on ticking.

Naturally, he complied, but when he determined that the only remedy for her condition was to pump her full of Dr. Adams' swollen root salve, that's what he did. Her condition was serious, so it took three times to assuage the situation. That was all the umph he had, the tube full of salve now being as empty as Al Capone's hidden vault, but it was sufficient to fill her with rapture and transport her into Dreamland.

Barlow must have accidentally rubbed some salve on himself while he was working up a sweat, because the Sandman rendered him into a masculine form of Sleeping Beauty. What about that?

All is well that ends well.

# CHAPTER 20

## Monday, June 7, 1971
## Sometimes Fate Favors the Undeserving

Joe Rag and Dick Wad were clueless as to where Gustavo Santana would go before he stopped for anything other than a red light. Unassing the laundry truck could be as dicey as sneaking on board. He might go directly to the laundry where he could have help offloading. Not good.

While they were in transit, movement and speech were an issue. The metal mesh shield between the driver's seat and the storage compartment did not allow for any privacy. Therefore, all they could do was wait, and hope, that Santana would be alone when he stopped to offload.

In point of fact, what happened was even better. The first thing Santana did when he got back to town was to stop for lunch at a Mexican diner. The tagalongs waited a minute for him to get inside, before they emerged from the pile of duffle bags. Joe Rag watched through the windshield for any sign of trouble, while Dick Wad searched until he found two CO uniforms that weren't too foul and would fit each of them. They took turns as lookout while the other changed clothes.

Fortunately, they were issued cheap, black sneakers since they were assigned to the laundry detail. Cons with no job wore shower clogs. They stashed their prison uniforms in one of the duffle bags, and buried it in the pile. Then they slipped quietly out of the truck. This metamorphosis and departure consumed fifteen very intense minutes.

They walked away from the diner as nonchalantly as they could, continuing until they spotted a strip mall with a parking lot full of cars. Joe spotted a well cared for metallic, light blue, 1966, Oldsmobile station wagon. It was practically lost to sight, buried in one of the middle rows. Dick was lookout, while Joe jimmied open the vent window on the passenger side, which was loose anyway, and reached in and unlocked the door. He slid in the front seat and hot wired the ignition. The Olds fired right up. Good! It had three-quarters of a tank of gas. Dick slid in the passenger seat, and away they went. Nobody noticed anything out of the ordinary.

Next, they drove around until they found a lower, middle class neighborhood. They needed some nondescript threads. Being Monday, there were lots of clean clothes pinned to clotheslines in back yards, drying in the hot summer sun. They had to make their selections from yards with some degree of concealment, nobody around, and no barking dog. Easier said than done.

They found such a yard, with two rows of sheets and pillowcases flapping in the breeze, which provided the concealment. In addition, there were two other rows of garments. Joe was more or less a standard size. Proportionate. Five-feet, eleven-inches tall, and 185 pounds. He found a short sleeve, red and white checked shirt, and a pair of jeans. He also grabbed two pairs each of white socks, drawers, and tee shirts. He was in and out in less than two minutes while Dick waited in the car, engine running, ready to sky up at the first sign of trouble.

Finding clothes for a baldheaded, 240 pound, five-feet, eight-inch, rapist was a bigger challenge. Finally, more than an hour and three neighborhoods later, Dick found himself three yellow tee shirts with Conrad's Cement, Hwy 105, Cleveland, Texas, printed across the chest in black, block letters. He also stole one pair of jeans, most likely belonging to a three hundred pound, five-feet, ten-inch, blue collar employee of the cement plant. He also copped three pairs of black, nylon socks, and screw the drawers. They were worn out tighty whities, and even though they were washed, you could still see the brown skunk stripe in the middle of the seat. Who needs underwear anyway? Just makes your balls sweat more.

They skedaddled out of that neighborhood before someone got wise to them. They drove 'up the down staircase,' otherwise identified as the exit lane of the Skylight Drive-In Theater, where they changed clothes. Then they drove around looking for an easy place to score a few bucks for some groceries. However, before they could accomplish that mission, they spotted a Goodwill center with a big metal dumpster, designed to accept donations after hours, so being charitable citizens, that's where they deposited the CO uniforms. Who knew the next time a bum might want to dress up like a prison guard? Maybe Halloween?

They only needed ten or twenty bucks to hold them over until they hooked up with Gravy Train tomorrow. They didn't want to cause any commotion. By now the Texas Rangers and the FBI would be looking for them. They didn't need the heat. Couldn't fade the heat. They had no compunction about snatching an old lady's purse, or rolling a queer for his money, or sticking a gun in the face of some fat cat to steal his watch and wallet. Nosiree Bob! That was all fair game. The problem was, robbery of any sort riled up the fuzz, like feeding cotton candy to a toddler, and the prowler car cops became more aggressive and shoved around anyone who didn't look like Mr. and Mrs. Beaver Cleaver, upright and uptight citizens. Anyone who didn't look, smell, and feel squeaky clean, would get snatched up on some chickenshit beef, like disorderly conduct, or vagrancy, or drunk in a public place, and tossed in the tank for a night. If Joe or Dick got busted on anything, even if the case were ultimately dismissed, they'd be back in prison, serving time in the hole within the week. So . . . . what to do?

Only one thing to do. Find an empty house that showed some promise and break in. Look for cash, handguns with ammo, gold jewelry, or as a last resort, food and alcohol. Strip a pillowcase off the bed, and fill it with whatever loot was worth the taking. In and out in fifteen minutes.

They found a single-story dwelling at the end of a street with an empty driveway, that was secluded from the neighbors, and had no dogs. Joe was the burglar, so he went in, while Dick waited in the car. First, Joe knocked on the front door three different times, just in case the occupant was asleep. No answer. Then he walked around to the back door. He was prepared to break a windowpane, but no need. It was unlocked. He let himself in and made a silent sweep of the house. No one home.

First, he checked the master bedroom. He found a loaded, .38 caliber, Colt Cobra, snub nose revolver, and half a box of bullets in a bedside table. He put the gun in his pocket, and the spare ammo in a pillowcase he stripped off a pillow on the bed.

He searched the chest of drawers and the dresser. He came up with a small leather change purse with a metal clasp, that had 22 two-dollar bills. Probably the homeowner's collection, since you don't see two-dollar bills much anymore. Put that in his pocket.

The other bedroom was set up for a little girl. He didn't even bother to look.

He checked the medicine cabinet in the bathroom. What do you know? A prescription bottle for one Harriett Clevenger, about a third full with ten-milligram Valiums. That might come in handy. Dropped that into the pillowcase.

Nothing of interest in the living room.

He checked the kitchen last. He stole two, sturdy, wooden-handled, Chicago Cutlery steak knives. Also a nearly full bottle of peach brandy, five cold bottles of Blatz beer, a jar of pickles, an unopened package of sliced bologna, a jar of mustard, a half box of Tony the Tiger's Frosted Flakes, a half gallon of milk, four apples, two oranges, a tin of homemade sugar cookies, a nearly full loaf of bread, a jar of salted peanuts, and an unopened box of Ritz crackers. He also found a half carton of Camel cigarettes, and several tabs of matches from Roxie's Billiard Hall.

Additionally, there was approximately a quarter of a dark chocolate cake with coconut cream icing, remaining in a glass cake pedestal on the countertop. It was begging him to eat it, so he did. He gobbled it all down with his fingers. Fuck Dick. Joe was taking all the risks. He should reap the larger reward. Dick's loss was Joe's gain.

Joe started to leave, and then he remembered. He went back to one of the drawers, and stole two teaspoons. Hard to eat Tony the Tiger chow without a spoon. Then he remembered the beer and stole a church key. He picked up his poke, and strolled out of the house like Santa Claus, only in reverse. When Joe played Santa Claus, he got all the goodies. Mmm! That cake was damn good!

They drove away. Nobody walking along the street or peeking out of windows. Clean getaway to a different neighborhood. They parked in the garage of a vacant house that sat on a small hill on an unmown, five-acre lot with a forlorn 'For Sale' sign in the front yard. They broke in through the back door. The house was empty. It was also hot and musty. Both the water and the electricity were cut off. Didn't look like anyone had checked on it for a long time. They hoped nobody did tonight. They would stay here until it was time to hook up with Gravy Train.

All in all, it had been a very good day. Very, very good. The taste of freedom was sweet, even in a sweltering, musty house filled with mouse droppings.

# CHAPTER 21

## Tuesday, June 8, 1971
## Hello the Beach

Sarah called her mom from a phone in the bank of pay phones in the lobby while Barlow checked them out of the hotel. Clarice was ecstatic to receive the call. Sarah was nearly breathless because she was talking so fast, while she gushed about all the things they had seen and done. She said they were taking a detour to Corpus Christi for one or two nights, probably two, so they could see the ocean. They would go to Houston in time to watch the Astros play the Braves.

Then her dad got on the phone, just to double check that they had not encountered any trouble. He was worried that Barlow's truck might not be up to the challenge for such a long trip. Sarah knew her father knew that Barlow was a first class mechanic, and that his truck probably ran better than a brand new one, let alone one of her dad's ranch vehicles. She also knew that the real reason he was worried was because this was the first time his baby girl had gone anywhere out of town overnight, unless it was with Mom and him, or else to go see family. She told him that she was in safe hands with Barlow and not to worry. He acknowledged same, and segued to a safer subject by telling her that Happy was doing well. It was painfully obvious that her dad sorely missed her and Barlow.

It was a comforting conversation for the three of them. She rang off after ten minutes, so she wouldn't have to deposit another fifty-five cents. She had the quarters, but not the nickel. The last thing she said was, "I love you. Call you all again in a few days." Then she met Barlow at the truck, and off they went to their next adventure.

They located a windswept motel called the Brown Pelican, right on the beach in greater Corpus Christi. Barlow wasn't sure of the name of the town they were in, but he was fairly certain it was not in Corpus Christi proper. It didn't really matter, he supposed. This was a small, circa 1950, single-story, adobe motel with neon lights shining brightly after dark - a motel which was largely overlooked by tourists, who preferred something newer, with more glitz and glamour. Nevertheless, it still wasn't cheap lodging because it backed up to the beach. Anyway, it met their needs just fine. By two o'clock, they were checking out the sand and the surf and the wind and the crabs and the seagulls, and yes, the brown pelicans, too.

Barlow and Sarah both pretty much looked like what one would expect of landlocked desert dwellers in their new bathing suits, only Sarah looked much better, and not just because of her curvaceous figure. Her face, neck, arms, shoulders, and legs below the knees, were tan. The rest of her unblemished body, which wasn't covered by her two-piece bathing suit, was a creamy white. Barlow, on the other hand, had a tan face, neck, and hands. The rest of him was alabaster white. He looked like he was from Norway or someplace where the sun never shines. Both were aware of their propensity for sunburn, so they lathered with Coppertone, and sat under a beach umbrella when they weren't frolicking in the surf. Besides, anyone who was paying attention could see that they weren't the only tourists who were unaccustomed to the summertime beach atmosphere. They stayed for two nights. Fun-filled nights.

# CHAPTER 22

### Tuesday, June 8, 1971
### Larry the Fairy Makes His Play

The Texas State Penitentiary in Huntsville was still in an enormous uproar, and heads continued to be systematically lopped off. Inmate or employee, serious shortcoming or minor mistake, it didn't matter. Not one whit! People would pay! Warden Cobb was humiliated. Senator Cobb was scrambling for cover. Darren Pinckney could see his empire crumbling before his very eyes. This must be salvaged! Blame must be assigned! Scapegoats had to be found! And if the escapees surfaced, it was hoped by all concerned that the cops would shoot them both dead and make this entire debacle go away.

The thing is, Joe Rag and Dick Wad were truly dangerous sociopaths. That's why they came to the attention of the authorities and the courts in the first place, and that's why they were incarcerated. However, that fine point was lost on the trio of greedy bloodsuckers. The important thing was to keep making money at the taxpayers' expense, and not to shine the bright light of proper public stewardship of tax dollars onto their shady little operation.

The way it happened, Joe Rag and Dick Wad had only been gone for an hour and change on Monday before management learned of their escape, thanks to Carter's Little Pills which made everything possible. That morning, Big Frankie's bowels turned him inside out. Each time he thought he was through purging, he had to drop trou and sit back down on the commode. He was unable to get out of the restroom. He was indisposed for a full thirty minutes! It was awful.

The smell kept seeping out from under the door of the john, farther and farther, until it was too toxic for anyone to come within ten feet of it. Inmates were gagging and making rude comments. The other CO assigned to the laundry, Roger 'The Creep' Sneed, who earned his monicker on account of his sneaking around trying to catch inmates doing something they shouldn't, went AWOL, and feigned important business in the library, which was the closest 'legitimate' CO fucking off place to the laundry. This is why the guards didn't wise up for so long. Both cats were away, and the mice did play.

Finally, six or seven pounds lighter, with an anus so raw that it felt as if he had rubbed it with Tabasco sauce, bathed in sweat, light-headed, and nose-blind (thankfully), Big Frankie emerged from the john, which ended up taking a whole day to air out. He wasn't fully aware of his surroundings, and the first absence he noted was the Creep's, not Joe's nor Dick's.

"Hey, any of you shitbirds seen Officer Sneed?"

No answer.

"Come on guys, where's he at?"

Still no answer, but one of the cons rolled his eyes in the general vicinity of the route to the library. Big Frankie picked up on the tip and headed in that direction. The air in the laundry was still foul beyond human endurance, but Big Frankie didn't notice, being nose-blind. Sure enough, the Creep was seated at a table in the library, flipping through a *Sports Illustrated* magazine, while Larry the Fairy was panting over the homo magazine, *Blue Boy*, which he successfully hid behind a *Look* magazine.

"Hey, Fucko, why aren't you in the laundry doing your job? You know I ain't feeling well."

"No shit, Sherlock, and on accounta you, ain't no one in the laundry feeling well."

"What are you talking about, shit-for-brains?"

"You're asking me? Did ya ever smell yourself, asshole? Did ya not spend the last thirty minutes shitting obnoxious, slimy, hyena turds in our one-hole laundry shithouse, until ya peeled the paint off the walls because of your poisonous odor, and then nearly croaking all of us in the laundry with that same eye-watering smell, that none of us can escape even from all the way over here in the library? Ya couldn't walk down the hall to the big shithouse with four stalls, and kill everyone there, instead of in our workspace? Fuck you, Frankie! In all my life, I never smelled anything so lethal! So who's the real shithead now, Frankie? Proud of yourself, are ya?"

"Geez, Roger, I'm sorry. I don't know what come over me. I still feel like shit, no pun intended. I didn't know it was so bad. Stay here long as you like. I won't blow the whistle."

"You're a real stand-up guy, Frankie. Ya know that? Tell ya what. I'll hang out here for a little while longer until I can see through the green fog that's hovering over the entire G compound area, thanks to you. And for Christ sake, don't light a smoke or you'll blow us all up to kingdom come! Go tend to our sheep - any that are still breathing, that is. But if ya fucking killed them all with that world-class asshole of yours, I ain't taking the fall with ya. You're all on your own. Rat me out. I don't care. I'll take my suspension at home where the air is clean, and I can drink a cold beer. Get the fuck outta here!"

Big Frankie was completely humiliated. He mumbled, "Sorry, Roger. I'll go back, and take care of the laundry," before shuffling out of the library and back to the 'scene of the crime.'

That's when Big Frankie first got the inkling that something was really wrong. He couldn't find Joe or Dick in the laundry, where they should have been. It wasn't time for them to begin their deliveries. Cementhead said he just saw them, but didn't know where they went. They didn't say. They're probably just sneaking a nap somewheres.

The other cons were just as evasive. Guards who had work crews, who fed the same time as the laundry crew, didn't remember seeing them at the mess hall, but then the guards weren't looking for them, either. "They're probably around just fucking off somewhere."

Big Frankie didn't think so. He searched high and low. He talked to everybody in and around G complex, but to no avail. The assholes were nowhere to be found.

Finally, as a last resort, Big Frankie called the front office and reported them missing. It wasn't his fault, but he'd take the fall. He knew that already. He'd probably be forced to retire on a partial, reduced retirement. He'd have to find another job someplace as a security guard just to make ends meet. His wife would be pissed! She would have no mercy. Hell, he'd need another job just to get away from her constant bitching.

That's when all Hell broke loose.

The emergency lockdown alarm began blaring. The loud speakers came on, ordering the COs to corral their charges and put them all in lockdown. All normal prison activities would cease, pending a top to bottom search of the prison. That meant nobody comes in, and nobody goes out.

A headcount was conducted, and fortunately, Joe Rag and Dick Wad were the only ones missing.

The search took three hours. No luck. Finally DPS and the Texas Rangers were notified. Ditto for the Walker County Sheriff's Office and the Huntsville Police Department.

The Texas Rangers assumed responsibility for conducting prison interviews. They started with Big Frankie. His alibi was quickly confirmed, but he was jammed up because he didn't call another CO to meet the laundry truck. Next, they interviewed the Creep. He was jammed up because he didn't fill in for Big Frankie. Nevertheless, he was cleared of any involvement.

They interviewed both the COs who worked the main gate. Lazarus Seguin remembered checking the laundry truck when it entered, and Bradley Porter remembered checking it when it departed. Both stated it was free of any inmates. Seguin was cleared. Porter was 'in holding' until it was determined if the prisoners escaped via the laundry truck. If that turned out to be the case, Porter was a gone pecan. Porter loved his job, and he was shitting razor blades.

Now the Rangers zeroed in on Cementhead. He tried to feign ignorance, but there was no way. They told the guards to isolate Cementhead in segregation for further interrogation. He was 'tuned up' or rather, he fell on the way to the hole and broke his nose. Accidents happen.

Next, the Rangers questioned Warden Cobb. They wanted all the details about the laundry service contract. Warden Cobb provided them with the log-in sheet for that day. It showed that the driver was one Gustavo Santana. The prison had no file on him. Sorry. Warden Cobb did, however, shit the name, business address, and telephone number of Pinckney's Stay Kleen

Laundry Services in Huntsville. He forgot to mention that Darren Pinckney was his brother-in-law. It didn't dawn on the Rangers to ask. The Rangers detailed two of their party to interview Mr. Pinckney and Mr. Santana. They kept Warden Cobb in tow so he couldn't warn them.

In the meantime, they had all the inmates assigned to the laundry segregated for interview. They wanted the warden present, mostly to keep him away from a phone, but they told him they needed his insight on the interviewees. These interviews were a total waste of time. They knew it would be, but it filled the gap while they waited for a call back from the Pinckney and Santana interviews.

Finally, they received it. Mr. Pinckney was extremely helpful. The Rangers watched while the prison duffle bags were examined. They recovered two inmate uniforms among the piles of guard uniforms. Pinckney almost fainted. Santana was shocked. He told them a guard in the laundry didn't come out, but Santana visually and verbally confirmed that Cementhead was authorized to sign for the laundry on this one and only occasion, since Big Frankie was in the bathroom with a bad case of diarrhea. Santana didn't personally know the guard, but thought he could recognize him if he saw him again.

They brought Santana back to the prison. He looked at the Creep, but said it wasn't him. He knew the Creep. At first the Rangers were dumbfounded. Then they walked him past the segregation cells with all the laundry inmates. Santana looked at them all, but never uttered a word. When they brought him up front to Warden Cobb's office, he said it was the inmate in the fourth cell. He had identified Sly Willie Peters. The Rangers thanked him, took his affidavit, and returned him to his job site.

They told Mr. Pinckney that he and Santana were both cleared.

They checked both escapees' prison files. Neither had received a telephone call. Dick Wad did not have anyone on his correspondence list, establishing that he had received no mail. Joe Rag had one correspondent. She was Alice Bolton from Del Rio, Texas. She did not have an arrest record. They copied her information.

They were about to leave, when Captain Norbert Eldridge whispered that an inmate named Lawrence J. Krebs, Jr., a/k/a Larry the Fairy, a prison snitch who works in the library, had passed him a note that he might have some information. He lives on the Honor Walk with the rest of the trusted inmates. Since all the inmates were still in lockdown, it was easy enough to have a CO escort him to the warden's office, unobserved by prying inmate eyes.

Larry was obsequious. He played the part of drama queen like the professional he was. He feared for his safety. If he told them what he had and anyone found out, he would be a dead man. (No shit?) He wondered what might be done for him, if his information proved to be true.

Warden Cobb assured him that his identity would remain secret, and said that after a reasonable amount of time, so as not to raise suspicion among the other inmates, he would get Larry an office job, if his information panned out. The Rangers didn't promise anything, but said if his information was as good as he said it was, they'd see if maybe the judge would reduce his prison sentence a little bit. That was everything Larry wanted to hear.

He pulled a folded newspaper page from his pocket and spread it out on the table. He pointed to a small wedding announcement, which was circled in blue ink. Warden Cobb,

Captain Eldridge, and both Rangers read the article. It didn't ring any bells.

Larry said, "The groom in this article is a Quayle County deputy sheriff who was ambushed by the Diablos Motorcycle Club a couple of years ago. He killed five of them in a shootout. He was also responsible for arresting Joe Rag and getting him 42 years to serve. Well, Joe Rag saw this article and said he and Dick Wad, who you know is a vicious rapist, would rape this bride and kill both her and the deputy, if they ever got out of prison. He also said he would make sure that I'd die a slow, painful death, if I ever told anyone. I think they broke out to do just what he said."

Warden Cobb asked, "Why didn't you tell us about this until now?"

"Heck, I didn't think they'd ever get out! They was in for life! Plus, I thought this prison was escape-proof."

Ranger Tyler said, "I certainly hope they were just mouthing off. We'll get on this right away. Thanks for coming forward. If your information is true, I believe we'll be able to help you out. Warden, we need to keep this information close to the vest. It's our best chance of catching them before they can carry out their plans. We'll keep you informed. We gotta go. Good day."

# CHAPTER 23

## Tuesday, June 8, 1971
## Reunion of Like Souls

It was 11:30 when Joe and Dick slipped out of the rental house. Boy, would the realtor be surprised when she came to check on the listing! The broken windowpane in the kitchen door would be the lesser of her concerns, compared to what Joe and Dick left behind in the commode that wouldn't flush because the water was shut off. Serves her right! A potential buyer might have to use the bathroom. Turning off the water is just wrong! Learn her a lesson, the tightwad bitch!

The First Baptist Church of Conroe only had one car in the lot. It was a faded green, 1962, Plymouth Valiant. Must be the preacher's. Joe and Dick both chuckled. They felt sorry for any SOB that was so bad off he had to drive that piece of shit! Joe parked as far away as he could get from it, at the opposite end of the lot, like the Valiant had a contagious disease. It was now 11:55.

Tick tock. Tick tock. 12:09. Come on! Hurry up, Grady! Their underwear was flapping in the breeze here (in a manner of speaking, of course, since Dick wasn't wearing any.)

Finally, a white, 1964, two-door, Chevrolet Corvair pulled into the lot and made a beeline for the Olds station wagon. Joe was afraid to look to see who was driving. They didn't need a confrontation with a cranky, geriatric, church deacon. Not today. Same with ancient, blue-hair church ladies. He wished the

Corvair would just go away. However, wishing did not make it go away. It pulled into the space adjacent to the driver's side of the Olds.

Joe feigned boredom. He made a slow, casual glance to see who it was. Screaming Jesus! It was none other than Gravy Train Triplett, hisself! How did he ever squeeze that big old, six-feet, four-inch, 280-pound body into that sardine can? Why would he embarrass hisself driving such a pussy ride? He was supposed to be driving a van. Joe finally pulled himself together. He swallowed his burning annoyance and asked, "Gee, Grady, how the fuck are ya?"

"Better than you peckerwoods, I s'pose. At least the cops ain't rousting everyone who looks like a biker, searchin' for me. Who's your friend?"

"This here's Dick Wad. We was cellmates. Who's car is that? Somehow, it's not what I would have expected, as in, it's not a van."

"No shit? It's Alice's. The van dropped the transmission, and I ain't had time to fix it. I didn't think this was the best time for me to show off my new hog. Good thing I didn't, seeing there's two of ya. I ain't got no other car. Whaddaya expect, anyway? A stretch limo? Besides that, I bet you didn't pay for that granny station wagon, didja, or is that your style now, a little light in the loafers since you been rehabilitated?"

"Nope. We borrowed it from in front of a whorehouse. Granny was busy pulling tricks. I bet she didn't notice it was missing until this morning. We was planning to ditch it here and ride with you, but now I'm not so sure. What did you bring us?"

"I didn't bring 'us' nothing. I thought you was all alone, remember? I brung you a .38 Smith & Western revolver and a pocketful of ca'tridges and five hundred bucks in small denominations. I'll even loan ya my sawed-off, 870 pump, if ya want. I got about twenty shells for it, double-aught and number sixes. What was you expectin' anyway?"

"That's a lot, brother. It sounds like Christmas to me. I couldn't exactly spell out my plans in them letters to Alice. We conversated in code, in case ya didn't ken that. Hey! You remember that greenhorn baby cop that arrested me and Screech in Quayle County?"

"How could I not? Only I never laid eyes on that son of a bitch, 'cause I wasn't there. Remember? I was in Mexico, but I heard all about it, over and over again. What about him?"

"Well, that punk got hisself married. He's on his honeymoon. He's most likely in San Antonio today. Supposed to go see the Alamo. Then they're going to see the Astros play the Braves. They got a four-game series beginning Thursday. Not sure which game or games he's going to. I'd like to be there for all of 'em if I can, but if we miss 'em in Houston, we can pick 'em up in the French Quarter. They're headed there next. Might even be easier in New Orleans. Me and Dick plan to grab him and his old lady, and ride her until she's all broke in. Do it while he's all tied up, and let him watch. Then we plan to make him bleed and feel some real pain before we snuff 'em both. It's payback time. You in?"

"Who told you all this?"

"Can ya believe it? It was in the newspaper. Said so in their fucking wedding announcement!"

"Sheeit! Of course I'm in. How you wanna play this?"

"First things first. How long it take you to drive here?"

"Well, it's about four hundred miles. I got up real early. Left around 2:30. Took my time. Besides that, this ain't the fastest car on the planet. Ate breakfast and a early lunch. We could make it back in seven, eight hours if we pushed it a little."

"I think we ditch the Olds here. Me and Dick will jump in with you. Go back to Alice's. She got a full time boyfriend now?"

"Whaddaya think? Ever met a man who could fuck ten or twelve times a night, every night? Course not! I take ya to her apartment tonight, she'll wear ya both raw. You'll need two or three days to recover to do what ya got in mind, but of course, you know that all ready. Besides, ain't you afraid the cops will check on Alice, being she was your pen pal? You all better stay with me across the river tonight. I'll ask her to stop by when she gets off work.

"Get your gear and let's go. Better wipe your prints off that Olds. You don't want the cops to know you were ever here. They're like bloodhounds. Once they pick up the scent, you'll never shake 'em."

"Good idea. Let's stop for some lunch on the way. Me 'n Dick ain't eat a McDonalds hamburger in a long time. We can take turns drivin'. Mebbe get there a little quicker."

# CHAPTER 24

Tuesday, June 8, 1971
Panic City

"Quayle County Sheriff's Office. Loretta speaking. How may I help you?"

"Miss Loretta, this is Texas Ranger Captain Orville Campbell. I'm in charge of Company F in Waco. May I speak with Sheriff Pratt, please?"

"Hello, Captain. One moment please, while I connect you.

"Sheriff, a Captain Campbell from the Texas Rangers is holding for you on line one."

"Captain, this is Sheriff Solomon Pratt. What can I do for you, besides sing the praises of Sergeant Trey Winfield?"

"Sheriff, call me Orville. I know Trey. He's one of our finest Rangers. Wish he worked in my company. Knew his old man, too. Let me see. As I recall, Trey was working with you all, when you tangled assholes with those rustlers up in New Mexico last year. I heard you killed 'em all. That was one helluva case."

"You got that right. We were flying by the seat of our pants on that one."

"Look. I apologize for being abrupt, but we may have a little situation on our hands. I was hoping you could help."

"Call me Sol, Orville. We will do whatever we can for you."

"I'll get straight to the point. You got a deputy named Barlow Adams working for you?"

"I do. He's only got two years on the job. You're not planning to steal him, are you?"

"No. Not that, but we may want to make a run on him in a few years. Is this the kid that waxed those Diablos?"

"The one and same. He's also eradicated a few other evildoers. We really would hate to lose him, Orville. In truth, it would break my back."

"I don't blame you, and that's why I'm calling. DOC had a prison escape yesterday in Huntsville. Maybe you heard. One escapee is a serial rapist named Richard Wadsworth, a/k/a Dick Wad. He's from Texarkana. A real sadist. Likes to torture, rape, and sodomize old ladies. The other is an absolute terrible excuse for a human being that I'm sure you all are familiar with. His name is Joseph P. Schitt, a/k/a Joe Rag, a/k/a Joe Shit the Ragman. He's from El Paso."

"We are all well acquainted with that oxygen thief, Orville. I didn't know he'd gone missing. I am very sorry to hear he's back on the loose. We definitely don't want that poke full of vomit back in our county."

"Look. We have credible information that these two douchebags have the newspaper itinerary relating to the honeymoon trip your deputy and his new bride are currently enjoying. Schitt said they planned to ambush your deputy and his bride, and rape her before killing them both. We have BOLOs out, but we don't have any information as to their whereabouts. Naturally, we suspect San Antonio or Houston. Do you know how to reach your deputy?"

"Orville, this is really terrible news. I don't know offhand where to call to leave a message for Barlow, but I will try to find out. Has anyone reached out to Arthur or Clarice Baker? Those are the bride's parents."

"No. I was hoping you would do that in person for me. Maybe they're getting telephone calls from their daughter."

"Oh boy. I surely hope so. I'll go see them, soon as I hang up. Also, I'll check with the deputies Barlow is closest to. Maybe he said something about where they were planning to stay. Give me a couple of hours, and I'll call you back."

"You got it, Sol. In the meantime, we'll disseminate photographs of these two assholes on TV. We're getting wanted posters made up for law enforcement. Just to be clear, we will not be releasing any information regarding their possible assassination plans. We believe that could escalate matters."

"I agree wholeheartedly. Maybe we'll get lucky, and Barlow will see Joe Schitt's mug on TV. That would definitely generate a call from him."

"Sol, they're honeymooning. They're screwing, not watching TV. But . . . . they might hear it on the radio, if they're in a car. By the way, do you know what they're driving?"

"I'm 99% sure it's Barlow's jade green, and I do mean jade, '65 Dodge, stepside pickup. That truck is spit polished like it's brand new. You can't miss it. I'll double check just to be sure. It has Texas plates on it, so I'm sure you can pull it up."

"Roger that. Talk to you later."

"You got it."

As soon as he rang off, Sheriff Sol called Deputy Archie Willis, Barlow's training officer. It was four o'clock, so hopefully Archie would be awake. He was the regular midnight shift deputy, and he had a tour of duty tonight. Sol got lucky.

"Willis residence."

"Are you fully awake yet, Arch?"

"I am now. What's up?"

"I just got a call from the Texas Rangers in Waco. Joe Schitt and another violent inmate named Richard Wadsworth, better known as Dick Wad, escaped from Huntsville yesterday. The Rangers have information that these two dickheads are planning to ambush Sarah and Barlow, rape her, and kill them both. Supposedly, they know Barlow's itinerary. Do you know where we can get ahold of him?"

"Those lowdown, dirty dogs! We should have killed that Schitt head instead of just breaking his arm! Damn!

"Let me think. I know Barlow had a list of hotels he wrote down in that little notebook he always carries. He wasn't sure where they would lodge, but he had this working list, first choice, second choice, etc. I think he got the list from AAA. He didn't want to make reservations without knowing what the hotels looked like. I need to think about it, to see if I can recall. What day is it?"

"Today's Tuesday the 8th."

"Well, he planned one night in Fredericksburg and two in San Antonio. He left Sunday, so he should be spending tonight in San Antonio. I know his first choice there was the Travis and Crockett. His second choice was the Crown Plaza, I think. You might try these two first."

"That's great. What about Houston?"

"I can't remember right offhand. But as I recall, he had several on his list which were within walking distance to the Astrodome. I know he planned to stay in the French Quarter in New Orleans, but I'd have to concentrate on that one a little more.

"Listen, Sheriff, why don't you let me go find 'em? I know Barlow better than anyone other than Sarah. I could be on the road in an hour. I promise you, I will find 'em, and if I get lucky enough and stumble onto those two rabid dogs, I will put 'em both down for good. Adiós pendejos."

"That would ease my mind considerably, Arch. I know you can find them if anyone can. Do you want me to send Slick or someone else to go with you?"

"No, Sheriff, I work better alone. I know the odds and what I'm up against. In fact, if I can find Barlow fast enough, we'll take down those two pricks together."

"Sounds good, but remember. Joe Schitt is a Diablo. He may have more than one partner.

"Look, I'm headed to the Bar B right now. Soon as I talk to Arthur and Clarice, I'll give you a call to let you know if they have any new information, so don't leave town until you hear from me. Also, you can take my car or Chief Alex's if you want. Also, stop by the jail and pick up the telephone credit card, because I want you to call me first thing in the morning, midday, and just before you go to bed. That way I can feed you any updates. Also, take one of the shotguns or rifles, whatever works best for you."

"Thanks, Sheriff. I'll take the calling card. Save me a lot of nickels, but I'll drive my trusty, old, GMC pickup. I'm used to it, and no way anyone would consider it a police vehicle. And, did you forget about my old Model 1901, Winchester ten-gauge, lever-action shotgun? Holds five shells in the magazine and one in the chamber. Got a 32-inch barrel. Puts Slick's double-barrel, ten-gauge to shame. I ain't blown anyone away with it since we chased them rustlers back across the border when I was just a tyke workin' on the old Whitaker spread. Must a been 1915, or thereabouts. Anyone ever tell you about it? We kilt five of 'em. The rest got away."

"I believe my daddy mentioned something about that, but it was a very long time ago. Okay. Soon as I learn something, I'll call. I'll try your house first and then the jail if you don't answer. Before I forget, tell Loretta to give you a couple hundred bucks out of the imprest fund. Get receipts so the supervisors don't jump my ass."

"Gotcha. Will do. Adiós."

Sol sped out of the jail parking lot, laying a patch of rubber twenty feet long. He broke the local land speed record to the Bar B. It took all his might to slow down to a ten-mile-per-hour crawl when he turned onto the gravel driveway. He saw Clarice watering some flowers in the front of the house. She looked so content. A Norman Rockwell picture in her blue and white striped cotton day dress, and her yellow and white checked kitchen apron. She was wearing white rain boots to keep her shoes from getting muddy.

"Hello, stranger. What's up. You look like you're in a hurry. Did you come to see Arthur?"

"Hello back. Actually, I was hoping to talk to you both."

"Gee, Arthur and Cordell are out on the back section. They might not return for another hour or so. Would you like to come in and have a lemonade or a beer or something?"

"Thank you. I will take you up on the something, if you have any bourbon. Otherwise, a lemonade will do nicely."

Clarice shut off the hose and rolled it up. She led Sol through the screen door into the kitchen. She took off her boots and put them in the mud room.

"Come on in. One bourbon on the rocks coming up. Have a seat in the parlor while I pour us both a drink."

A couple of minutes later, after Clarice had washed her hands, checked on her hair, and straightened her dress, she entered the parlor with two bourbons on the rocks. She handed one to Sol, who was seated on the couch. They clinked glasses. She took a seat across from him in her rocker.

"Okay, Sol. What's going on? I know something's up."

"Clarice, I'll be blunt. Sorry. I just got off the phone with Texas Ranger Captain Orville Campbell from Troop F in Waco. He says Joe Schitt and another inmate escaped from Huntsville yesterday. According to an informant, the escapees have the article from the newspaper with Sarah and Barlow's honeymoon itinerary. I know you remember Joseph Schitt. Supposedly, he said they were going to find Sarah and Barlow and kill them. Schitt obviously has a vendetta. I'm sending Archie to go and find them, just as soon as I learn if you know where they are, or where they'll be staying next."

Clarice seemed to shrink as she listened to his words. She began to weep quietly. She placed her glass on the end table, and began to shake. Then she closed her eyes, and folded her hands. Sol watched while she prayed silently. Sol thought his own silent prayer. After a minute or so, Clarice opened her eyes, wiped the tears away with a tissue she pulled out of her apron pocket, and smiled weakly.

"Sol, this is just dreadful. Sarah called this morning. It was the first time she's called. They drove to Corpus Christi today. They were looking for a motel on the beach. I don't know where, because this wasn't planned. She said there was a good chance they'd spend two nights. Sarah's never seen the ocean, and she was all excited. I probably won't hear from her until they go to Houston. I think they plan to see two games there against the Braves, but I'm not sure. Also, depending on the price, they may stay at the hotel nearest the Astrodome. Otherwise, they will look for lodging within walking distance. That's all I know.

"I just don't see how we can sit here while they are in danger. Arthur and Cordell and I need to go find them. What would we ever do if those animals hurt them? I couldn't stand it. I know Barlow's a wonderful man and he's savvy and quite capable of defending them, but what if they catch him by surprise? The only gun he took with him, so far as I know, was the little one you all gave him when he graduated. I know this is all in God's hands, but I just don't think I can bear to sit by without doing something to help."

Then she broke down in deep, choking sobs.

Just then Angel knocked on the screen door. Sheriff Sol answered it and said, "Angel, go find Mr. Arthur just as fast as you can. Miss Clarice is very sad, and she needs him. I'll wait here until he returns. Hurry!"

"Sí, Señor." He was off in a flash.

Sheriff Sol used the kitchen phone while he waited. He called Archie's house. Arch answered.

"Arch, we caught a break, and maybe bought a day or two reprieve. Barlow and Sarah left San Antonio for Corpus Christi this morning. Not sure if they will stay one night or two. They were hoping to find a motel on the beach. Since this wasn't on the itinerary, the shitbirds won't be looking for them there.

"If you don't find them in Corpus, they may stay in a hotel at the Astrodome. Somewhere, I heard they had one. If not there, check any motel within walking distance. They planned to see one or two games with the Braves before going to New Orleans."

"Thanks, Sheriff. I was just about to walk out the door. I'll call you later tonight. I'm used to working mids, so I will probably drive all night. Catch you later."

Next, Sheriff Sol called Captain Campbell, and passed along what he knew. Captain Campbell said he would send a couple of Rangers to Corpus to see if they could locate Sarah and Barlow. They would also look for Archie. He wanted to know what Archie looked like, and what type of vehicle he was driving.

Sheriff Sol replied, "Archie is a rangy, 71-year-old, five-feet, ten-inch cowboy, with a wavy mane of white hair and a full sweeping mustache. His eyes are bright blue. He'll be easy to identify, because he wears a cartridge belt full of .45 Long Colts for his six-inch, Colt Peacemaker, which has carved ivory grips, that he wears cross-draw on the left, and on the right, he wears a well-used, bone-handled sheath dagger with a seven-inch blade he carried when he was in the Army during The Great War. However, he's partial to his Winchester, Model 1901, lever-action, ten-gauge shotgun. I think he said the barrel is 32-inches long. Wouldn't surprise me none if he was also wearing a bandolier full of ten-gauge buckshot shells.

He'll be dressed in bluejeans, a jean jacket, and brown, high-heeled Tony Lamas with scuff marks on the heals from wearing spurs. It goes without saying that he wears a Stetson. It has a vertical crease in the front like a cunt. It's mostly beige, but it does have some wear on it.

"When he's not on horseback, he drives a faded, white, 1960 GMC pickup truck with a red interior. It has a set of longhorns mounted on the hood from a steer that nearly gored him. I think that sums Archie up in a nutshell."

Captain Campbell asked, "Sol, are you sure a man of his age, no matter how much law enforcement experience he may have, is up to this assignment? He sounds a mite long in the tooth to say the least, although I do fancy his style."

"Orville, Archie has something like 47 years on this job. He's a bonafide World War One combat veteran of trench warfare, who slipped through razor wire, and killed many Germans who were armed with mustard gas, heavy mortars, grenades, and machine guns, not to mention more conventional weapons like rifles and pistols. He sneaked up on them in the middle of the night and slit the throats of dozens of them, just to sow fear in their ranks, and make them afraid to go to sleep at night. Besides that, he and Barlow made the arrest on Joe Schitt that got him 42 years to serve, so Archie knows Joe Schitt on sight.

"Also, before our time, when Archie was a wrangler on the old Whitaker spread, which was about 200,000 acres, he and two other Whitaker hands chased a dozen or more cattle rustlers across the river into Mexico, where they got into one helluva gunfight. Archie was credited with killing three. They recovered every head of cattle, because all the other rustlers skedaddled empty-handed as a result of the gunfight. I'm telling you straight up, it won't be a fair match for Joe Schitt, or his comrades, if Archie finds them before your guys do. This is not to take anything away from any of your men. I know they are all the best of the best."

"Well, Sol, I know you know your man. I'll ask my boys to keep an eye out for him, too. With that description, I doubt anyone would mistake him. By the way, since we don't know what type of vehicle the escapees are driving, I think checking San Antonio for them would be a long shot at best, so we'll go straight to Corpus. I'm also sending some guys to Del Rio to check out Joe Schitt's prison pen pal."

"Who's the pen pal?"

"Some barmaid. I forget the name. I can find out and call you back."

"No. That's okay. We didn't know he had any contacts there. That's all."

"Okay. You on board with bypassing San Antonio?"

"Yep. No point now. I'll stay in touch if we learn anything."

"Likewise."

Messages passed and understood in both directions, they said goodbye and hung up.

A little while later, Arthur and Cordell came running into the house.

Arthur said, "Sol, what's up?"

"Why don't you go talk to Clarice? I'll fill in Cordell, and then we'll meet you in the parlor."

This entire affair was almost as bad as making an unexpected death notification. Besides that, these were Sol's dear, lifelong friends. Sol felt like the Bakers were blaming him but he knew, in his heart of hearts, that they were not.

Everyone concluded that it would be best for the Bakers to stay near the phone to relay the warning to the kids, and to ask them to return home immediately, if they called. Sheriff Sol promised to keep them updated with respect to the manhunt as he received information.

They all prayed for a miracle.

# CHAPTER 25

## Tuesday/Wednesday, June 8/9, 1971
## Things Turn Ugly

Gravy Train and the boys made good time. They arrived in Del Rio at 8:45. Dick wanted to eat. Joe wanted to stop by the Wagon Wheel Inn and Restaurant, where Alice was waitressing. They could eat there, and line up fun and games for later on that night. Kill two birds with one stone. Gravy Train said it was too fucking risky. The cops could have Alice staked out, hoping Joe would stop by. In the end, they compromised by stopping at a Steak and Shake, where they ate like this was their last meal on Earth. You know. Like being on Death Row.

After they ate, Gravy Train called the Wagon Wheel from a payphone out in front of the diner. They put him on hold. In less than a minute, Alice picked up. He told her he was back in town, and Joe wanted to get together.

Alice asked, "Are you freakin' crazy? Two Texas Rangers have already been to my apartment looking for Joe. I told 'em, I didn't know nothing. They didn't believe me. They wanted to know where my car was. I said I loaned it to a friend, who needed to pick up some shit in Ciudad Acuña. One of them said, 'Likely story, unless your friend needs it to bring some dope across.' They said they'd lock me up if they found out I helped Joe escape. Get me for harboring a fugitive. Hell Grady, Joe's face and the other dude's are plastered all over the TV!

"Look. I walked to work. I seen they was following. They're

in a white Dodge Charger. It looked new. I don't know if they're still out there or not, and I suggest you don't try and find out."

"That's what I figured. I told Joe, but he wasn't listening. So, we'll go back to my pad in Acuña. Want me to come back and pick you up? The boys are real horny and claim that you'll cry uncle before they do. Besides that, I need to return your car."

"Sorry, Grady. I got three young studs lined up for tonight. Besides that, I'm afraid to be anywhere near you or our friend. I don't even want you to return my car right now. I think the cops are still watchin' me. Why don't you line 'em up with some of those young whores you're always banging over there in Acuña? How much they charge?"

"Usually fifteen bucks for the whole night. They do it as many times as you want, any way you want. Sorta like you, Sis, except you do it out of the goodness of your heart and not for filthy lucre."

"Well, tell the boys if they can get it up tomorrow and keep it up long enough to ring my bell at least twice by both of 'em, maybe I'll stop by before I go to work and give 'em a ride. In the meantime, you better scout out the bridge before you start to cross. Those Rangers might have promised to make the Border Patrol agents heroes if they bust the extremely violent escapees trying to flee the U.S. That's what they called them on TV! They also might have bribed the policía to roust every American male between twenty and forty who comes across the border. Did you all think of that? No, of course not!"

"No. You're right. Thanks for the heads up. Okay. Talk to you tomorrow. Call before you come. Not sure what they have planned."

He rang off and explained the scenario to the extremely

violent escapees. For once, Joe sat up and took notice. He asked if there was a backdoor way to sneak across the border. Grady said it was easier and a lot safer to cross at Eagle Pass, which was about sixty miles farther south. Then they'd have to double back on the other side to get to the rancho where he worked in Acuña, but at least they wouldn't be dead or in jail. Once they got there, they'd call some Mexican whores to spend the night at his digs. He does this all the time. Cost 'em fifteen bucks a head.

Dick was all in. Joe wanted to know if the whores were good looking and clean. Grady responded, "Joe, I never seen you pass on a piece of pussy as long as I've known you, and some of those skanks you fucked was downright butt ugly. Tell me what you like, and I'll know who to get for you. I've done fucked them all. Besides that, I always ride bareback and I ain't caught the clap yet. That good enough for ya?"

Joe responded, "I'm in. I like 'em young with a little meat on their bones, not fat, but definitely not boney. I like the ones what squeal when ya give it to 'em. They gotta have all their teeth and hair down to their shoulders. Any of 'em fit that bill?"

"Oh, Hell yeah. They all fit that bill. The youngest one is sixteen, but she ain't very good at fucking yet. The oldest is 25. If Lolita is available tonight, I'll get her for ya. She's my favorite. If not, any of the other ones except the youngest one will do."

It was after midnight when they finally arrived.

Grady lived on a 250,000-acre rancho in an ageless, sixteen-by-twenty-foot, adobe cabaña, which was set off all by itself under a copse of ancient live oak trees. A hundred or so years ago, this had been housing for a caporal de la hacienda, or ranch foreman, one of many, when this rancho was an agrarian enterprise in which money was honestly acquired by herding sheep and selling thousands of pounds of wool and mutton, rather than the current illegal business model of cultivating cannabis and distributing thousands of pounds of primo marijuana.

The cabin had one door and two windows in the front and two windows in the back. It even had some modern improvements, circa 1950, like electricity, a flush toilet, shower, ceiling fan, and a wall phone. A single bed was pushed up against the right wall. A small table with two chairs and a small chest of drawers were up against the opposite wall. The casa also sported a small, two-burner, propane-gas stove, sink, and a 1950-model Frigidaire that was still humming and keeping things cool even after all these years.

Open shelves held a few pots and pans, dishes, canned goods, and boxes of grub. The stove was home to one iron skillet and an enamelware coffee pot. Three plates, each with different patterns, two enamelware cups, four ten-ounce glasses, a bottle of Palmolive, and another of Pine Sol were also sitting on the shelf above the sink. There were pegs along the wall with jeans, shirts, jackets, hats, and other, sundry items hanging up. Grady's sawed-off 870 pump shotgun was also hanging on the wall, held in place by its sling, next to a cartridge belt full of twelve-gauge shells.

Not bad. Joe had resided in digs, some better, but most far worse than Grady's. Dick too, but nearly all worse. The good news was that it was rent free, with an abundance of privacy, far away from prying eyes. Other belongings included some towels, and four old quilts for extra bedding folded up on the floor, plus two-and-a-half quarts of mescal sitting on the table waiting to be consumed. They began right away. Get a head start on the women.

Roughly an hour later, a worn out, 1954 Buick station wagon arrived. It farted when the driver turned off the ignition. The boys were all outside, sitting on wooden benches waiting. Gravy Train stood up and greeted the driver, a plump 45-year-old madam named Reina, or Queenie, your choice, with a hug while the other three whores seductively exited the vehicle. Lolita even flashed a beaver shot, although you really couldn't see much on account it being dark and all. Nevertheless, it was well received by all three horndogs.

Money changed hands and the party was on. Joe took Lolita, and Grady took Teresa. Reina offered Isabel to Dick, but he said he'd prefer to fuck Reina. Reina said she didn't turn tricks anymore, but for another thirty bucks, she'd haul his ashes all the way back to the Rio Grande. She said Dick never had a pussy as sweet as hers. Preliminaries exchanged, Grady paid her another thirty bucks and she pulled off her dress like a magician and grabbed Dick by his namesake. She said she didn't fuck on the floor anymore, so Grady told Dick to take the bed. Then Joe said he would take Lolita and Isabel. Isabel perked up and said she was happiest doing a man and a woman, both at the same time.

For more than an hour, they seven were happy campers all. Drinking. Cavorting. Screwing in all the female orifices. More drinking between sessions, which lasted just as long as it took a female to coax any available resting male component back into the game. Swapping females to see if the ride was better. Truth is, it was all good, because these were properly motivated and aroused females, each of whom was an artist in her chosen profession. For a straight man, who had been bereft of female companionship while serving time in the joint, this was like having all the holidays on the very same day. Fireworks, presents, and bunnies, all flipping your switch simultaneously.

And then suddenly it wasn't.

Dick couldn't hold his liquor. Then his perversion to abuse women began to rear its ugly head. He got rougher and rougher with Reina. Finally, she had enough. Dick slapped her hard enough to black her eye when she was going down on him, so in return, she tried to bite it off. Nearly did, too! It was squirting blood like a garden sprinkler! He screamed, and began choking her with all his might. Reina was kicking her legs and trying to pull Dick's hands from her throat, but she didn't have the strength. She was seconds away from having her larynx crushed.

Joe was taking a leak outside. He heard the commotion, but paid it no mind.

Grady disentangled himself from both his holiday treats. He scrambled over and tried to pull Dick off, but he was out of his mind with rage. He was hellbent on killing Reina, who might have decommissioned his cock for the rest of his miserable life! He bit Grady hard on his arm, adding to the blood that was already being shed.

Enough is enough! Grady pulled his shotgun down from the wall and chambered a round of number six shot that he used on vermin. He walked up until he was about three feet away. He pointed the shotgun directly at Dick's head. Grady yelled, "Stop!"

Dick glanced over at him, as if to say, "Don't bother me," except he never uttered a word. His eyes were filled with rage and hate. He turned back to concentrate on the savagery he was committing on Reina. He hadn't quite finished the job.

Grady pulled the trigger. Dick's head all but disappeared in a deafening boom, with smoke, the smell of cordite, and a massive, six-foot spray of flesh and brains and eyeballs and teeth and bone. Nobody could hear. Their ears were ringing like fire sirens going off inside the station. Besides that, it was almost impossible to see. The headless corpse was still straddled across Reina with his hands around her throat. She was not moving.

Joe rushed into the casa and said, "What the fuck, Grady?"

Grady said, "Help me with Reina! That bastard might've choked her to death! Who the fuck does he think he is? Besides being my compadre, she's the cousin of the patrón. If she's dead, so are we my friend. Help me! I don't think she's breathing."

Even in death, they still had a hard time prying Dick's fat sausage-like fingers off Reina's neck. They didn't want to aggravate the injury. The three whores were freaking out. Shrieking. Piercing everyone's half-busted eardrums. Grady screamed, "Silence!" All went quiet. Not even a whimper leaked out.

They shoved Dick to the floor. Joe dragged him outside before he bled completely out all over everything. What a fucking disaster!

Reina was conscious. She blinked her eyes several times. She was gasping for air, and gradually she recovered. She asked for a sip of water. They gave her a sip. Her neck was bright pink. The bruising was already turning a deep blue, but she could turn her head gingerly, and she could speak, so she apparently did not have any broken vertebrae or a crushed larynx. She whispered, "Gracias, Señor Grady. This was an evil man. I do not hold this against you. We will help you bury this piece of shit where nobody will ever find him. None of us will ever speak of him or this night ever again. Sí, señoritas?"

"Sí, señora."

They dragged his headless body fifty yards behind the house to an old shed that was about to fall down. The earth was soft. They dug a shallow grave and dumped him and all of his stolen clothes in with him. Grady pissed on his body. Asshole! Then they emptied a half sack of powdered lime all over him. Grady threw the empty sack into the grave. Then they filled the grave with dirt and tamped it down hard. Grady poured kerosine all over the shed, inside and out. Reina lit the fire. It burned with a frenzy. The wood was old and brittle. The boards and roof fell onto, and encompassed, the grave site. Though they lit up the sky, there was no fire department within fifty miles to respond. No busybodies either.

They drank more mescal. Finally, the bottles were empty. The women piled into the station wagon and left.

Grady and Joe cleaned the interior of the cabin as best they could. Pine Sol is great and so is Ajax, but they don't eradicate blood stains. The mattress was ruined, along with the bedding and some clothes. They burned the debris on top of Dick's funeral pyre. Grady said they needed to paint the walls today, before anyone noticed. Joe agreed. The hunt would have to wait. They could drive to Houston tomorrow or the next day.

It was already a long day, on top of a long night, on top of the previously long day and night.

So endeth the saga of Dick Wad. His body was never found. He was never missed by anyone. Not even the cops.

# CHAPTER 26

## Wednesday, June 9, 1971
## Archie Makes Up Distance

It took Archie nine hours to cover the four hundred miles to Corpus. US 90, to US 83, to TX 44. The only open gas station to refuel along the way was in Del Rio. The GMC's 351 cubic-inch, V-6 engine got good gas mileage, but Archie always brought along two five-gallon jerry cans filled with fuel for long trips in the outback. You can't be too rich. You can't be too thin (if you're a woman). You can't have too much ammo, and you can't have too much gasoline if you're driving in the outback. Same for coffee. That's why he also had his 'don't leave home without it' Stanley thermos on the seat next to him. It proved to be a long, but uneventful drive.

He found a 24-hour Phillips 66 truck stop on the outskirts of Corpus at the intersection of TX 44 and US 77. He chatted up a friendly and well-preserved, fifty-year-old waitress named Twyla for information about reasonably-priced motels on the beach. She said the Holiday Inn had good beds if he were interested in a romp. Then she said she got off at six - from work that is, in case he was feeling a little randy. He said he was definitely of that mindset; however, he needed to locate a friend and his wife who were on vacation just as soon as possible because the wife's mother was extremely ill and probably dying. They were supposed to be here on the beach, assuming they didn't already up and go to Houston. He needed to find them before the old lady passed away. Be that as it may, he crossed his heart and hoped to die if he didn't stop by the diner just as soon as he accomplished his mission. Then, if she still wanted to rodeo, he'd take her out for a long ride and work out all her kinks, but it might be a couple of two or three days. Perhaps even a few more, if things didn't go well.

She told him where to start his search. Then she wrote her name and telephone number on a napkin and leaned across the table, and stuffed it in his shirt pocket. The neck of her dress was wide open in a V. She had the most gorgeous melons caged in a lacy bra that he had seen in a very long time. Too long, in fact. He felt Roscoe beginning to rouse up. He smiled and said, "You've got my complete attention, Missy. I'll call you, just as soon as I can."

She left the check on the table. Then she smiled, licked her lips, and sashayed away. The swing in her caboose was mesmerizing. He left a five-dollar bill for a buck sixty-nine breakfast.

Archie checked all the way up and down the beach twice. He drove over two hundred miles doing just that. He cruised through all the back parking lots. He looked behind dumpsters, tractor trailers, signs, and anything else that could hide a pickup. Barlow's truck was simply nowhere to be found. This was more difficult than he had imagined.

At three o'clock that afternoon, he got a room at the Days Inn a block off the beach. He was all worn out and frustrated. He called Sheriff Sol to check in. Neither one had any additional information or insight. Arch said after he got some sleep he'd search the strip again. Then, if he couldn't locate them, he'd move on to Houston. They'll be all right.

# CHAPTER 27

## Wednesday, June 9, 1971
## Barlow Calls Another Audible

When Barlow and Sarah woke up, they were both in pain from dry, sunburned skin. They overdid it on the beach, beyond what they thought. Neither was blistered, but of necessity, today was going to be a timeout from the sun so far as it was possible in Texas, unless they remained indoors all day. One might suggest that most honeymooners spend their time indoors, but that rule of thumb does not apply to lovers who are too sunburned to rub their bodies together, even gently.

Before they left for breakfast, Barlow walked to a nearby drugstore to purchase a lotion with aloe to soothe their burning bodies. The lotion helped, but they still had a hard time putting on their clothes. Barlow's waistline was particularly touchy on his right side, where he carried his new revolver in the inside-the-waist holster. Guess he learned a lesson. He didn't go around nearly half naked in Texas like he had done in Vietnam, so his body was no longer accustomed to this much sun.

They ate breakfast at a small diner near the motel named Lizzie's. Supposedly, it was world famous for its eight-ounce Lizzieburger which was marinated in, you guessed it, Lizzie sauce, with its nine secret ingredients, just like Colonel Sanders' fried chicken. Too bad it wasn't lunchtime.

During breakfast, Barlow finally figured out that the motel wasn't in a city, but was located in unincorporated Mustang

Island. He picked up a newsprint pamphlet for tourists and browsed through it while they gobbled their sausage and eggs, which were not marinated in Lizzie sauce. They were yummy just the same.

He saw an advertisement for a museum located on the King Ranch in Kingsville, which was about fifty miles southwest. Supposedly, the King Ranch was the largest ranch in America. It had a long and storied past according to the ad. They both had heard of it, but knew nothing about it. They decided to spend the day there while they were recuperating. Tomorrow, they would drive to Houston. The first of the four-game series with the Braves would begin tomorrow. They might listen to tonight's game with the Reds on the radio, if their bodies had not recovered by then, but if they were recovered, they would have more intimate matters to attend to. Use your imagination. Barlow certainly was. Either way, Barlow planned to be at the Astrodome in person for the game tomorrow night.

They turned on the radio en route to Kingsville. They were only half listening to the music. When the news came on, they heard a report about "an escape from the Texas State Penitentiary in Huntsville by two extremely violent prisoners who are still on the loose, whereabouts unknown. They are identified as Joseph P. Schitt of El Paso and Richard Wadsworth of Texarkana. There is a statewide lookout on both of them. The Texas Rangers request that the public be on alert and to report any sightings of these fugitives. Do not attempt to detain these men if you see them. They are considered armed and dangerous. Call your local police department right away. The forecast today in Corpus Christi is . . . ."

Barlow asked, "Did you hear that?"

"What? About the escape? I didn't pay it much attention."

"Remember Joe Shit the Ragman? He was one of the escapees. This is not good. He's a stone cold killer."

"Oh my gosh! You don't think he'd come back to Mosby for revenge, do you?"

"Well, I wouldn't put anything past him, but if I were him, I'd book it straight to Mexico. His life won't be worth a plugged nickel if the Rangers catch up with him. Even so, the joke's on him if he goes to Mosby looking for me. Not so much if he's looking for Archie, but Archie can take care of himself."

"Think we ought to stop and call Sheriff Sol?"

"Baby, Sheriff Sol doesn't need me. He's got plenty of deputies who can handle Joe Schitt, if it comes to that."

"Not really, except for Slick. Maybe Archie, but he's always on midnights. You really think Ernie, or Chunk, or even Chief Alex could take on Joe Schitt and survive? Barlow, this is a very scary man. I won't rest peacefully until he's back behind bars or dead. You know he has a vendetta against you and Judge Sweeney! I think you should call the sheriff. I mean it!"

"Tell you what. Joe Schitt has no idea where we are. We're as safe as we can be, as long as we aren't in Mosby. Besides that, now we know he's out there running loose, we'll take precautions. Next time you call home, ask your mother. See what she says. If she says I ought to call the sheriff, I will, but I really doubt we'll see Joe Schitt sitting next to us at the Astrodome or on a barstool drinking Hurricanes in the French Quarter."

"Well, I guess it depends on how much he really wants to kill you. He's bad to the bone and everyone knows it. I couldn't stand it if he hurt you."

"Okay, okay. I'll call Sheriff Sol tomorrow after we check in to our new hotel, but who says he wants to kill me? I'm sure he has freedom on his mind, more so than trying to get revenge on me. Satisfied?"

"Satisfied, although I think today would be better."

"Good girl. Now let's go have some fun. Act like tourists. I need to find my Hawaiian flowery shirt before we leave the truck."

"Shut up, Mr. Smartypants."

They had a great time. On the way back to the motel they stopped and had a scrumptious fried chicken dinner at a place called Aunt Jemima's.

The parking lot was full when they returned to the Brown Pelican. Barlow had to park in an overflow lot, a block away behind a bowling alley. No biggie. They were young, and the moon and stars were bright, and the wind was balmy. They sat in lawn chairs on the beach in front of their motel room, holding hands, sipping on some Old Grand Dad, while Barlow smoked one of his pricey cigars. It just doesn't get any better than this, especially if your sunburn quits hurting. That's because you know what's coming next before the Sandman puts you to sleep.

# CHAPTER 28

## Wednesday, June 9, 1971
## A Fun-Filled Day - Not

Grady left Joe back at his cabin scrubbing down walls and sanitizing everything in sight. Joe wasn't happy about it, but Grady told him to knuckle down and wash away every morsel, every trace of evidence that Dick the Fuckass Wad had ever set foot in his cabin or they would part ways forever. Joe could hitchhike his way to wherever the fuck he wanted to go and good luck to him. Don't turn around and never look back. Their ties of brotherhood would be severed forever.

Joe had a screaming headache. He regretted not killing Dick in the rental house and meeting Grady alone. Dick wouldn't make a pimple on a Diablo's ass. Joe apologized to Grady for the third time and said the walls and floor would be as clean as Ajax and elbow grease could make them. However, he wasn't promising the bloodstains would be completely gone. That seemed to mollify Grady.

Grady rode his new chopper across the bridge to Del Rio without anxiety. Cops weren't looking for him. Nobody seemed to be on high alert. He rode over to the hardware store and bought a couple of gallons of semigloss white paint, brushes, and a quart of paint thinner. Then he found a payphone and called Alice.

He told her what happened. She said she wasn't surprised. He said he and Joe were going to clean everything today and head out for Houston on Thursday. He didn't say what for. Then he asked if she had seen the Rangers or noticed any other nosy cops watching her. She said she hadn't. She thought the heat was off of her. She told Grady to be careful with whatever it was that he and Joe were up to. He said he would. He would give her a ring when he got back.

Before they hung up, she said, "Grady, I like Joe and all that, but I don't want to see him again. Whoever is with him when he goes down, will go down with him. I don't want to be there, and you shouldn't either. You know he isn't going back to prison, plus the cops don't plan to take him alive anyway. Sooner or later, the cops will turn him into Swiss cheese, just like they did with John Dillinger. You already know that. You're not wanted. There's no paper on you. You got a sweet gig. Don't throw all that away because of Joe. You don't owe him nothing."

"I hear ya. I promised I'd help him out on this one little thing, then he's on his own. I owe him that much. He came back and got me and carried me on the back of his scooter when I got shot robbing that liquor store. He could've left me to die or rot in prison. To this day, the cops don't know I done that. You know all this. That's why I gotta do this one thing with him. Then he's on his own. Love you, Sis. Call ya when I get back. Probably won't take much more'n a week. Hopefully less. Bye, now."

When Grady returned to his cabin, all was spic and span. Most of his stuff had been moved outdoors. The big stuff was shoved in the middle of the room. They each grabbed a bucket of paint and went to work. It didn't take as long as Grady thought it would, even with putting things back. They were done by four o'clock. Time to unwind.

Grady rode his new hog and Joe rode Grady's old one. They

went to a cantina called Eduardo's, which was situated right on the river on the south side. They ate at least one of everything on the menu. They drank a half-dozen, frosty-cold, Dos Equis each. The entire meal, beers and all, didn't cost ten dollars American. They stayed away from the hard stuff, since they had a long drive ahead of them tomorrow. Not only that, they had to steal a vehicle to carry them there. No problemo. Grady had that covered. He knew exactly where to steal a pickup truck in Del Rio, where the old man that owned it always left his keys in the ignition. He hoped the truck ran as good as it looked.

They were both racked out with a mellow buzz at eight o'clock. They had been up for two straight days. It was almost like old times.

# CHAPTER 29

## Thursday, June 10, 1971
## Next Stop Houston

A rchie got a big head start on Joe Schitt and on Barlow. He was up and out the door of the Days Inn just after midnight. One final check along the strip was another bust. He had considered checking the rear parking lot of the Mustang Bowling Alley, but he didn't. It was closed. There was absolutely no good reason to believe that Barlow would park there, so Arch cruised right on by.

Next stop was Houston, roughly 225 miles away. He didn't think Barlow would be there yet, but Joe Schitt might be. Archie had absolutely no idea how many partners Joe would have. It could just be Dick Wad or he might have recruited some of his Diablo brothers. Or both. The only thing he was fairly certain of was that Joe and fellow denizens would not be riding on window-shattering, fume-spewing, bone-jarring, teeth-rattling, heat-generating Harley Davidson motorcycles. Anything else short of a horse was a definite maybe. Archie needed the time and the relative emptiness of the streets around the Astrodome in the early morning hours to come up with the best plan possible to find Barlow and Sarah.

It was an easy drive, which got more congested the closer he got to the Eighth Wonder of the World, otherwise known as the Astrodome. It was an absolute marvel. Archie loved baseball and he looked forward to seeing a game in this Space Age, geodesic dome. The first thing he did upon arrival was to buy a ticket for tonight's game. There were plenty of seats available, so he picked one midway up, about halfway between first base and right field.

There was one hotel and three motels on the grounds, all within walking distance to the Dome. They had the nine-story Astroworld Hotel, major bucks no doubt, plus a Holiday Inn, Sheraton Motor Inn, and a very modern, orange-roofed, Howard Johnson's, which allegedly was designed to look contemporary with the new Space Age that the modern world had embarked upon. Really? Did they plan to play baseball on the moon? Was this supposed to be like the Jetsons or Buck Rogers? Who knew? Either way, it was just downright hideous. A brand-new, modern-day eyesore. The good news was that the parking lots had plenty of empty spaces, so he knew lodging would not be a problem. He checked into a normal motel, specifically the Holiday Inn, getting a room near the stairway on the second floor.

Archie spent very little time checking other motel sites. He knew any of these four, full of vacancies, would fill Barlow's needs nicely. Instead, Arch ate an early lunch at the HoJo just to check it out. The food tasted better than the decor looked, inside or out. Green eggs and ham weren't on the menu. The waitress wasn't dressed like an alien. They even accepted greenbacks as currency. Afterwards, he called Sheriff Sol. No news yet. He gave Sol his room number and the telephone number of his motel. Then he took a little siesta.

He awoke to a start with the phone ringing. The phone even had a blinking red light! It was a little after four o'clock. Game time was at seven. Stadium was open at 5:30. He was still groggy, trying to figure out where he was.

"Hello."

"Arch, it's Sol. We got a call!"

"Well, that's great. Lay it on me."

"They checked in at a Howard Johnson's by the stadium. They're in room 113. They still plan to go to the game tonight, but they promised not to go until they heard from you, or you stopped by. They're going to eat at the motel restaurant tonight about five o'clock."

"I know where it is. I'm almost next door. I'll try to catch them in the restaurant. Better there than in flagrante delicto."

"You old dog, you."

"Well, I ain't dead yet, Sol."

"Any sign of Joe Schitt yet?"

"No, but I wouldn't expect to see him or his buddies at any of these Astrodome motels where the civilians stay. They'll be staying at some cockroach motel located next to a biker-owned titty bar where the dancers turn tricks and the bartender sells meth. Don't worry. I know what Joe looks like. I also seen a newspaper picture of Dick Wad. I'll be on overwatch at the game tonight. We'll be just fine.

"Look, I better get busy if I'm gonna get cleaned up before I meet them. I'll call you tonight, most likely after the game so as to give them, and me, an opportunity to sort things out. Tell the Bakers not to worry. We got things under control here."

"Easier said than done. Clarice wanted to fly to Houston just as soon as she heard her baby was there. Both her babies. She doesn't even know the plan is to rape Sarah before the killing begins. Ignorance is bliss. Savvy? Keep me informed. Talk to you later. Bye."

Archie cleaned up as fast as he could, to make himself

presentable. He actually put on clean underwear and a clean long sleeve shirt. It was 96 degrees outside. No problem. What else is new in June in Texas? However, 96 percent humidity on top of 96 degrees? That was downright uninhabitable, even for a thin man. Mother Mary, have mercy!

He slipped his unholstered Peacemaker under his jeans in the small of his back, padded by his tee shirt and drawers. Made it troublesome to sit down, but it had to stay concealed, else some pantywaist would see it and start hollering for the law. Never even consider that he was the police. Cause him some embarrassment. He put five spare cartridges in his right pants pocket. Doubt he'd need 'em, but you never know. Then he put on his jean jacket and Stetson and walked out the door. At least the motels and the Dome had refrigerated air. This damn humidity made him ever so thankful that he fought his war in France and Belgium, and not in Vietnam or the Pacific. How on Earth did Barlow or Slick adjust to fighting their wars in Asian jungles? Hell, his glasses steamed up here every time he stepped outdoors. How you s'posed to shoot somebody if they're lyin' in wait, when your glasses fog up soon as ya step outside? Ridiculous!

Archie beat them to the restaurant. He took a seat in a booth about halfway back, in the front dining room facing the hallway entrance. The exterior plate glass window was to his left.

He saw them as soon as they entered. They both lit up with big smiles. Sarah ran over and gave him a hug. She smelled so good, too. Then Barlow and he shook hands vigorously, like they were making a milkshake. They slid in and took seats across the table, Barlow first, up against the window.

"Did you have a hard time finding us?"

"Not here. Somehow I missed you all in Corpus Christi, so I just on and upped myself here. Where did you all stay there?"

"At the Brown Pelican on the beach."

"I know that place! I went by there no less than four times, to include sometime after midnight this morning."

"Well, we went to the King Ranch yesterday. When we got back, there wasn't anyplace to park, so we had to park behind the bowling alley as overflow."

"Darn it! I knew I shoulda looked back there! Well, at least we're together now. You all been enjoying yourselves, or is that too nosy a question?"

Sarah replied, "Why, Mr. Archie, whatever do you mean? Are you trying to make me blush? Do you suppose our carnal desires have consumed both our days, and our nights? Oh my goodness, Barlow! What have you been telling Mr. Archie about me?"

"Oh, nothing special. Just the same things I tell the rest of the fellas when they ask. You know. Manly man talk. Things like that."

"Well, I reckon that's all right then. Long as it wasn't anything embarrassing. Mr. Archie, Barlow didn't say anything embarrassing about me, did he?"

"Well now, Missy, I reckon you've turned the tables on me and now I'm the one what's embarrassed. My apologies."

"That's quite all right. I'm just teasing. Truth is, we've been having the time of our lives. We've seen so many things we never saw before. We've just come and gone whenever the mood struck us. I wish we could go on for a whole month like this. I feel so free, even though I do miss my folks and friends back home.

"Before you say anything, don't get upset when I tell you that we are not going back until we've had all the fun we can stand, or we run out of time. We are not letting that creepy Joe Schitt or his new pervert buddy to get in our way. We will do whatever we must if they do show up. Besides, if they don't locate us here, they'll just find us back in Mosby. It's not like they don't know where we live."

Arch looked over at Barlow. "You agree with the missus? One for all? All for one, you all being both the one and the all? You all will handle this situation all on your lonesome?"

"Archie, we're not running. Once you start, you can't stop. What would that say about me as a man, or better yet, as a cop? I'd rather pick the location for a fight, but I don't have the time to sit around, waiting for them to show up. We refuse to live in fear or trepidation. We have lives to live. We hope that you, of all people, would understand. We don't expect that her folks will, and we get that. They just have to trust us, to understand that we know what we're doing."

"You all don't know the whole story yet, because we didn't tell Clarice. They're not just stalking you all to kill you. Oh, no indeed! They plan to ambush you both, and carry you off someplace quiet so they can rape Sarah until she wishes she was dead while you watch, before slowly killing you both. You would be embarking upon a lethal odyssey of cat and mouse. You all are the mice.

"Sarah, does this give you pause for reconsideration?

"What about you, Barlow?"

Sarah replied, "The only thing I wish is that we had more firepower. Barlow's got his .30-30, but we can't walk around carrying that everywhere we go. He's also got his new .38, but I don't have my gun. It's at home. We might have to go buy me one tomorrow."

Barlow replied, "The only thing that changes for me is that I will kill them both just as soon as I see them. I won't even try to take them alive. Not taking any chances like that. Plus, like Sarah said, now I gotta go buy her another gun, one she can conceal and carry everywhere she goes."

Archie chuckled and said, "I figured as much. That's why all I did was promise to find you. I never said I'd bring you home against your wishes. However, you both know your parents and Sheriff Sol will probably come down on us hard if we don't turn around and head back tomorrow. Are you both prepared for the grief we'll have to endure, if we decide to stay?"

They both nodded. Then Barlow asked, "You're staying with us?"

"We're pards, ain't we? You'd be there for me if the shoe was on the other foot, wouldn't ya? Even if it meant ya might get jammed up at home or at work?"

Barlow said, "I would, Arch. You're blood to me. I would never turn my back on you."

Sarah said, "That goes for both of us. What did you have in mind, exactly?"

"I was pretty certain you all would feel this way."

Archie reached into his jacket pocket, and pulled out a red bandanna wrapped around something hard. He handed it to Sarah. It had some heft. He said, "That belonged to my dearly beloved Opal, who died twelve years ago, as I'm sure you remember, Sarah. I'm giving this to you. Don't unwrap it in here.

"It's a beautiful little, nickel-plated Browning, .25 caliber, semiautomatic pistol, with mother-of-pearl grips. They call it the Baby Browning. The magazine holds six rounds. It didn't come with a spare. It's only four inches long. It has a two-inch barrel. It weighs less than ten ounces. It shoots a fifty-grain bullet with a muzzle velocity of 820 feet per second and a muzzle energy of 75 foot-pounds. It's not a lion killer, but Baby Brownings saved many a French Resistance troop in World War Two during the Nazi occupation.

"I want you to have it. You can hide it anywhere. One word of advice, though. It doesn't have a safety, so if you choose to carry a round in the chamber, keep that in mind. If it's chambered and you pull the trigger, it will fire. Oh, yeah, there's also a box of cartridges in the hanky."

Sarah was stunned, "Mr. Archie, are you sure you want to do this? I'd be happy just to take it as a loaner until Barlow can get me a pocket pistol."

"Nope, I want you to have it. I bought it in 1952. Opal didn't carry it very often. She kept it in her nightstand drawer. That's why it's in such good condition. Not a scuff on it. In all the years we was married, no one ever threatened to rape or kill her. I know she'd want you to have it."

"Well, thank you so very much. I'm absolutely floored and honored. I feel safer already. Do I need to load it?"

"You do. You could probably do that in a stall in the ladies room. Before you load it, jack the slide a few times and then pull the trigger each time, so you know what it feels like. The trigger pull is crisp, but stiff, so it's safe to carry a round chambered, in my humble opinion. I mean, if you are being attacked in close quarters, and that's what this gun was designed for, do you really have the time to jack a round, aim, and then shoot?"

"My sentiments exactly. Be right back. I need to make a trip to the restroom."

While she was gone, Barlow asked, "What's your plan?"

"Tonight, it's simple. I got a seat halfway up between first and right field. You all get seats below me, at least by several rows, hopefully right in front of me, but close enough so I can see you. Keep your wits about you, but have fun. I will make several forays around the stadium to see if I can pick them up. If I do, I'll let you know. If that happens, we'll have to play it by ear. Otherwise, after the game is over, I'll shadow you back to your room. I'll call you when I get back to my room to make sure everything's okay. We'll talk about tomorrow over breakfast.

"Make sure Sarah understands that gun. It's easy peasy to learn, but her life or yours may depend upon it."

"Roger that. Thanks for everything."

When Sarah returned, they paid their check, and walked over to the Astrodome. It was fabulous! Not a bad seat in the house. The game was close, but the Braves won two to one. Maybe tomorrow would be different.

There were plenty of empty seats, so Archie had easy access to walk around and watch the fans. He never saw anyone who resembled an outlaw biker, and especially not Joe Schitt or his cohorts. Nevertheless, the Adamses and he were all extra tense walking back to the HoJo, with Archie pulling drag, halfway expecting to be ambushed outside the stadium by assassins too cheap to buy a ticket.

Nada. Joe Schitt didn't show tonight. That was a good thing, theoretically. However, when you're out on the prairie, and you know the Indians are on the warpath, not seeing an Indian is not always a good thing. He might be the very last guy you never see.

After Archie made his check-in call with Barlow, he phoned the sheriff. He reported, "Sheriff, all is well. If Joe Schitt or Dick

Wad were here tonight, we never saw 'em. I was on overwatch. I walked through every square inch of the stadium. After the game, I followed the kids back to their room. I just called them to be sure they didn't have a problem after I left. We're meeting for breakfast at nine o'clock."

"What about tomorrow.? Are you bringing them back?"

"Nope. They're not coming home until after they're done honeymooning. They said they ain't runnin' or hidin'. They pointed out that Joe Schitt knows where they live, and if Joe don't find 'em here, he'll just find 'em home in Mosby. I couldn't argue with that. Besides, I'm staying, too. I gave Sarah that little .25 I bought for Opal back in the day. She knows how to use it. I'll be on overwatch the whole time. We hope to scare 'em up, and settle the score once and for all."

"How you gonna do that? You can't stand outside their motel room all night long and then scout for assholes all the next day."

"No, I can't. How about you scare us up a Ranger for the night shift? Tell 'em Sarah and Barlow volunteered to be bait. Might even get our old bud, Trey."

"Well, I'll call Captain Campbell tomorrow. I can tell you now, that if he agrees, it won't be Trey. Trey doesn't work for him. Wouldn't surprise me if he wants you on midnight shift, being that you are out of your jurisdiction. What about that?"

"Ain't gonna happen. Me and Barlow is blood. If that's the way it's gonna be, we'll just handle it ourselves, which is what we planned to do all along, anyway. If the Rangers want to send someone, tell 'em they can tag along independently, so long as they look like citizens and not like Texas Rangers."

"I could get our old pal, State Senator Darnell Sweeney involved."

"Oh, please don't do that. The Rangers would never forgive us."

"Tell you what. You all sleep on it tonight. Call me after you all have had breakfast."

"You got it, Sheriff. Adiós."

"Adiós."

# CHAPTER 30

## Thursday, June 10, 1971
## Two Malefactors Get Serious About Crime

It was nearly noon before Joe Schitt and Gravy Train finally headed eastbound to Houston. First, there was the matter of scoping out the bridge to Del Rio for the better part of an hour, looking for signs of extra Border Patrol vigilance due to the prison break. Eventually they determined that nothing was amiss, so they ventured across riding double on Gravy's old hog. They rode it, instead of the new one just in case. Grady didn't want to risk his new ride getting seized.

As it turned out, crossing back into the US was no problem. Apparently no one was looking for an escapee from a Texas prison to sneak back into Texas from Mexico.

Next, they needed to steal a truck. That was also a cakewalk. Grady dropped Joe off a block away from the target residence. Joe was looking for a pale, mint green, adobe house in the middle of the block on the left side. Grady's instructions were, "A dark green, '68 Ford F-100, with an unpainted aluminum topper should be parked under the carport. The keys should be in the ignition. Joe Bob Tinsley, the owner, works the midnight shift at the Ford dealer as a security guard. He should be rattling the pictures off the wall with his snores by now, but he does have a revolver, and he is known to shoot, so be careful."

Grady's intel was solid, and the theft came off with nary a hitch. The truck was a plain Jane, but it was well maintained and spotlessly clean. It had a straight six, 300 cubic-inch engine with a three-speed shift on the column. No carpeting. No air conditioning. Vinyl seats. AM radio. No FM. Only 22,000 miles showing on the odometer. Joe fired it up without a problem. It purred like a happy kitten.

Joe followed Gravy Train to an old, empty house with an unattached, wooden, weather-beaten, single-car garage. The doors were partially open. He parked his hog in there. Then he pulled the saddlebags from the rear fender. They were stuffed with their few travel essentials. Things like a toothbrush, socks, tee shirts, and ammo. He locked the garage with a padlock onto a loose-fitting hasp, threw the saddlebags in the bed and jumped into the stolen chariot. He told Joe to head towards San Antonio. Joe drove through the city until he found US 90. They turned east and made their getaway.

"How's come you know so much about the owner of this truck?"

"He's a friend of mine. Known him since high school. We play poker together a couple of times a month. He'd never loan me his truck, so I didn't ask. He'll probably figure out I'm the one what took it. I'll have to do him a solid when we get back to stay in his good graces. You know. Buy him some Cherry Bomb mufflers or an FM radio adapter kit. Something like that. He loves this truck. Hafta make sure we return it shiny and clean, and full of gas. He'll get over it."

"What the fuck kinda friend are you, stealing a man's truck? I'd feel much better about stealing a car from someone I didn't like or didn't know."

"Forget about it. I told you, I'll make it up to him. Besides that, he bangs my sister every chance he gets and I ain't sore about that."

"That's because it ain't your pussy. It belongs to Alice. She don't care if you approve or not. You benefit from what she does anyway. Some of the guys balling her probably don't like you, but put up with your shit just to stay in her good graces. Just don't steal any of my shit, okay? I don't have much now, but I will, and just come and ask me if you want something. I'll most likely give it to ya. Understand?"

"Understood. By the way, do you know exactly how to get to the Astrodome? Where we gonna stay? It can't be where the TV family, 'Father Knows Best' stays."

"We'll follow the signs once we get into Houston to find the Astrodome. It ain't like they're trying to hide it. I know a motel on the northwest side, a little ways out on Business 90 called Lucille's Motor Court. It's next to Big Red's Saloon, which is a biker bar. Maybe you heard of it. You'll probably see someone you know there. Could be a friend. Could be a foe. And, just so you're warned, this place is a lot rougher than ours was. A lot more blood been spilt here. Buckets more. That's why, if the cops show up due to some disturbance, they come with plenty of reinforcements. If you hear sirens, you better split. We'll meet at our motel room."

"If the place is prone to cops buzzin' around, why you want to take the chance? You got everything to lose."

"Grady, I been cooped up for two years. I give myself an early out. I know the cops are hunting for me. They will shoot me on sight if they recognize me. I want to kick up my heels. Live life to its fullest. When I go, it will be with guns a blazing. I know I'll never make it to a ripe old age. Don't worry, though. I won't drag you down with me. You're my best friend, who is either still alive or not serving life without parole. You sittin' in the catbird seat. I would not jeopardize that for you. Promise."

"Thanks, Joe. I 'preciate that. I really do. I'm willing to do whatever it takes, so long as we have an exit strategy. I don't wanna die, but I also don't wanna go to jail even worse."

"Savvy."

It was some bit over 350 miles to Houston. They made good time. The game had already started by the time they arrived. Being that this was the first game, they decided to grab a bite to eat. Afterwards, they would stakeout two of the ground exits looking for the newlyweds to come out. Whoever spotted them would trail them back to their truck or motel. Then Grady and Joe would meet back at their truck. They'd wait until about three in the morning to bust into their room and make the grab.

If they didn't spot 'em tonight, they'd come back tomorrow and buy some tickets. Go in. Walk around. Keep an eye out for them. It would be the same drill once they had 'em located.

This was not Joe's nor Grady's day - or night. They covered the wrong exits. They left empty handed. No worries. They checked in at Lucille's. They drank some brewskis at Big Red's. They didn't see any friends or enemies. They closed the bar down, and fell into bed at Lucille's.

Tomorrow would be another day.

# CHAPTER 31

## Friday, June 11, 1971
## Calling Home

Archie met Sarah and Barlow for breakfast at the HoJo. It was convenient and inexpensive for a tourist area, and the grub was well above average, especially for a space station. Who knows? Maybe an alien from Mars or a Soviet cosmonaut would come in for a meal. Maybe order up a slice of green cheese.

Arch recounted his late night conversation with the sheriff. Barlow, in particular, didn't want anyone guarding his door while he slept, especially someone as exalted as a Texas Ranger. He had no qualms if they shadowed his and Sarah's movements, provided the Rangers wanted to use them as bait. That would be just fine. He'd even give them a schedule and try to stick to it. Also, just to be clear, he wasn't taking his eyes off Sarah, except for her to use a public restroom while he waited just outside the door.

Barlow concluded with, "Arch, you know I plan to kill Joe Schitt and anyone with him, just as soon as I lay eyes on them. I'm not taking any chances that they might snatch Sarah or blindside me. I don't give a hoot if someone kills them before I do. That would be fabulous. I just don't want anyone holding me back from protecting Sarah, or myself, if we see them first."

"What if you cross paths and Schitt is unarmed?"

"I already naturally assume that he is armed, if he's looking for me, but if he isn't, I'll cross that path when I come to it. Sarah put it to me a couple of days ago something like this. Joe Schitt - and I extend this to anyone else who travels in his sphere of influence - is bad to the bone. He's a rabid dog, who needs to be put down before he bites somebody. As long as Joe continues to draw a breath of air as a free man, neither Sarah nor I are safe from him or his minions. Like she says. Bad to the bone. That's exactly what he is. Ergo, in a case like this, a man has to do what a man has to do. You know that better than anyone."

"Okay. Sarah, what about you? What do you plan to tell your folks? They are not gonna want to hear this."

"I'll tell them how much I love them; that this is something Barlow and I must do if we want to live free; that I am no safer in Mosby than I am here; that Barlow and I are either predestined to our day of reckoning with these awful criminals, or we are not. It's in God's hands; therefore, they should fear not; that we will see them in about a week, once we get back. Now, we've spoken our piece. What do you have to allow, Mr. Archie?"

"Well, I'm glad it's you calling your folks and not me. Of course, you're absolutely right, both of ya, but telling your folks you're not gonna take sanctuary on the Bar B, but instead, you're plannin' ta go dragon huntin' a two or three-day drive from home in uncharted territory with nothin' but a .38 and a .25 auto, and an old coot like me, when you could get half of Quayle County to stand by your side. I dunno, it sounds kinda idealistic, where you all risk everything just to make a point. Mind you, I know with absolute certainty that we can turn the tables on Joe and his pals, but it will be bloody and we may not all of us come out of this completely unscathed. Me, I'm ready to slay some dragons. I've slayed dragons before, and Barlow, you have, too.

"Sarah, do you fully comprehend how gruesome this will be

if we do meet up, face to face? It won't be a pretty sight once the smoke has cleared."

"I love you, Mr. Archie, and I know what you say is true. I may not have any combat experience and I may be a girl, but as long as I am with Barlow, and now you, I know I'm as safe as I can be. Not only that, I just might surprise you and help save all of us. Just ask Barlow. I'm a pretty fair shot and now I am a motivated shooter. Thanks again for the gun."

"You slay me, Sarah. I love you, too. If it comes down to nut cuttin', I know you'll meet the challenge with tremendous determination and grit.

"Okay. This is what I propose: Barlow, you and Sarah go make your call to Clarice and Arthur. I'll go call Sheriff Sol. He can do however he chooses with the Texas Rangers. Tell them our motels and room numbers. Let 'em know what we drive, and generally where we're parked.

"You all meet me in my lobby in, say thirty minutes. I'm gonna call the Harris County Sheriff's Office and find us a place to buy more ammo, and also to practice some with our pistols. I'm sure they got a range they'll let us use. We go shoot. Maybe eat some lunch. Call the sheriff back after we eat. Go to the game about six o'clock, and handle it just like last night. Maybe have a siesta between lunch and suppertime, unless there's something else you all wanna do here in this urban rainforest. That sound okay to you all?"

Barlow replied, "Roger that."

"Good. See ya later, alligator. Also, think about when y'all wanta go ta New Orleans."

Sarah and Barlow both spoke with Clarice and Arthur. The decision to press on was encountered with fear and tears. Her parents pleaded fervently, and it grieved both Sarah and Barlow deeply. Finally, Barlow explained their rationale in a way that neither Clarice nor Arthur could counter.

He spoke softly and earnestly. "You all both know that when Sarah and I wed, it was the happiest day of our lives. I would do anything to protect her, and I know she would do the same for me. Consider this. We know with a very high degree of certainty, that Joe Schitt and some of his compadres are looking for us to kill us. They don't know that we've been alerted. This gives us a huge advantage. Also, on the road, we are not stationary targets. They have to seek to find us. If we were in Mosby, the advantage would be all theirs. They know where we live, where we work, and probably have figured out the best places to ambush us. But away from home, they don't know where we're staying. We don't have a work pattern, so the advantage is ours.

"Not only that, we've got Archie covering our back - a tremendous advantage that we'd only have sporadically, or not at all at home. Plus, we haven't told you yet, but Archie gave Sarah Opal's .25 caliber semiautomatic pistol. It's small and concealable. Nobody but us knows she's even carrying a gun. Soon as we hang up, we're all going to a range to practice. If we see these stalkers tonight, we will be prepared. In fact, we will carry the fight to them. It won't be the ambush they've been planning to spring on us.

"Lastly, if we don't run into them before our honeymoon is over, we will hunker down at the Bar B with you all until Joseph Schitt is either dead or back in prison. That's a promise."

All was quiet for a minute or more. They could hear Clarice quietly sobbing. Finally, Arthur responded, "Barlow, you're a good man. We know you're a true sheepdog. We trust that you and Archie know what's best. Take care of yourself. Do what you have to do. If you run into that, that, that villain, finish it, once and for all. Just bring our daughter back home to us safe and sound. Oh, one more thing. Call us each morning, Okay? We love you both."

"We love you all, too. Try not to worry. If it's God's will, we will prevail. Talk to you all tomorrow. Bye."

Archie was waiting for them in the lobby. Barlow asked, "What did Sheriff Sol say?"

"He said he'd call Captain Campbell and tell him where we are staying and where we like to park. That's all. He said to stay alert and come home in one piece. He said what we already knew, that being, if the Rangers see Joe Schitt, it will be his last day on Earth. What that means is, it's open season on these polecats in Texas. Louisiana is a whole different situation. Savvy?"

"Savvy."

"Good. You all ride with me. Harris SO gave me the name of a gun dealer who's in the police reserves. He gives a ten percent police discount. Also, I got directions to their range. Nobody's using it this morning, so we're good to go. Just gotta check in with a Lieutenant Gormley when we get there."

Sarah bought a cleaning kit, a garter holster, and two boxes of shells for the Baby Browning. At the range, Archie saw for himself that she was a fast learner. Anyone within fifteen feet would definitely feel some pain if she shot at him. Push that back to about 25 feet, if she actually had time to aim.

Sarah really loved this gun. It boosted her confidence and Archie's confidence in her. Nothing changed for Barlow, except it made him happy for her. He already had beaucoup confidence in her shooting skills. He also knew she had the mental toughness to pull the trigger, if it ever came down to that. He hoped that Joe Schitt would be lined up in his sights, before he was in Sarah's. Time would tell.

# CHAPTER 32

### Friday, June 11, 1971
### A Loose Cannon on the Gun Deck

Joe Schitt and Gravy Train slept until three p.m. They were in no big rush. They went to a Ponderosa Steak House because of the all-you-can-eat buffet, which augmented the Texas-size, half-inch thick, tough-as-shoe-leather, select-grade, well-done, tasteless round steak smothered with A-1 sauce, served with a baked potato the size of a peewee league football, and dripping with a half cup of melted margarine. This particular restaurant did not serve beer, so they washed it down with a quart and a half of truly delicious sweet tea, all for $2.95, plus sales tax and tip. Of course, they never tipped unless the waitress was less than sixty and she let them cop a few feels. Today's was willing, but she tipped the scales about the same as Gravy Train, so they both decided not to engage. Too bad. They didn't know what they were missing. The bigger the cushion, the better the pushin'. At least that's what the boys said who rodeoed with her. They never voiced any complaints.

En route to the Astrodome, they happened upon a small, corner tavern named the Sidewinder's Hideout. The building was at least seventy years old, constructed of brick, dingy, too dodgy for the average Joe, and for good reason. Had anyone ever taken the time to scroll through the police and crime section articles, covered for decades in the local newspaper and long since relegated to obscurity in the newspaper morgue, they would have been mesmerized by the tawdry saga of homicides, knifings, shootings, barroom brawls, arrests, closings and re-openings, most likely accomplished by greasing all the right palms.

The interior was narrow with a heavy oak bar and tall stools running the length of the building on one side and small, scarred, two-person tables, and worn-out, wooden chairs on the other. It was dimly lit. The sign on the wall said 'Occupancy - 34 Persons.' The only other decoration was a stuffed sidewinder striking at a chipmunk, which was hanging above the bar. Most of the fur had long since fallen off the doomed chipmunk.

The restrooms were on the opposite end from the entrance. Two one-holers, which hadn't been upgraded since they were installed. At least they both still flushed. Smelled just like you would imagine, with overtones of Clorox wafting through the air. The ladies had a semi-melted bar of Lifebuoy soap dried onto the sink, and the linen towel roller still had clean cloth on the roll. That's because a true lady seldom patronized this joint. The men's room was bereft of soap or any clean towel left on the roll.

This was a whiskey bar, not a frou-frou bar. The only beer they served was a slightly chilled Shiner Bock on draft. A ten-ounce glass cost a quarter. No wine. The only distilled spirits were four brands of bourbon: Early Times, Heaven Hill, Ancient Age, and for the high rollers, Jim Beam. A quarter-a-shot for the first three and thirty cents for Jim Beam. Don't even think about a mixer. Even ice was begrudgingly doled out. Two cubes per glass. Customers who asked for ice were eyed carefully for symptoms of deviance or perversion.

This was exactly Joe Schitt's type of bar. He was right at home as soon as he and Grady walked in. Grady begrudgingly followed Joe's lead. He preferred loose women in the establishments he frequented. Nary a one of those hanging around here. What he did see were three hard cases trading shots down at the end by the restrooms, a couple of winos nursing shots at this end (hoping someone would spring for another), and a loner who looked like trouble sipping a draft in the middle. Grady could smell trouble a mile away, and this guy's karma emanated that, plus a whole lot more. Although both Grady and Joe were packing, he hoped that Joe wouldn't start any shit. In a place like this, most of the patrons were armed and dangerous. Not only that, the barkeep nearly always had a sawed-off shotgun under the bar.

Naturally, like a moth to a flame, Joe bellied up right next to the loner and ordered shots all around. He slapped a five-spot on the bar to cover the damage. The bartender smiled and poured himself a drink first. Before swallowing it, he saluted Joe with the glass held high in the air. Then he poured the round and passed them out. Everyone had something nice to say except for the loner, who kept to himself and continued to look down at his beer.

Grady could see where this was headed. He slammed his shot. He slapped Joe on the back and said, "Come on, Joe. We got someplace to be."

Joe said, "In a minute. Let everyone drink up first, then we'll be on our way."

The loner was the only patron whose glass was untouched. Grady said, "Come on, Joe. Not everyone's a fast drinker like you and me. We need to shove off."

"Not so fast. It's insulting, if someone won't have a drink with you. It's like saying, 'You're not good enough to drink with me.'

You think that's what this dude is thinking to hisself? That he's better than me? That he doesn't like my looks? Like maybe he wants to kick my redneck, hillbilly ass?"

Finally, the loner looked over at Joe. He spoke softly. He said, "I don't drink whiskey. Thanks just the same. Maybe someone else would like it."

Both the bleary-eyed winos said, "I'll take it, Mister."

Joe said, "Not so fast. Drink up, asshole, or I'll wash your face with it."

The loner slowly swiveled his barstool so he was facing Joe directly. Then he stomped on Joe's left foot with his right foot. A split second later, he kneed Joe in the balls as hard as he could, like a left jab and a right cross, only done with his legs. Joe crashed to the floor in grueling agony. He was writhing around like a snake, except moaning, not hissing. Everyone else was perfectly still, except for the barkeep, who was pointing his double-barreled scattergun at Grady. He said, "Mister, I appreciate what you done trying to defuse this situation, but I don't know you. I'll ask you just once to drag your partner out of my bar. I don't want neither one of you to ever come back. You will regret it if you do. Savvy?"

"Savvy. Thanks, Mister."

Grady helped Joe to his feet, and gingerly led him out the bar. He had to help Joe climb up into the cab of the truck. He closed the door. Then he got in himself and slowly meandered towards the Astrodome. "Damn, Joe. Why you have to go do that? Act like an asshole. We're lucky we both got outta there in one piece. You still wanna go find the boy cop, or should we go back to Lucille's?"

Joe was rubbing his crotch. His balls throbbed but they

weren't busted. He replied, "He sucker punched me, Grady, or I'd a mopped up the floor with him. He wasn't that much. Don't be such a pussy! And Hell yeah, I still want to go find that boy cop. If I can't fuck tonight, we'll just have to gag 'em and hold 'em over until tomorrow. They will pay dearly. I promise you that. Maybe when I'm done with 'em, I'll come back and take care of that jerk who fights with his knee and foot instead of his hands. I bet that shitbird fucks with his face, too."

"Joe, you'll never see your next birthday if you don't start using your head."

"Maybe not. Come on. Let's get a move on, so we can get there early, buy our tickets, and scope the place out."

"That's what I'm talking about."

# CHAPTER 33

## Friday, June 11, 1971
## First Contact

Archie, Sarah, and Barlow took their seats in the Astrodome just before the first pitch was delivered. That's because the restaurant in the Astroworld Hotel had absolutely some of the best country ham and au gratin potatoes any of them had ever tasted. It was served with a tossed salad, corn on the cob, biscuits, and cherry pie á la mode. Arch washed his down with black coffee, and the Adamses washed theirs down with sweet tea. Everything was so good, they lost track of time and just lingered at the table too long.

They purchased seats almost exactly where they sat the night before. The crowd was double the size of yesterday's. Everyone was festive. Barlow and Sarah became absorbed in the game, which was close, and, for awhile, they forgot they were being hunted by rabid dogs.

Fortunately for them, Archie did not forget. The larger crowd meant that it was easier to hide, and harder to find. Cat and mouse, but that was a two-way street. Archie was so busy, his ass barely touched the seat. He cruised the stadium like a killer whale searching for great white sharks. He was so focused that he lost track of the game until the seventh inning stretch. While everyone else was engrossed in singing 'Take Me Out to the Ballgame', Archie was standing in one of the passageways to the seats on the upper level, scanning for men unengaged with their surroundings.

Bingo! Patience paid off. He saw Joe Shit the Ragman, who was standing on the same level, but about a third of the stadium away. This was proof solid that the information from the prison informant was true. Of course, it didn't mean anything legally, except for the fact that a prison escapee was in the stadium. No way one could prove beyond a reasonable doubt that Joe was stalking the Adamses to commit mayhem and murder.

Joe was standing next to a tall, heavyset dude, with a bushy dark beard, who was clearly an outlaw biker, but he wasn't wearing his colors. He was about the same size as Joe's old partner, Screech, only it wasn't Screech. As far as Archie knew, no one knew where Screech had landed. Also, Archie was 99% sure this wasn't Dick Wad. The newspaper photo showed that he was balding with short, light-colored hair, plus he was clean shaven. This dude had dark, shaggy hair like Charles Manson. Also a scraggly beard. Both outlaws were dressed in jeans, biker boots, white tees, and jean jackets with the sleeves cut off wife-beater style. Also, today's outfits were actually clean and not soaked in piss. Joe and company thought they were incognito because they weren't wearing Diablos patches on their jackets. Hell! Their arms were all covered with tats. Even a dimwit only needed one glance to intuit that they were predators.

Joe and his partner were still scanning the stadium seats, obviously looking for Barlow and Sarah. At least they were looking in the wrong direction for now. Archie kept looking for Dick Wad or other outlaw bikers, but he saw neither. This presented somewhat of a dilemma. He could either break contact and alert Barlow, or he could maintain contact and leave Barlow in the dark.

It was a no-brainer. He decided to maintain contact. If he fouled up and lost sight of them, then he would contact Barlow. The situation was, Joe knew Archie. If Joe spotted him, he would probably come out shooting. His partner would probably follow suit. Archie's advantage was that he saw them first and they were not looking for him. If they locked eyes, it might take Joe a few seconds to wise up. Also, Arch figured that he was more proficient with his long-barreled Colt than either of them would be with whatever handguns they were carrying, especially at a distance, like, say fifty yards. It was doubtful they could consistently hit anything past fifteen. Of course, that was also the Adamses' handicap with the firearms they were carrying. Distance was his friend, and his alone.

The second half of the seventh inning began and the fans took their seats. The outlaws stayed together, taking the steps down one level and moving closer to centerfield from left. Archie paralleled from their rear.

The rest of the seventh and the eighth innings went fast. Three up. Three down. The ninth was a nail biter. In the end, the Astros pulled off a five to four win. The crowd went wild. Everyone was up on their feet cheering. The song 'Deep in the Heart of Texas' began blaring over the loud speakers. It was next to impossible to locate anybody. That included the Adamses finding Archie. They decided to make their way back to the motel, assuming that Arch would shadow them. Even so, sensing danger, their hackles were up and they proceeded with caution.

Archie followed the outlaws out to the parking lot. They split up. The big guy took a position outside one gate, watching the crowd as it exited. This was a good thing, because this was nowhere near the gate the Adamses would use, assuming they followed yesterday's path. Joe Schitt, on the other hand, decided to push his way through the crowd, going against the flow. Archie followed him from a distance. It wasn't easy. If Joe's timing were good, he would intersect with the Adamses. Fortunately, it was not. Archie didn't see the Adamses, either.

Once the crowd thinned out, Archie had to exercise more caution. He did not want to get made by Joe. Fortunately, the police presence picked up and he watched the outlaws make their way back to a pristine Ford pickup. He copped the plate, TX 454711, as they drove away. When they were out of sight, he walked over to the Howard Johnson's Motel and knocked on the Adamses' door. Barlow answered, gun in hand.

"What happened, Arch? We couldn't find you."

"Then that would be a good thing. I found Joe Schitt and another guy, who I'm sure is an outlaw biker. He looked a lot like our old friend, Screech, only he wasn't. Also, I never saw Dick Wad. I don't think he came with, at least for tonight. I saw Joe and his partner leave in a '68 or '69, F-100, black, or dark green, or maybe blue, not sure, with a bright silver aluminum topper. The plate number is Texas 454711."

"Arch, you should've come got me. I'd have helped you take 'em down."

"I know you woulda liked to, but if I'da broke off, I probably woulda lost 'em. Then maybe they'd a turned the tables on us and got us from behind. You know that. Heck, it was so crowded, I couldn't find you all when the game was over. Now we know what they're drivin', plus I know what Joe's pard looks like. Before I call Sheriff Sol, tell me what you all wanna do. Are you all ready to move on or do ya wanna see if we get a repeat of tonight's performance? Understand, a baseball stadium is not a good place for a gunfight, assuming you're the good guy."

Barlow looked at Sarah. "What do you think, Sarah? Stay one more night, or go to the French Quarter?"

"I agree with Mr. Archie. It's better for us to pick our battlefield, if we can. I don't want to have to defend myself in a crowd. A lot of innocent folks could get hurt. Besides, now we know what they're driving. With that shiny topper, it should be easier to spot. We could even let the Rangers know what they're driving. I vote we go to New Orleans in the morning."

"I'm agreed. That okay with you, Arch? Do you have a better idea?"

"I'm agreed. Let me call the jail first, while I'm here, and get whoever's on the desk to run this plate. Then I'll call Sheriff Sol."

Archie placed his call.

"Sheriff's Office. Deputy Carruthers speaking. How may I help you?"

"Dewey, this is Arch. Got a minute?"

"Well, you old hound dog, taking a vacation on the county's dime. How the Hell are ya?"

"We're all three doin' just fine. Thanks for asking. How are you and Elsie and the kids?"

"Couldn't be better. Now that school's out, the kids are helping their mom and their Aunt Hyacinth at the second-hand shop. Thanks for asking, yourself. I know you didn't call just to chew the fat. What can I do for ya?"

"I need ya to run a registration and wanted check on a plate. It's Texas 454711. I saw Joe Shit the Ragman and another outlaw biker get in this truck at the Astrodome tonight. The second dude was not Dick Wad. Maybe the owner of the truck is Joe's unknown partner."

"Hot damn, Archie! This ain't no joke no more. Hang on while I run the checks. Be just a minute."

Tick tock. Tick tock. Tick tock. The virtue of patience is not easily attained.

"Archie, ya still there?"

"Yep."

"The plate comes back on a 1968 Ford F-100, green in color. It's registered to a Joseph Robert Tinsley, of 877 Purple Sage Street in Del Rio. The truck was reported stolen yesterday by Mr. Tinsley, hisself. He probably didn't steal his own truck, but if you want, I can call DMV and see can they pull his information up, unless you would happen to have his DOB, which I highly doubt."

"Tell you what. That's probably not our guy. Thanks anyway. I'm fixin' to call Sheriff Sol and let him know what happened. I expect he will pass this along to the Texas Rangers. They may be able to light a fire under DMV's asses and get them to track down Mr. Tinsley, DOB unknown, faster than we can. The important thing is, now we know for sure the information is valid, that Joe Schitt is hunting Sarah and Barlow, and we know what stolen vehicle he's driving. By the way, that truck has a bright aluminum topper. It ain't painted. That might make it easier to find."

"Roger that, good buddy. If ya don't need nothin' else, I'll letcha go."

"Thanks, Dewey. Bye."

Next, Archie called Sheriff Sol and passed along all this new information.

Sheriff Sol said, "This is great work, Arch. I'm gonna call Captain Campbell at home and wake him up. I'm sure he'll get

DMV to check on Tinsley; hopefully, even send a Ranger to conduct a personal interview. Last time I spoke to Orville, he was inclined to just wait and see. Now he may want to assign a Ranger to go with you all to New Orleans.

"It's interesting that you didn't see Dick Wad. Maybe they parted ways. If so, all the better for us.

"Call me in the morning before you all check out. I'll fill you in."

"You got it, Sheriff. Barlow and Sarah say 'good night.'"

"Tell 'em 'good night' from me, too. Adiós."

# CHAPTER 34

## Friday/Saturday, June 11/12, 1971
## Staying One Step Ahead of the Law

Not locating the boy cop and his bride tonight was no big deal. Sooner or later the odds would change in his favor. Besides, Joe knew where they lived. He just figured it would be cleaner to do them away from family and friends, most notably cop friends. Cops from another tribe wouldn't work quite as hard to affect a rescue as those who were truly his brothers from the same tribe. Those cops would press on until they found their brother and his bride or their bodies. Joe didn't have a death wish. His plan was to do the dirty deeds and then bug out of town as a person or persons unknown.

They drove back to Lucille's Motor Court and parked. They walked over to Big Red's Saloon. It was nearly midnight and the place was hopping. You could hear the country music a block away. Apparently, nobody objected.

They walked past a drunk taking a leak against the wall and a guy getting a blow job in the front seat of his truck, which was parked just outside the front door. This was Grady's favorite type of bar! He was definitely partial to a target rich environment, full of loose women. Even if he didn't score, there was plenty of eye candy.

They sauntered in and elbowed their way through the crowd up to the bar, where they took stools near the end. The noise was deafening. Hard to hear yourself think, and forget about carrying on a conversation unless you could read lips. Also, the smoke extended from the ceiling all the way down to the bar, making the dim light hazy. About the only thing one could see well were the neon lights, notably the ones which flashed.

The bartender who served them was a bleached blonde with size 38D hooters being held in check by the skimpiest of string bras. The straps must have been made by Goodyear. Ain't them the guys who make steel-belted radial tires? Her nether parts were barely covered by a tiny bikini, also held in place with just a string. What a voluptuous body! Only the parts required by law were covered. That didn't include the perfect curve of her calves and ankles. Problem was, she was wearing white go-go boots to match her white bikini. She was also wearing glossy red lipstick that looked like it was dripping wet and cobalt blue eye shadow. She smiled, licked her lips, and said, "What can I get for you two, luscious, stud muffins?" The way she said it brought Grady to mind of a cat which was purring.

She licked her glossy red lips, smiled, and leaned across the bar. Her gorgeous melons were mesmerizing.

Joe got straight to the point. He asked, "Are those real?"

"Of course they're real! Whaddaya take me for? Are ya drinkin' or just lookin'?"

"Both. Can you bring us two glasses and a bottle of Jim Beam?"

"Sure I can, but it'll cost ya 25 bucks."

Joe peeled off the cabbage and placed it in her hand. She tried to break away to fetch the bottle, but he squeezed her hand and held on tightly. He leaned over and whispered, "How much it cost to feel those puppies, just to satisfy myself they're real?"

"Five bucks, but if you squeeze too hard and bruise 'em, I'll call my boss and he will make you sorry that you hurt me."

Joe smiled. He peeled off another five-dollar bill and placed it in her hand. He whispered in her ear, "Promise to be gentle. Cross my heart and hope to die." He was being his most charming self.

She smiled, and leaned over. He slipped his hands up under the bra, and ran his hands all over them. They were real, all right. Nice and firm, too. He brought his hands out, and she readjusted her bra. She smiled and asked, "What do ya think? Are they real?"

"Oh, they're real, all right. They're absolutely fabulous. Maybe we can get together tonight when you get off from work."

"We could get together, but it won't be off work. I'm what you call an independent commercial enterprise. My meter will be running. Thirty bucks a half hour; fifty bucks a whole hour."

"What can a guy get while your meter is running?"

"Regular, French, no Greek. Nothing kinky. Just remember. If you bruise the merchandise, my boss will bruise you. Sound like something you might be interested in?"

"Oh, I'm interested. I'll take an hour. What time are you available?"

"Soon as we close at two o'clock. Meet me out front."

"You're on."

"What's your name?"

"They call me Miss April 1969, but I answer to just plain ol' April, if I like you."

April walked down the bar and returned with an unopened bottle and two glasses. She set them down in front of Joe. She smiled, and left to check on the other customers. Joe and Grady cracked the seal and began sampling Mr. Beam's wares. Mmm.

Tasty. Joe was counting the minutes. Grady was concentrating on getting drunk. Guess it was just bad karma. Neither of them got where they wanted to go.

About 45 minutes later, Joe said, "Hold down the fort. I gotta go take a whiz."

Grady replied, "Don't take too long, or this bottle may be a dead soldier by the time you get back."

"If it is, you're buying the next one."

The restrooms were in a narrow corridor across the room from the bar. Joe had the men's all to himself. He had to go so bad, he could have drowned a fish. Mission accomplished, he opened the door to leave. When he did, he slammed it into a well built guy, about six-feet, four-inches tall, coming in. Joe started to apologize a split second before he and the guy recognized each other. As it turned out, this chance encounter was bad karma for both of them.

The guy said, "Well, if it isn't Joe Shit the Ragman, hisself, standing before me here, in flesh and blood! You're a dead man, asshole!" As he spoke, he reached into his waistband, and pulled out a nickel-plated, Colt Commander, .45 auto. He was just one second too late. Joe pulled out the Colt Cobra .38 he stole from the house in Conroe and shot the rude name caller under his chin. The shot blew the top of his head plumb off. Brains and blood dripped off the ceiling tiles and all over everything. Smelled disgusting. He fell dead as a mackerel without making another sound.

His partner, who Joe had not seen until now, had been standing directly behind the rude name caller, out of sight. He was shorter and less muscular. He was also unprepared and in serious shock. He never quite got his gun out. The hammer spur of his Smith and Wesson, .38 caliber revolver, snagged on the inside of his pocket. It was the last thought he ever had. Joe didn't know this dude; didn't hate this dude. His problem was simply a matter of being in the wrong place, at the wrong time. Joe shot him four times in the chest. That was three shots more than he intended, but his nerves were frayed. Couldn't control himself. Then he walked hastily out of the corridor in long strides and stepped into the barroom.

Joe's ears were ringing, but the band had never stopped playing, so he assumed the shots had not been heard by anyone else. He walked up to the bar, and put his hand on Grady's back. He said, "Come on. We gotta get out of here, pronto!" Then he pivoted abruptly, and was adiós amigo before Grady could even react.

Grady grabbed the bottle, but forgot the cap. He put a five-dollar bill on the bar and headed out the door. Joe was halfway to Lucille's. Grady ran up and said, "What the fuck? I thought you were going to get laid."

"No questions. Just get your shit. We gotta get outta here now."

They went into their room and grabbed all their stuff, which took every bit of thirty seconds since they were traveling so light. Grady left the room key on the table. They locked the door and skedaddled. Grady fired up the truck and backed out slowly. Two minutes later, he turned onto US 90 and headed east. Joe, who had been holding the bottle, took a couple of long pulls. They hadn't gone two miles when they were passed by three marked, city police cars going Code Three, their sirens breaking the tranquility and flashing red lights illuminating the coal black sky.

"Joe, what did you do?"

"I defended myself! That's what! I'm lucky to be alive! Gimme a minute. My mind's going a hundred miles an hour."

"Sure."

Several minutes passed.

"You remember that bikers' rendezvous that we all went to outside of Ft. Worth a few years ago?"

"Yeah."

"Well, I got in a little hullabaloo there with this dickhead in the SOS."

"Spawns of Satan?"

"You got it! There was this prick there named Dennis Eggleston. They called him Rotten Egg, or just plain Egg, on accounta the rotten farts he's famous for. The dude is six-feet, five-inches tall if he's an inch. A fuckin' bruiser. Built like Charles Atlas, hisself. He was from the Dallas Chapter.

"Anyway, they brung their whores with 'em to the rendezvous. They was pulling tricks, making a shitload of money. I screwed a foxy lookin' chick called Rainbow Girl. Her real name was probably something less delightful, like Jane Snodgrass or Doris Griswold. She was a hippy chick they picked up somewheres. Supposedly from Wisconsin. She was a full-time pot head, plus she'd drop acid every chance she got. She really was a good-looking chick and a great lay, but man, her mind was fried. She was living on another planet. Anyway, she was completely stoned when I fucked her. She was really groovin' on me. She wanted me to take her with us when we left town. Hell, I couldn't take that crazy chick! Besides that, she was the property of Egg. Anyway, long story short, I told her I couldn't do it. Man, she went off the rails! She hid the twenty bucks I paid her, and told old Egg I stiffed her. He believed the bitch! Can you believe that? He wouldn't listen to me. He wanted twenty more bucks and I told him to get it from Rainbow Girl because I already paid her! Said I wasn't payin' twice.

"Well, that was the wrong answer as far as he was concerned, so he pulled this big old Jim Bowie knife on me. Said he would start by cutting off little pieces of me, 'til I was ready to pony up. He was stoned out of his mind too, only on meth. I said 'fuck that' and pulled out my little hideout gun, this 1906, Colt .32 auto. He kept advancing, so I emptied the clip. Shot him seven times in the chest. I thought I killed him, so I jumped on my scooter and headed back to El Paso all by my lonesome. Nobody seemed to notice, just like tonight, and the cops never came lookin' for me, so I thought my worries was over.

"I was wrong. They weren't. When I stepped outta the john tonight, that asshole was coming in. We recognized each other right off. He called out my name and said I was a dead man. He pulled out a Colt Commander, and I pulled out my .38. I shot that douche before he could shoot me. I hit him right under his chin. Blew the top of his fuckin' head off! When he fell, I saw he had a backup behind him. Never saw that guy before. He went for his rod, but it caught on his pants. I shot him four times in the chest.

"Nobody except us was in that hallway. No eyewitnesses. End of story."

"Hell's bells, Joe! Gimme that bottle! I need another taste. Better reload your shooter before something else goes wrong."

"Good idea."

The drive the rest of the way to New Orleans was anticlimactic after this.

# CHAPTER 35

### Saturday, June 12, 1971
### The Prey Follows the Predators

When the honeymooners and Archie walked into the HoJo diner for breakfast, they spotted the Texas Ranger right away. He was seated in a booth, sipping a cup of coffee. He was wearing traditional Texas Ranger garb, consisting of khaki trousers, a white western-cut, long-sleeved dress shirt, bolo tie, wide-brimmed, beige Stetson, brown lizard skin, Tony Lama, pointy-towed, cowboy boots, and a brown, hand-tooled belt, with a sterling silver buckle, belt slide, and tip. His silver star, circumscribed by a circle which proudly proclaimed DEPT OF PUBLIC SAFETY on the top, TEXAS RANGERS on the bottom, and CO F in the middle of the star, was pinned above his left shirt pocket. The badge was made from a genuine, antique silver, Mexican peso, from an era when a peso actually had some value.

This particular Ranger was about forty years old. He had black hair, brown eyes, and was clean shaven. He stood probably six feet tall, and weighed about 180 pounds, consisting mostly of bone, gristle, and muscle. He was wearing an El Paso Saddlery gun belt with a holstered, nickel-plated, Colt, Government Model 1911, .45 ACP caliber, semi-automatic pistol on his right hip. His ammunition pouch, with two spare magazines and a handcuff case, were on the left. He made the Mosby crew right off the bat, and motioned for them to join him.

He smiled and said, "Hi. I'm Jarvis Reeves. Captain Campbell asked me to see if I could be of any assistance to you all. I understand we have a common interest."

He extended his hand, which was firmly shaken by all three. Then they sat down a micro-second before the waitress brought them each a menu. They all ordered the Number One, scrambled eggs, grits, bacon, biscuits, orange juice, and coffee. Less interruption and confusion, while they were getting acquainted, and making plans. When breakfast came, they continued to talk while they ate.

Archie replied, "I'm Archie Willis. This here is Barlow Adams, and his wife, Sarah. We are all very pleased to make your acquaintance. I'd say we do have a common interest, besides law enforcement in general, and that interest would be a no-good scoundrel by the name of Joseph P. Schitt."

"Bingo! I heard you saw him in the parking lot here last night with a person unknown. Surprised to hear it wasn't Richard Wadsworth. We got a Ranger headed to Del Rio right now to locate the owner of the stolen truck they were in. Maybe he could shed some light on this."

"We certainly hope so. Did they tell you we are planning to go to New Orleans today?"

"They did. Please excuse my bad manners. Sarah, Barlow, congratulations on your wedding. I am sorry to interrupt your honeymoon, even though I am very glad to meet you both. This escape business with Joe Schitt couldn't have come at a worse time for you all. That's why Captain Campbell cleared me to stay with you, wherever you all go, at least until you return to Mosby. Before you all get nervous, I'll be wearing jeans and a short-sleeved shirt before we leave for the French Quarter. I thought it would be best to meet you in my standard outfit first. Also, I'm driving an unmarked, white, '70 Dodge Charger, so I can fit in most places."

Sarah said, "Thank you very much. You are so kind, Ranger Reeves. We're both glad you're coming with us. Normally, I would say we'd be mixing work with pleasure, but if that poor excuse for a human being manages to insert himself in front of our sights, we'll just be mixing pleasure with pleasure. You do understand that we won't be safe until he's either dead or behind bars, except behind bars just doesn't seem to be enough deterrent these days, or so it appears to me."

"Please call me Jarvis. We're all on the same sheet of music. I must say, Sarah, you exhibit more grit than I would expect from a woman as young as you. I assumed you would be . . . scared to death."

"I am scared. This devil tried to slice my husband up with a great big knife just because. Barlow and Mr. Archie got the best of him. I witnessed his trial. I know everything that happened. He's bad to the bone. A rabid dog that has to be put down. I know what he said he plans to do to me, before he kills us both.

"I'm also scared of rattlesnakes, but I know what to do when I see one. Mr. Archie gave me a hideout gun and I know how to shoot it. Besides that, I grew up with guns. I've been shooting for ten years now. I have my own revolver, but unfortunately, it's at home. I just want to be clear on that. I can shoot well. I will give this lowdown varmint no quarter if I see him."

Barlow added, "Jarvis, we both feel that way. If we don't meet him on this trip and put his lights out, he'll just follow us home and try to ambush us there. Maybe sneak into our home when we're out. Who knows? Besides that, Joe Schitt will never surrender to law enforcement. You all know that."

"And that's exactly why I'm here. Hopefully, Archie or I will snuff his lights out so neither of you two have to. If push comes to shove, I'm positive that you're both up to it. Also, Barlow, I'm well aware of your encounters with the Diablos. Also, with Ranger Winfield and the rustlers last year. I want to make it perfectly clear that I am not here because you aren't up to the job. Every Ranger in Texas knows you are. Same for you, Archie, but you may be outnumbered and they sure won't face you square on. It'll be an ambush, when you all are most vulnerable. Rest assured that you will be granted no quarter by them."

Archie said, "Our hats are off to you, too. Everyone knows you don't get to be a Texas Ranger unless you've already demonstrated your skills in vanquishing the bad boys, and I don't mean just once or twice. Many a time.

"Let's talk about our plans for today. I wanna see Marie Laveau's House of Voodoo. Got someone I need to put a hex on. The sooner the better."

Barlow responded, "Archie, I didn't know you believed in that stuff."

Jarvis interjected, "Just one last thing. Houston PD got a call of a double homicide at a biker bar late last night. Happened in the restroom, I think. Nobody saw or heard a thing. The decedents were both members of the Spawns of Satan. Both were armed and shot up close. Whoever did it got clean away. Makes me wonder. Could this be Joe Schitt, perhaps a little frustrated because they didn't find you all last night? Don't know. Today probably is a good day to go see a voodoo house in New Orleans."

Barlow said, "Wouldn't surprise me in the least, if it turns out Schitt was the doer. My recollection of him is, he's a mean drunk, quick to inflict pain on anyone who isn't fast enough, or savvy enough, or tough enough to do him first. That's why we won't be waiting around, if we see him, following Marquis of Queensbury rules. We'd never stand a chance then. We know he is unencumbered by scruples or rules."

Sarah suggested, "After we settle the check, why don't we meet back here in the lobby in an hour? Give everyone a chance to clean up and make a call if he needs to. Jarvis, if they didn't tell you, we plan to stay at the Bienville House. It's in the French Quarter at the intersection of Decatur Street and Bienville Avenue. They say it's elegant. I think it's three stories tall. It's two blocks off Canal Street, which is the main drag downtown. It's supposed to be close to the U.S. Customs House. They say you can't miss it. Takes up a whole block. Also, Canal is a real wide street and separates the regular part of New Orleans from the French Quarter. We made our reservations yesterday. Maybe you could make yours before we leave this morning. We only made reservations for two nights. We figured we could extend if we needed to."

Archie followed up and said, "Jarvis, why don't you get your change of clothes, and follow me across the street to the Holiday Inn?"

He replied, "I am at your service."

It was a hot, steamy drive to New Orleans. Once they got into Kenner, a small city on the west side of New Orleans, they got turned around. Some might even say lost. Several crucial road signs were missing. Traffic sucked. They wound up for a stretch on Jefferson Highway in a little town called Harahan. They had been on Airline Highway, but somehow found themselves on Jefferson.

It didn't help that the Mississippi River meandered back and forth like a snake. Impossible to keep north, south, east, and west straight in your mind. The roads certainly weren't true, nor were they consistent. If you asked for directions, you were inevitably told to go towards Lake Ponchartrain, or towards the river. The only absolute, was that the lake was north of the city.

The river meandered in all four directions. You could be on the West Bank of the river, and be north of the East Bank. Or not. It could be just the opposite. The streets tended to parallel the river, meaning they were serpentine and aggravating, if you didn't know your way. Also, there weren't that many bridges to cross the river. Some places you had to take a ferry. Logic was simply not a part of the equation. It only made sense to a local, and they loved to tease the tourists who got confused.

What Sarah and company also didn't know was that they drove right past the muddy, potholed, junky, vermin-infested street where Joe and Grady were staying, in a century-old dump, owned and identified as a clubhouse by the Crescent City Jacks, a local outlaw motorcycle gang friendly to the Diablos. In fact, Snakebelly Crabtree affiliated with the Jacks once the Diablos fell apart, so they had an in when they arrived at six in the morning and woke up all the happy campers recovering from their hangovers.

Eventually, the Adams/Willis/Reeves three-car motorcade found US 90, which was called Broad Avenue. It intersected with Canal Street, their landmark, but too far towards Lake Ponchartrain. Nevertheless, they eventually located the French Quarter, also known as the Vieux Carré, and finally, their hotel, which was an Old World gem. Getting there was so complicated! They would never find their way home! They hadn't thought to drop kernels of corn along the way to retrace their steps.

Simply stated, they were all frustrated. First, you could not rely on points of the compass to find your way anywhere. Second, nearly every other road sign was missing or turned around. Third, left turns were not allowed at traffic signals. You were forced to drive past the street where you wanted to turn and get into a designated U-turn lane, or you had to square the block, few of which were actually square, and some of which went on and on, with curve after curve, before you could find a one-way street the direction you wanted to go, but by now might not be in the right direction. Fourth, some streets went only one way, and then suddenly, without warning, they changed to one way in the opposite direction. Fifth, how do you pronounce a street spelled T-C-H-O-U-P I-T-O-U-L-A-S? There were others nearly as bad. Enough!

Finally, they found it! The hotel was absolutely fabulous, so in the end, at least to Sarah, well worth the frustration of trying to find it on a busy Saturday afternoon, in nearly hundred-degree heat and ninety-percent humidity. Both Sarah and Barlow were melted by the time they arrived. Archie, too, but he wouldn't admit it to them. Jarvis' auto had air conditioning, but even so, he was bathed in sweat.

The Adamses were assigned to room 303. Archie was in 216, and Jarvis was in 112. They decided to meet in the lobby at seven o'clock to go to dinner. Everyone stayed inside until then, sucking up the refrigerated air, except for Archie, who went to Marie Laveau's House to buy a voodoo doll to put a hex on someone. He was being contrary and refused to say whom.

Later, they walked to the Port of Call for a steak dinner. It didn't taste like a steak from Texas. Too many unusual herbs and spices, but it sure was tasty. Good thing they gorged, too, because afterwards they walked to Pat O'Brien's to see what the big deal was about a manmade Hurricane.

They found out real fast. It was still ninety degrees. The humidity had to be one hundred percent. The breeze was ever so slight. Maybe two miles per hour. No more. They were parched by the time they arrived. Soaked with sweat. The Hurricanes were ice cold, and delicious, and extra large, and went down like you were drinking sweet tea or Kool Aid. Yummy. No one ever told them just how many shots of rum were in each one. Like four. Six ounces! Couldn't taste it, but it was definitely there.

They were all hammered after the first one, but nobody realized it because they slammed it so quickly, quenching their thirsts brought on by the sweltering walk over, so they each ordered a second one to sip on. Sarah couldn't finish hers, so Barlow came to her rescue like a good bridegroom. Bad mistake. Archie and Jarvis had to hold him up, as they all staggered back to the hotel. No taxi tonight. They all needed to walk it off.

Praise the Lord! The creepy crawlers stayed home tonight.

Lesson learned. Don't tangle assholes with a Hurricane, even if it is manmade.

# CHAPTER 36

## Sunday, June 13, 1971
## In Furtherance of Mayhem and Murder

Saturday was shot in the ass, so far as hunting for the boy cop and his bride was concerned. First of all, Grady and Joe were wasted from being up all night, plus from being hungover. It's unknown how much Joe's close brush with death by a .45 ACP, had affected him. Probably a lot more than he let on. They slept on mattresses on the floor in an empty bedroom until two p.m. When they woke up, it was time to forage for food and get to know their hosts. See if the Crescent City Jacks were the real deal, or just a sorry crew of wannabes, or as they say in Texas, all hat and no cattle.

Snakebelly Crabtree had been a reliable and faithful Diablo, but he was limited in the thinking department. He took orders and never questioned them. He knew better. They used him for gofer jobs and backup in dicey situations. He was good at both. He didn't get to count the money or do any of the planning or ordering around. His reward for doing what he was told and not fouling up, was having a secure position at the lowest level of their totem pole and having free access to the ugliest and skankiest bitches in their stable. He didn't dare touch the primo stock. Ergo, neither Joe, nor Grady could rely on Snakebelly's assessment with respect to their welcomeness during their temporary and unannounced layover with the Jacks.

They were quite hospitably offered grub. It came in the form of a leftover pie from Pizza Hut and ditto for a half bucket of Kentucky Fried Chicken, which someone from the Jacks picked up for lunch earlier in the day for anyone interested. They washed it down with tepid and slightly flat Dixie beer from a keg. Beggars can't be choosers. Apparently, this was the breakfast of champions for wasted outlaw bikers at the Crescent City Jacks clubhouse, unless, of course, you planned ahead or rousted some of the stable girls to make biscuits and gravy, as a flavor pairing to complement their boudin and tar-like coffee. However, the girls were much better at fucking than cooking, so that really wasn't the best option.

While they were sitting around chewing the fat, they bonded with the Jacks. Before long, it became obvious that all the hullabaloo about the prison escape never made it as far as New Orleans. Joe was relieved that it hadn't, because he was sure that the cops had put a bounty on him for information leading to his arrest. He wouldn't put it past some slime ball from this crew to dime him out and cash in.

The topic came up as to why he was hellbent on locating the boy cop and his bride.

Joe said, "It's like this. That fucker is responsible for me and one of our brothers getting popped. Me and Screech was having a few brewskis in this crummy little, one-horse town in West Texas. There was this sniveling, whiney puss of a man in the bar who was giving Screech and me the hairy eyeball when he thought me and Screech wasn't looking. We fronted him and he started bawling like a little bitch, so Screech and me poured his drink over his head to let him know just how much we truly cared. What a girly man! Someone must've called the cops and complained.

"This boy cop, still wet behind the ears, looked about sixteen to me, confronted us. Never did see him come into the bar. Don't know where he come from. Screech turned on him when he trash talked us and scared that punk cop half to death. He broke bad though, and damn near poked a hole in Screech's belly with his billy club. Fucked Screech up pretty good. Put him on his knees gasping for air. I went over to check on him and by the time I got there, Old Screech was barfin' like an active volcano and all because that asshole cop panicked. Later, he claimed I was fixin' ta cut him with this knife I was wearin' on my belt, no different than half the men in Texas carry.

"Lyin' prick! He swung at me with that club, and busted my arm into eighteen pieces. I ain't kidding! Look at it! It's still crooked. I can barely use it! The nerves still keep goin' off on me, like lightning bolts when I move it too much. That was two years ago! Then his partner, this broke down old geezer, sneaked up on me from my blindside and snatched both my arms behind my back. He cuffed me so hard my wrists was bleedin'. He liked to have twisted my broke arm completely off. I ain't kiddin'!

"Me and Screech was taken by complete surprise and done in by uncalled for, and devious means and we ain't even done nothin' worth mentioning! Both of us wound up in the hoosegow, but they ended up givin' Screech probation, and I got the time.

"Whatever become of old Screech, Gravy?"

"Tell ya later."

"Well, the boy cop was the main problem. He framed us good. We heard he got married and was goin' on his honeymoon here in the French Quarter. I owe him big time. I aim to sneak up on him and his old lady like he done me and Screech and put the grabbola on 'em, and take 'em somewheres out of the way and ride her like a bronc while she bleeds and begs until it's all she wrote. It wouldn't even matter to me if she was fat or ugly. I'll make the boy cop watch until it's all over. Then, I plan to put a bullet in him and dump 'em both where the buzzards will pick their bones clean. Anyone who's interested in helping can ride the bitch, too, but I get first crack."

Bruno 'The Vampire' Morgan, King of the Jacks, asked, "What do they look like?"

Joe replied, "The dude is about my size, brown hair, short, wears a mustache, dresses like a cowboy. Probably wearing a Stetson and cowboy boots, jeans, long sleeve shirt. I would say blue jean jacket, but it's too fuckin' hot here for that. Think cowboy. That's what he looks like. A fuckin' hayseed cowboy.

"The broad looks like . . . remember the Mamas and the Papas?"

Bruno interrupted, "Christ, Joe! We ain't interested in fuckin' Mama Cass!"

"No, you moron! Like the other one, Michelle Phillips. Long brown hair, fuckin' gorgeous. That's what she looks like!"

"Well, all right then. We're in. You can do 'em here. We got a spot for the bodies down in the swamp in St. Charles Parish. Whaddaya need?"

"Well, we could use some boots on the ground, watching the tourists in the French Quarter. They're on their honeymoon, so they'll be alone, holding hands, making goo goo eyes at each other, shit like that. Me and Gravy will find a bar on Bourbon Street to hang out in. Anyone sees 'em, follow 'em. If they roost, send someone to get me, so I can make the ID."

"Why ain't you gonna be workin' the crowd?"

"'Cause they know me on sight. If they see me first, they'll sky up."

"Gotcha. Okay, I'll send a few guys."

"Oh, yeah, this dude drives a snot green, five or six-year-old Dodge pickup. It'll have Texas plates. Maybe someone could check the parking lots."

"We got a couple of teenagers with bikes we can send to do that. They'll never get made. What's their names, in case we find 'em?"

"Barlow and Sarah Adams."

"Okay. Let's get a move on. I'll wait with you all at Poppy's Candy Store on Bourbon Street. My guys will report to me there."

"Sounds like a plan."

# CHAPTER 37

## Sunday, June 13, 1971
## Touring the French Quarter

The first thing they did Sunday morning upon leaving the hotel was to attend a mass at the St. Louis Cathedral in Jackson Square. The cathedral held numerous masses on Sunday, normally one an hour for six hours in a row. Most were abbreviated to attract the tourists. On one mass each Sunday, out of tradition, the homily was spoken in Latin. That worked out just fine for the Texas crew, because none of them were Catholic. Protestants all: Baptist, Methodist, and Presbyterian.

The service only lasted forty minutes. The choir was phenomenal. Sounded every bit as good as the Mormon Tabernacle Choir. The ambience within the church was majestic, with its architectural design, its crosses bearing our Lord and Savior, elegant murals, lifelike statues, gold leaf trim, arches, and so forth. The priests were ornately adorned, as were members of the choir, the altar boys, and all the other mass participants. It was meant to be awe-inspiring and it succeeded. Collectively, the totality of the worship service inspired sinners and saints alike to experience and succumb to the reverence and majesty of the Lord of Lords. When it concluded, these four Protestants and certainly many other attendees, felt like they were washed clean of all their sins, or at least until next Sunday, when it would be time to renew themselves all over again.

Church service concluded, they opted to eat the breakfast of yats - yat being a slang term for a native of New Orleans, allegedly derived from Irish English, 'Where ya at?' Of course, this is also a favorite breakfast of tourists at Café du Monde, located across the street from Jackson Square. Café du Monde is an old landmark, more outdoors than not, but covered by a roof, and famous for its coffee and beignets. The coffee has chicory in it, which runs off the uninitiated and faint of heart, and no doubt about it, the flavor is stout. Many people order a café au lait to temper the strength just a tad, but the coffee is tame for anyone who served in the Army or Navy and learned to drink their coal black, acidic, asphalt-like coffee.

The beignets are heavenly clouds of white powdered sugar covering a deep fried, hollow, yet chewy pastry. Very light and extremely addictive. Barlow provided comic relief when he exhaled just prior to taking his first bite and until he was brushed off, was every bit as white as Casper the Friendly Ghost.

Afterwards, they strolled up and down all of the streets in the French Quarter, some more intently than others, sampling various cuisines such as Aunt Sally's pralines and Central Grocery's muffulettas. They browsed all through the French Market, Jackson Square, the Cabildo, Bourbon Street, of course, and particularly Royal Street, with all the fine antique shops and oil paintings, enjoying every bit of the French Quarter's very unique charm.

Sarah took two rolls of photographs, including one with all four of them, snapped for her by another tourist, standing in front of Andrew Jackson's statue in Jackson Square. Sarah said this picture was for posterity, because she wanted everyone to know she went on her honeymoon with three handsome men.

In mid afternoon, Archie asked, "Is it just me, or has anybody else noticed the three outlaw bikers I've seen in the past hour?

"I saw one on a scooter wearing his colors, the Crescent City Jacks as I recall, when we were on Bourbon Street. Didn't think a thing about it at the time.

"Then I saw one without his colors, but he had every other marker: the long greasy hair, covered with jailhouse tattoos, wife-beater shirt, filthy jeans, run-down Harley Davidson boots, chained wallet to his belt, long sheath knife on his side, couple of domed rings on his fingers with a spike on the front of each one, for that vicious little advantage in a fist fight. I could smell that rat bastard a mile away.

"And now, I saw another one loitering in the French Market, like he would actually purchase some groceries, unless you consider beer a food item.

"They was all unpleasant to behold, scary looking you could say, which made 'em easy to spot in the crowd. Bet they smelled just as bad, too. Most folks was trying to avoid eye contact with 'em. Just walked around 'em like they was Moses parting the Red Sea or a fresh, steamy, cow patty on your front porch. In fact, the one in Jackson Square was so ugly, if I had a face like his, I'd shave my ass and walk backwards. He was just hanging around like a virus, eyeballing everyone he saw, one of the usual suspects who needs to be rousted by the local gendarmes, and lodged in the Crossbar Hotel in the name of crime prevention."

Jarvis responded, "I saw two of them and was wondering the same thing. You think Joe has recruited some of the local biker douchebags to help locate Barlow and Sarah?"

Barlow asked, "Where would he get the money to pay them? How are people who've never seen us supposed to identify us? Joe's the only one who's seen all three of us, although he probably would not remember Sarah. The only time he saw her was in court. He had other, more pressing things on his mind. Nobody else saw us! Our photographs were not in the paper."

Archie said, "We could just walk up to one of these assholes and ask him. Grab him by the balls and squeeze the truth out of him. Would that help? How could we believe anything he coughs up?

"I don't have any answers to your questions. On the other hand, how could your antennae not be up when: (a) Joe's an outlaw biker; (b) he's set out to kill you; (c) I saw him in Houston two days ago where you were way far away from home; (d) he knows from the newspaper, just like in Houston, that you all were coming to the French Quarter; and (e), we've seen three outlaw bikers in close proximity within the last hour here in the French Quarter, even though they might not be Diablos. Hell, Dick Wad isn't a Diablo!

"We don't know who Joe's recruited to help him do his dirt. You know damn well he isn't going to do it all by hisself. He has to have at least one butt boy to assist. After all, he's the big dog, the so called alpha male. For all we know, he may have some of those renegade, broke-dick dogs from the Diablos with him. Maybe some of them skedaddled to Louisiana to escape the heat from the police in Texas. They'd help him for free.

"Besides that, I'm sure Joe knows what you're driving, since every other Diablo in Texas seemed to know. Plus, he'll know you got Texas license plates. That will help to narrow the odds some, too. He even might have guys looking for your truck. It would be easier to locate than getting lucky looking for you two lallygagging on the street in the Quarter somewhere. Once he finds your truck, he stakes it out and waits. If he's really intent on rape and torture, he's got to do a snatch, not just an execution. That takes us back to him needing assistance; but, if any of us saw the snatch coming, we could take the fight to him and end it then and there. It could get bloody real fast and we all might not come out of this unscathed. Even so, that's better odds for both of you than if he was successful in pulling off a kidnap."

Barlow asked, "What about the bikers we've seen in the crowds? Why would they be out on the street if they're looking for my truck?"

Archie, exasperated, rolled his eyes. "Some of them might be looking for your truck. They could have some of their crew scanning the crowd and others looking for your truck. Think how we would do it if we was seriously looking for them.

"Barlow, you gotta focus. Any of those bikers could be in it with Joe. They might not be, but one thing's for sure. They got more outlaws here in the French Quarter today than I seen in any one day since Joe's trial. Is that a coincidence? Was it a coincidence I saw Joe at the ballgame? I think not.

"That shithead's here and he's looking for you and Sarah and we all know it. I can feel it in my bones. We gotta keep our eyes open. We may run across him yet, in a restaurant, or a bar, or worse still, in an alley where he could set up an ambush. I always heard that NOPD knows how to take care of business, but we're from Texas, and we might not get home cookin'. Know what I mean? We don't know how they'd react if we had to punch Joe's ticket, or any other outlaw's ticket for that matter."

Jarvis said, "Probably give us a medal. Listen, I got an idea. When we head back to the hotel, what if I break off and walk over where we got our vehicles parked? I'll act like I'm getting something out of my car. Maybe I'll be able to tell if someone is watching your truck. After all, I'm parked right next to you. If someone's watching, it might spark some interest."

Archie replied, "That's an outstanding idea. Let's put this to rest, just for a moment. Now that it's past six o'clock, anyone thought about supper yet? I'm starved. Barlow, you or Sarah got any restaurants scribbled in your little notebook we should consider?"

Sarah replied, "I was thinking about the Court of Two Sisters. It's on Royal Street. We just passed it. In the event that we don't stay a third night, or if this winds up being my last meal on Earth, I'd really like to eat there. It's supposed to be fabulous."

Jarvis replied, "Sarah, if this is going to be your last meal, it will be ours, too. None of us will let them grab you, especially Barlow. I'm famished, too. Sorry, but I couldn't make myself choke down that half muffuletta at lunch. Too many of them dern green olives! Thought I scraped them all off, but little bitty pieces of them were hidden everywhere."

Their timing for supper was perfect. They had no wait. Walked right in and got a table. The menu was extensive and full of unusual items that concerned them all, but Sarah, in particular, pretended otherwise. After all, this was her idea. They began with a carafe of the house red while they studied the menu. After the conversation they had just had, everyone needed an adult libation, but nobody was in the frame of mind to dull his wits or his reflexes tonight. They all were in a state of undeclared war with Joe Rag and his confederates.

They decided to challenge their palettes with a couple of hors d'oeuvres to share. Archie selected grilled alligator sausage and Sarah selected corn-fried Louisiana oysters. Barlow was appalled at both selections, but he didn't see anything else that looked more appetizing. Nevertheless, he kept his thoughts to himself. This was very important to Sarah, and the guys were all being good sports.

When they were served, Barlow ate two small pieces of gator sausage. The meat was pink and chewy, just like a rubber ball. It was impossible to fully masticate. He finally swallowed them whole, relying on his gastric system to break them down into a digestible format. Good thing he didn't wear dentures. On the other hand, the oysters were pretty darn good. He could have been a pig, but he checked himself. Way to go, Sarah!

Next, they were served their salads. Everyone but Jarvis selected the Court of Two Sisters dinner salad. Basically, it was a bed of weeds, bitter leafy things that a cow might chew on and turn into a cud, otherwise described on the menu as seasonal greens, which were covered with sliced boiled eggs, tasso (which turned out to be thin, salty ham slices), and pecans, with a Creole French dressing. Barlow was surprised. It was good, but would have been better served on a bed of real lettuce, like iceberg. Jarvis played it safe and ordered the lettuce wedge with thousand island dressing. He was the real winner.

By now the carafe was empty and they ordered another. So much for willpower. Nevertheless, if they got into a gunfight tonight, it would still be skill and hours of practice pitted against blind rage and raw, brute force.

Next were the entrées. Sarah had the Louisiana crabmeat au gratin. Archie had the corn fried des, otherwise described as catfish and crabmeat. Jarvis had the shrimp and grits, which was served with the spicy andouille sausage. Barlow selected the roasted duck, which had a sweet jalapeño cornbread. The sauce was made from a cane syrup glaze. They were all well satisfied with their selections, and ate every morsel.

The best is always saved for last. Sarah had crème brûlée; Jarvis selected pecan pie à la mode; Archie had Bananas Foster; and Barlow selected bread pudding with a whiskey sauce. This was the finest meal any of them had ever eaten, period, even considering the weeds. They were all well sated when they departed.

On the walk back, Sarah and Barlow took a direct route to the hotel and waited for Archie and Jarvis to meet them in the lobby. In the interim, they ordered a nightcap. Barlow had a Makers Mark and Sarah had an Irish cream.

Archie walked to the parking lot and found a secluded spot to watch where their cars were parked.

Jarvis waited about ten minutes for Archie to set up. Then he walked to his car and took his old, sweet time time, eventually retrieving a small gun cleaning kit.

Both of them watched for persons of interest. What they both noticed was a white, teenage boy on a bicycle who entered the parking lot from across the street, cut through the row Jarvis and Barlow were parked in, and departed out the back exit. He pedaled right behind Jarvis' and Barlow's vehicles while Jarvis was rooting around in his trunk. The youth glanced at Jarvis, but nothing more. The thing was, it was out of his way to ride down the aisle where they were parked. Completely unnecessary.

So this was the lookout tonight. Game on.

Jarvis and Archie made their ways back to the hotel, double checking along the way to make sure the kid wasn't following, nor anyone else. They met Sarah and Barlow in the hotel bar. Jarvis ordered a draft Jax Beer. Archie opted for a gin and tonic.

They discussed the juvenile lookout. Archie and Jarvis waited for Sarah, in particular, to mull it over. After all, it was her honeymoon which had been sabotaged by an ass wipe they both hoped to erase from the gene pool. They knew it was a tough decision.

After a second round of drinks, Sarah looked in the eyes of all three of her protectors, and gave them an appreciative smile. She said, "You all are the best. I'm indebted to you for everything you've done to allow us to enjoy this trip unmolested. I think it's time to go home. Better if we face our demons on our own soil in Texas. My folks, and Sheriff Sol would feel better if we did. Barlow and I can come to New Orleans another time, like in the winter when it isn't so hot and muggy, but definitely not during Mardi Gras, to see the things we didn't get to see on this trip. On our way back home, maybe we could stop at the YO Hotel in Kerrville. It's on a big old ranch where they have all kinds of exotic game people pay big money to go hunt. I think you fellas would enjoy it."

Archie said, "Girl, you are wise beyond your years. I think that's a great idea. What do you all think?"

Jarvis replied, "I've been to the YO. You'll love it. Be prepared to eat the best steak you've ever had. The hotel is like a museum of stuffed game animals and cowboy artifacts. In fact, I'm pretty sure I saw some Peacemakers there on display that are at least twenty years newer than Archie's."

"Watch yourself, young fella. A disparaging remark like that regarding the pistol that damn near every Texas Ranger carried from 1873, until mebbe 1963, could get the smartass who said it run off from the Rangers, and rightly so."

"Touché. I know it must be a touchy subject for an old coot, who probably couldn't handle the modern Colt .45 like me and a bunch of the younger Rangers are now carrying."

"Modern, my ass! They don't call it the Model 1911 for nothin'. We had them during the Great War, when you wasn't even a gleam in your daddy's eye. I had one. No complaints, except my Peacemaker fires a bigger ball that goes a lot farther with greater accuracy. I realize it don't hold as many bullets, and it's a might slower to reload, but if ya hit what ya aim at the first time, ya don't have to waste ammo tryin' again and again like a peckerwood."

Barlow interrupted, "Hey, Captain Frank Hamer and Marshal Wyatt Earp, you both have history on your side! Both of your preferred sidearms have lived up to their reputations time and again. Maybe we can set up a contest between you two pistoleros when we get back to Texas. What about tomorrow? How do you all want to handle our strategic withdrawal?"

Archie replied, "Spoken like a true rifleman. What I think is this. We come down and eat a real cowboy breakfast just as soon as they open up at six o'clock. Then I go out to the parking lot after we're done and get my truck. Drive it right up here to the front door. Sarah, you and Barlow load up and take off. Get on Canal and turn right and drive to the overpass where the new interstate, I-10, is. Pull over on the right side of the road just before the ramp. It's probably not more'n a mile. Once you've gone, Jarvis and I will walk out together. I'll drive your truck and Jarvis will be my wingman. He'll cover my ass if need be.

"We'll meet you at the interstate. When you see us up behind you, pull on out. We'll follow. We'll take I-10 as far as it goes. If it peters out, we'll jump on US 90. If we make a clean getaway, we'll switch trucks the first pit stop we make. Also, after we make the stop, I'll lead and Jarvis will take trail. Just make sure you don't lose sight of us. If we do get separated, we will meet in Lafayette in the parking lot of the sheriff's office, wherever that is. Both the interstate and US 90 go to Lafayette. That's why I picked it. Study your roadmap before we saddle up tomorrow. Everyone good with this?"

Jarvis said, "Sounds good to me."

"Us, too. Six o'clock it is. Sarah and I both bid you adieu."

# CHAPTER 38

## Sunday, June 13, 1971
## Pay Dirt

It was between three-thirty and four o'clock by the time Joe and Grady and their new associates from the Crescent City Jacks set up in the French Quarter. Executive management, consisting of Joe, Grady, and Bruno the Vampire, swilled semi-cool, draft Dixie beers and made salacious comments to the strippers at Poppy's Candy Store, who got paid handsomely in tips by egging it on with their strip teases and maybe by making a date on the side. In the meantime, Snakebelly, Sylvester the Cat, and the Hunchback did the grunt work and took up surveillance posts in the hot sun.

Snakebelly got the funnest job. He rode his chopper up and down the Quarter, being as cool as he knew how to be, looking for either Barlow's truck or young Texas lovers who could be Barlow and Sarah. Sylvester the Cat trolled the French Market, also a pretty good job because the market was under a roof. The Hunchback drew the short end of the stick because he got an assignment without much shade. He was in Jackson Square, hoping to locate the lovers, but really, all he did was gross out the small-town, middle-America, Mr. and Mrs. Beaver Cleaver type tourists who saw or smelled him. The Hunchback was truly hoping to hit pay dirt because he was gross and he knew it. The only way any woman would have anything to do with him was if he took her by force. He'd done that more than once, but it was a real hard way to get laid. He knew karma was a bitch. He always feared some type of painful retribution, so he only preyed on the weakest women who didn't have a big brother or a pimp.

Besides the dynamic trio, Joe hired two teenagers named Rodent and Cathead, both of whom had bicycles, which were undoubtedly ripped off from some unfortunate, smaller kids. Joe paid them ten bucks each, in advance, to canvass the parking lots, with a promise of ten more if they found Barlow's truck.

By six o'clock, all the foot soldiers had had all the fun with this silly reindeer game that they could endure. None of the dynamic trio had seen anyone who resembled their individual interpretations of what a young, Texas cowboy couple would look like. Snakebelly had been too busy trying to look like Peter Fonda in Easy Rider to actually scout the parking lots. All three of the outlaws were sweltering, disgruntled, and thirsty. One by one, they each beat feet to Poppy's Candy Store to report failure. Not Rodent and Cathead, though. They actually did their jobs and they did them well.

Rodent located Barlow's truck where it was parked in a lot especially contracted for by the Bienville House. He took up a perch in the shade near a decrepit building undergoing renovation and waited for Cathead to cruise by. When Cathead eventually did show up, Rodent signaled for him to come over. He pointed out Barlow's truck and told Cathead to ride to the bar and fetch Joe so they could both earn their ten-dollar rewards. Cathead was all over this like white on rice.

Fifteen minutes later, management arrived and decided that, yes, this has to be the truck. Joe ponied up the reward, plus he offered the teenagers another ten bucks each, just to sit on the truck until he and Grady relieved them around midnight. The street urchins jumped at the offer. This was the first time either of them had earned thirty bucks in a single day for doing honest work. Besides, it was easy. No heavy lifting.

Joe needed the time to return to the clubhouse so they could pick up their gear. Also, he needed to acquire some rope, duct tape, and other miscellaneous items, such as non-perishable foodstuffs, beverages, etc., in the event they were forced to follow the prick and his woman out of town. Better yet, for when they captured them and holed up for a few days, making them bleed and suffer. Joe didn't want to be completely dependent upon the Jacks. Now, he wished they had stolen a van instead of a pickup. He suddenly realized that he was totally dependent on the Jacks to transport their prey, unless he or Grady could jack a van before midnight.

Joe worried for naught. The Jacks had everything he needed, except for the victuals. They loaned him a white, nondescript, 1964, Ford Econoline panel van, in which the only windows, other than those in the cab, were in the two back doors, and both of those windows had curtains. The van had a rack on the top with two ladders tied on, disguising it as a work truck instead of the rolling meth dispensary that it actually was. The Jacks also had yards of rope and duct tape which they readily provided. Joe still had Grady throw their gear into the van on the off chance that they wound up doing the snatch someplace other than in New Orleans.

Bruno had some undisclosed business that he and several of his Jacks needed to transact. He wished Joe happy hunting and said he and a couple of his boys would meet them in the parking lot in the morning.

Everything was falling into place. Joe and Grady departed the clubhouse about eight o'clock in the borrowed van. They bought the grub, to include four cases of Jax beer, which they iced down in a huge, borrowed, 160-quart fishing cooler. Then they ate at a greasy spoon on Airline Highway called Thibidaux's Cajun Cooking and loaded up on étouffée, cracklings, and cold Jax.

Time passed quickly. It was nearly eleven o'clock. They arrived way early at the Bienville parking lot. They lucked into a great surveillance spot a row behind and four cars down from Barlow's truck. Then they relieved the Rodent and Cathead from duty, after asking them to come back in the morning.

The adrenaline was flowing. They could smell victory. Joe could hardly contain himself. Grady mostly wanted it to be over with so he could go back to Mexico and resume his life as paid muscle for the Coahuila cartel. He had so much more freedom to operate in Mexico than in the U.S., especially with his cartel connections and the poorly paid and corrupt police. Too bad Joe was so consumed with revenge and hatred. He could do very well for himself in Mexico, getting paid to convince people who were crossways with the cartel, the error of, sometimes the fatal error of, their ways. The only problem with this pipe dream, was Joe hated greasers and thus, would not survive for very long in Mexico with his bad attitude.

By midnight, Joe and Grady decided to while away their time by draining a few of the brewskis down their gullets. The beers were ice cold and glided down their parched throats like a fat kid on a sled on a steep, snowy hill. A few morphed into a lot. All the while, they carried on a conversation which was less inhibited than any they had had since meeting in Conroe.

Joe eventually asked, "Whatever become of Screech? I really liked him."

Gravy said, "Not sure, exactly. He wasn't the same after the Hairlip and Wingnut picked him up in Quayle County after your little dust up. A few days after he got back, he cleaned out his secret stash and packed up all his shit. He said he was done outlawin'. Jaybird took him to his ex-old lady's apartment and dropped him off."

"You don't mean that skinny little bitch named Polly Something-or-Other? The one who could suck the chrome off of a bumper hitch."

"That's the one. Her name was Polly Warnock before they got married. She's a redhead. Kinda fixy. Worked as a beautician. And you're right. She was a natural born head job artist. Made really good money at it, too. They had a kid she named Dallas, 'cause that's where Polly claimed she was conceived in the backseat of her daddy-in-law's DeSoto Firesweep station wagon at a drive-in theater while they was supposed to be watchin' James Bond whip the Russians in 'From Russia with Love' instead of fucking. Screech probably shoulda stuck with the blow jobs. That way he wouldn't have become a daddy."

"How you know all this?"

"Screech told me a long time ago. Anyway, Jaybird dropped him off, but decided to wait in case Screech stepped into a big pile of shit and needed to be dragged outta there before the cops showed up and pissed all over his parade.

"Jaybird said that Screech told Polly he was quittin' the outlaw business. Said he was movin' to Las Vegas, where he could get a fresh start. Claimed he already had a job lined up as a mechanic in a fancy, custom bike shop. Said the owner and him was friends. Anyway, he asked Polly if she and Dallas wanted to go, too. Said things would be different this time. Said he was straight and that he learned his lesson.

"She asked, 'How we gettin' there, hotshot?' Said she didn't have enough money to eat at McDonalds, even if they accepted S&H Green Stamps as payment. Screech said he had enough money to buy bus tickets and cover their needs for a month, until he could start drawin' a paycheck.

"She told him to show her the money. He pulled out a thick wad of bills and fanned it out like a deck of cards. She reached in and pulled out about a half dozen twenties and stuffed 'em in her bra. Said that was her gettin' back home money in case he welshed on his promise. Then she asked if Jaybird could give 'em a ride to the Greyhound Bus Station. He said he could and she said for him to hold on, that she'd be packed in a jiffy.

"That was that. Jaybird dropped 'em off. About a month later, he got a letter from Screech. Return address was in Henderson, Nevada. Screech said they rented a little house. Polly was workin' in a beauty shop and he was makin' four dollars an hour doin' engine work on custom Harleys. Dallas was in the second grade and doin' well. He sent Jaybird twenty bucks for haulin' them around. That's the last I heard. Oh, yeah. I forgot. He said they started goin' regular like to the Catholic Church. That he was thinkin' about gettin' saved."

"Blow the man down! I never woulda thunk that of old Screech. He always was the best wrench in our club. Guess it wouldn't do no good to look him up. He's for sure a goner now. Well, well . . . ."

The conversation lapsed for a very long time. They continued to get hammered. Finally, Grady asked, "What about you, Joe? What're your plans after this is all over?"

"Not sure yet. You know I can't hide out in Mexico. I hate

greasers. End of statement.

"Another thing. I probably won't make it 'til the end of the year, unless I go to someplace like New Hampshire or Key West and I couldn't tolerate no place like that. I'm plannin' to get me a scooter. Think I'll cruise the open road in any part of Texas that ain't so humid, like Houston or San Antonio. I'll ride free, long as I can, until the law catches up with me. We'll eventually tangle assholes and I might win for awhile, but one day I won't. I know that. I just want the sun and the wind in my face for as long as it'll last. I've made my peace with it."

"You could go do that now. What you've got planned, might put you back in the limelight with the fuzz. Could shorten your time livin' the dream."

"Nope. That punk railroaded me, plus he's the reason why I have this bum arm. I can't do no forty more years in the joint. That's why I busted out. Simple as that. Before I give up the ghost, I'm payin' that asshole back in Spades. Then, me and him will be even. But, if by some quirk of nature, before I rub him out, someone gets the best of me and bumps me off, so be it. That's how the cookie crumbles. I been a dead man walking since the day I broke outta Huntsville.

"Thing is, I was already dead inside my soul while I was in the joint. I was breathin' air, but I was obliged to do whatever the Man told me to do, when he told me to do it, and how he told me to do it.

"'Eat shit, convict!'

"'Yassa, Boss. Shakin' it here, Boss.'

"'Assume the position, yardbird.'

"'Yassa, Cap.'

"No more. Never, ever again! I'll die, but I'll take as many with me as I can before I go."

Tick tock.

Time passed. It got later. Much later. The empty beer bottles kept piling up. They pissed on the tires of the cars parked on either side of them several times. What a hoot! Who gives a shit? Not them.

Conversation lagged. Then it stopped altogether.

It began to rain and the wind began to bluster. About four o'clock they both drifted off to sleep in a drunken stupor. They forgot why they were parked there in the first place. They never noticed the storm.

Tick tock.

# CHAPTER 39

## Monday, June 14, 1971
## Leaving New Orleans Gets Dicey

Barlow and Sarah were up with the chickens at five o'clock. Both had lain awake for awhile. It was still dark outside and it wasn't getting any lighter. A semi-tropical thunderstorm, with lightning and thunder and torrential rainfall had trumped dawn and forced day to remain in darkness. The sounds of heavy field artillery, coupled with the staccato and blinding flashes, which were charged with thousands of volts of electricity, reminded everyone of the omnipotence of God and the power of His wrath.

Barlow pontificated, "Mother Nature is celebrating the birthday of the United States Army with these bursts of celestial cannonry."

Sarah responded, "Spoken like a true artilleryman. It's also Flag Day, my patriotic veteran."

"I knew that."

"No you didn't! You're making that up."

"Well, maybe I am. You need to consider this, though. If it wasn't for the Army, especially the field artillery, plus the Navy and all the other branches of the service, our flag would not be flying free today."

"True. Speaking of flags, look at your flagpole. It's standing at attention. I better salute."

"And why shouldn't it? We're still on our honeymoon, if you

haven't forgotten, and you are a heavenly body to behold in your nudies. You're wearing my absolute favorite outfit."

"Guess I'll have to take care of that before we shower, so you won't embarrass yourself when we go downstairs and meet the others."

"You think I'm embarrassed about this? Take a harder look."

"Hard, huh? Shut up. You're wasting time. Show me what you got, Mr. Artilleryman."

"I got enough to put a smile on your face that'll last all day."

"Well, get to it then. Cock your cannon, Mr. Artilleryman. Let's see whatcha got."

When they were done, it looked like an escaped Bengal tiger, maybe the one named Mike at Louisiana State University, had torn up the bed and the sheets. They had to scramble to meet Archie and Jarvis in the dining room on time.

This morning's breakfast consisted of eggs Benedict, smoked sausage links, freshly squeezed grapefruit juice, cantaloupe slices sprinkled with shredded coconut, a solitary strawberry, and a carafe full of Community Coffee with chicory. They certainly don't serve this at the Waffle House!

Archie asked, "Everybody clear on the drill today? The weather could very well complicate things. I hope this ain't the beginnings of a hurricane. You all remember Hurricane Camille two years ago, what tore the whole Gulf Coast to ribbons, don't ya? We don't wanna get trapped here. I ain't got any gills, and neither do any of you."

All three nodded in the affirmative, because they were gobbling down groceries as fast as they could and didn't want to pause to speak. Archie left most of his breakfast untouched and was already done. Apparently, he would have preferred something titillating like Quaker Oats or Shredded Wheat.

"All right, then. Hurry up. Soon as you're done, grab your gear, and let's go. You all meet me under the awning. I'll pull my truck up."

None of them thought to bring their slickers with them, so they were all going to get soaked. Might as well have stayed in their birthday suits, for all the good clothes would do this morning. Archie held onto his Stetson, and trotted off into the blinding rain, headed for the parking lot.

As he scurried down his aisle, he noticed two assholes standing on either side of a white van pissing on the cars parked next to them. He got a good look at the first asshole, who was built like a hairy refrigerator. Couldn't recall seeing him before, at least initially. He only got a glimpse of the other one. Nothing registered until after he backed out and took a closer look. He and Joseph P. Schitt made eye contact and locked into a joint death stare, which shouldn't have, but did take them both by surprise, such that it jolted them both all the way down to their toes. Archie shifted to second gear and sped away, trying his best to hold down the hive of angry honey bees buzzing in his stomach, which he would never, ever, confess to anyone.

Joe would have pissed himself, but his bladder was already dry. He shrieked, "Shoot that motherfucker!"

Grady yelled, "What? I can't hear you!"

"It's him!"

"Who, the kid? That wasn't him. Just an old man."

"Not the kid, dipshit! The other cop who helped bust my arm! Deputy Willis! You let him get away! Hurry up! We gotta follow him!"

"Now who's the dipshit? We follow him, we miss the kid

coming to get his truck!"

"Fuck! Get in the van! Got your gun handy?"

"I will in a minute, if you let me dry off, and get it out of the glovebox. I swear, Joe, sometimes you are such an imbecile! Where's your gun? Why didn't you use it?"

"I got it now! It was under the seat. I can't believe I saw that piece of shit and didn't have my gun!"

"Did he make you?"

"Damn right he did! My guess is, he didn't have his gun handy either or he woulda shot."

"Well, he's probably with the kid. Sit tight, and see what develops. The kid's gotta come this way to get his truck."

"By God, he better, or I'm liable to shoot the next person who comes by out of sheer frustration! Where are them damn street urchins when ya need 'em?"

"Joe, would you stand out in this monsoon for ten bucks? If so, you're dumber than I thought."

"Well, we ain't got nobody to tail that asshole! If we do it, we gotta leave the truck."

"Exercise a little patience, would ya? Trust me. He's gotta have his truck. He'll be here. I promise."

In the meantime, Archie pulled up under the awning at the hotel. He said, "I just saw Joe Schitt and that huge outlaw with him. They got a white Ford van with two ladders in a rack on top. They saw me, too. Bastards were taking a leak on cars next to the van. I'm surprised they didn't get it together and follow me over here. We don't have much time. Let's put all our gear in the back of my truck. I'm pretty sure it'll stay dry, double wrapped in this canvas duck.

"Jarvis, when we leave to get the other vehicles, you might

want to draw that very modern, Government Model Colt ahead of time. We may be throwin' lead before we can saddle up. That's why we're puttin' all our gear in this truck, so our hands will be free."

Barlow said, "Archie, Sarah and I can't just drive off and leave you all to fight our battle!"

Archie replied, "Barlow, we already worked this out. Stick to the plan!"

"No! Sarah's gonna drive. I'm riding shotgun. Loan me yours. I know it's in here. I'd use my .30-30, but it's in my truck. We'll give you all a minute to get a head start. Then we'll drive on the street running along the parking lot, and stop. If we hear shots fired, we're comin' in hot!"

Jarvis said, "Good idea, Arch. Give him the shotgun. We may need the help."

"Well, all right then. Just don't get my truck all shot up. The shotgun's behind the seat. It's loaded but you'll need to chamber a round. They're all double-aught buck."

"Thank you. Try not to let those assholes perforate Jade, either."

"I'll do my best. Once we're all behind the wheel, just play follow the leader, no matter who's out front. We'll sort things out down the road. We all go together or we all stay here together, except going is better than staying. Got it?"

It didn't take much time to stow their gear. Archie and Jarvis unholstered their hardware, and held it down along their right legs. The rain was still coming down in buckets. Archie knew exactly which van he was looking for and where it was parked. They were still nearly twenty yards away when he put a round through the right rear tire. Grady, the refrigerator-sized outlaw, started to open the passenger door. Archie sent another round through his window, shattering the glass, and the door slammed shut.

They kept walking. Briskly. When they were behind the van, Jarvis sent a round through one of the back windows. The round went all the way through the van and out the windshield. Nobody got hurt, but it was another wake up call. Simultaneously, Archie shot the left rear tire. This van wasn't going anywhere for awhile.

Jarvis yelled, "Start the truck. I'll hold 'em here until you back out!"

Archie started to object, but his own pickup came squealing around the corner. Barlow was hanging out the passenger window. The barrel of the shotgun was sticking out in the rain. He shouted, "Come on guys, let's go!"

Grady was hugging the underside of the dashboard as far as he could get, but Joe was not. He was going to kill these assholes! He swung his door open wide, and as soon as he did, Barlow let loose with a load of buckshot. The door paneling and window were perforated and shattered, respectively. Not only that, Joe took a ball through his wrist. He snatched his arm back into the van, screaming, "Ahhhh!"

Barlow stepped out of the truck into the pounding rain and yelled, "Come on! We got these bastards! I'll kill 'em both!"

Jarvis yelled back. "Get back in the truck and let's go! This ain't our town! We'll settle this back in Texas!

Archie shouted, "Barlow, follow the plan! Now!"

Sarah pleaded, "Come on, Barlow! Please! Let's go!"

Reluctantly, Barlow got back in the truck and slammed the door shut. He had blood in his eye, and Sarah saw it. It frightened the heck out of her. She understood in a flash the transformation that made him so deadly in a fight.

It devastated Barlow's soul to run, but run he did, along with the rest.

Sarah pulled in behind Arch. Jarvis pulled in behind Sarah. Surprisingly, after all the fireworks and adrenaline, Archie took it slow, but he was wise to do so. The rain was still pouring out of the sky in sheets. They were all sopping wet. They should've brought an ark. Not only that, it was still dark, like dusk, not morn. Both their headlamps and their windshield wipers were losing the battle to enhance vision. The windows were all fogged up and the defroster was virtually useless. They were driving half-blind due to fogged-up windows, sliding precariously close to parked cars, and splashing rooster tails of rainwater three-feet high in the air on potholed streets filled with standing water because the gutters were overwhelmed.

They crept onto I-10 and headed west. They were going home. Just like that, the long anticipated confrontation was over, only it wasn't. Not even close. Barlow knew he had the winning hand against those sidewinders, and he wanted to finish it conclusively, then and there. He knew they would regret it later because he didn't. Joe Schitt would never stop until one of them was dead. The miles ticked away. Slowly.

Nobody but the antagonists heard or saw the lopsided, unfinished, completely inconclusive, gunfight. The thunder covered up the sound of gunfire. Nobody else had ventured outside in the monsoon. No cops. Not even a duck. At least there was that.

Joe was vibratingly furious. His wrist hurt like Hell. The nerve endings of his shattered bone were throbbing in revolt. He was holding it tight to stop the bleeding. Grady was rooting around for something to make into a bandage. Joe needed something strong for pain. They never even got off a shot! Not one! Those assholes had been in complete control and very easily could have finished them off. Too bad for them they didn't. Joe knew exactly where they were going. He was going there, too. Payback's a bitch.

Grady was thankful to be alive. He knew that by all rights, they should both be dead. He just wanted to get back to Acuña. Now what? Bruno's van was full of bullet holes. The two rear tires were shot flat. All they could do was wait for Bruno and company to show up. He hoped the Jacks had a friendly doctor for Joe's sake. It was his left wrist, too. That boy cop had already maimed Joe's right arm. Now the poor bastard couldn't jack off with either arm. A fate worse than death, unless your pecker was shot off, too. That would really be worse than death. He thought to himself. Joe's snakebit, but he ain't got that figured out yet.

What a day, and it was only seven o'clock!

# CHAPTER 40

## Monday, June 14, 1971
## A Perilous Drive

Archie and party stayed on I-10 to Metairie, where they stopped at a Gulf gas station to regroup. It was still raining in torrents and the wind was still blowing in gale force, but they needed to powwow. Even more importantly, Archie was jonesing for coffee.

While they refueled, Archie spoke with the proprietor, an ancient, withered, bald headed coonass in bib overalls with a missing forefinger on his left hand, regarding the route out of Louisiana. Should they stay on I-10 as far as it would go, or should they take US 61, otherwise known as Airline Highway, to Baton Rouge? What about taking US 90 to Lafayette?

The proprietor suggested US 61. He said I-10 was normally quicker, but it traversed a swamp for about twenty miles and the water was rising. Besides that, he knew there were areas which had been under construction. He didn't know the status. He recommended taking US 61 to Baton Rouge, where they could pick up US 190, the northern route, all the way to US 171, where they could pick up LA 12 to Beaumont, Texas. If they took US 90, the southern route, they would likely be forced to turn back due to flooding.

Archie passed this information along to the group. They unanimously agreed that the northern route would be best. Now they were all determined to get back to Texas as quickly as possible. Archie said once they arrived at Beaumont, they would decide whether to spend the night or continue on. He estimated the distance at three hundred miles, which they could normally drive in six or seven hours; however, unless the storm abated, it would likely take a few more.

Barlow was glad to return to Jade, just as Archie was glad to return to his longhorn beast. The first thing Barlow did, was to chamber a round in his .30-30, place it on half-cock, and stand it on the floorboard between him and Sarah. Not taking chances anymore. A man has a God-given right to protect his family and himself, whether he is in Louisiana or Texas! Barlow was on the warpath and would be deterred no more.

Neither Archie nor Jarvis blamed him. They both knew this wasn't over. It's just that, having more experience in law enforcement, they knew Texas authorities were on their side and would be relieved actually, if Joe Schitt were killed in a gunfight with the cops. They couldn't be certain of that in New Orleans. There was a hint of corruption about the way things were done in NOLA, and it wasn't worth the risk that an official might be on the take and work against them.

It was a long, soggy, miserable drive. They finally arrived at six-thirty. They ate supper at Woodrow's Barbeque House. It was adequate, but uninspiring. Not much conversation at supper. At least the beer was ice cold.

They found lodging at the Texas Motor Lodge. 1950s quaint. They were all tired and a little bummed out. At least they had driven out of the rain. Now it was just steamy.

That night, while they were cuddled up in bed, Sarah told Barlow what she had been thinking about all day. "Barlow, I was really scared this morning."

"I was, too."

"I wasn't scared that they would hurt me. I was scared about what you were gonna do to them. I've never seen you so . . . . enraged. If left to your own devices, you might have emptied that shotgun into them, even after they were dead. You know. Like beating a dead horse. You were on a rampage."

"I know. That's what fear does to me. That's how I stay alive. I get focused, and don't stop until all the bad guys are completely obliterated. It's instinctive. I don't think about it. I just go until the gettin's done. I should've killed those guys. Now we both gotta look over our shoulders until it's done. You know they're still comin' for us. What if they ambush you when you're all alone? I can't make it without you. Blowing them into itty bitty pieces would not be anywhere near enough. It would never bring you back."

"That's how I feel about you. Once we get back to Mosby, we'll be all alone. Everyone will give us moral support, but in the end, I know it will be just you and me. I'm afraid to go back."

"I know. Me, too. What scares me the most is that I can't protect you when either of us is at work. You have to keep your eyes wide open and carry that .25 with you everywhere you go. You can never leave it behind. And if they attack you or try to grab you, or even if they do grab you, you gotta pull that gun and try to shoot them in the heart or the gut. You gotta keep on pulling the trigger until you're empty. You gotta get mean, just like me, to survive. Also means you gotta wear a skirt or a dress unless you're on horseback. Easier for you to hide the gun, and to get to it in an emergency."

"Barlow, I'm sorry I told you to get in the truck. I was just so scared. Maybe we'll get lucky and see 'em on the road before we get home. At least, we'd have some help."

"Sarah, it's highly unlikely we'll see them again until we're in Mosby. However, I'm not letting that .30-30 get more'n a couple of feet outta reach, just in case."

"Hold me until I fall asleep."

"I will."

He thought, hopefully tomorrow will be a better day than today. He prayed for it. Eventually, he drifted off to sleep, too.

# CHAPTER 41

Monday, June 14, 1971
Bailed Out by the Jacks

It was eight o'clock or a little after when Bruno the Vampire and his segundo, Max Arce, pulled up in a fire engine red, 1963, Cadillac Sedan de Ville Park Avenue. Normally, Joe would have been green with envy, but his wrist was taking up nearly all of his attention. Besides, it was dark and the rain was still coming down in buckets.

Bruno rolled down the window a crack. "What the fuck happened here? My van's a mess! Show me the dead bodies who done this."

Grady, who was still sitting in the passenger seat in the rain, didn't have a window to roll down because it had been shot out. He replied, "They sneaked up on us early this morning. We was ambushed. They shot Joe in the wrist. They got away. We'll pay for the damages. You all got a friendly doctor? Joe's in a lot of pain and he can't afford questions by the cops. Can you help him out?"

"Yeah, grab your stuff and get in the back. I'll get Leo and Stumpy to bring the wrecker to tow the van back to our shop. What was ya doin'? Sleepin' it off?"

"Something like that."

Bruno drove them to a seedy brick building somewhere on Carrollton Avenue. Eventually, they were buzzed in. They walked up a flight of stairs and then down a dark hallway to an office where Dr. Jekyll, at least it looked like him, was standing in the doorway in a soiled and wrinkled white lab coat. He didn't look that clean himself, but beggars can't be choosers. He stood about six-feet, two-inches tall, very thin, weighed about a buck forty, had stringy black, greasy hair, long bony fingers with untrimmed, dirty nails, hollow eye sockets, looked like a heroin addict. He was smoking some kind of brown, rank smelling cigarette. Smelled like it came from the Soviet Union, or some other garden spot. Probably made from cabbage leaves mixed with mouse droppings. Dr. Jekyll greeted Bruno, and invited them into his dingy, spartan, waiting room.

"I wasn't expecting any patients this morning. I was just stepping out to breakfast. What do we have here?"

Bruno said, "Some cocksucker shot my friend in his wrist. Can you fix it?"

"Most assuredly. Can your friend pay? Off hand, no pun intended, I'd say it would cost five hundred bucks, unless we run into complications."

Grady responded, "I can pay."

"Excellent! Why don't you all have a seat here in the waiting room while your friend and I go back to the surgery?"

After Dr. Jekyll led Joe into his lair, Grady took a seat. He looked at the magazines on the end table for something to while away the time. He found what he was looking for in spades. Apparently, Dr. Jekyll was a different kind of doctor, or perhaps few of his patients ever learned to read. All his magazines were studies on the female anatomy, with substantially more photos than words. He had Playboy, Penthouse, Club, and a plethora of glossy, porn magazines from Europe and Asia, which made the American magazines look tame. Knowing how to read was really quite unnecessary.

The first thing Dr. Jekyll did after he got Joe situated was to give him a shot of morphine. Joe didn't pass out, but he may as well have. He entered *The Twilight Zone* all by himself. Rod Serling wasn't there. Woozy and warm with no pain. Not a worry in the world. Bliss.

The good doctor got down to business and scrubbed the wound clean. First thing he observed was that the bullet had gone clean through. That helped.

He didn't have an x-ray machine, but he didn't really need one for this injury. He saw where the radial bone was fractured and noted that the bullet had chipped away a small piece of it. No biggie. The bone would still knit back together, but it would probably never be as good as new. He set the bone, stitched the skin back together, and put a plaster cast on it.

Under the circumstances, this patient was extremely lucky. Normally, he would want the patient to return in six weeks, so he could see how he was doing, make sure there was no infection, and to remove the cast. He knew, however, that he would never see this patient again. He was obviously on the run from the law or something worse. Dr. J. wrote a prescription for fifty Percocets with one refill. He couldn't complete it until someone provided a patient name. Then he helped Joe up on his feet and out of the surgery into the waiting room.

He said, "This will be five hundred dollars."

Grady got up and peeled off ten fifties.

"Thank you. He's heavily sedated on morphine right now. It will wear off in a couple of hours. Then the pain will come back with a vengeance. I've written a prescription for fifty painkillers with one refill. What name should I list it in? He will have to have identification to pick up the medicine."

Grady asked, "Doc, don't you have some pills we could buy from you here?"

"I'm afraid not. In this neighborhood, I would be robbed every other day if I kept medicine on hand. I've already had several break-ins, but fortunately, there was nothing in my clinic for the dopers to steal. I store what little morphine I keep on hand where no one would ever find it."

"Write the prescription in the name Grady Triplett."

"Grady Triplett it is. I suggest you fill this as soon as you can. Like I said, the morphine will wear off in a couple of hours."

"Thanks, Doc."

"Thank you."

They stopped by a pharmacy and filled the prescription on their way back to the clubhouse. Joe was still out of it, so now the burden of what to do, and where to go, and how to pay for it, was all Grady's. He had fronted Joe five hundred bucks the day they met. He paid Joe's doctor bill. Now, he had to pony up for the damage done to the van. In addition, he'd already spent more than a hundred bucks on the trip for gas and meals and lodging. He had less than five hundred bucks left in his pocket. Being Joe's friend was an expensive, one-way operation.

Bruno asked, "You all gonna call it quits and go back home?"

Grady said, "I'd love to, but then I'd have to kill Joe. He just doesn't know when to quit. He can't even put it off long enough to heal. I got a bad feeling about this, but I owe him. Once this is over, me and him are quits. Right now, I don't even care if he reimburses me for what I've already shelled out for this fucking boondoggle. Speaking of costs, what do we owe for the damages to the van?"

"Gimme two hundred, and we'll call it even."

Grady peeled off four more fifties. "Thanks, Bruno. Maybe our paths will cross again. Guess I'll load up the pickup, and we'll be on our way. Wish this fuckin' rain would stop."

"Not so fast. You don't wanna return the way you come. Take 61 to Baton Rouge and jump on US 190. You can get to Beaumont from there. It's out of your way, but it'll save time because I-10 and US 90 will likely be flooded. Also, I'm sendin' Tee Beau and Junior with you all, in that old, faded green Plymouth over there. The trunk's big enough to hold two bodies."

"What year is that car, anyway? It looks all wore out."

"It's a '61. It's supposed to look all wore out, but it ain't. It ain't got a speck of rust on it nowhere. Runs like a gazelle. It'll still be runnin' when that Ford pickup you're drivin' is rusting away in some salvage yard. Don't make 'em like that old Plymouth no more. Used to belong to a dentist with six kids. Him and his old lady used to pile all them kids in the backseat and drive to Chicago each summer to visit his in-laws. Can't do that in a pickup truck."

"Nope. You're right. This truck is stole anyway, so it don't really matter to me."

"I guess not. Look, When it's all done and over with, I told 'em to follow you back to Mexico and fill that trunk up with weed. You good with that?"

"That's a boatload of weed."

"We want a lot. Have your contacts give 'em a price. If it's agreeable to me, I'll wire 'em the money via Western Union. Safer for the boys and for me that way. They won't be holdin' all that dough getting ideas or mugged. Capeesh?"

"Capeesh. Hasta la vista."

"Adiós."

They drove all the way to Kinder, Louisiana, before calling it a day. Joe was getting on Grady's nerves. He complained all the livelong day. No doubt he was still in pain, but that didn't give him the right to whine like a little bitch. Grady was already thinking. Maybe Joe would agree to ride in the back seat of the Plymouth with Tee Beau and Junior. He could sleep the whole way. Probably not!

Another day like today and he might just pop Joe in the back of his head and dump his body in a swamp somewhere along the way. You can only put up with this shit for so long. Something's gotta give.

# CHAPTER 42

## Tuesday, June 15, 1971
## Another Day Older, Another Day Closer

It was a glorious, sunshiny day in Beaumont when the crew met for breakfast at the restaurant next door to the Texas Motor Lodge. It was aptly named Mavis' Texas Cafe. Mavis greeted them at the door with a smile and a carafe of coffee in her hand. She ushered them to an empty booth and poured them each a steamy cup of stout coffee. Cream and sugar, salt and pepper, and silverware wrapped in paper napkins were already on the table. She pointed out that the paper placemats had the breakfast menu printed on the top. (Lunchtime menu was on the back.) Then, all five-feet, two hundred pounds of Miss Mavis, stuffed in a pink, formfitting, short-sleeve work dress with her dyed-blonde, Texas 'big hair' bouffant hairdo, sashayed back behind the counter from which location she ruled her fiefdom.

Lenora, the eighteen-year-old high school dropout, wife, and mother of one, brought four ice waters on a tray and placed them on the table. She took her pencil and receipt book out of her apron and prepared to take their orders.

Archie wanted to know what she would recommend. She said she was partial to the pancakes and link sausage, but mostly they served bacon and eggs with grits, or biscuits with white sausage gravy. She said the portions were large. Also, the cantaloupe was fresh and sweet. She said the orange juice came from concentrate, but the grape juice was Welch's and tasted real good.

Sarah and Barlow ordered the pancakes and link sausage with grape juice. Archie had the biscuits and gravy, cantaloupe, and grape juice. Jarvis ate the cowboy platter with three fried eggs, patty sausage, bacon, grits, biscuits, and a small orange juice.

Over breakfast, they discussed the day's agenda. Everyone was in favor of spending the night at the YO Hotel in Kerrville. It was probably twenty miles out of their way, but they could take I-10 to get there. It was roughly 350 miles away, not a great distance, but they had to drive through Houston and San Antonio to get there. The traffic was terrible in both cities, as they all knew from recent experience.

Archie reminded everyone to be alert. Nobody knew where Joe and his friends were, but it was certain he wouldn't give up.

Breakfast was surprisingly tasty and it was cheap. Lenora filled their thermoses with scalding hot Maxwell House coffee. They left generous tips. They were on the road by nine o'clock.

They pulled into the YO a little after five. They met in the lobby outside the restaurant at six-thirty. They were all refreshed and in good spirits after hot showers and the donning of clean clothes.

The hotel and restaurant were rustic, Texas elegant. Sarah was thrilled to spend the last night of their honeymoon here. It was close enough to Mosby that they could come back for a couple of nights on a long weekend sometime.

For supper, they each ordered a wedge salad. Archie and Barlow both had the ribeye with baked potatoes. Jarvis had the ribeye with onion rings. Sarah had the rainbow trout with roasted red potatoes. For dessert, Archie had the fudge brownie à la mode. Barlow and Sarah had pecan pie. Jarvis had the turtle molten cake. Every bite of it lived up to its reputation.

Afterwards, they repaired to the saloon for a nightcap or two. Tonight, it was Old Grand Dad all around.

Nobody talked about tomorrow. Archie smoked his Lucky Strikes. Barlow offered, and Jarvis decided to try one of Barlow's H. Upmann, Maduro Churchill cigars. Conversation was scant. Everyone was lost in his own little world. Sarah and Barlow were the first to say good night after only two drinks. Jarvis and Archie needed more time and bourbon to unwind. Besides that, neither of them were getting laid tonight. They both felt bad for Sarah, in particular, that her honeymoon turned out this way.

What they didn't know was, it was perfectly all right with Sarah. She enjoyed their company. She still got to do everything she wanted to do, to include making her first trip to the ocean. She was having a wonderful time. So was Barlow. They were alert, but tried to put Joe Schitt out of their minds. They had planned to stay a couple more days, but going home didn't mean they were returning to work early.

It was all good. In fact, life was very good. They both knew God was taking care of them. They had everything they needed. What more could you ask for?

# CHAPTER 43

Tuesday, June 15, 1971
Laser Focused on Revenge

It was ten o'clock before Joe and company finally got back on the road. The weather was pleasant with lots of sunshine. A solid night's rest, tasty coonass grub, dry clothes, and a good shit improved everyone's mood. Joe, in particular, was in a much better frame of mind than he had been yesterday. He still had some serious pain off and on, but the Percocets made everything mo' better.

Good thing too, because, although Joe never suspected it, Grady had definitely decided to cap him if he acted like he did yesterday. Some folks might think that was a little over the top, but Grady knew that you couldn't part ways with Joe without making a mortal enemy. It's just the way he was built. Everything became a vendetta with him.

Grady had long since regretted helping Joe after he broke out of the joint. Had Grady kissed Joe off, Grady would have become Joe's enemy for life. However, without some outside help, the probability of Joe not getting gunned down by the police would have been slim to none. However, assuming that Joe would have eluded the police, Grady knew Joe would have never dipped down into Old Mexico to seek revenge for leaving him hanging. He hated Mexicans too much. Besides that, Joe didn't speak Mex. The only loose end would have been whether Joe would have killed Alice to get back at him. It's likely he would have. This was all water under the bridge since he did help Joe. No use dwelling on it, but Grady would have had his life back now without all the drama, if he'd just stayed home in Mexico. Fuck Joe.

Different from Joe and Grady, Tee Beau and Junior were both happy campers. They were following behind in the big green machine, oblivious to all the drama. They were thrilled to be on this important assignment. Bringing back a trunk full of weed was a major league deal. It meant that Bruno really trusted them. Killing a dude and raping his woman was lagniappe, so long as she wasn't ugly. They had their standards. They were told she was not. They would wait and see. Merrily, they tagged along in a state of nirvana, listening to zydeco music in the eight-track player Junior had installed under the dash, munching on a bag of pork rinds and smoking cigarettes as they whiled away the miles. This was a holiday to them.

They stopped for lunch in Sealy, Texas, at a Mexican diner. Joe and Grady were right at home. Not so much for Tee Beau and Junior. Three ice cold cervezas each, helped them wash down the mystery meat tacos and the ABC (already been chewed) frijoles without too much anxiety or trepidation. In fact, everything tasted great! After all, every coonass knows that gumbo is made with mystery meat, and sometimes even roadkill! What's the big deal? Same-same. Just a different culture. Meat is meat.

It took them all day to drive to San Antonio, which was a trip of only 350 miles or so. They stopped for the night at a Motel 6, the chain where Tom Bodett 'promised to keep the light on' until you arrive. Only cost six bucks a night. Left more money for beer at The Green Armadillo Saloon. They let off a boiler full of steam and got wasted. Everyone forgot about Barlow and Sarah.

Everyone except Joe Rag.

# CHAPTER 44

Wednesday, June 16, 1971
280 Miles to Home

It was a clear blue, hot day, with no clouds, no humidity, and no breeze. This would be a short day. They only had 280 miles left to return home. Both Sarah and Barlow were a little melancholy, but neither mentioned it. They'd probably have to stay with her parents for awhile. It was their best option.

Archie was anxious to get back to Mosby. He felt like keeping the Adamses safe until they were both at home was his responsibility alone. He knew better, but that's the way he felt. The closer they got to home, the more convinced Archie became that he should have let Barlow kill Joe and his partner in crime when they were in New Orleans. Think of it. They were lying in wait! Too fucking bad for them that the tables were turned on them and that they were unprepared for it. The police would have probably seen it Barlow's way. No matter which way it went down, it was truly self defense, even if he had had to put a gun in the hand of each bandit (which would have been a million-to-one odds against.) Besides, Joe was a dangerous escapee. Not only that, there were no other witnesses to say otherwise! Zero! The Texas Rangers were on board and they have beaucoup clout. Now, as things stand, neither Sarah nor Barlow, nor their loved ones, including Archie, would rest until the day of reckoning arrived. What if it didn't go their way? He would never forgive himself.

Jarvis was rolling along on a completely different plane. He didn't know how he felt today. On one hand, it would be nice to get home and see his family. He missed them terribly. On the other hand, he knew this saga was far from over. Besides that, he really liked Sarah and Barlow and Archie. Both Archie and Barlow were great law enforcement partners. Jarvis always had a partner when he was a cop on Dallas PD. Good ones, too, but the Rangers did a lot of stuff alone. A partner was pretty much a luxury. He loved being a Ranger, but he missed not having a permanent partner. He decided he'd like to hang out for a few days, or a week, in Mosby. He believed with all his heart that the showdown would happen very soon. His captain may not agree and might not authorize it. He would hate himself if he left and the very next day Joe Schitt attacked the Adamses.

They departed the YO at ten. They drove something over a hundred miles west on I-10, and stopped at a rest stop a couple of miles past Sonora. Actually, Jarvis didn't quite make it. His right rear tire blew out, almost directly under the sign which announced that the rest stop was two miles away. Jarvis was pulling drag when it happened, but both Barlow and Archie saw him stop, so they pulled over, too. Barlow and Sarah waited in their truck, while Archie walked back to see what was going on.

Archie and Jarvis examined the damage. The tire was flat as a bosom in a double A bra, but it didn't appear to be anything out of the ordinary. Archie offered to help change it, but Jarvis said he had a brand new spare and that he could do it himself in ten or fifteen minutes max. He said he would meet them at the rest stop.

Archie said, "I hate leaving ya here on the side of the road, but if that's what ya want, I will. However, if ya ain't up at the rest stop in twenty minutes, I'll be back here looking for ya."

Jarvis replied, "I'll be there. Y'all get on outta here."

Offered and declined. Archie was of a mind to stay put until Jarvis was operational, but he had to pee something awful, so he didn't. Archie didn't know it, but Sarah was in the same boat, so Barlow left also.

As soon as they pulled up and parked, Barlow could see that this was a really nice rest area. The reason it looked like it had just been constructed was because it had. The building was a rectangle made out of tan brick. It had a slightly peaked, corrugated metal roof, which was erected about a foot over the eaves to allow for circulation. The building was divided into three sections, with the men's room on the left and the women's on the right. In between, was an atrium with rafters spaced about six inches apart, which functioned as a quasi-roof, and which allowed the sun to shine through. Rain was so infrequent, nobody had even considered it in the planning stage. There were two park benches and a map of Texas hanging along the back wall. A pin with a red plastic head was sticking in the map with a little piece of paper which read, "You are here." The atrium also contained a water fountain, trash can, and a payphone.

Both restrooms were designed to accommodate two people at the same time. The men's room had one stall, one urinal, a stainless steel mirror, and two sinks. The women's was identical, except it had two stalls and no urinal.

The rest stop was vacant, except for a blue Ford Maverick with a New Mexico license plate. It was parked just to the right of the walkway to the women's restroom. Barlow pulled into the space to the left of the walkway, which was the width of a parking space. Archie parked two spaces left of Barlow, which put him just to the right of the walkway to the men's room.

Sarah and Archie made beelines to the restrooms. Barlow lagged a little behind, in case the men's room was a one-holer. He went inside once he saw that it wasn't.

Unfortunately, both stalls of the women's were occupied, so Sarah stood cross-legged in front of the sinks, praying for a speedy deliverance. Finally, a fortyish woman vacated one. Sarah and the woman smiled and greeted one another as they traded stations.

Sarah and the second woman, who was approximately twenty, finished at the same time. The older woman had already stepped outside and was studying the map in the atrium, while Sarah and the younger woman washed up.

While everyone was inside the restrooms, Tee Beau pulled up and parked the Plymouth on the right side of the Maverick with one space in between. Junior and he were a couple of minutes ahead of Joe and Grady, who had dawdled to see why a new Dodge Charger was parked along the highway. As soon as they realized that the Charger was not left unattended, they moseyed on down to the rest stop.

Tee Beau and Junior both recognized Jade as soon as they saw it, from the description that had been passed down to them. Tee Beau, all five-feet, five-inches and 135-pounds of him, carried a Sears and Roebuck, sawed-off, double-barreled, twenty-gauge shotgun as his weapon of choice. Maybe he suffered from 'little man's syndrome.' He grabbed it when he got out of the car. Junior, on the other hand, five-feet, ten-inches tall, and 260 pounds, carried a .38 Special caliber, Colt Police Positive revolver, with a four-inch barrel, which he carried in his right jean pocket. Tee Beau walked over to the right side of Jade and ducked down, keeping an eye on the men's room. He planned to capture Barlow.

The twenty-year-old daughter of the older woman finished washing up before Sarah, and she walked out of the restroom. She was slender and had long, brown hair. Junior spotted her right away and was convinced that she was Sarah. He ran up and grabbed her and began to half carry, half drag her towards the Plymouth, with the intent to stuff her into the trunk. This was just too easy. Joe would be pleased.

The young woman began screaming and kicking and flailing her arms in an effort to break loose from Junior's bearlike grasp. Her mother looked up in horror and began shrieking like a run-over dog. Sarah had just stepped out of the restroom. She saw Junior carrying off the young woman and realized instantly that Junior snatched the wrong victim and that this was a terrible case of mistaken identity. This was so wrong! She fumbled under her skirt, trying to retrieve her .25 auto from its garter holster.

Junior was impeded by the young woman's resistance and he stopped to get a better purchase. In the meantime, Sarah had retrieved her little pistol. She took aim and shot three, carefully placed rounds into Junior's torso. Those were the only clear shots that she had. It had been difficult not shooting the woman by accident because Junior was twisting every which way to control his squirming, hysterical victim. Problem was, his injuries didn't seem to slow him up one bit, even though Sarah could see that he was bleeding.

Junior had, indeed felt the impact of the bullets. They stung like Hell! He was hurting, but not disabled. He could see that he had sprung three leaks, but he was a kidnapper on a mission. He was going to violate this woman every way he could think of until she could breathe no more, even if it was the last thing he ever did.

The gunshots had drawn Tee Beau's attention away from the men's room. At the same time, the shots scrambled both Archie and Barlow outside with guns drawn. Unfortunately, Fate threw them another curveball, because Joe and Grady pulled up and parked between the Maverick and the Plymouth.

Junior managed to get the hysterical woman under control, down the sidewalk, and all the way to the rear of the Plymouth. He dug the car keys out of his pocket. She continued to kick and flail her arms. She bit him as hard as she could on his left arm, tearing a chunk out of his flesh. He stuffed her violently into the trunk and slammed it shut. Then he pulled his revolver from his trouser pocket and began walking back up the sidewalk. He was looking for the primary target. Sarah was standing close, and she was the bitch that shot him, but he was looking for Barlow.

Joe Rag and Grady watched it all. These coonasses were dumber than a box of ten-pound hammers! Joe and Grady scrambled out of the stolen pickup truck. Joe yelled, "Stop! Stop! You grabbed the wrong woman! It's the one with the gun!"

It took a few moments for this to sink into Junior's lizard brain. His injuries were beginning to take their toll. He stood dumbfounded. How could this be?

Tee Beau, having seen Sarah shoot Junior, locked in on her with the shotgun to even the score. He was gonna turn that bitch into roadkill.

Joe saw it and yelled, "No, you idiot!"

At the same time, Barlow assessed the threats. Nothing mattered except Sarah. He shot Tee Beau from an angle, hitting him in the chest twice. Tee Beau never saw it coming. He stumbled to the right side of Jade and fell down out of sight.

Barlow shifted his focus to Joe. He was the cause of all of this.

Barlow didn't realize it, but Archie focused on Joe, too. Bad mistake. On another day, each would have called his shot, so as to cover both threats simultaneously.

Too late! Grady, who was standing on the sidewalk just six feet from Sarah, took aim at Archie with his .38. He fired, but missed what he was trying to hit, which was Archie's chest, though he did manage to shoot Archie in his right thigh. Archie fell to the ground, but he returned fire as soon as he landed, hitting Grady in his face with a 250-grain lead bullet. It demolished all of his distinguishing features and most of his head. Too bad for Grady. He was shoveling coal in Hell before he even knew he was dead.

Archie's thigh was pumping thick squirts of bright-red, arterial blood, eight inches into the air. He knew this was a fatal injury if he couldn't stop the bleeding. He clamped down over the bullet hole as hard as he could. He was feeling a little woozy. He knew if he lost consciousness, he was a dead duck.

Out of the corner of his eye, Barlow saw Junior, who went from dazed and confused to apoplectically enraged by Tee Beau's demise. He was carefully sighting his revolver with both hands at Barlow to snuff out his lights. Barlow slammed face down into the dirt, dodging Junior's bullet a split second before it came whizzing past where he had been standing at the time Junior fired. Archie let up from his compress just long enough to return Junior's fire. Another of Archie's 250-grain, .45 caliber balls hit its mark, slamming into the center of Junior's rotund body. The impact sent him flying four feet into oblivion, as if he had been hit by a charging rhinoceros. Lights out for Junior. No more zydeco. Now he was just a deflated slab of raw, red meat.

Suddenly, Joe realized that this situation had deteriorated

into a soupy, shit sandwich. He was all alone now, and retreat was his best option. Live to fight another day. Besides, his wrist was pinging like a marching band parading over hot coals.

He tried to cover his withdrawal from the battlefield by snapping off a hasty round in Barlow's direction. He knew it was not well aimed, but that was okay. He urgently needed to cut a chogie back to his truck and then boogie the fuck out of there. He was just trying to cover his retreat and buy some time. His shot landed somewhere in the same zip code, but otherwise it was way off the mark.

Barlow's reciprocal shot was not. His 158-grain, lead ball hit Joe in his side, just below his right armpit, missing his ribs, but ripping a jagged hole through his heart. Joe's wretched soul was shaking hands with Grady in the pits of the fiery inferno in the blink of an eye. At the very same instant, Joe remembered just how thirsty he was when he found himself standing in Hell. He was so parched! A cup of cold water, which was just out of reach, would taste so good. Too bad. He should have thought about that earlier. Joe would remain unquenched. Forever. Ad Infinitum.

Tee Beau was busy crawling on the ground by Barlow's truck, hoping to remain unseen. He knew he was hit bad and that he probably wasn't going to make it. He slithered like a snake to get into position. He wanted to acquire a worthwhile target before he kicked off. He painstakingly managed to lift himself into a crouch, using the hood of Barlow's truck as a bench rest. He and Barlow saw each other at the same moment. Barlow fired first. His aim was a little off. In the rush to be first, he hit Tee Beau in the right shoulder, which did some damage, but was inconclusive. Then he sent a follow up shot to Tee Beau's Adam's apple, for the coup de grâce.

Barlow was out of bullets. He had thought all the bikers were dead, but he had been wrong about Tee Beau. It took Barlow two minutes to reload from the leather, zippered pouch in his pocket. Then, he walked over to each bandit and kicked them viciously in the face to be sure. All except for Grady, that is. No more playing possum.

Barlow realized that Sarah was saying something to him, but he couldn't hear what. She was struggling with Junior's body. He knew she was uninjured, so he yelled, "Wait! I'll be back with you in a minute. Archie's hurt bad!"

He turned around, and found Archie trying to keep the blood from spurting out of his right thigh. It was obvious that he had been hit in an artery. This was serious!

Just then, Jarvis came barreling up the driveway. He jumped out of his car and said, "Oh my God! I'm so sorry I'm late! Is everyone okay?"

Barlow said, "Arch has a femoral artery wound. He's lost a lot of blood. Hurry! Help me to make a tourniquet!

Jarvis replied, "I have one in my first aid kit!"

Jarvis dug around in his trunk for just a moment. He ran up and set the first aid kit on the ground. He pulled out a flat, thick, black, rubber strap, which looked a lot like a bungee cord. Barlow recalled that the Army used Ace bandages with a stick to cinch a wound up tight. This was different. Jarvis placed it above Archie's wound, and wrapped it twice, pulling it as tight as he could before he clamped it. By now Archie was beginning to lose consciousness.

Jarvis said, "I gotta get him to a hospital, pronto! The nearest one I know about is in Del Rio. That's close to a hundred miles from here. I'll call the Rangers soon as I leave. I'll ask them to send someone here and to call the sheriff. I think we're in Sutton

County, but I'm not sure. Look it up in the phone book and give 'em a call yourself. It can't hurt. Call your own sheriff, too. Have him send someone to meet me at the hospital. Come on! Gotta go! Help me get him in the car. Put him in the front seat."

Barlow assisted him in walking Archie to the Charger and carefully placing him inside. Archie queried, "Ain't this a pickle? After all them years. See ya when ya get done here."

Barlow replied, "Archie, you saved my life. I couldn't stand it if you up and died on me. Ya gotta hang on!"

"That was my job, Barlow! I asked for it. You were my rookie. Besides, ain't no buzzard like that sorry rodent over there gonna plant me in the ground. Wusser men than him have tried. Bring me some chocolates when ya come ta see me."

Jarvis said, "Gotta go. Reach out for me when you're all done." Then he burned rubber as he scrambled out of the lot code three, red light and siren scaring all the local jackrabbits into high gear.

Barlow ran over to Sarah. She said, "Help. I can't roll him over. I gotta get his keys, so I can let that poor girl out of the trunk before she suffocates or dies of heat stroke."

Once they retrieved Junior's keys, they ran over to the Plymouth. Sarah unlocked the trunk and Barlow lifted the girl out. She was very wilted, pale, and suffering from shock, but otherwise she had no visible injuries. Barlow carried her to one of the park benches and gently set her down. Her mother was so hysterical that she nearly tripped him while he was trying to carry her there.

Barlow looked at Sarah. She was trembling and fighting back tears. He drew her aside and took her into his arms.

"It's okay. It's all over. You probably saved that girl's life. You done good, Girl. Your momma and poppa are gonna be so proud of you. I'm proud of you."

"Barlow, I was so scared. What if I accidentally shot her? What if they shot you? What if Archie dies? I'm so sorry this happened. I love you so much. How do you do this and stay so . . . . normal, like it's no big deal?"

"I love you, too. It's because of you that I can do this to keep you safe. To keep us all safe. The folks in Quayle County. I couldn't be me if I let predators like this bunch run over folks and hurt them anytime they took a notion.

"Look. I gotta call Sheriff Sol and the local sheriff. See if you can comfort these ladies. I think they need a woman's touch right now. Find a cloth to wet down and put it on the girl's forehead. Help her cool off."

"Okay. Of course."

Barlow used the payphone to call the Quayle County Sheriff's Office. Loretta answered on the first ring. As soon as he identified himself, Loretta exclaimed, "Hey, Stranger! When are you two lovebirds coming back home?"

"Soon, I hope. Look Loretta, this is urgent. Is Sheriff Sol around?"

"Sure is. Let me get him. See ya soon."

"Hey, Barlow, what's up?"

"Boss, I'm at a rest stop on I-10 just west of Sonora. Joe Schitt and three of his buddies jumped us here. Archie and I killed them all, but Archie took a round in his right thigh. Hit the femoral artery. We put a tourniquet on it. Jarvis is taking him to the hospital in Del Rio. Sarah and I are okay. I gotta call the local sheriff soon as I hang up. What do you want me to do?"

"Are you sure, you and Sarah are okay?"

"I'm sure."

"Okay. I'm sending Chief Alex to Del Rio. I'm coming to the rest stop. I know where it is. I'll be there in a couple of hours, maybe less. You're in Sutton County. I don't know the sheriff there. Be cooperative with him and his deputies, but don't offer too much information beyond the obvious until I get there. I need to talk to you first. I'd like to see the crime scene. If the sheriff insists on taking you back to his jail, do what he says. If you're not at the rest stop when I get there, I know where to go. And tell Sarah to button up. She's not to answer any questions until I get there. They might trick her into saying something harmful. Tell her to claim shock if she has to."

"Oh, yeah. I forgot to mention that Sarah shot one of the bad guys, who snatched a woman he thought was her. She didn't kill him. Archie did. Still . . . ."

"Nothing's changed. Tell her to be polite, but to keep her mouth shut."

"You got it, Sheriff. Thanks. See you when you get here."

"Roger that."

Next, Barlow called the Sutton County Sheriff's Office. The dispatcher said they had just been notified by the Rangers. She asked if they should send an ambulance.

Barlow replied, "A young woman was kidnapped here and put in the trunk of a car. We got her out. You might want a medic to check on her. Her license plate says she's from New Mexico."

"She's not trying to leave is she?"

"No. I was just thinking that she may be in shock."

"Of course. We'll send Doc Dollinger to check on her. Sheriff should be there in ten or fifteen minutes. Bye."

"Bye."

# CHAPTER 45

## Wednesday, June 16, 1971
## The Preliminary Investigation

When Barlow rang off from the Sutton County Sheriff's Office, he told Sarah to keep an eye up there by the restrooms, while he waited for the sheriff down closer to the highway on the entrance ramp. The last thing they needed right now was for a carload of passersby to pull in and contaminate the crime scene. He needn't have worried. He didn't wait very long.

A three-car motorcade showed up. It consisted of the high sheriff's unit, a white, unmarked, 1970 Ford Galaxie, driven by Sheriff Roy Groth himself, who was carrying his chief deputy, Rodney Peoples. Next in line was a white, marked, 1965 Chevrolet Biscayne, driven by Deputy Rufus Littleton, who was carrying Deputy Otto Heine. Last in line was a metallic, blue-green, 1968 Buick Special, driven by Doc Euliss Dollinger.

Deputy Littleton was assigned to block off the entrance. Deputy Heine was a rookie, who was there to do whatever grunt work he was told to do. Doc Dollinger was there to check on the young woman and to lend a physician's eye to the decedents, as sort of a pre-autopsy. Chief Peoples was there to conduct the crime scene investigation, and Sheriff Groth was in charge of everything and everyone. Fortunately, he was smart, competent, and charismatic.

Sheriff Groth was about fifty years old. He stood roughly five-feet, nine-inches tall, and weighed about 160 pounds. He was balding with thick silver hair peaking out from under his Stetson. He had bright blue eyes and a thick, walrus mustache. Sutton County Sheriff's Office personnel, to include the sheriff, wore dark brown trousers with tan shirts. They wore gold stars on their chests. Sheriff Groth carried a nickel-plated, Smith and Wesson, Model 29, .44 Magnum revolver with a six-inch barrel, in a western-style, cross-draw gun belt, with two dozen cartridges in loops. He was the real deal.

After introductions were made, he said, "I received a call from the Texas Rangers. I was told two deputies were attacked by four outlaw bikers who had been stalking one deputy and his wife for about a week. Four bikers are dead, one of which is the notorious escapee from Huntsville. One deputy is injured, being transported to the hospital in Del Rio by a Texas Ranger, and the other deputy is standing by for me. That must be you. That about right?"

Barlow responded, "Yes, Sir."

"No offense, son, but you look a mite young to be a deputy. How old are you, anyway?"

"I'm 22, Sir. I've been a Quayle County deputy for two years. I'm post certified. My boss, Sheriff Solomon Pratt, said for me to let you know that he's en route."

"Glad to hear it. Any sheriff worth his salt would be. You wanna walk me through this while we're waiting for him? I can't close down this rest stop forever. The next one ain't for another hundred miles. We can't have motorists pissing all along the highway, can we?"

"No, Sir."

"Well, all righty then. Show me where it all started. Rodney, you ready to take notes?"

"You bet, Sheriff."

"Yes, Sir. It started in Quayle County two years ago. The injured deputy, Archie Willis, who was my training officer, and I arrested Joseph P. Schitt, this man over here, in a barroom ruckus."

"Shit, huh? This man's legal name is Shit? Whoever heard of having the last name, Shit? Why not Dickhead, or Asshole? This some kind of a joke?"

No, Sir. His name is spelled different. S-C-H-I-T-T. His street name was Joe Shit the Ragman. He was a member of the Diablos Motorcycle Club. He had a long felony record. The judge sentenced him to 42 years hard labor. Part of that was for a conviction in our court on the Habitual Offender Act.

"Anyway, he found out I was getting married. Someone must have showed him the wedding announcement in the newspaper. A prison snitch reported that he broke out of prison to rape my wife, Sarah, and to kill us both as revenge, while we were on our honeymoon. He escaped with an inmate named Richard Wadsworth. I've never seen Wadsworth. They must have parted ways. When Sheriff Sol found out about this, Sarah and I were already on our honeymoon. He sent Archie to find us and ask us to come home.

"Archie caught up with us in Houston on Thursday. We decided not to go home, so Archie was assigned to stay with us as protection, just in case. Friday night at the Astros game, Archie saw Schitt, and I think this enormous biker without a face over here, in the stadium. He saw them leave in this stolen, green Ford pickup truck parked over there. That sighting confirmed the snitch's information, so Texas Ranger Jarvis Reeves was also assigned to accompany us.

"We went to New Orleans on Saturday. Sunday we noticed three local outlaw bikers, each wearing Crescent City Jacks colors, everywhere we went. These two other dudes are probably Jacks, since Archie didn't see them in Houston. Not sure about this faceless fella, who he is, or if he has an affiliation. Anyway, we figured the three Jacks in New Orleans were buddies with Schitt, so we decided to leave early Monday morning. Sure enough, Schitt, and the big faceless dude were sitting in a white work van just a few spaces over from where we were parked. We shot out two of their tires and took a powder out of there.

"We spent last night at Kerrville. Just before we got to the rest stop here, Jarvis had a flat. We all stopped, but he told us to go on and that he would meet us here. That Maverick with the New Mexico plate was already here. Archie was driving that pickup over there with the horns on the hood, and that jade green truck is mine.

"We all went to the restroom. It wasn't but a few minutes when Archie and I heard three shots. We came running out of the restroom. This other big palooka here had snatched that young woman sitting up there in the light blue dress. (The older woman is her mother.) Pretty sure Palooka thought she was my wife, Sarah, who's wearing the yellow dress over there. Sarah came out of the restroom and figured out what was going on, so she shot this guy three times with her .25, but he never stopped. He put that young woman into the trunk of the green Plymouth parked over here.

"After that, it gets a little confusing. I saw this little cockroach here aiming this sawed-off at my wife. I shot him twice in the chest and he went down. I thought he was dead. Oh, yeah, this was about the same time that Joseph Schitt and the faceless dude showed up. The faceless dude shot Archie in his leg and Archie shot him in the head. Then Schitt fired a shot at me and missed. I shot him in his side and he died. I thought they were all dead, but this little dude with the sawed-off shotgun popped up again. He was pointing that shotgun at me this time, so I shot him two more times. That's when he died.

"Then Jarvis rolled up, but it was all over. We put a tourniquet on Archie, and Jarvis took off with him to the hospital. That's all I know. Oh, yeah. My wife and I got that young woman out of the trunk of the Plymouth."

"You using that little hideout gun you got in your waistband there?"

"Yes, Sir. It was a gift from the department. It saved my life. Five shots. Five hits. I reloaded it afterwards."

"What was Archie using?"

"A Colt Peacemaker in .45 Long Colt."

"I should have guessed. Very well. You can have a seat in your truck while we process the crime scene. We'll wait for your sheriff. What's his name again?"

"Quayle County Sheriff Solomon Pratt."

"Oh, yeah. Okay. We'll send your wife over here to you, just as soon as we finish talking with her."

"Yes, Sir. Just so you know, she might not be up to it right now. She's pretty shook up. I asked her to look after the two ladies up there. They're really upset."

"Don't worry, Deputy. We're not going to try to ambush her. We just need to see if she can fill in some of the details you may have failed to mention. Okay?"

"Yes, Sir."

Sheriff Sol showed up before Chief Peoples was done processing the crime scene, so Sol got to see it while the bodies were still where they fell. There were no surprises regarding the gunfight. Barlow's rendition matched physical evidence from the crime scene, and statements, more or less, from the women. The older woman was hysterical and the younger woman had spent most of her time in the trunk of the Plymouth, so their reports were sketchy. Sarah was a great witness, but she was also a participant, and potentially biased as Barlow's bride.

Chief Peoples radioed his office and told the secretary to run DMV, NCIC, and NLETS record checks on the four decedents. They all had a driver's license on them except for Joe, and Barlow had already identified him. Faceless dude turned out to be a Diablo named Grady S. Triplett, with an address in Del Rio. The other two bodies were both Crescent City Jacks. The little one was Ramón Petard, also known as Tee Beau. The big one was Rémy A. Harvey, Junior, who went by Junior. Both were from New Orleans. All three had at least one felony conviction, not to mention convictions for assorted misdemeanors.

Sheriff Sol also met Sheriff Groth. They got along fabulously, as if they had grown up together and played baseball on the same team in high school, and served on the same Navy submarine, and married twin sisters. It was as good as.

Before they left to go to the Sutton County Sheriff's Office, Sheriff Groth said, "Sheriff, since Archie took his keys with him, I will have my guys tow his truck to our storage lot until someone can pick it up for him. Tell him there will be no charge."

Sheriff Sol replied, "Thanks very much."

The two New Mexico women, Francine Meadows and her daughter, Muriel, and Sarah and Barlow, were lodged at the

Sonora Siesta Hotel for the night, courtesy of the Sutton County District Attorney's Office, so they could testify before the hastily summoned Sutton County Grand Jury in the morning. The Siesta was a very pleasant, old-timey hotel. Bonnie and Clyde or their nemesis, Texas Ranger Captain Frank Hamer, could have stayed there. It was that kind of place.

They all ate supper together with Sheriff Groth, Chief Peoples, and Sheriff Sol at Granny Jenkins' Pie in the Sky Restaurant. The beef stew, biscuits, coleslaw, and sweet tea were all very good, but the lemon meringue pie á la mode was out of this world.

Sheriff Sol stayed through supper, then the first chance he got, he vamoosed to Del Rio to check on Archie.

This was a long, wild day of reckoning. That night in their room, sipping Wild Turkey over ice, Sarah and Barlow prayed that Archie would be okay. They thanked God it was over, and that they were not the ones pushing up daisies. Barlow cleaned both their guns before reloading them and putting them back in their holsters.

After Sarah fell asleep, Barlow wondered. Was it truly over, or would the Crescent City Jacks come seeking revenge?

# CHAPTER 46

## Thursday, June 17, 1971
## What About Archie?

Both Barlow and Sarah testified before the Grand Jury. Barlow was first. He pretty much repeated what he had told Sheriff Groth the day before. Sarah did, too. Then Muriel Meadows, then Francine Meadows, then Chief Peoples, and finally Doc Dollinger.

The Grand Jury deliberated for twenty minutes. They returned a verdict that all four homicides were lawful and justified. Truth is, they could hardly wait for the next of kin to come claim the bodies. They really didn't have room in either of their cemeteries for out-of-town trash like this. Nobody could remember if Sutton County had ever had four outlaws killed on the same day. Probably not. The last time four people got killed by violent means on the same day in Sutton County, as far as anyone could recollect, was over a hundred years ago during the Indian wars. Things was different then.

Sarah and Barlow were southbound to Del Rio by eleven o'clock. They picked up US 277 south and arrived at the hospital sometime just before one. Barlow had to stop by a pharmacy before they arrived to pick up a box of Whitman's Sampler chocolates to keep his promise to Archie.

To their relief, Archie had just been moved from ICU to a semiprivate room, which currently did not have another patient. Archie's daughter, Colleen Pendleton, and Sheriff Sol were both visiting.

Archie looked pale and haggard. He was hooked up to a rolling IV. He was woozy, but he was grinning like his pet pig just learned how to square dance. His eyes said happy. He said, "Well, I swear. Look at you two honeymooners. Colleen, this here is Mr. and Mrs. Barlow Adams. Mrs. Adams goes by Sarah. Barlow, Sarah, this here is my daughter Colleen. She drove all the way here from Oklahoma City, because someone told her I was dying."

Colleen said, "Well, gettin' four pints of blood might have caused someone to think the Grim Reaper was standing by in the shadows. Hey, you all! I'm so glad to finally meet you. Daddy talks about you two all the time. No, I lied. He doesn't talk. He gushes about you two."

Sheriff Sol stood up and said, "Arch, I gotta get back to the salt mine. Glad you're feelin' better. Don't get out of bed 'til they make you. Call me if they release you before I get back over here. Barlow, stop by the jail and see me before you go home."

Barlow answered, "Yes, Sir."

Archie replied, "Thanks, Sheriff. I expect to go home Saturday. Sunday at the latest."

"I hope so. Bye y'all."

Once Sheriff Sol was out the door, Sarah said, "It's so nice to see you again, Miss Colleen. The last time I was still in elementary school. You probably don't remember."

"My gosh, I think I do! I don't get back this way very often. That must've been the time my husband wanted to ride a bull in the Cowboy Days Rodeo. Almost broke his arm. Daddy, you and Barlow go ahead and visit. I think I'll go get a cup of coffee. Sarah, would you join me? I think Daddy wants a few moments alone with your hubby."

Sarah replied, "Of course."

Archie asked, "How did the Grand Jury go?"

Barlow replied, "About the way you'd expect it to. Everything's copacetic. You don't even have to go testify. Next time you're up that way, stop in the sheriff's office, and tell 'em who ya are, and they'll probably give ya a free cup of joe.

"Tell me the truth. How are you really doing? Are you gonna be gimpy, or die of a blood clot, or are you gonna be okay, and come back to work? Please tell me your dick didn't get shot off."

"Well, Deputy Adams, if it turned out that my willy was shot off, and that I do hafta sit down to pee, aren't ya glad I didn't have to embarrass myself and confess that in front of that beautiful wife of yours?"

"Oh my gosh! Tell me it ain't so!"

"It was a pretty close call. I'm gonna be fine. I might be a little gimpy for a while. Not sure yet. That's not why I want to talk to you in private."

"What is it then?"

"Barlow, I'm fixin' to retire. Not right away, but before the year's end. The only other person who knows, besides Colleen, is Sheriff Sol, and he's on board. I told him the day you graduated. I had considered retiring before then, but I wanted to hang on until you got POST certified. I feel like a proud papa. Now that you're a bonafide deputy, with far more experience than anyone else with your tenure ever got, I can retire knowing I left the Sheriff's Office better off than when I first joined up in 1919. For the record, I was only nineteen years old. Course, them was different days. Not as many bandits, and if one got shot because he had it comin', oh well . . . . "

"Archie! Come on! Whatever will I do without you? You taught me everything I know about being a deputy. You're my mentor! You're like blood to me!"

"Well, I ain't moving away. You can come over and visit anytime ya want. Ask me anything ya want."

"Why are you retiring? You're not having health issues, are ya? What will you do?"

"Barlow, I'm 71 years old. I been a deputy over 46 years. My health is just fine. I'll draw 92 percent of my salary. I want to enjoy it before I can't. Understand? I still have horses to train. I can do it full time now."

"Yes, but . . . "

"Barlow, consider this. My son, Malcolm, is fifty years old. Did you know he joined the Army Air Corps in World War II? He was a a gunner on a B-26. Fought in Africa and Italy. Got shot down over Anzio. Took some shrapnel in his chest. Had to bail out. Lucky for him he landed in an American zone. Got a Purple Heart. Anyway, he stayed in after the war. Transferred to the Air Force in 1947. He was a crew chief on B-52s. Retired as a master sergeant in 1968, at Offutt Air Force Base in Omaha, with 26 years of service. That was three years ago! Now he drives a school bus, and hunts and fishes the rest of the time.

"Colleen's 49. Her husband is 52. After he got out of the Army, he got on with the Oklahoma City Fire Department. He's got 25 years. Five more to go for a full retirement.

"Barlow, I'm twenty years older than both of them. It's my time to retire. I've had a great run. You should be happy for me."

"I am, Arch. I'm very happy you're okay. Sorry. Guess I've only been thinking about myself and how much I'm gonna miss you. Reckon I'll have to stop by your place whenever I need some advice. Congratulations. I'm really happy for you, that you're able to retire and enjoy the fruits of your labor. I won't tell anyone but Sarah, and she won't spill the beans, either."

"Barlow, I'm not retiring tomorrow. We have time to figure things out. Besides, you don't have to wait until you're in a jam to stop by. You can stop by anytime."

"Thanks. I will. Guess I better track down Sarah, so I can see what Sheriff Sol wants."

"Well, don't go away mad."

"I ain't mad. Just choked up a little bit, I suppose. I didn't see this coming. I just need to wrap my arms around it. I'm okay. I need to talk this through with Sarah. That's all."

"Good idea. See ya in a couple of days, after they sew my pecker back on."

"The Hell, you say!"

"Ha! Gotcha!"

The last 120 miles home were the longest of the trip. Barlow told Sarah all about Archie's secret. She was as surprised as he. She could tell her husband was hurting. She promised not to tell anyone.

They decided that she would drop him off at the jail, so she could go to the grocery. She would pick him up when she was done.

Sheriff Sol was in his office when Barlow arrived.

"Good trip?"

"Mostly. Yes. We got to do what we wanted. Sarah's happy. Me, too. The drama took us by surprise. Our honeymoon was one for the record books, I guess. We'll be talking about it for years."

"How's my goddaughter?"

"She's fine. She's stronger than you might imagine. This scary shadow looming over us is finally gone. We don't have to look over our shoulders anymore. Even though, it will be a cold day in Hell before Sarah goes anywhere without that little .25 that Archie gave her."

"I don't blame her. She stepped up and took the bull by the horns when she saw that genetic garbage grab that poor girl. I don't know of any other woman who would have been so brave."

"Yep. Sarah's full of spunk. She also knows that, except for the grace of God, she would have been the one stuffed into the trunk. It still gives her and me both chills."

"Understood. If either of you need anything, let me know. On another note, did Archie share a confidence with you?"

"He did. It bowled me over, but I understand. Archie's an institution, in and of himself. I can't imagine him not being around to guide us all."

"I feel the same way. He had at least thirty years on when I signed up. Soon, I'll have to look for a replacement. Might be a brand new hire like you were. Someone who has to take the course. If so, I might need you to talk the newbie through it. How would you feel about that?"

"I would feel fine about it, especially if I don't have to work midnights all the time. Have you got someone in mind?"

"I might. If so, it's not somebody anyone around here knows. The person I'm considering might face a few barriers initially. If I do select this person, it would be for the very same reason I selected you. I could see that your head was screwed on straight and that you had the heart of a lion. Some folks thought I was crazy bringing on someone so young. They quit thinking that a long time ago. Now I may be inclined to, once again, hire a stranger who is outside the boundary of conventional, non risk-taking thinkers. If I do, would you be on board with me?"

"I trust your judgment, Sheriff. You took a chance on me, and I will forever be in your debt. I will assist whomever you hire in any way I can."

"Thanks, Barlow. We have some time. I may see if the Board of Supervisors would let me bring on a new hire before Archie retires. Give us some overlap while the newbie is in training. It would be a big help. And Barlow, I will do what I can to give you more shifts on days or afternoons. You've more than earned it. Problem is, I don't have any volunteers for nights besides Archie. Kirk is the last one hired before you and he has four years seniority over you. Nevertheless, I'll see what I can do."

"Thanks, Sheriff."

"Okay. That's all. Get out of here. If Sarah isn't waiting, get Slick to ride you home."

"Roger that. I'll be back Sunday night to hold down the fort. Probably see you Monday morning."

"You bet."

# CHAPTER 47

Friday, Saturday, Sunday, June 18, 19, 20, 1971
At the End of the Day . . . .

Home at last. The trip seemed so short, but it also seemed like they had been gone forever. So much had transpired. It was as if they were different people now. Time to pick up the pieces and get back to work. Fast forward beyond their nightmare, and resume where they left off, except for being married. Sort things out. Sweep away all the leftover anxiety cobwebs and the what ifs.

Sarah hardly let Barlow out of her sight. She was pensive, anxious, jumpy. She carried that .25 on her person everywhere she went, even to the bathroom. It was like a child's teddy bear or blanket, except designed for an adult. Woe be to the person who came up behind her silently, before making himself known. He might get shot.

At night she stayed cuddled up next to him as close as she could get. It had nothing to do with sex.

On Friday, they aired out the house. Put things away. Gave Jade a thorough cleaning and detailing. After lunch they went to the Bar B. It was a happy reunion with Happy. It was a joyful reunion with everyone else. Sarah and Clarice were so overcome, they wept with joy.

Cordell and Darla were also there. They all got caught up on the grapevine news from both directions. They grilled steaks and gorged on all the trappings, including baked potatoes, corn on the cob, and peach pie, like it was Thanksgiving. In a way, it was.

The men stayed outside under the copse of live oak trees sipping on bourbon, and the womenfolk clustered in the kitchen sharing a bottle of rosé wine. That's the only way it was possible for Sarah and Barlow to tell the complete saga of their being stalked by Joe Schitt and his cadre of vicious criminals. They both gave mostly Archie, but also Jarvis, credit for keeping them safe. Arthur and Cordell said they were happy that the hoodlums were all dead. Sarah showed the women the gun that Archie gave her. Explained that it belonged to Opal before her. Both Clarice and Darla could see that, besides her wedding and engagement rings and wedding necklace, it was the most precious thing she possessed. It frightened them a little.

It was a great visit by any set of standards. Sarah actually relaxed and enjoyed herself. Things were improving for her psyche.

They returned on Saturday, all day, to ride horses and shoot. Happy got to go, too. It was almost like old times. They barbecued chicken, and had potato salad, a tossed salad, and sweet tea. They topped it off with rice pudding.

Church was on Sunday. Everyone was glad to have them back in the fold. No one mentioned "the incident," although everyone knew about it.

Barlow waited too late to take a nap. He was already tired when he relieved Deputy Meacham at work. By midnight, he was missing Archie like a first grader misses his mother on the first day of school. He hoped Arch would make a full recovery and live to be a hundred.

Time to get to work.

He decided to clean all the long guns, beginning with the Thompson submachine guns.

Boy, did he love his job!

# Postscript

## Friday, June 25, 1971
## A Letter Arrives at the Jail

RR1, Box 375,
Arlo, Texas
June 21, 1971

Dear Barlow,

Greetings from a long lost friend. It's been over four years. Sorry we lost touch. I mailed this to the Quayle County Sheriff's Office because I didn't have no better address.

I got out of the Marines two weeks ago. I served two tours in the Nam. I heard you was in Nam, too.

Came home with a Purple Heart and a tattoo and no desire to ever leave Texas again. Looking for a job. Hope to get on as a truck driver for Star Transport over in Baileyville. I have a commercial truck driver's license. Learned how to drive big rigs in the Corps.

Sorry to hear about your grandma. She was the sweetest lady. Everybody misses her. Mama put some flowers on her grave.

I'm sending this article from the Amarillo newspaper. Mama cut it out. I bet you haven't seen it. Everyone here's talking about it. You and your police partner are stud ducks. I can't believe you all made it through this firefight. Sounds about as bad as the Nam. You and your new bride are amazing. Wouldn't surprise us none if they make a movie about it.

Let me know how you're doing. Everything's changed since I

left for basic. It's hard to explain. It's like I'm feeling my way around in the dark. I'd really like to see you or hear from you anyway.

Best Wishes,

Your Old Pal,

Claude Perkins

P.S. My phone number is 806-277-1191.

## Making Mountains Out of Molehills

- Author: Earl Snort
- Publisher: TotalRecall Publications
- Paper Back: 9781590954324
- Ebook: 9781590956533
- Number of pages: 320
- Publication Date: 2019

It was 1969. Barlow Adams, age 20, was a recently discharged veteran. He was driving late at night on a lonely stretch of highway in the Trans-Pecos region of Texas. He stopped to render assistance to a motorist with a flat tire. What he stepped into was a vicious attempted rape. He rescued the victim, which catapulted him into an appointment as a deputy sheriff.

Along the way he encounters an enchanting woman who will change his life forever. In addition, he will be confronted by a gang of outlaw bikers who are obsessed with killing him while he is still learning the ropes of becoming a lawman. Will they succeed?

This is the story of a young man in the 1960's, an era which has long been forgotten except for those who lived it.

## When Dreams Come True ~ Sort Of

- Author: Earl Snort
- Publisher: TotalRecall Publications
- Paper Back: 9781648830006
- Ebook: 9781648830013
- Number of pages: 320
- Publication Date: 2020

The year is 1970. Barlow Adams is a young deputy sheriff in a rural county in the Trans-Pecos region of Texas. He's a rookie still learning the ropes. Up until now, his experience has been limited to working in the jail and performing routine patrol work that is anything but routine when bad men decide to exert themselves in furtherance of their wicked ways.

In recent months, a gang of rustlers had begun to prey on the livestock of unwitting ranchers. The sheriff has decided to stop them cold wherever he finds them. He employs all the limited resources at his disposal to achieve this goal. One of those resources is Deputy Adams, who learns new law enforcement skills in teamwork, criminal investigation, surveillance, and undercover operations.

Barlow also learns something else. The crime may be solved and plans may be hatched to catch the evildoers, but, in the end, there's usually a joker in the woodpile who upsets the applecart and then suddenly Life becomes a free for all.